AGENCY

Sean Fenian and Robert Auerbach

Fenian House Publishing

COPYRIGHT DECLARATION:

DISCLAIMER:

This is a work of fiction. All of the characters<u>hund</u> in this story are fictional. Some of them, however, may have been *inspired by* real individuals. If you're reading this book and something looks really familiar, you most likely already know about it. Some organizations and corporations mentioned are (obviously) real, but have no *actual* connection to any persons or events described in this story—none of which have happened yet anyway.

Any mention in this book of any present-day established trademark is not a challenge to that trademark.

And yeah, yeah, we've taken a few liberties here and there with The Way Things Work. Because "And then we handed everything over to the FBI and went home" *right up front* doesn't make for a very satisfying story... but in the words of Detective Inspector 'Dirty' Harry Callahan, "A man's got to know his limitations," and there comes a time when it is *stupid* to do anything *BUT* take everything you've learned and hand it off to the professionals to take it the rest of the way.

References? *Of course* there are references.

PUBLICATION HISTORY:

0.9.9 — Late 2024 — Advance Reader Copy (ARC)

1.0.0 — January 2025 — First Electronic Edition

1.0.1 — April 2025 — Cumulative corrections

1.1.0 — October 2025 — First Print Edition

Soft Cover ISBN 979-8-9926260-4-9

FORMATTING CONVENTIONS AND PACING:

This novel is intended to be styled like storytellers at the bar, spinning a yarn that's so good nobody is willing to challenge its veracity.

Where you see a single line of vertical space, as is above this line, imagine the narrator stopping for a breath—or the characters pausing to order their thoughts—before speaking again.

A larger double-line space, such as here, is akin to the raconteur pausing to replenish with half a pint and some pretzels; or, within the story, for an extended break in dialogue between the characters that usually does not involve a change of viewpoint or scene. Now might be an ideal time to make a cup of tea, if you're so inclined, or otherwise attend to life.

═══════════════

Finally, a double horizontal bar like this one denotes a scene or perspective break within a chapter: the scene or the viewpoint has changed, but no lengthy narrative pause is *necessarily* implied (although there *usually* is one).

Of course, we at Fenian House strongly advise you to read how you want, on your own schedule. The above is our guide to how to read our *intended* pacing of the text; but our suggestions are just, only, that. You paid good money for this book; we are your humble bards.

Agency

ACKNOWLEDGMENTS

SEAN:

First and foremost, my esteemed collaborator **Robert Auerbach**. I am *delighted* to be able to work closely with Robert on this book. He has given me invaluable guidance on it almost from when I first started work on it over eighteen months ago. Were it not for his expert knowledge, I would have made a great many mistakes about the internal workings of law firms, the legal system, and related matters—and that's just the beginning of the places I would have gone wrong, not to mention the many, many plot refinement suggestions. Not only are there scenes which Robert sketched out for me in detail after I showed him what I was trying to do, and made them *better*, there are many passages and even entire chapters which we worked on together. It is a far better and more convincing book for Robert's assistance, and I have learned a lot from him.

I've seen a fair bit of Robert's writing by now, and he sets a consistently high standard which often leaves me envious. He writes things I could not write.

His many contributions to this book do not disappoint.

ALSO:

To fellow author **Mackey Chandler**, for early self-publishing advice, rubberducking, and general support and encouragement;

To my growing team of beta readers, including **Ralock Kaltan**, **Douglas King**, **Sam Latham**, and **Jeff Geauvreau**, for proofreading and being sounding-boards;

And to **Cymru Llewes**, for the idea of using LoJack to track rental cars. (No, it's not made up, and yes, it would work.)

ROBERT:

When it comes to thanks I should begin with my lucky stars. I'm not sold on notions of karma, fate, destiny, or an interventionist God, but often some thread of nearly-transcendent order is visible running through the utter chaos of my life. If this is just my flawed perception, don't correct me. If it's not, well—whomever the weaver is, I'm listening. Give me a ring.

Ruth Michaud, who taught me to love writing well.

Sean and his entire family. Family are the people who show up, and they've done so repeatedly. Peace to House Fenian.

My father. In the twilight of his days we've at last reached mutual understanding. I love you, Old Man.

BOTH OF US wish to thank **Irene Kenyon**, formerly Director (Acting) of the Office of Illicit Finance at the United States Department of the Treasury, for sanity-checking the mechanics of the financial crime central to this book's plot. Any lingering madness is, of course, entirely our fault, and is largely necessitated by the need for our protagonists to be able to discover and trace it without being able to utilize any of the official resources normally used to detect and unravel such schemes. Irene notes that as described, the scheme is somewhat stupid in parts—but let's face it, in the real world, *that has seldom stopped anyone* from committing a crime.

And likewise our thanks to **Wendy S. Delmater**, Editor-in-Chief of Abyss & Apex Magazine, for lending her professional editing skills to this book.

A Word To The Wise

(And even more, to the unwise):

The portrayal of intelligence and counterintelligence operations presented here is a mix of real-world tradecraft that's been tested in the hardest places, and plausible-seeming Rule of Cool stuff that will get you killed if you try it. We strongly advise that you just enjoy the story and not try to use any of these techniques for real.

Agency

Prologue: The Secret Life of Syria

I was on my way back from a forward base in Syria as a civilian contractor. No, I'm *not* going to tell you where in Syria the base was, or which specific military command it was under, or who I was under contract to. You don't need to know any of that. Suffice it to say that I had been sent there with one specific objective—well, okay, *two* objectives; I had accomplished them; and I was now on my way back home. I was riding in a convoy along with about a dozen other technical contractors being rotated out. It *should* have been a routine trip, just like the ride in had been.

I was in the fifth of seven vehicles; two Humvees in the lead, three Suburbans with three-row seating carrying us contractors, two more Humvees bringing up the rear. We were making a reasonably good pace down a road that wasn't even all that bad really, northeast of Damascus, headed for Beirut and a flight back to the United States. The trip had been calm and uneventful so far. There was occasional casual chat among the contractors, some of it shop talk about how our respective trips had gone, some of it about what each of us was going to do once back stateside, some of it the inevitable griping. But most of the time, most of us just sat and watched the landscape roll by. It all got to look the same after a while.

The convoy slowed a bit as we encountered a rougher stretch of road. It looked as though this stretch had been bombed or shelled, and then the craters filled more or less level, but not really graded. The jouncing threw us around a little, but that was par for the course. On average, the ride so far had been better than most. We were only in the bad stretch for maybe five minutes, then it smoothed out again and the convoy sped back up. We were probably two hours from Beirut, not counting the inevitable delays at the Lebanon border.

About ten minutes past the rough spot, I heard the *crack, crack* of high-velocity bullets passing nearby. The radio crackled. I caught the words "taking fire." I looked outside but couldn't see any movement. The minigun atop the Humvee behind us was traversing back and forth as the gunner looked for a target. Flame stabbed from the muzzles, visible even in the bright Syrian sun, as I saw and heard him rip out a few short bursts, but I suspected it was just suppressive fire. There was intermittent probing fire from both lead Humvees as well, and the gunners *could* have seen something I couldn't, but since the bursts were so brief I presumed they were just firing a few rounds into spots where they thought the fire *might* be coming from. There was no indication that anyone had an actual target. Whoever was firing at us wasn't close enough to easily spot, and they had a tactical advantage over us, because we were an easy-to-see target while they weren't.

Still, we'd be out of their field of view pretty soon, I imagined, and the incoming fire hadn't had any real effect, though I saw there was a fresh star mark in the rear window of the Suburban ahead of mine. Seemed like nobody was getting anything much out of this desultory little exchange of random fire. Welcome to Syria. Beirut, here we come.

There was a BANG as our driver's window starred, but nothing penetrated the bulletproof glass. He swerved slightly, but kept going, pretty much unperturbed. This clearly wasn't his first time under fire.

Then a sledgehammer hit me in the upper back, throwing me forward and right.

"Cole's hit!" I heard someone say. A moment later, the driver picked up his mic.

"Fox Alpha, courier three, we have a casualty, need a medic."

"Can't break here," I heard the reply. "Five mikes."

I heard another, longer burst from the tail Humvee's minigun, then the firing tailed off a minute or so later. I was leaning against the seat in front of me. I wanted to sit back upright, but I couldn't. I coughed, and it hurt like fuck. There was a spray of blood on my hand. Well, shit, *that* wasn't good at all. My back felt wet and sticky.

After a couple more minutes, we stopped. Almost immediately someone opened the door next to me. I felt hands steadying me.

Someone reached in and unfastened my ballistic vest, then cut my shirt open.

"Came in through the side," I heard someone say. "Sheer bad luck it slipped past the edge of his vest."

"What's his status?"

"Collapsed lung, smashed rib, losing a lot of blood." I felt a sting in my arm, then someone started putting a dressing on my back.

"Medevac is on the way," another voice said. "Rendezvous at waypoint India, fifteen mikes."

Hands gently leaned me back against the seat and pulled my seatbelt tight.

"Hang in there," someone told me. The voice sounded slightly unreal somehow. "We've got you. We'll get you out of this."

A few moments later, we got under way again. The pain didn't seem as bad, but I was short of breath, and felt woozy. The medic had given me a shot of something, I realized. Probably morphine.

I wasn't really aware of much until the convoy pulled over again. Zoned out, I guess. I heard the distinctive heavy thrum of a Blackhawk's main rotor, and a loud rattle of sand and pebbles on the side of the Suburban. Then someone opened my door, and a couple of people carefully lifted me out and laid me on a stretcher. I felt myself being strapped down, lifted and passed up, then heard the side door close. Someone put an oxygen mask over my face. I distantly heard the pilot throttle up.

The last thing I was aware of was a dark face wearing desert goggles leaning over me, and a voice with a Georgia accent saying, "You're going to be okay, man, you're going to make it, we've got you, just try to relax." Then everything faded to black.

I woke up in a hospital bed. There was an IV in my arm, and my back hurt. I didn't try to move. I just lay there. It was easier to breathe now, but breathing hurt a little.

After a while, a nurse came by and noticed I was conscious.

"Good, you're awake," she told me, perhaps unnecessarily. "Don't worry, we patched you up, got all the bullet fragments out, you're going to be fine." She checked my vitals, then left.

A few minutes later, a doctor appeared, an older man with iron-gray hair. He had an MP in tow.

"Welcome back, Mr... Cole," the doctor said. "I'm Doctor Aaronson. You had a close call, but you're going to be fine.

"It seems there's some issue with your paperwork, though. You're lucky we typed your blood for verification before we transfused you. You're O negative. But your paperwork says you're type AB."

Uh-oh. This might be a problem.

"I've always been O negative," I mumbled in reply. It was unsettling how weak my voice sounded. "If my papers say AB, they're wrong."

"We'd figured out that much," the MP said. "What we'd like to know is *why* you have the wrong papers."

Well, crap. I knew perfectly well the papers that I'd come into Syria on weren't mine. It's a long story. They were a close enough match that probably only something like this would have given the game away. I was going to have to brazen this out. Not something I really wanted to attempt while still drowsy.

"Don't ask me that," I said tiredly, "ask whoever prepped my paperwork for this trip." I paused for a moment, acting a bit more woozy than I actually felt. "...Wait, you said wrong *papers*. What else is wrong with my papers? Besides my blood type?"

The MP looked hard at me.

"I'm going to ask you a direct question," he stated. "You get one chance to give me an honest answer. Are you Nathan Cole?"

"...What?" I feigned confusion. "It's *mac* Cool. And it's not Nathan, it's Ciáran. Who's Nathan Cole?"

"Nathan Cole is who your papers say you are," the MP said.

"What the fuck?" I mumbled. "That's bollocks. That's not me."

Then the easy gambit was to stop fighting the drowsiness and just let my eyes close again.

=====

When I next woke up, Doctor Aaronson was back, along with a couple of orderlies and another MP.

"You're stable enough to be moved," he told me. "So we're getting you out of here. You've missed your flight home by several days, I'm afraid. We're going to put you on a flight to Germany, to Rammstein, and you'll be transferred to a regular hospital there to recuperate. You'll be under guard until we figure out why your papers don't match up."

"Sure," I nodded weakly. "Makes sense. Oh, and Doc? Thanks for fixing me up."

"You're welcome, son," he said. "Try not to make us do it a second time, huh?"

=====

Well, the long and the short of it is, they put me in another helicopter, which delivered me to a transport plane somewhere, and the plane took off an hour or so later. I slept through most of the flight and didn't wake up until landing. An ambulance ride from there took me to a proper military hospital. As Dr. Aaronson had told me, I was under guard the whole way, and an MP was stationed outside the door of my room.

A couple of days in, when I was a bit more awake, I had a visitor. He introduced himself as Lieutenant Haskell.

"I believe you already know that your paperwork doesn't match who you actually are," he told me. "I'm here to find out why." I nodded.

"Let's start with your real name. Which is not Nathan Cole, is it?"

"No, sir, it isn't," I replied. There was a bit more strength to my voice now. That was good. "Ciáran mac Cool. They said something at the field hospital about my paperwork being wrong. I don't remember it very clearly."

"Your paperwork says you are Nathan Cole," Haskell said. "Nathan

Cole is a civilian contractor who was assigned to perform a certain maintenance upgrade. But you know that part. We've done a little checking, and you performed the upgrade perfectly, exactly according to spec."

"Of *course* I did. That was my job."

"A job which was supposed to be assigned to Nathan Cole," he replied. "Don't get me wrong, we're not criticizing the work. But Cole didn't show up, and you showed up in his place, carrying his papers, and we'd like to know how that happened."

"Honestly, damned if I know. Truth is I didn't even look closely at the ID on the paperwork packet they sent me. It never occurred to me they might be wrong. They've always been correct before. Why should this trip be any different?"

"Didn't it ring any alarm bells for you when people called you Nathan?"

I looked back at him and sighed.

"Nobody ever *did*," I answered. "Look, I'm a civilian contractor. I don't know anybody else on this deployment. Never previously worked with anyone I met here. I'm not on a first-name basis with anybody I've run into on this trip. And by now, believe me, I am thoroughly used to people dropping the 'mac'. All too often 'mac Cool' becomes just 'Cool'. And more than half the time, people pronounce even *that* wrong, even if they get the 'mac', and rhyme it with 'pool'. So I was just happy that on this trip most people seemed to be at least *pronouncing* it right.

"When your name is mispronounced *all the time*, you take your wins where you can get them, and don't think too deeply about it. You know?"

Haskell looked at me, then nodded slowly after a moment.

"Okay," he conceded. "I guess I can see that."

He had a lot more questions for me, but most of them I had no worries about because I knew my cover had been carefully set up. Everything in the files would show me as just another civilian contractor, in the same specialty as Cole. The one thing that couldn't be faked was the actual assignment, or I'd have just gone under my own name in the first place. I knew that Cole had been chosen because he looked plausibly like me, had a similar name, and had an assignment on the right forward base, that I could step into his place and complete without any difficulty. So all that had been necessary was to intercept his assignment and the papers for it, and route them to me instead. I'd showed up in his stead and flown to the Middle East in his place, done his job, and the rest was history.

...Oh, and one evening, as I was finishing up the day's work in the admin building that I was already supposed to have access to for the job I was officially there to do, I casually walked into an office I wasn't supposed to be in, while nobody was looking, and moved one file folder from that office to the in-tray in a different office. There'd been a guard stationed outside the door of the second office, but when I told him all I needed to do was deliver that one folder, he'd glanced at my pass, then let me in and watched while I dropped it into the in-tray. I was only in there five seconds, and his eyes never once left me. And *that* two minutes had been the purpose of the entire caper.

Anyway, since my *actual* identity checked out against the subcontractor's records, I was able to eventually convince Lieutenant Haskell over the course of the next few days that the identity mismatch was *someone else's* paperwork screw up, that I had no idea I had another contractor's paperwork and assignment, and it was simply an oversight that I hadn't checked it closely enough myself to catch the mistake.

"It looks like this entire screw-up happened internal to your employer," Haskell finally told me. "We've been in communication with them, and they don't understand how it happened, but they're taking full responsibility. So you're off the hook.

"You realize that since all of your *paperwork* says you're Nathan Cole, it's Nathan Cole who will get paid for the work you did? Unless you can manage to straighten that out on your own with your employer?"

I sighed.

"Truth is, I kinda needed the money. But who knows. Maybe Cole needs it worse. I hope he appreciates me taking his bullet."

Haskell nodded understandingly.

"Shit happens," he agreed. "Sorry it worked out this way. We'll take care of getting you back Stateside, once you're recovered enough to travel. We can do that much for you."

"Thanks, Lieutenant," I replied.

They kept me about another week and a half before declaring me fit to travel. By that time I was able to walk, and indeed Physical Therapy was getting me up twice a day and having me walk around under supervision. I'd recover faster with activity, they assured me. Then they discharged me, and I got a ride back to Rammstein and a free seat on a MAC flight back to the United States.

I got home nearly two and a half weeks later than the original plan, but I got home, only a little the worse for wear, and under the circumstances I was willing to settle for that. It beat coming back in a body bag.

Prologue II: Last Week Tonight

I was on a mission from the Box. Not from God; it wasn't dark, I didn't have a half pack of cigarettes, and I wasn't wearing sunglasses. And I don't look anything like either of the Blues Brothers, anyway.

At least, I was *reasonably* sure the Box wasn't any kind of god.

I was slowly approaching a medium-sized industrial plant, from the back side.   There were two reasons for this.   The first was that my information said it was back here somewhere that some kind of illegal discharge was happening. The second was that it would be much easier to get into the plant from this side.

I was dressed to look the part of a chemical engineer, hard-hat and all. But over the top of those clothes, I was wearing what amounted to a single-use disposable ghillie suit, made mostly from tissue paper.   It didn't need to make me invisible; just inconspicuous until I got close. It only needed to fool the cameras watching the fence. I'd put it on before I started my approach, a half mile back into the woods that ran up the face of the line of gentle hills that I'd reached the bottom of about two hours ago.   Since then I'd been quartering back and forth looking for something that shouldn't be here.

The ground was pretty uneven back here. There'd been a lot of fill dumped after the ground the plant sat on was cleared, and it had been ignored and left to get overgrown. Over the years, brush had moved in and taken over. That provided an abundance of concealment, but also by the same token made it pretty hard to find anything from any distance. But I thought I was onto something now. I kept catching a whiff of something acrid from upwind when the wind shifted just right. So I was slowly working my way in that direction, trying not to miss anything.

About half an hour later, I found it. The chemical smell got stronger and steadier, until I came upon a small depression in the ground, masked from a distance by the surrounding brush. The undergrowth around the depression was stunted, sickly. The ground was slick, sodden, waterlogged, discolored with foul-smelling slime in shades of yellow-green to red-orange and brown. There was a sluggish stream near here, I knew. I'd crossed it three times. It fed into a creek, that in turn fed into the river from which the town got its drinking water.

I worked my way around the edge towards the plant, careful not to step into the ooze, and in about thirty yards or so I came upon what I was looking for, a pipe protruding almost horizontally from a slight swell in the ground. Multicolored slime oozed from the pipe. The vapors made my eyes water and my nasal passages burn, despite the activated-charcoal filter mask I was wearing.

I took a bundle from a pocket and unwrapped it. It contained a small jar made from chemical-resistant polysulfone plastic, a waxed-paper funnel, a handful of wipes, a couple of ziplock bags, and a set of neoprene gloves. I gloved up, slipped the funnel into the mouth of the jar, and extended it toward the pipe, capturing about half a jar of the effluent, being careful not to spill any down the side of the jar. When I had enough, I backed away a dozen steps or so. I didn't want to stay close to that pipe and the stinging fumes any longer than I had to.

I capped the jar, set it down on the ground for a moment, then opened the wipes and wiped down the outside of the jar just to be sure. I pulled out my phone, accessed its sensors, and read off the exact GPS coordinates, then took out a permanent marker and carefully copied them onto the label on the jar. I marked it "S1", added the date and time, then slipped it into a ziplock bag, rolled the bag around it and sealed it, then put that into a *second* bag and did the same. Then I put the double-bagged jar away.

There was dirt piled over the top of the pipe, forming a long, low mound about a foot and a half high. I wasn't surprised at all that it appeared to lead almost directly toward the plant. I started following it back, as closely as cover allowed. About twenty yards away from the fetid spill I poked a hole in the ground next to the pipe with the toe of my boot, and buried the waxed paper funnel and the used wipe. Not the ideal thing to do, but it would be a bigger risk to carry them with me.

Now that I was heading directly for the plant, it only took me about another fifteen minutes before I was in reach of the back fence. It was a pretty good fence, really: twelve feet of chain link topped with two strands of actual razor wire. It'd be fairly difficult to get over in a hurry, and there were closed-circuit cameras on poles inside the fence every hundred yards or so.

That was fine by me, because I wasn't planning on going *over* the fence. I worked my way along the fence a little way in the bushes looking for a likely spot, and it didn't take me too long to find one. I looked around the area and identified the closest two cameras. Looked like the ones I'd previously designated K and L. Of the two, I was closer to K. I'd determined from prior observation that the cameras all scanned back and forth on the same two-minute cycle, but that occasionally a camera would jam and skip a sweep. It didn't seem anyone paid the jams any attention unless a camera stayed stuck; then someone from the security company would come out and unjam or replace it. A couple of times a day an actual security guard walked the fence, but he should have made his previous pass over an hour ago and shouldn't be back for nearly another two.

Still in the bushes, I scanned the edge of the plant for any movement. There was nobody in sight. I tore off the paper ghillie suit, buried it shallowly under one of the bushes, then checked for movement again. Still clear.

I took out my phone and sent one message. "Simulate jam camera K, next cycle." Then I waited for the response. Breaching the security system had been easy; there was a known hard-coded vendor default password on a gateway device that had made it trivial to gain access to the system. Security in SCADA was a joke, and my strange collaborator would be breaching the system again right now, like a hot knife through butter.

I waited, and watched the camera. It swiveled through its slow scan, looking my way, hesitated, swiveled slowly back the other way to the far extent of its arc. Stopped. My phone bleeped. I checked the screen. A single word. Go.

Camera L, the next over, was now looking directly towards me. I waited for it to track around far enough that I was outside its field of view, then scurried out of the bushes and went straight to my target spot on the fence. With camera K briefly disabled, I had about a minute of blind spot to work with. Compound-action cutters out. Clip one strand, two, enough to loosen the bottom edge of the fence. Camera K should have tracked back this way by now, if it didn't have a simulated "jam." I threw myself flat on the ground and rolled *under* the fence against only moderate resistance, tugged the fence back into place, hooked it back together with the pieces I'd clipped, got up, and walked away from the fence and directly into the nearest cluster of pipes, making certain I was in shadow. Then I stopped and watched the cameras.

Camera L had almost reached its full traverse back towards me. I'd be on the edge of its vision now if I wasn't concealed among the pipes. As I watched, L stopped and reversed, tracking away again... and, on the other, closer pole, camera K jerked and resumed its scan.

One brief, not-unexpected "jam" that wouldn't raise any alarms, and nobody had seen a thing. I was now inside the plant, and headed for my next objective with nobody the wiser.

Taking care to watch for anyone else moving around and not to step out into the open where another camera might see me, I started working my way between the tanks and pipes, looking for the right set of markings on a pipe. I knew roughly where I was in the plant and had studied both the available schematics and a detailed set of drone photos, so it didn't take me too long to find the right pipe. I started following it to the junction I needed to reach, where there was a valve on the right pipe line that should have a gland.

Of course, it *figures* there was somebody already there. Two somebodies, in fact. I approached as closely as I could without breaking cover. They looked as though they'd just been working on the valve. They were wearing gear just like mine, and one was holding a large open-end wrench. It was very late afternoon by now, nearly shift change time. I got close enough, without breaking cover, that I could hear their voices.

"The leak's getting worse," one man griped. "We're going to need to drain this line and re-pack the gland before it gets out of hand."

"I'd sooner replace the valve," the other answered. "Who knows what kind of shape it's in inside?"

"Yeah, well, so would I, but we both know Tomlinson won't go for that. And with the shit that's in it, I don't really want to open this line if we can avoid it."

"You're right there," the second man sighed. "Well, I think it's tight again for now, but I want to check on it again in an hour or so before we call it good. I need to file a... well, okay, I need to *check in with* Burroughs and let him know it's deteriorating further. And I can't book overtime for an undocumented problem that we *all know* doesn't officially exist."

There was a pause.

"You ever worry about who we might be poisoning with this shit?" the first man asked.

"I don't make enough money to ask questions like that," the second replied. He didn't sound like he really believed his own answer.

"Yeah, I hear you. Tell you what, I've got to come back this way myself after I do the leak check on tank 41. Leave the wrench, and I'll get it on my way back."

"Thanks, Ed. Catch you at Slim's later?"

"Sure."

The second man hung the wrench up near the valve, and the two of them headed off in opposite directions. I gave it about five minutes, then warily approached the valve myself. There was a splash of fluid on the concrete below the valve. I sniffed. Yup. Same smell.

I looked around, all ways, then pulled out another jar and another waxed paper funnel. Grabbing the wrench so conveniently left there, I cracked the gland nut off until it started to seep, then held the jar under it and loosened it a bit further one-handed, until a narrow jet started trickling thickly from the gland. Again, I collected about a half jar, then tightened the gland again, holding the jar in place to catch anything else until the flow was reduced to slow drips. Then I put the jar down in a dry spot, tightened off the gland nut the rest of the way, and hung the wrench back up exactly as I'd found it.

I wiped and sealed the jar, took out my phone, and copied the GPS coordinates onto the label again. I marked this jar S2, then double-wrapped it like the first one and put it away. This time I also took a photo of the valve, from a few feet away so that enough nearby markings were visible to locate exactly where it was. I bundled up the funnel, the used wipe, and my disposable mask, and departed the scene before 'Ed' came back. Then I headed unhurriedly toward the front of the plant. I made a detour to take one more sample along the way, which I labeled S3, handling it exactly as I had the other two.

I started encountering a few people as I got nearer to the front of the plant, but I was careful neither to get too close to anyone, nor to obviously *avoid* anyone. You can get away with a lot by just looking like you belong there. Don't ask how I know. I casually tossed my bundle of used wipes and such into a convenient dumpster, then walked into the front lot, got onto a park-and-ride shuttle bus along with a crowd of others, and just sat there looking boredly out the window. Nobody paid me much attention.

After a few minutes, the bus pulled out and went straight out the front gate without any problem. Nobody checks IDs of a busload of people *leaving* a plant. Nobody in the commercial world, anyway. If they weren't *supposed* to be there, they'd have been stopped on the way *in*, after all.

"You new?" asked a voice from across the bus aisle, as we were probably half way to the park-and-ride. "Don't think I've seen you around."

I shrugged without turning around.

"Been here about three weeks," I replied unconcernedly. "I keep to myself."

"New, huh? Who hired you in?"

"Burroughs," I replied. Based on what I'd overheard earlier, that name would probably discourage much in the way of further questions.

"Huh. Well that figures," my questioner said. "Tight mouth on that one. What's he got you doing?"

"Tank inspections." I'd anticipated I might have to answer a question like that if someone got curious.

"Huh. *Those* tanks? Rather you than me. Well, good luck with it."

"Thanks," I replied. Then the shuttle bus was pulling into the park-and-ride. As soon as the doors opened I got up and was among the first off the bus. Not waiting for anyone else to strike up an unwanted conversation, I strode off heading towards the corner where I'd parked. I went straight to my car, got in, and left.

When I got back to the motel I was using as base camp, I washed my hands thoroughly, put on a pair of disposable nitrile gloves, then took the three sample jars and wiped them down again. I used a portable inkjet printer I'd paid cash for two days earlier to print the photos I'd taken, copied them to a fresh USB thumb drive I'd also bought with cash, clipped the thumb drive to the photos, and put those in the box as well. Finally I printed a map section and a satellite photo of the plant, marking on both the exact GPS coordinates where I'd taken each sample. Again, I labeled the spots S1, S2, and S3. I wrapped the jars in bubble wrap, packed everything up in a box, and sealed it. Then I marked the box with the date, and the name of the plant.

With all *that* done, I went and got a long, hot shower to get the remaining traces of chemical stink off me, then changed my clothes and went to find some dinner.

═══════════

The next day, I put my package in the car and headed for the regional EPA headquarters at the Federal building in Omaha. It was about a ninety minute drive. I parked nearby, walked in carrying my package, and went through the metal detectors.

"What's in the box?" asked a security guard.

"Site samples for EPA," I replied. "Actionable evidence of illegal toxic waste discharging." He nodded, then swiped the top and a side of the box with an explosives detection swab. It came up clean, of course.

"Go ahead, sir."

I headed for the elevators. I already knew the EPA office was on the third floor. So up I went, and I walked into the EPA office, and just put my box on the front desk. The woman behind the desk shot me an inquiring look, and started to open her mouth to ask who I was.

"Please see that these samples reach the appropriate department head," I said, before she could speak. "They were taken yesterday at Longwillow Industries and prove that Longwillow is illegally discharging caustic organometallic waste. There's documentation in there to show exactly where and when each sample was taken."

She seemed a little taken aback, which was exactly what I wanted. I wanted her on her back foot, because my plans didn't include sticking around for a long explanation.

"Uh, let me call someone to come and take care of you," she

answered, flustered. "Who shall I say brought these in?" I was already turning away.

"Report it as coming from an anonymous whistleblower," I told her. Then I just walked out before anyone thought to stop me.

And then, as they say, I went home. This assignment was done, and my time was my own again. For now.

═══════════════

It turned out I got nearly a week of being left to my own devices—*mostly*.

HEIGHTENED THREAT LEVEL, the Box told me, on my second day back. PLEASE BE PREPARED FOR POTENTIAL ALERTS AT ANY TIME.

I didn't know what exact 'alerts' or 'heightened threat' the Box was referring to, and it wouldn't tell me. But it had never led me wrong... yet. So just as a precaution, I didn't leave the house unarmed except to run. Every time I went out, it was with my favorite pistol—a Laugo Alien in .40 Smith and Wesson—in a shoulder holster under my jacket. And just because *you never know*, I took its Helix suppressor with me as well. Better to have it and not need it, than need it and not have it.

Was I overreacting? I didn't know. But by this time, if the Box told me 'heightened threat,' you bet your ass I was going to take it seriously.

It was six more days before my phone went *Bleep!* again, just as I was about to make a grocery stop. I pulled it out and read the message.

MAXIMUM PRIORITY, the message read. Then it gave a street address, and just one single instruction: REACH THE UPPER FLOOR BEFORE DARK.

Well, *crap*. I pulled up the location in GPS. I was going to have to hurry to be there and inside before dark. I pushed it up five more on the speedometer to be sure.

1: The First Day

The Box had told me to be here, so, here I was, approaching a smallish suburban house, not much bigger than a two-up-two-down, in what was clearly a fairly respectable, if not overly expensive, neighborhood. There was no real traffic on the street at the moment, and the houses, most of them modern-built mock-Victorians, were set back from the street. I scanned for entry routes, observers, and possible threats as I approached the house. Like most of the houses on the street, it had a fenced-in back yard. I could see a gate in the fence, beside the house. That was good.

It was near to dusk. Lights were on inside the house. I really hoped that didn't mean a problem. Looking as casual as I could, as if I belonged there, I walked up and turned in on the side path. I didn't know whether I had time to look for a less visible way in. I walked directly up to the gate, put my hand on the latch, pushed down, and it opened without resistance. It wasn't locked. I heaved a sigh of relief. That saved me having to do things which might be awkward if I were noticed, like climbing over it. I wished once again I'd had a little more lead time to let me properly recon the area.

Keeping a wary eye out for security cameras, either on the house or its neighbor, I walked around to the back of the house and found the back door. Next to it, what looked like a small outside storage shed was built onto the back of the house, nicely blocking any possible view of the back door area from *that* side. There was another gate in the back fence. I inferred it opened onto the back service alley I now remembered seeing earlier as I pulled into the loop. God forbid deliveries should come to the front of the house. But I'd bet ninety percent of them did anyway.

The door was locked, but seriously, come on, American contractor-grade residential back door lock. I pulled out my lock picks, and was inside in less than a minute. It was twenty minutes to seven. I could have *broken* the lock faster, but it would have made more noise, and anyway, I had neither the need nor the desire to break anything. That's seldom a good start to making friends and influencing people.

"Reach the upper floor before dark."

Okay. I was in a back hallway. A door on my right looked like a closet. I didn't bother with that. An open doorway ahead of me led into what was obviously a kitchen, and ahead, past a small dogleg, it was a straight shot to the front door. Just inside the front door on the right, a staircase with a turned wooden banister led upstairs. There was an open arched doorway on the left.

I listened for sounds of movement or occupation, but heard nothing. I scouted my way forward, pie-slicing the kitchen and front room as I passed their doorways. Nobody. But the hallway light was on. Well, whatever. Not my circus, not my monkeys. Maybe whoever lived here just wasn't a fan of coming home to a dark house. Couldn't blame them, really. I didn't like it much either.

I reached the stairs and went upstairs. The top landing was small. A door to the side led to a room with nothing in it but a folding table and several neat stacks of boxes. Most of them looked like file boxes. Straight back led into a rather busily-furnished room with a computer on a desk. Ordinary-looking compact desktop machine, moderate size monitor, probably not a power user. It looked like a cluttered home office. The computer was on, nothing else was. Behind that was a fairly tidy bedroom, with a large picture window facing the back of the house, and to the right beyond that, the master bathroom. Good. Target area achieved.

There was little in the way of good concealment in the home office. The bedroom, though, had a large, freestanding dark wood wardrobe opposite the end of the bed, near the back end of the wall to the left of the door. The corner behind it was in deep shadow. I hoped that would be good enough. I looked out the window, which was hinged outward, and saw that just below it was the roof of the attached shed or storage room I'd seen. The roof looked solid. That might be important. I made certain that the window appeared fully closed, but was not latched. I might need to go out through it in a hurry.

A dresser near the window had a large mirror. I adjusted it just slightly so that from behind the wardrobe, I could see through the office out to the landing and the very top of the stairs.

It would have to do. I had no idea yet why I was supposed to be here, but... the Box had told me, so here I was. It had never steered me *wrong* before, not exactly, but there had been some... tense moments. And it very seldom told me the full details in advance of *why* it gave me the instructions it did. I got to figure that out for myself. It had been particularly terse this time, though. As though it was in a hurry. I fitted the suppressor to the Laugo, as a precaution.

Just past seven, I heard a small car pull up outside. Then the front door opened, and closed again a moment later.

Almost immediately, the hallway light—the only light in the house on—turned off. Okay, that was... *odd*, but probably worked in my favor. Maybe. I had no idea what the fuck was going on and was totally playing it by ear. What light there was now came from the window. A moment later I heard footsteps on the stairs. After a few seconds, a young woman dressed all in white came into view up the stairs. Looked pretty.

She slipped her pumps off on the landing and left them lying there, then walked barefoot through the office and into the bedroom. She started shedding clothing on her way through the bedroom, first undoing and taking off her shiny white sleeveless top as she walked past me and into the light from the window, and casually tossing it aside. She didn't glance my way. Yeah, really pretty girl, and looked classy. About average female height. Late twenties, at a guess.

There was nothing under the discarded top but a white soft-cup bra, which I couldn't help but notice was well filled. Her blonde hair came down to the middle of her back. She undid her skirt as she walked into the bathroom, then stepped out of it and dropped it on the floor. She turned towards the shower, turned the bathroom light on, then took a couple of steps to her right. Standing directly in front of the glass door, her back to me, she took off her bra and dropped it, leaving her in a pair of high-cut white satin panties, then she shucked the panties off and stepped out of them, tossed them away with a toe, opened the glass door and stepped into the shower. She turned the water on and stood under the spray.

Still no clue what I was here for. But I could see into the shower from my chosen spot, and she was damned easy on the eyes, so I idly kept *half* an eye on her showering while I waited for any clues that would let me figure out *why* the Box had sent me here. I hoped like hell there was going to be some kind of enlightenment before she came out of the bathroom. Please, let this *not* be the time the Box led me astray and set me up to look like some kind of creeper.

Then I saw movement in the mirror. *Uh-oh.* A burly man in what looked to be a somewhat ill-fitting suit was coming up the stairs. I hadn't even heard the front door open and close. *That* was suspicious in itself. I had the immediate feeling he was up to no good.

He walked quietly into the office, taking his time, yanked a cord off a table lamp, and wrapped it around his hands, then headed for the bathroom. Oh, *crap*, I did not like how this was shaping up one bit.

He crossed the room without looking into my dark corner, and paused just out of sight outside the bathroom, right about the time the girl shut the water off. She stepped out of the shower and passed out of my line of sight. Ugly Brute stepped stealthily in behind her. Yeeeeaaaaah, doubleplus ungood. *NOW* I was suddenly certain why I was here. Not on *my* watch you don't, buddy.

I stepped out from behind the wardrobe, moving quickly but silently, drawing out my Laugo .40 as I circled the room to regain line of sight. I was glad I'd had the foresight (*ha, ha*) to fit the suppressor.

I'd only managed two steps before I heard her cry out. Abandoning stealth, I sped up, and by the time I cleared the corner, Plug Thugly had his improvised garotte around her throat and her feet off the floor. She was still struggling and making noise, but she wouldn't be for very much longer, if I didn't act fast and effectively.

I had a clear shot right there and then, so it was an easy, instant decision. I dropped into a Weaver stance, aimed carefully, and double-tapped him in the head. Even with the suppressor, the two shots still echoed in the tiled bathroom. No matter what Hollywood might tell you, a suppressor on anything significantly more potent than a subsonic .380 ACP does not make a gun silent, or even *nearly* silent, it just brings it down from 'immediate permanent hearing damage loud' to merely loud. The sound wouldn't carry far, though, this far in the back of the house.

This close, it would have been hard to miss. Blood and brains splattered across the floor and far wall. Thugly froze for an instant, then folded like a puppet with its strings cut, the garotte pulling the girl down with him, but the muscles that had been tightening it suddenly limp. She ripped it away from her throat with a shuddering half-sob and struggled free on her hands and knees, looked at the bloody wall, looked down at her dead assailant. One hand went towards her mouth and she drew in a shaking, horrified gasp that sounded like it was going to turn into a scream at any moment if she could manage to stop hyperventilating. I stepped forward quickly as I holstered my pistol, deliberately making enough noise for her to hear, not making any attempt to hide. Her gaze snapped to me and she froze. Wide, terrified eyes met mine.

I stopped moving and showed her my now-empty hands, fingers spread wide.

"I'm here to *HELP* you," I said quickly. "Please don't scream. Are you all right?"

Her mouth moved, but for a moment no sounds came out.

"Listen: you're alive, and he's dead. The first is what we wanted, the second was its price." I kept my voice low and calm, trying to calm her in turn. "We can argue gunshot capitalism later, but for now, we need to go. Can you manage that?"

Then she found her voice.

"*WHO ARE YOU?*" she demanded, her voice shrill. She was clearly frightened out of her skin. And why wouldn't she be?

"A friend," I reassured her, trying to keep my voice low and calming. "I was sent to protect you." *I think*, I mentally added.

"To *protect* me?" She clearly didn't entirely believe me yet, but at least she wasn't screaming. She seemed to suddenly notice that she was still naked, grabbed at a bath towel on the floor that she had apparently dropped there when Thugly grabbed her, and held it in front of her, still on her knees.

"Who *sent* you? Where did you come from? ...Where did *HE* come from?" She was visibly shaking. I didn't blame her in the least.

"Look," I said, trying to sound as calm and reassuring as I could, "I know *you* don't know *me*, I don't know *you*, and I'm pretty sure *neither* of us knows *him*." I pointed towards Thugly. "But we're very short on time, and right now, until further notice, please consider me your personal bodyguard. I've danced this dance a few times, and I can tell you already, there is no doubt in my mind that this was a professional contract hit, not some random weirdo who followed you home from the gas station."

She looked at me, then at the thug who'd just tried to kill her, then back at me. She started to climb to her feet, still holding the towel in front of her. I didn't distress her further by pointing out that it was still half-balled and wasn't really covering much. It was a nice view. She was a *really* pretty girl.

Don't get distracted, I told myself sternly.

"That means two things," I continued, keeping my eyes determinedly on her face. "First, it means someone probably spent quite a lot of money to have you become dead." She gasped again, her eyes still wide and frightened.

"And second, it means that we should assume that this thug *probably* has backup, and that his backup is *probably* going to arrive very shortly if he doesn't show up back outside pretty soon.

"And *THAT* means we need to get you out of here, *right now*, because we don't know what or where his backup is, or how much, or when it's coming. So can we please hold lengthy explanations for later?"

She hesitated for a long moment, then nodded her head vigorously.

"What do I need to do?" she asked shakily. She still sounded scared, but was obviously fighting to get herself under control.

"Good girl." Reassurance first was always a good tactic. "I need you to get clothes on, quickly. Dark, casual, inconspicuous. Comfortable clothes you can move quickly in, that will keep you warm and protect you from minor abrasions. Shoes that you can run in if you need to. No heels. Anything but heels or sandals."

She nodded. Went to towel herself off, stopped, looked at the towel, and flinched like hell. She froze for a long moment, then dropped the towel like there was a scorpion in it. Then she looked at me, and walked quickly past me, naked and still wet, one arm across her breasts, her lower lip trembling. There didn't seem to be any blood on her that I could see, which was good. I didn't want anything to nudge her towards losing it. I needed her functional to get her out of here safely. She was holding it together well so far. I hoped that would continue.

She opened a drawer and took out a clean bra and panties, quickly put them on with her back to me, grabbed a pale blue T-shirt and pulled that on over her head. I kept her only in the corner of my vision as she dressed, just as I had while she showered, keeping watch towards the stairs and front door.

"Should we call the police?" she asked, as she pulled out what turned out to be dark grey leopard-print jogging pants, then sat down on the end of her bed and started pulling those on too.

"No time for that," I replied. "When seconds hang in the balance, the police are only minutes away. *If* you're lucky. Also, their job is to *investigate* crimes, not prevent them, and the Supreme Court has ruled they cannot be held responsible for failing to protect you."

She nodded.

"Right. I know that," she agreed, nodding. Her tone suggested an unspoken *'And I should have thought of that myself.'* As soon as she had the joggers on, she grabbed a Harvard sweatshirt off the back of a chair and pulled it on over her head.

"Good choices," I nodded approvingly. She finished up with short socks and a set of blue Adidas running shoes. It all took her maybe three minutes.

"Fantastic," I declared. "We're out of here."

I went to the window and peeked out, particularly looking out over the back fence for any sign of light or motion. I saw nothing and no vehicles in sight. Hopefully that meant Thugly's backup was out front. Meanwhile she had picked up the vest she'd discarded earlier, pulled a phone out of it, and was about to slip it into her pocket.

"No!" I said, more sharply than I'd intended. She looked at me, the question obvious on her face. "Leave the phone. Please. It can be used to track your location. Even when it's turned off, it's not *really* 'off'."

She thought about that for a moment, looked at the phone, then dropped it on the floor and kicked it under the bed. Good, this girl was a smart cookie. That improved her chances enormously.

"Right, we're going out this window."

"The window?" she asked.

Then I heard the front door open again.

"We're out of time," I whispered, holding a finger to my lips. "Window. *NOW.*"

I turned and opened the window as silently as I could, then helped her out the window and down onto the shed roof. There were footsteps on the stairs and voices in the hall.

I positioned the latch carefully, then vaulted after her, reached up, and pushed the window closed. I heard the latch snick home. Good. That might delay pursuit from considering the window as our escape route.

I jumped down off the shed, tucked and rolled the landing, then stood and held my arms up to her. She squatted on the edge and then jumped, landing just in front of me. She stumbled, but I caught her and steadied her. She looked into my face for a moment, then looked away. I led her straight to the back gate and opened it as quietly as I could, alert for any movement from the other side. There was nothing but trash cans and a couple of dumpsters. Fucking amateurs. This was the obvious discreet way in and out, if you knew it was here. Professionals with time to scout out the scene beforehand would have come in this way. I would have used it myself, if I'd known about the back gate. Honest.

Behind us, there was a shout from the house. They'd probably just found Mr. Bad Example.

"Clear," I told her. "Out, quickly." She ducked through without hesitation. I followed her out and closed the gate behind us, then set off down the service road at an easy jog, staying close to the side. She followed immediately.

"This way," I said, perhaps unnecessarily. "Try to stay about ten feet behind me. Stay near the fences. If any shooting starts, drop flat, roll over next to the fence, and cover your face until I tell you to move. Get behind a dumpster if you can."

"Got it," she answered tensely. "Flat next to the fence, dumpster for cover if I'm near one, hide my face." She sounded afraid and shaken, but she had it together. Damn, I was starting to like this girl already.

When we got near to the mouth of the service alley, a dozen houses down, I slowed to a walk, approached the corner of the last fence, then stopped. She took the cue and moved quietly up behind me.

"My car is parked over there," I pointed out quietly, indicating the silvery-gray SUV I'd arrived in, parked under trees across the street. "You're going to wait here, just in case there's anyone on watch in front of your house. I'm going to walk across to my car, get in, and make a U-turn which is going to put me right *there*." I pointed to a spot about twenty feet in front of us.

"The doors will be unlocked. As soon as I reach that spot, you open the door, get in, and we're gone. Got it?" She nodded twice.

"Right then," I said. "Thirty seconds."

I stepped out from the corner and unhurriedly crossed the street, walking directly up to the gray XC60 I called the Gray Ghost. I could hear a sizable engine idling up the street. I scanned the street quickly as I walked, without breaking step. There was a small import sedan in her driveway, a Honda I thought, presumably hers. There was also a dark full-size SUV parked in front of her driveway, blocking the Honda in, headlights off, looked like maybe a Cadillac Escalade from here. Couldn't see much detail.

"Fucking amateurs," I muttered aloud.

I reached the car, opened the door and got in. I turned the car on but left the lights off, hit the unlock-all button, and pulled a gentle, slow U-turn that put me six inches from the curb on the other side, right where I'd told her I would be. The passenger door would be out of line-of-sight from the Escalade and from her front yard. The girl was already in motion, and was pulling the door open almost before the car had fully come to rest. She climbed in and closed the door in a single motion, then reached for her seat belt. She continued to impress me.

I put my foot down and eased us away, not smartly enough to make noise or attract attention, then turned the lights on. The car had only been stopped for two, maybe three seconds. Even if whoever was in the Escalade had been looking this way, they probably hadn't even noticed me stop. We went straight out to the main road, and I turned right on the red and pulled away firmly, but not dramatically. Once we were away clean, I pulled on my own seat belt, and the car stopped complaining at me.

"A bodyguard driving a *Volvo*?" she asked me, her voice brittle with stress.

"It's a Polestar XC60T8," I replied. "I call it the Gray Ghost. Hybrid-electric drive train, engineered by Volvo's semi-secret high-performance division. It's inconspicuous, doesn't stand out, nearly silent at low speeds, all-wheel-drive, makes over four hundred and fifty horsepower, goes like stink compared to nearly anything else in its class, and has a sensor suite that would give a lot of third-generation jet fighters feelings of inadequacy. It's not a serious off-roader, but it will go *pretty nearly* anywhere in nearly any weather conditions, including white-out snow—slowly—if necessary."

She thought about that for a moment, then nodded.

"Where are we going?" she asked, a quiver still in her voice.

"My house, first," I replied, "if that's okay with you. I had no time to plan or set up anything else, but we have no reason to believe whoever wants you dead even knows I exist, so it's as good a safe-house as any other until we know more, and a lot better than most. Also, taking you there will simplify some explanations a lot." And complicate others, I thought to myself. "I could take you to a hotel, but I'd be a lot less able to protect you there.

"Right now, though, I need to be certain *first* that we don't have a tail. I'm pretty certain we got away cleanly, unheard and unseen, but I don't want to be bitten in the ass by assumptions." She nodded silently.

I took a semi-random evasive course through the nearby area for the next few minutes, working generally towards the highway, planning my route real-time using the GPS map, staying on side streets but avoiding any dead ends or one-way-in-and-out loops and carefully watching the rear view, trying not to remain stopped at lights, until I was certain we weren't being followed. Then I headed straight for the nearest highway on-ramp in the right direction, watching behind us to see that nobody suspiciously loitering near the ramp followed us up, and set the cruise right at the speed limit. We had about fifty miles to go.

"Great," I said, once we were on the highway, starting to relax. "We're clear, clean, and should be all but untrackable, unless the bad guys have eyes in the air.

"So. As I told you earlier, this was clearly a contract hit. There was backup, they were sitting right out front of your house in an Escalade, they came in as soon as their man was late getting back out, but they didn't watch the back service road or the back door. So a paid hit, with money behind it, but not really professionals, *definitely* not state-level actors. My first guess is mob or other organized crime.

"Which leaves a lot of questions unanswered. My, uh... dispatcher operates very much on a need-to-know basis, and, uh, there's a lot about you it apparently felt I didn't need to know yet." That was perhaps a slip, but she didn't seem to have caught the 'it'.

"So, first priority: Do you have any idea who might want you dead?"

In hindsight, it might have been a bad time to ask that. Her hands started to shake, her lower lip trembled, and she shook her head violently, then began sobbing. Tears streamed down her face. Dammit. The adrenaline had worn off and the reaction had just hit her, *hard*, and

I hadn't helped that at all. The attempted hit and subsequent escape had primed her, but I was the thoughtless jerk who'd pressed the 'Fire in the Hole!' button. I mentally kicked myself, *hard*.

"I'm sorry," I offered gently. "That was clueless of me. This hasn't been your greatest day, has it?"

"No," she choked out between sobs. *"Fucking HELL no."*

I took my right hand off the wheel, and rested it on the center console where she could easily reach it if she wanted to. After a few moments, she grabbed my hand and held on tightly. That was a good sign that I hadn't completely blown her trust. I squeezed her hand softly.

"You're alive, and you're safe," I reassured her. "We're at least one jump ahead, we have the initiative, and I'm not going to let anything happen to you if I can help it." I paused. "What's your name?" Always a good safe grounding question.

"Sharon. Sharon Kielic." Her voice was shaky, but starting to steady.

"Hi, Sharon. What do you do for a living?"

"I'm an associate. At a corporate law partnership."

"Okay, Sharon. Here's what we're going to do. We're going to get you to safety, first of all. I want you to drop out of the picture, don't call anyone, don't go online, don't access anything, don't use any credit cards, until we know more." She gave a little choked-off nervous half-laugh.

"Credit cards?" she said. "I've got the clothes on my back. I didn't think to pick up anything else."

"That's fine. I've got your back. Anything you need is covered. Within reason."

"Thanks," she sniffled. "I hope I don't have to take you up on that too much."

"Don't worry about it," I replied. "And then, we're going to see if we can figure out what this is about. My guess is this was set off by something you saw, something that you perhaps don't *know* you know, maybe even something they only *think* you know, some piece of legal information that someone doesn't want coming to light."

<hr>

We drove north as dusk turned into night, turning off the highway after just over forty miles. Another fifteen minutes, and we turned up a short, tree-lined driveway, looped around behind my house, waited a few seconds while the garage door finished opening, and drove in. I shut off the car, hit close on the remote opener, and got out. I went straight to the charger connector, unhooked it, and plugged it into the charging port, as she went around the back of the car. I thumbed the inside garage door unlocked as she approached, but before I could open the door, she walked straight up to me and threw her arms around me, burying her face in my shoulder. After a moment of surprise, I put mine around her and gently held her close. Her breathing slowly became more even.

After a couple of minutes, she loosened her grasp and looked up at me.

"Thank you," she said, her voice unsteady. "I needed that. I still *really* want to know why you were in my house, but it's because you *were* that I'm alive. I couldn't have held out much longer."

"I'm... glad I was there," I answered. "Though to be honest, until a few seconds earlier I didn't know why I'd been sent there." She gave me a quizzical look. "I apologize for breaking into your home, by the way."

She laughed sharply. Good. That was probably healthy.

"I'll let you off this time, all things considered," she said, "but don't let it happen again, all right?" She had the ghost of a smile.

"I'll try," I replied. "And I will explain as much as I can, as soon as I can. For right now... are you hungry?"

She thought about that for a moment.

"Not... very," she said. "My stomach feels like butterflies are holding a rave in it. But I should probably eat."

"Are you good with fish and chips? Not fancy, but fast; I can just throw them into the oven."

"Sure," she replied. "I'm good with that."

I led the way into the house, a fairly modern split-level with some custom modifications, passing first through the small storeroom—well, actually it was meant to be a mud room, but I used it as a storeroom—between the garage and kitchen, stopping to grab a bag of frozen seasoned fries and a package of beer-battered fish fillets out of the big chest freezer. Then through into the kitchen. I turned the oven on, pulled out a large baking sheet, put a wire tray on top, and spread fish and chips across it. I put them in on fan bake, and set a timer. They'd be done within a few minutes of each other.

Then I led her through the kitchen, across the hallway, toward the back of the house, and down the stairs to the lower floor. There were four doors off the small hallway at the bottom of the stairs, two on one side, one at each end. I opened the first side door and walked in. She followed me hesitantly.

There wasn't much in the room. Just a big square abstract painting hung on the back wall, an overhead light, and a low platform built out of six-by-six pressure-treated landscape timbers. On top of the platform was the Box. She looked at it, and stopped in her tracks. I could see her gaze scanning it. Then she looked questioningly at me.

"I promised you explanations," I told her. "The explanations start here, with the Box."

The Box was roughly cubical, a little over a meter on a side. I'd stood a small flat-screen TV on top of it. The TV wasn't plugged into anything.

The surface of the Box was deeply detailed, a fractal pattern of triangular facets and triangular holes, and between all the triangles there were more triangles, and more triangles between those, and more, and more. Somewhere deep inside, there was light, a formless pale glow. Here and there, it leaked out through the holes.

She took two slow steps closer and peered at it close up. She went to put her hand on it, then stopped suddenly and drew her hand back.

"It's safe to touch, if you want to," I reassured her. She turned to look at me, a question on her face. "And yes, it's triangles all the way down. I've looked at it with a jeweler's loupe. Just... more triangles within triangles. I looked up the pattern. It's... something similar to a 3D version of a fractal pattern called a Sierpiński gasket. It looks the same at every scale. It goes on forever, as far as I can tell. Theoretically the ideal Sierpiński gasket has infinite detail. It's relatively easy to program a 2D version on a computer screen that goes down to sub-pixel-level detail, and zoom in on it, and just keep zooming in. This? I don't know. Finer detail than I can figure out any way to see.

"And it never gets dusty. Dust won't settle on it. Or on that TV, now that I put it there. It just drifts off." I pointed to the slight line of dust that started an even two inches *away* from the Box, on all sides.

"What... *is* it?" she asked.

"I don't honestly know," I answered truthfully. "I call it the Oracle Box. It was just... *here* one day. I found it in the middle of the hallway. I moved it down here, because... it's an awkward thing to explain to visitors. Precisely because I *don't* have a good answer to the question you just asked."

There was a faint electronic *snap* from the TV on top of the Box. It lit up on its own, and words appeared on its screen.

HELLO, SHARON, said the Box, in blue letters.

She stepped, almost leaped, back towards me and grabbed my arm in a death-grip.

"How does it know my *name*?"

"It seems to know a great deal," I told her. "But it is very sparing at times with what it knows." I gestured towards it. "*This* is what told me to go to your house this evening."

She looked at me as though I was mad, and started to shake her head, but the words on the screen changed, and she caught the flicker out of the corner of her eye and turned to look at it.

YOU ARE SAFE AND UNHARMED, the Box said. MISSION ACCOMPLISHED. Then the text changed again.

PRIMARY ASSIGNMENT CONTINUES. FIND EVIDENCE.

She read it, repeated it to herself, turned to me.

"Find evidence?"

"I am going to infer," I answered slowly, "there is something that you perhaps know, or have access to, that involves you, and is in some way important to the Box's ends. I'm going to go out on a limb here and *guess* that it is *probably* the same thing that resulted in someone trying to have you killed." She flinched.

"The Box's ends?" she repeated doubtfully.

"I told you it was complicated. The Box doesn't share its rationales for the assignments it gives me. I don't know who, or what—if *anything* —is behind it. But it has never given me an assignment that was... well, *on balance*, illegal, though a couple have shaded the edge pretty hard, and every assignment it gives me ends in, in some way or another, making *something*... better. I mean... it has me do things at times that technically violate laws... but never, *so far*, in any way that would not be covered by the Doctrine of Culpability. I think."

"Like breaking into my house to save my life," she observed.

"Uh-huh," I agreed. "Exigent circumstances, is the legal term of art, I believe?"

She stared at me for a long moment, then backed off a couple of steps, shaking her head, arms wrapped around herself. It was obvious she was still in a very fragile mental space. Not that I could blame her in the slightest for that. I was, in fact, *incredibly* impressed with how well she was holding up with all of this. She was one in a hundred. Or maybe a thousand.

"You realize how *crazy* this sounds?" she asked.

I nodded in emphatic agreement.

"Oh, I know full well," I replied. "Believe me, you don't know the *half* of it. At one point I even went and had myself checked out by a shrink, one I hadn't used anything connected to the Box to choose or find, to make sure I wasn't delusional or hallucinating. Without, you know, mentioning the Box at all; just said I'd been under a lot of stress and I wanted a mental-health checkup to be sure I wasn't losing it. He ran me through a two-day battery of tests, and gave me a clean bill of health. Just told me I should get out more, get more social contact, maybe find a hobby, or get a pet. And I never told the Box where I was going.

"I got home after he gave me his assessment, and the Box said, Are you convinced now?"

She looked dubiously at the Box.

"That's... a bit creepy," she remarked.

"Can't entirely argue with you," I agreed. "Though it *did* just direct me to save your life. A directive, I note, of which I *FULLY* approve."

She opened her mouth to speak, then hesitated. After a long moment, she nodded slowly.

"I... can't truthfully claim to have any complaint about that," she said. "You know, *aside* from the whole attempted murder thing in the first place."

YOU ARE WELCOME, said the Box. Then, THIS IS IMPORTANT.

Sharon stared perplexed at the screen for a long moment, then began to laugh. There was a nervous edge to her laughter. Not surprising, really.

Right then, I heard the sound of the kitchen timer.

"Sounds like supper's up," I pointed out. "Let's go eat, and we can talk about Weird-Shit Fractal Boxes With Opinions while we eat. Now that you know—well, at least, have some tangible *evidence*—that I'm not some crazy dude just making shit up."

I turned around and we headed back upstairs to the kitchen. I let her go up the stairs ahead of me.

When we reached the kitchen, I pointed her to the cupboard that held my plates, tore a paper towel off the roll and lined a table bread-basket with it, then pulled the tray of fish and chips out of the oven and dumped them all into the basket. I took the basket to my dining room table, then came back for condiments.

"Where's the silverware?" Sharon asked. I pointed to a drawer. She opened it, scanned it, and reached in. Meanwhile I collected ketchup, tartar sauce, and malt vinegar. By the time I got back to the table she had set two places, side by side, and was sitting on the left waiting for me. I'd been going to set them opposite, out of courtesy, but didn't dispute it. I set down the condiments, sat down next to her, and offered her the basket. She took one piece of fish and a handful of fries, I took two, and we settled down to eat.

"So," she asked after a little while, "what sort of things does your... box... get you to do?"

"Besides rescuing fair maidens in distress?" I asked. She swallowed uncomfortably.

"Well, let's see. For example, just over a week ago, it had me go and collect some samples of some very nasty-looking illegally-discharged shit at a chemical plant in Nebraska, then drop them off at the regional office of the EPA. Probably not newsworthy. And most likely wouldn't have hit the news yet in any case.

"Something you might possibly have heard of: About three years ago, it had me pay a visit to a tower block on Ninth. Told me where to go, exactly what to look for and photograph, and how. It involved picking the locks on a few maintenance doors. Then it had me send the photos and a detailed description of precisely where each one was taken to the city building inspector's office."

"Wait," she interrupted. "Ninth avenue, three years, tower block... 440A South Ninth?"

"That's the one," I agreed.

She shook her head for a moment, then looked levelly at me.

"Harris Magnusson, the law firm I work at, handled the liability and malfeasance case against the contractor for substandard workmanship and materials after the 440 South Ninth project was condemned," she said. I blinked in surprise. "I've read the case file. Nobody ever knew where the anonymous tip came from. The building was only eight years old, it wouldn't have come up due for its first routine inspection, post-opening, for another twelve years. Hundreds of people could have died if it had collapsed while it was occupied.

"That anonymous whistleblower was you?"

"The very same," I confirmed. "I've been a *number* of anonymous whistleblowers, on the Box's instructions." Then I shook my head briefly in bemusement. "Go figure. Hell of a coincidence, us both being involved in that one." Then I hesitated.

"...At least," I added, "I'm *assuming* it was pure coincidence."

She considered that thoughtfully.

"I wasn't actually directly involved," she corrected me. "The case was opened before I joined Harris Magnusson. I only saw the tail end of it. But I read all the files. Edrick Magnusson told me it was a great textbook case for me to read up on."

I nodded, and went on.

"Let's see, what's another good example... Do you recall the bombing attempt against Avianca Honduras at DFW last year? The one where the airport police caught the guy in the act of placing a bomb in the landing gear well?" She nodded. "And do you remember someone in the airport administration mentioned on the TV news reports how *weird and fortuitous* it was that the patrol schedules and routes had been changed, with no advance notice, for just that one night, and how they'd never have caught him if they'd been on the regular schedule, because he'd have been gone by the time the patrol got there on their regular routine?"

She looked at me, an eyebrow raised.

"Let me guess," she said, "another anonymous tip?"

"No," I replied, shaking my head. "Not exactly." I held up my right hand as though swearing an oath in court.

"Confession: The Box had me hack into the airport security computer system and change the patrol schedule."

"You're a computer hacker *AND* a bodyguard?" Her expression was skeptical.

"Nope, not I. I'm pretty good at *searching for* information, I'm not bad at scripting, I can build tools to maintain and secure and customize my own systems reasonably well—especially with occasional help from the Box—and I can follow a set of detailed instructions accurately; but nope, I couldn't 'hack' my way out of a wet paper bag unaided.

"The Box gave me detailed instructions on exactly what tool to download, from where on the dark web, where to point it to get access to the airport system via a software vulnerability, and what admin credentials to use to break into the patrol schedule without breaking anything. Then it was just a matter of rearranging a few of the night's patrol routes exactly as it told me to. All the same places covered by all the same teams, just in a slightly different order with different timing that put a team at that exact location at the right time."

"So your box gave you complete step-by-step instructions to hack DFW, and you just followed the instructions?" She eyed me quizzically.

"Yup," I agreed. "Dotted every i, crossed every t, double-checked every step."

"And somehow it knew exactly *when* a patrol needed to be *where*."

"Yup. I've never managed to get it to tell me *how* it knows these things."

"And what if the instructions it had given you had *created* the opening to let the bomber get in and plant his bomb undetected?"

I paused, then took a deep breath and let it out. This was a question I had sweated a hundred times. I gazed out the window into the darkness.

"You're not wrong," I confessed at last. "I lose sleep over possibilities like that. What if the Box is malicious, and gaining my trust only to play me for a patsy on something REALLY important some day? A long game? What if there are unintended *consequences* to one of its assignments? Collateral damage? Or I screw up, the assignment goes pear-shaped, and people die? Or what if I screw up on one of its assignments and *that one* turns out to be crucial?"

I sighed and shook my head ruefully. I'd thought of the same questions myself, and I didn't have any answers.

"I'll tell you honestly," I continued, turning to her, "about the time you were in the shower, right *before* Mr. Bad Example waltzed his Matilda up the stairs, I was really starting to wonder whether it had gone off its rocker, or set me up for reasons of its own to be arrested as some peeping-Tom pervert as part of some Grand Master Plan. It told me *not one word* about why it wanted me to go to your house. *Only* that I had to be upstairs in a specific house, preferably concealed, before dark. And it *barely* gave me enough notice to get there in time."

"Uuuuuh-huh," she said, slightly skeptically. "Aaaaaand you had a gun with you *why*, exactly?"

"Sharon," I replied seriously, "the Box told me a week ago that there was a heightened threat, and that I needed to be ready for priority alerts at any time. So I haven't left the house unarmed in a week. When the Box sends me out on short notice, with minimal details, after warning me to be on heightened alert, I *ALWAYS* assume that it's *likely* I'm going to get shot at. And I'm too often right."

"How many times have you had people shooting at you?" she asked, slowly.

"Seven times," I said without hesitation. "Being shot at in earnest is not the kind of thing you forget easily, if you don't do it for a living. Most of them, I didn't need to shoot back. The best way not to lose a fight is to evade it."

"Have you ever... actually *been* shot?"

"Three times." Immediate concern showed on her face. "Two minor flesh wounds, pistol calibers; one sucking chest wound, probably from an AK or AKS, maybe a PKM, on a road somewhere north of Damascus. A sucking chest wound is Nature's way of telling you to slow the fuck down."

"Damascus...? Syria?"

I nodded.

"What were you doing in Syria?"

"Two words," I replied grimly. "Mass graves."

She shuddered. I gazed out into the night, remembering.

"Sometimes," I mused slowly, "it's not the one bullet with your name on it. It's the six hundred marked 'To whom it may concern' or 'Because fuck you, buddy, that's why.'"

After a minute or two, she took my left hand in both of hers. I turned and looked at her, surprised.

"I'm glad you were there tonight," she told me. "Really, *really* glad. And I'm glad you made it out of Syria. And I *don't* think you're any kind of peeping pervert.

"But if I ever *do* need a peeping pervert who I know I can trust with my life, I'll be sure to call you. Okay?"

I couldn't help it. I burst out laughing. After a moment, she joined in. I couldn't help notice that she had a lovely smile, and that I liked the way she laughed.

"It's a deal," I got out eventually. "I'll be sure to keep a spot on my busy schedule open for you." We sat together smiling for a little bit longer, then I got up and cleared the table, put the dishes in the dishwasher, and put everything else away.

It was getting late, but not that late, yet, and I for one was still kinda keyed up—and she *clearly* was as well, to nobody's surprise—so I led her into my living room. She curled up in the big comfy overstuffed chair that sat apart from everything else. Yeah, I could see why she'd be needing space right now.

"I have another quick cleanup job I need to do," I said. "Will you be all right here for a few minutes?"

She nodded.

"I could use a little time to myself to think," she replied. "What do you need to clean up?"

"This," I said, patting the Laugo under my jacket. "I fired it today. Needs cleaning."

"Do guns need cleaning every time you fire them?" she asked.

"Not really every time. But it's a good idea every *day* that you fire them."

"...Because when you need it, you need it to work *every* time," she guessed. I nodded.

"Exactly right," I agreed.

I went downstairs and let myself into my small armory, field-stripped the Laugo, quickly cleaned it, then reassembled it. It took me maybe fifteen minutes. I replaced the two rounds I'd fired. It would have been nice if I'd had time to pick up my brass, but, well, life is a bitch. I was already certain Sharon was a hell of a lot more important than two fired cases anyway.

I went back upstairs, locking up behind me, and parked myself on the short couch opposite the chair she'd picked. I wanted to be sure I gave her plenty of space.

"So," she asked after a few minutes, "what happened in Syria? If you're willing to talk about it?"

I sat there and gathered my thoughts a bit.

"A *lot* of really bad shit went down in Syria," I began after a minute or two. "Not all of it made the news. Sometimes it was deliberate, sometimes people screwed up. Sometimes it was us, sometimes it was the Russians, occasionally it was the Peshmerga—the Kurdish militia. The Russians mostly didn't give a shit anyway. The Syrian regime *certainly* didn't; I think they *enjoyed* it. The Syrian military were randomly bombing villages using drum bombs—improvised chemical weapons. The Peshmerga were mainly looking out for ethnic Kurds, and that necessarily meant fucking up Da'esh wherever and whenever they could find them, because Da'esh had it in for the Kurds, and especially for the Yazidis, whom they regarded as heretics. But by the standards of the region the Peshmerga are a professional military, and they did what they could to prevent civilian casualties. There were only a few hundred of them in Syria at any one time, anyway. They really weren't interested in the civil war. They just wanted to protect their fellow Kurds and encourage them to come to relative safety in northern Iraq." I paused.

"Da'esh?" Sharon asked.

"Better known as ISIS, or the Islamic State. But I prefer Da'esh, because it pisses them off. It's actually an acronym for their name, in Arabic—*ad-Dawlah al-Islāmiyah fī 'l-'Irāq wa-sh-Shām*—but the short version is, uh, considered derogatory enough that they'll flog people for using it.

"Anyway, one day, someone on *our* side fucked up and YOLO'd an air strike on a large group of presumed militants gathered on the bank of a river."

"...Who turned out to be friendlies?" she asked. I shook my head hard.

"Worse than that. The target was badly mis-identified. It was women and children, doing their laundry." Her hands flew to her mouth and her eyes widened in horror.

"That air strike wiped out two thirds of the womenfolk of a village. Wives, mothers, daughters. And then the military *covered it up.*"

She stared at me for a long moment, speechless, before she found her voice.

"And... you... the Box? How were you involved?"

"The Box gave me a long series of exacting instructions, which got me into Syria in the place of another civilian contractor who *should* have gotten the assignment, who happened to be assigned to perform a task on the correct forward base; got me into the admin building one evening, and told me exactly where and when to enter which office and move which specific file folder to which in-tray in which other office, so that key information about the strike would be seen the next day by different eyes in a different chain of command. It took me about three weeks, all told, to get there and move one file folder.

"The next day, the base commander demanded to know why he hadn't seen that file sooner. And all of a sudden, within forty-eight hours, the military went from covering it up to investigating it, without ever publicly admitting there had been a cover-up."

She nodded.

"And then the Box got me back out again. But as my convoy was passing near Damascus, a group of... maybe Da'esh, maybe a Syrian patrol, doesn't really matter who, randomly sprayed us with automatic rifle fire. *Insh'allah* marksmanship—'*It will strike the target, if it is the will of Allah.*' And right as it was tailing off, a bullet came through the side of the Suburban I was riding in, barely slipped past my vest, and hit me right below the left shoulder blade."

She winced, then looked back at me.

"How bad was it?" she asked quietly.

"I was coughing blood," I answered. "I wasn't going to make it to the civilian flight out of Beirut that I was supposed to ride back to the States. Let alone survive the flight.

"The convoy pulled over and laagered for ten minutes a few miles down the road, while a combat medic slapped a field dressing on me to limit the bleeding, and hit me with a vial of morphine. A Blackhawk rendezvoused with our convoy at the next waypoint, and they took me out of the convoy and flew me to a US field hospital, where they took the bullet out and patched up my lung and the rib the bullet smashed. Then two or three days later, once I was stable enough to travel, they medevac'd me to Rammstein, Germany, on a MAC flight. Military Airlift Command.

"There was a lot of confusion and awkward questions because I didn't match up with who my paperwork said I was supposed to be. The documents the Box had sourced for me were good, but they weren't expected to face that kind of close examination. I had to do a lot of fast talking and professing innocence, but I managed to convince them that I had no earthly idea why I'd been given the wrong paperwork and didn't even know it was wrong. Why would I even look at it closely? It had always been right before. Why would I *expect* it to be wrong?

"They wrote it off in the end as a bureaucratic error by the contractor, doubtless helped by the contractor admitting the error appeared to have been their fault. I don't know whether that part was the Box's doing as well. Then they flew me home two weeks or so later on another MAC flight, after I was recovered enough to walk unaided."

She thought about that for a long time.

"The Box couldn't have predicted that you'd get hit by a random shot," she observed, at last.

"No," I agreed, "no it couldn't."

"So it's not omniscient," she concluded.

"No," I agreed again. "There are limits to its... mysterious knowledge of events."

She thought some more.

"I think," she said at length, "that *sort of* makes me feel a little better about it. In a way. Though it still leaves a lot of questions unanswered."

"I think I know what you mean," I replied. "Omniscience is a troubling concept."

"Have you ever figured out any *pattern* in the tasks it gives you?" I shook my head.

"None I've ever spotted. Except that some way or another, it always seems to end up preventing something bad from happening, or ensuring that some wrongdoing does not go unpunished. And it kind of feels like I *learn* something new nearly every time."

She was quiet again for a while.

"You could easily have died there in Syria, couldn't you?" she said, after a time. It wasn't really a question.

"Yeah," I replied. "I could have. If the bullet trajectory was just slightly different, or if they hadn't been able to get me to a field hospital in time."

"And then I'd be dead now," she said.

I didn't know what to say for a moment.

"Let's just be thankful that both of us are here," I managed, after a few seconds.

She nodded agreement. Then she climbed out of the chair, walked over to the couch, sat down next to me, and cuddled up against me. For a moment my hindbrain gibbered and chased its tail, then my cortex gave it a good hard rap, and I put my arm around her shoulders. It felt nice, even though I could feel she was shaking slightly. Needed some physical comfort, I guessed, and I couldn't say I blamed her at all.

"You know something?" she remarked after a little bit. "You haven't told me *your* name yet."

She was right, I realized. We'd kind of had other priorities on our minds.

"Ciáran mac Cool," I replied. "At your service." She lifted her head and looked at me, interest evident in her expression.

"Mac Cool?", she repeated. "Like the legendary hero Fionn mac Cumhaill, from Irish mythology?"

"Yeah," I agreed, pleasantly surprised. She'd pronounced both correctly. "You're well read. Family, uh, *legend* says we're descended from him. Of course, half the families in Ireland that aren't Viking probably claim descent from either Fionn mac Cumhaill or Cú Chulainn. Which is problematic, considering the legend says the Cú had no surviving children."

She sat up a little straighter so that she could look at me straight on, gently pushing my face from one side to the other with her fingertips. It was the first time, really, that I'd looked at her face close up in good light. I noticed that her eyes were deep blue, and very pretty.

"I think I could see you as a mythic Celtic hero," she told me musingly, "a blessed warrior doing the bidding of the Fenian gods."

I chuckled.

"Are you telling me that box might be a Fenian god?" I asked jokingly.

She grinned right back at me.

"Do you have a *better* explanation?"

"Weeeeellll..." I hesitated. "You know, you have a point. I'm not sure I *like* it, but you do have a valid point."

"Clarke's Law," she told me. "Any sufficiently advanced technology is indistinguishable from magic."

"I'm pretty certain there's no magic involved here," I replied. "Magic—or the supernatural in general—is an explanation I'm not prepared to accept. I'm sure there has to be a rational explanation there somewhere. I just don't know what it is."

"But in the meantime, you're willing to keep taking on assignments of unknown provenance?"

I thought about that one for a long time.

"As long as they keep on doing good, I guess, yeah," I replied at last. It was an uneasy line of thinking, but not one that was new to me.

"See," she replied, grinning again. "Mythic Celtic hero."

I chuckled.

"Just don't ask me to pull off Cú Chulainn's battle warp."

"Yeeeaaah," she agreed. "That *would* be pretty terrifying."

It got late.

"Ready to catch some sleep?" I asked.

"Sure. It's... been a rough day."

"Especially for you," I said, thinking to myself that 'rough' was putting it mildly.

I led her upstairs, stopping on the upper landing. I opened the door on the left.

"Spare room," I told her. "Not much furniture in there, but there's a good sound bed and a clean chest of drawers. Might want to turn the bed back and let it air out for twenty minutes or so. I change it from time to time to keep it fresh, but it hasn't been used in a while. It's yours for as long as you need it."

I pointed at the middle door, straight ahead. "Bathroom. Consider it your private bathroom, I have my own. And I'm on the right." I opened my door.

"You'll probably be wanting something to sleep in." She nodded gratefully, and I pointed.

"That dresser, anything in the bottom two drawers. There's both silks and cotton flannel in there, pick whatever you feel the most comfortable in. They'll all be big on you, but tomorrow we can go and get you some clothes that actually fit you."

I headed for my bathroom and left her to it. When I came out, the drawers were closed, and so was her door. I left mine ajar and turned in.

I heard her tossing and turning for a while. But eventually, the house became quiet.

2: The Second Day

In the morning, Sharon was up before I was. I heard her in the bathroom. I went and used the bathroom myself, not making any particular attempt to be quiet, then picked out clean clothes and got dressed.

She beat me downstairs. I smelled the savory aroma of bacon and mushrooms cooking before I was half-way down the stairs. When I got to the kitchen, I found her making breakfast, with eggs already waiting on the counter ready to go into the pan. She'd found the orange juice, too, and that was sitting out ready to be poured.

"You'll have to make the coffee," she told me, her voice perhaps just a little too bright. "I don't know how to use your machines."

"You didn't have to make breakfast, you know," I said. "You're the guest here."

"Yes, I did," she said urgently. "Because I needed to *do* something to get my mind to stop thinking about things I *don't want to think about* right now. My brain keeps trying to drag it back up. Let me do this, please."

"Fair enough," I replied, without hesitation. "You take sugar?"

"One," she replied. So I made coffee, one sugar in hers, a little more in mine, and pretty soon we sat down to coffee and breakfast. She picked up her coffee and held it just in front of her face.

"Mmmm. Smells good. Luxurious." She visibly relaxed a little, and took a sip. "Mmm. You always make coffee like this?"

"Life is too short to drink bad coffee when you have a choice about it," I declared. "It's Sumatra Mandheling this week."

She nodded, and we dug into breakfast.

"First order of the day," I told her in between bites, "should, I think, be to take you shopping for some clothes. Can't risk going back to your house for your own. Too dangerous. The opposition could be watching the place."

She nodded.

"I'd appreciate it," she said. "Got anywhere in mind?"

"There's some outlet stores not far from here. Includes a bunch of clothing stores. Major brands—Nike, Ralph Lauren, Banana Republic, LL Bean, Levi Strauss, Old Navy, several others... should be plenty of choice."

"Works for me," she replied. Then an odd expression crossed her face.

"If you... work for... that Box," she said slowly, "what do you do for money? Do you get *paid* somehow?"

"All the bills are on autopay," I answered. "I have a couple of accounts at different local banks for expenses. Money just... *appears* in the accounts. Never too much at one time. Just like a regular direct-deposit salary. The transfers come via a holding company. I have no doubt it's the Box's doing, but probably couldn't prove it if I tried. And my taxes are filed for me, and they're always either just a small overpayment or just a small underpayment, not enough to earn penalties. Ordinary, boring tax returns, always the standard deduction, always scrupulously correct, nothing in them to ever trigger an audit. Nothing to see here. These aren't the droids you're looking for."

She giggled.

"As mysterious as everything else," she said, with a smile.

I picked up the tablet I'd brought to the table with me and looked at the local news.

"No reports of unexplained goings-on in suburban houses," I commented, after a quick scan. "That's *probably* good."

Then a name caught my attention.

"Wait, hello, what's this..."

I tapped on the story.

"Two-alarm fire early this morning at the law offices of Harris Magnusson Partners," I read aloud. Sharon gasped and went pale. "Extensive damage to the building. No-one believed to be in the building at the time." I centered the main photo and slid the tablet over to her. She took it hesitantly and studied the photo, then laid the tablet flat on the table.

"This corner?" she said, pointing to one of the worst-damaged parts of the building. I nodded.

"That area is my boss's office and the library where I work."

"Crap. Well... that seems to support the theory that this is about some document that you saw. Or that the Black Hats *think* you saw."

She looked pensive, then went to push the tablet back towards me. As she did so, her finger touched the Back button. She glanced down at the change of screen, looked away, then her attention snapped back to it. She paled again and pulled the tablet back toward her, tapped on another story, then read from it, her voice unsteady.

"Philip Bartholomew," she read, "a senior partner with the law firm of Harris Magnusson Partners, died last night in an apparent single-vehicle accident." She read a bit further. "Responding Highway Patrol officers stated that some of his injuries *were not consistent with the accident*."

She looked at me, her hand shaking.

"My boss," she said quietly. "They killed him, didn't they?"

I looked back at her, then took the tablet from her hand, set it down, and took her hand instead.

"That seems the obvious conclusion," I agreed, "given what else we know. And—"

I stopped before I said more.

"...And?" she asked.

I sighed, wishing I hadn't started to voice that thought.

"And if 'some of his injuries' were incongruous enough that the Highway Patrol mentioned it to the press... I think we have to assume he was probably tortured before he was killed."

Her hand clenched in mine. I held on gently.

"Thank god he wasn't married," she said. "Oh, *god*. Poor Philip."

Then she looked at me.

"Should we... should I...?" She trailed off.

"Try to call anyone and warn them?" I completed the question for her. She nodded, her eyes frightened. I took a deep breath.

"I know you want to," I said, nodding. "And I respect that, I truly do. But it's a bad idea. For two reasons.

"First, if there was anyone *else* they were targeting, available evidence says *they probably already got to them*.

"And second, if you *do* contact anyone and warn them, and the Black Hats—who, remember, undoubtedly *already know* that something went sideways with the hit on you—*find out* that you talked to someone..."

"...Then I just made them a target, didn't I?" She put the pieces together herself. I nodded agreement. She'd got it.

"Oh, god," she muttered, after a moment. I squeezed her hand. This couldn't be easy for her. It was a big change in her thinking about the world, and she was having to make it very suddenly. I could see her thinking it through.

"People from work are probably trying to get hold of me," she said. "And they won't be able to." She looked me in the eyes. "They probably think I'm dead too. Don't they?"

"It's... a definite possibility," I answered carefully. "But I wouldn't assume anything yet."

"And I can't try to tell them I'm safe, without putting them in danger."

"Right," I agreed.

She closed her eyes and just sat there. I wished I knew better how to help.

We finished breakfast and cleaned up, then got ready to go out. It took us about twenty minutes to reach the outlets. I just turned her loose and followed, letting her lead the way, staying close by her for safety but giving her enough space for comfort. I intentionally paid with a different card at each store to help conceal any buying pattern. Five four-hundred-dollar-average women's clothing purchases spread out across five cards is a lot less visible in financial records than two thousand dollars of women's clothing purchases in a couple of hours on one account.

She bought a few dressier pieces that she could mix and match, and two pairs of shoes, one with more heel than the other, but also plenty of casual, serviceable clothes that wouldn't stand out. She was continuing to really impress me. She also stocked up half a dozen or so sets of underwear, and a couple of sets of pajamas that actually fit her. She asked for my opinion on a couple of the dressier pieces, and some of the lingerie, as though we were a couple. *Smart* girl. I made a mental note that she liked silky, satiny things, not frilly lacy things. We picked up some bathroom necessities for her, too.

At the last store, along with a couple of silky blouses, she picked out a smart pale-blue jacket, and a darker blue evening dress that could pass as business wear if she wore the jacket over it. This, like a couple of other previous pieces, she tried on before she was sure. I waited next to the changing rooms while she tried it on.

She was out in a few minutes, looking satisfied.

"Okay, I think I'm done," she declared. "All set." We went to check out.

On the way, we passed an in-store jewelry display, and something caught my eye.

"Hold up a moment," I said to Sharon. I stopped and looked at the display. Where was—ah, *there*. That's what I'd caught. A flash of that same deep blue. It was a simple short necklace, almost a choker (careful, I thought to myself, careful, that *might* be a sensitive concept), a couple of strands of fine white-gold chain studded with small pale brilliant-cut zircons, from which hung an understated but elegant deep-blue stone the size of my thumbnail.

"Could I see that a moment, please?" I asked the attendant, on a sudden impulse. She got it out for me and I looked at it. It seemed to be well made, by a mid-tier jeweler. I didn't recognize the name.

"The central stone is a tanzanite, an unusually blue one, they're usually more purple than this," the attendant told me enthusiastically, "and the side stones are blue zircons." It was six hundred dollars... but I was pretty sure that big tanzanite was a close match to Sharon's eyes.

I turned to Sharon.

"Anna," I said clearly, looking her directly in the eye, "come over here a moment, please." She came closer, a curious expression on her face, and I held the necklace against her where it would hang if she were wearing it. Her mouth opened in surprise. I looked back and forth a couple of times quickly between the stone and her eyes, verifying that they were almost perfectly the same blue, then, still holding it in place, I slowly stepped out of the way just barely behind her shoulder—

deliberately *not* all the way behind her—and directed her gaze into the mirror on the counter. She looked at it, and lifted her hand to touch it.

"Do you like it?" I asked.

She hesitated. She looked at the necklace, then over her shoulder at me, a question in her eyes, then back at the necklace in the mirror.

"Do you *like* it?" I repeated.

"It's *lovely*," she answered hesitantly, "but—"

"But nothing," I said. "You *know* it matches your eyes. And it'll go perfectly with the blue dress you just picked out."

She hesitated a moment longer, then flashed that brilliant smile again, slightly uncertainly.

"We'll take it, please," I told the attendant, who was watching us with a big smile of her own. She retrieved a small box and put the necklace away in it, wrapping it carefully in tissue.

"I *do so love* to see people in love," she declared. "It's what we're here for." Then she handed me the box, and we went and checked out.

<hr>

"Ciáran," Sharon asked quietly as we walked back to the car, her voice serious and slightly tense, "*why* are you buying me jewelry?"

"Several reasons," I answered carefully.

"One, verisimilitude. You've been running clothing purchases past me for approval as though we're a couple. I'm playing along with it." She nodded.

"It *is* your money I'm spending," she pointed out.

"That means I get to buy you jewelry. It's one of those things couples do."

"That's... fair, I guess," she conceded, after a moment. She didn't really sound convinced.

"Two, misdirection," I counted off. "If it should ever come up, if someone is showing a picture around here and asking if anyone's seen you, Sharon Kielic, missing person, that store attendant will now remember you as Anna, shopping with her partner, not as Sharon, single woman." She gave me a puzzled look for a moment, then understanding dawned.

"Confusing our trail," she said, nodding in understanding.

"Yup," I agreed. We were almost at the car.

"Three, if we go anywhere where that dress you just bought—nice dual-use, by the way—is appropriate as an evening dress, I expect you are going to look absolutely *stunning* in it, but it'll seem odd if you're not wearing at least one piece of matching jewelry. Now, you have one." I hit the power hatch release on the key fob as I spoke.

"And four," as she turned to me, before she had a chance to speak, "you have lovely eyes, and the tanzanite really does match them perfectly, and I wanted you to have it. I'm your *de-facto* bodyguard, but I'm not blind... Humor me?"

She'd been about to speak, but she stopped, then looked down for a moment. When she looked back up, she was smiling. This time, there was no uncertainty in her eyes.

"Thank you, Ciáran," she said softly.

I loaded our purchases in and closed the hatch, then we got into the car.

"And there's another thing," I continued, as I turned on the car.

She looked at me, her eyebrows raised.

"I was *really enjoying* playing along."

She just looked at me for a moment, then her smile spread.

We pulled out of the parking lot and headed back home, hopefully not having left any clear trail behind us that could be used to find her.

<hr>

We made one more quick stop on the way back to buy more eggs and bacon, and a few other groceries—I'd already been low on bacon, and we were going to be going through twice as many eggs now. A fresh bag of onions was also in order, and I grabbed a cryovac center-cut pork loin. Cheap, versatile, a lot I could do with it, and we'd get half a dozen meals out of it. It was four in the afternoon by the time we got back.

We unloaded everything, then Sharon asked where the washing machine was. I showed her to my laundry room, and she started washing all the new clothes she'd just bought before she wore them. I left her to it, went to the kitchen, and put away the groceries. Then I headed downstairs.

Of the four doors downstairs, the closest door to the stairs led to the Box. The one at the far end, the reinforced door in the concrete wall with the biometric lock, was my armory. Weapons, tools, workbenches, ammunition storage, and more.

The one in between those two was my office. It was the second largest space in the basement by a small margin, only a little larger than my small armory vault. In one corner was a nineteen-inch rack holding network gear, a large uninterruptible power supply, and a storage server with a flash array. There was a desk in the middle of the room with a curved thirty-five inch widescreen monitor on it, connected to a tower PC under the desk. Another PC against the wall, with two video cards, fed a row of twenty inch monitors, each displaying a particularly trustworthy and useful news channel. There was a single Aeron office chair at the desk. Sometimes I ended up sitting here for hours at a time, day after day. That meant my chair needed to be comfortable for hours, and stay that way.

I sat down at the desk, thought for a while, and then launched a few web spiders, all of them carefully routed through distant exit points to try to prevent anyone easily back-tracing them. They would crawl around on their own and send me anything interesting they came across. One I set to search for any stories or articles in the last year related to Harris Magnusson Partners. Another, I set to background research on every company, person or entity named in any case Harris Magnusson had taken in that same period. A third looked for any of *those* names connected in some way to the name of any known organized crime figures. The last, I tasked with researching all mentions of Philip Bartholomew.

About the time I finished setting the parameters for the fourth, I heard Sharon calling my name.

"Down here," I called back. "Second door."

A few minutes later she walked into the room, in jogging pants and T-shirt. She'd shed the sweatshirt. She half-perched on the corner of the desk, and I showed her what I'd set running.

"Anything else you can think of?" I asked.

"None of these are likely to find any newly filed cases," she replied. "Whatever we want, it's most likely some new case, but it's also possible it could be new discovery in an old case. So the case search *might* turn up something. So might the cross-connections.

"Can you get into Westlaw from here?"

"Well, yes," I said, "but I don't have an account."

"No problem," she replied, "I do."

"I'm sure you do, but—"

"Oh." She stopped. Then she buried her face in her hands. "Right. I don't dare use it, do I?"

"Exactly," I agreed. "If anyone's watching for that access..."

"...It'd be like sticking my hand up and calling, 'Hey, here I am!'" she finished for me.

"You got it," I agreed. "So we can't do that. I won't put you at risk if I can avoid it. I'm being as careful as I know how to with these webspiders. It's why I'm not running them from here."

She looked at me.

"You know," she replied slowly, after a long pause, "at some point you might *have to* risk me."

I looked back at her.

"Only as a last resort," I said. "Only if there's no other way."

We spent the next half or so brainstorming ideas for how we could find out more, then the washing machine declared mission complete. Sharon went to go move her first load of laundry to the dryer and put her second load in, while I looked through the results the webspiders had brought in so far. Which was nothing of any obvious use, yet.

Sharon was back shortly. We searched, scratched our heads, drew lots of blanks, and generally failed to come up with anything very much.

After another hour, I called a halt.

"We need to be thinking differently about this," I said. "Beating this dead horse isn't going to get us anywhere. We need an angle, and we can't progress until we figure out what it is.

"So I'm going to get supper started."

"I can get behind that," Sharon agreed. "But I think my first laundry installment should be done by now, and *I want clean clothes.*"

"Go, girl," I told her. "Get comfy. I'll take care of supper."

There went that smile again. We both went upstairs, she headed for the laundry room to change over her things, and I went straight to the kitchen. I set up the rice cooker first and started it, then pulled out the pork loin I'd bought earlier. I cut a usable-size chunk off one end to give a nice, clean, square end, cut a dozen even ⅛" slices off, then put the rest of it away and started rummaging for ingredients. I pulled out a small onion, grated about a third of it, then set the rest aside to be thinly sliced later and started building my sauce.

When Sharon reappeared, the rice had about twenty minutes to go and I was nearly ready to start cooking the pork. She was wearing a soft, shimmery dark green shirt and close-fitting blue jeans with batik patterns around the bottoms. She looked good in it, and I told her so.

She sniffed the air.

"I smell... ginger. And is that sake?"

"It is," I replied. She clearly knew her way around food. Was there nothing—

I clamped a muzzle on that line of thought, put a large skillet over high heat, splashed in a little oil, and left it a few minutes to heat. Then I got to work. We chatted idly while I cooked.

"By the way," she said a few minutes later, "I approve of your taste in knives."

Right, I wasn't letting it go *this* time.

"You cook?" I asked.

She shot a grin my way.

"Even a law student's got to get *some* fun," she said. "We don't spend our *every* waking moment memorizing legal precedents and rules of order."

I grinned back.

Fifteen minutes later, the rice cooker sang the song of its people. Without hesitation, she popped the lid, picked up the paddle, and started fluffing the rice. When she was done, she closed the lid to let it finish steaming.

"You have a serving bowl I can put this into?" she asked.

"Uh, far upper cabinet the other side of the fridge," I replied, "lower shelf."

She found the serving bowls, selected one, and put it by the rice cooker, then got out plates from the same cupboard and took them to the table. Once again, she set places side by side. She'd picked out the black Mikasa set. Well, if we were doing fancy tonight, I could work with that.

A few minutes later, I was done cooking. Instead of taking the pan directly to the table, I went to the same cabinet and pulled out a matching serving platter. She began scooping rice from the rice cooker into the serving bowl as I started layering the cooked pork onto the platter. We reached the table at the same time, as it turned out. It looked pretty elegant.

"So what are we eating tonight, Master Chef?" she asked.

I chuckled.

"I'm far from being a master chef," I demurred. "An enthusiastic amateur, is all. This is pork shogayaki, Japanese ginger pork. Or my best attempt at it. This is my fourth try. I think I'm starting to get the hang of it."

I looked at the table.

"We do need one more thing, though."

"Oh?"

"I need to complete what you started. I'll be right back." And indeed, a minute or so later, I was back with a black iron candlestick with a single white candle in it. I placed it in the middle of the table, lit it, and turned to see her regarding me with a little smile and a raised eyebrow.

"Candle-lit dinners now, is it, Mister?" she said archly.

"Don't blame me, missy," I replied with the same smile, "you started it when you picked out the fancy Mikasa."

She laughed. I liked it when she laughed.

"So," she asked, "is there wine with dinner?"

I thought a moment.

"Pretty sure I have a Roscato chilled that would work," I said. "I know it's supposed to be white wines to serve with pork, but I don't care. Give me a couple more minutes. Pick us out some wine glasses? That cabinet there."

She fetched the glasses, I got the wine and a corkscrew, and we sat down to eat. I let her serve herself first, then took some for myself. I caught a look of pleased surprise on her face at the first bite of the thin-sliced pork. There was just the least hint of bite to the gingered pork, not enough to be overwhelming, but enough to add depth to the flavor and the aroma.

"This is really good," she declared after a little while. "Do you have a particular cooking specialty?"

"Interesting," I replied.

"Interesting?" She shot me a puzzled look.

"I like to cook interesting food. Curries. Jambalaya. This shogayaki. Lohikeitto."

"Lohi-what?" she asked. "What's that?"

"Finnish salmon soup. Well, they *call* it a soup, but it's almost more of a stew. A salmon chowder, I suppose. It's really good. Supposedly considered one of the world's eight great soups. Of which I know how to make three. Four, if I cheat."

She looked thoughtful.

"Which four?"

I counted them off on my fingers.

"Lohikeitto; avgolemono, which is Greek chicken-and-rice soup with egg; borsch, beet soup, which most people think of as Russian but is actually Ukrainian. Those three, I make from scratch. For tom yum—Thai hot and sour soup—I cheat and use prepared tom yum paste. But honestly, so do most Thai restaurants. It saves a huge amount of time, and it's just as good. Somebody else did the work of making the paste, that's all."

"Salmon chowder sounds tasty," she said. "I don't suppose you could be persuaded to make it, sometime fairly soon...?"

I chuckled.

"Twist my arm," I replied, with a grin.

"So you said eight great soups. What are the other four?"

"Tom kha, Thai hot and sour coconut-milk soup; mulligatawny; Italian wedding soup; and Chinese hot-and-sour egg drop soup.

"Of course, lists vary. I've seen lists with as many as twenty-five world's greatest soups on them, but at that point it's getting close to 'Every distinctive soup you can think of.'"

Sharon nodded agreement.

"Right," she said, "they can't *all* be the greatest."

<hr>

After we finished supper and cleaned up, Sharon went and got the last of her laundry out and put away upstairs. I retired to the living room again and sat down on one end of the couch, thinking over other possible ways to find a lead. It was quite a while before she returned.

"Ciáran?" I heard Sharon call softly from behind me, and turned to look.

My jaw dropped.

She was standing on the third stair, one hand on the banister. She'd put on the blue evening dress, and the black pumps, and she'd put her hair up and pinned it, and she was wearing the tanzanite choker, and simple silver hoop earrings that I hadn't seen her pick out.

"...Wow," I managed eventually. Then I ran out of words, so I got up, walked over to the bottom of the stairs, and offered her my hand. She took it.

"You said I'd look stunning in this," she said hesitantly. "So... I had to try it out."

"Stunning," I answered after I caught my breath, "turns out to be... an inadequate word."

I gave her hand the slightest tug, more just a light pressure toward me, and she came down the stairs the rest of the way. The heels weren't anything excessive, but they added about three inches to her height. That put her eyes only an inch or two below mine. As she stepped off the bottom stair, we were briefly eye-to-eye. It was nice.

"Is there more left in that wine bottle?" she asked.

"Should be," I agreed. "We only drank about half of it. You want another glass?"

"Please," she said. So I went and poured more wine, and when I came back, she'd settled herself comfortably into one corner of the couch. I handed her one glass, then took the other corner, half facing her. She raised her glass and held it out toward me. I raised mine expectantly.

"To surviving," she offered quietly.

"To surviving," I agreed. Then we clinked glasses, and drank.

"Was this unfair?" she asked me, after a few minutes. I raised a questioning eyebrow, and she waved her free hand vaguely up and down herself.

"Unfair?" I shook my head. "*No.* Not in the least. Just unexpected. I figured you had a good reason for buying the dress. I wasn't expecting to see you in it so soon. But... just... *wow.*"

"I wasn't *planning* on wearing it this soon," she replied, looking at me very seriously. "Buying it was mostly a contingency preparation. And dual-use, as you said. If we need to go and visit law offices, whether mine or any other, I'll need to look professional. For which this dress, with the matching jacket over it, will work nicely.

"But a girl really needs to feel... *appreciated* sometimes."

"Especially a girl who just narrowly escaped death?" I asked gently.

She nodded.

"Got it in one," she agreed, a catch in her voice.

"Well in that case, Miss Sharon Kielic," I said after a moment, "I am going to venture bravely out on a limb, and voice a few thoughts I've been repeatedly biting my tongue to keep to myself because I thought it might be inappropriate to speak them out loud.

"You are one *smart* cookie; you are sharp as a tack, and you think well on your feet. I never have to point anything out twice to you, and seldom more than nudge you in the right direction. You're brave, resourceful and resilient. Even after what you've just been through, you just pitch right in. You look good even in scruffy jogging togs, and dressed up like this you look... fabulous. I already knew you were pretty as... uh, heck, I'd have to be blind not to; but when you *want* to be, my *god*, girl, you are *beautiful.*

"And I personally appreciate the *living heck* out of you."

She looked down for a long moment, then back up at me. When she looked back up, she was smiling. There were *dimples*, and her eyes were moist.

"Thank you, Ciáran," she replied, quietly yet fervently. "And for the record, I appreciate the hell out of you, too, my warrior Fenian."

Wait, I thought after a moment, *"my" warrior Fenian?*

The couch wasn't all that long, almost closer to a love seat really, and if I switched my wine glass to my left hand, I could reach most of the way to her with my right. So I did that. She reached out, took my hand and held on tight. We sat and looked at each other, and held hands, and sipped our wine.

"So I had a thought, while you were upstairs," I said after a while. "An angle. I... know this guy who works in the intelligence sector. Three-letter agency. Don't ask me which one, please. Can't say more than that for obvious reasons." She nodded. "We do favors for each other occasionally. He visits sometimes. I could ask him if he's run across anything on the grapevine—anything *unclassified*, that is—that might involve Harris Magnusson.

"It's a long shot, but it might shake something loose. Too late to do anything tonight. But I could drop him a line tomorrow."

She thought about that.

"If—" she began, then hesitated. "If any part of the Federal government *is* involved in some way—if there's already some related ongoing investigation—then it's big. But we can't just officially *ask*."

I nodded.

"We already know it's big enough that the Black Hats were prepared to firebomb your offices, kill your boss, and try to kill you," I observed. She nodded in turn.

"They didn't reckon on you or the Box," she replied. Then she looked at me, and pulled gently, but insistently, on my hand.

I put my wine glass down on the coffee table and scootched over closer to her, and she put hers down and slid a little my direction, and we met in the middle. Sharon pulled my right arm around her and snuggled into my shoulder. I took her right hand in my left, and held her close.

"That said," I remarked, "I don't believe for a moment that any US state actor is behind this. The attempt on you was too sloppy, too half-assed. But if it involves anyone government agencies are *watching...* there's a chance Judson might be able to tell us something useful. Point us in the right direction. As long as it's not classified.

"If it *is*, he couldn't tell us even if he wanted to. We're not cleared. But it's worth the shot."

She nodded.

We sat there for quite a while, not talking much, just enjoying each other's presence and finishing our wine. But eventually it got late.

"We should get some sleep," I suggested. She nodded, and got up. I let her go up the stairs ahead of me, and I'll be honest, it was because I wanted to watch her walk up them. She stopped on the top landing and waited for me. I caught up to her, and she took my hand again, and stood looking up at me. Then she reached up and put her other hand behind my neck, pulled my head down, and kissed me quickly, soft and gentle. I returned it, enjoying the softness of her lips.

"Goodnight, Ciáran," she said. "And thank you again." Then she let go my hand, turned, and went to her room.

"Goodnight, Sharon," I replied before she closed the door. "Sleep well."

I thought I heard her cry out in the middle of the night once. But I wasn't sure. I listened for a while just in case, but there was no repeat.

3: The Third Day

In the morning, we made breakfast together, as we had the day before. I gave her a quick run-through on how to operate the Baratza coffee grinder and the Breville espresso machine, then we skimmed for news articles as we ate breakfast. I found only one relevant item, a news segment from a local station. But it was *extremely* relevant.

I propped the tablet on the table between us and started the video.

"Investigators have determined yesterday's two-alarm fire at the downtown law offices of Harris Magnusson Partners to have been arson," the brunette anchorwoman stated. "The perpetrators are currently unknown. Many records, both on paper and electronic, were destroyed in the fire. There is currently no known motive.

"Additionally, the death yesterday of Harris Magnusson senior partner Philip Bartholomew, initially reported to be a single-vehicle accident, has been reclassified as a homicide. Police said in a statement that there is an extremely high likelihood the two events are related.

"Sharon Kielic, a legal associate at the firm, has officially been declared missing today. Police entered her home early this morning at the request of senior partners in the firm, when she could not be located. She is not considered a suspect, but a police spokesman stated unequivocally that foul play was involved in her disappearance.

"They also stated that someone was killed in the master bathroom of the house, and the body removed. It is not known for certain yet whether that person was Ms. Kielic, but no other theory has yet been offered. It is known that she worked in the office of Philip Bartholomew, and there is speculation that she may have been murdered about the same time he was and for the same reason, whatever that reason may be. Police are on the lookout just in case she is still alive, but the chances seem slim.

"We will continue to follow this case and report on it as new information becomes available."

Sharon looked at me, and I at her. She looked on the edge of tears, and I took her hand.

"They think I'm dead, don't they?" she asked brokenly.

"It's... likely," I admitted. "We know now that the backup team removed their man's body before anyone saw it. Not surprising. They'd want to not leave any clues that could be traced back to them.

"It's also apparent they didn't take the time to clean the bathroom, or at least not well, and we can assume they may also have tossed the house looking for anything they didn't want found.

"Unfortunately none of this new information is really very useful to us."

Sharon shuddered.

"The police probably think all of that blood and... *brains*... in the bathroom is mine."

Her hand clenched convulsively, and the tears spilled over. I switched hands, and put my arm around her shoulders. I was doing that a lot. I wished it was for different and kinder reasons.

She looked up at me.

"I didn't realize there were—were *brains on the towel* at first," she said, her voice breaking, "until I went to start *drying myself* with it."

Ouch, I thought. *Goddamn. No wonder* she broke down in the car. She'd held it together until then even better than I'd thought. Thank the gods she'd spotted it *before* she started smearing someone else's blood and brains on herself. She might have completely lost it, and I couldn't have blamed her at all. And then I probably wouldn't have been able to get her out, without a shootout that I'd been badly under-prepared for, and which would have put her at still further risk.

I pulled her a little closer.

"I'm *really sorry* you had to go through that," I told her sincerely. "But it's over now. If there's any way I can help you to... get past it, please just ask. Anything you need. Just say the word." She just looked at me silently, then nodded very slightly.

"At any rate," I continued after a pause, "it seems pretty certain now that the backup team didn't clean up. Forensics will be typing the blood to try to confirm whether it was yours. And if they have enough tissue for DNA testing, which they almost certainly do, they'll quickly find out that it came from a male. Chromosomes alone will tell them that. Then *that* cat, at least, will be out of the bag."

That seemed to console her a little.

"Then the question will become who was murdered in my bathroom, I suppose," she said, sniffling slightly. "And by whom."

"Doubtless," I agreed. "And you never know, they *just might* figure that out, if Forensics is able to match to an existing DNA sample. That's probably a one-in-a-million shot.

"But there's another thing in the meantime."

"What's that?" she asked.

"The report said the police are deeming you a person of interest. As I'm quite sure you're aware, when persons of interest avoid talking to police, the police tend to move them over into the 'suspect' category.

"We don't want that to happen. It would be bad all around. So if you know a good criminal defense attorney whom you trust, we should consider reaching out to them, telling them the story—at least the sane part of it—and having them go to the police on your behalf. Then you're not evading the police at all; you're actively cooperating.

"That means it's much less likely your average beat cop is going to pull a gun on you and escalate the situation if they spot you while we're out and about.

"Now, it's your call. If you would *prefer*, you can keep your head down hard and not risk exposing yourself to another attempt. That means staying in the house or immediately nearby, avoiding any dense concentrations of people wherever possible. But we're already doing that anyway.

"If you talk to the police, through a lawyer, it's one less thing we have to worry about. We *ought* to be able to impress upon them the importance of not revealing your location or the fact that you are alive. It's not something that comes up every day, I'm sure, but equally I know damned well they're no strangers to the situation.

"It's up to you. Whichever way you feel safer."

She thought about that for a while.

"I want to stay here," she answered at length. "I feel *safe* here. And your... box..."

"My weird, opinionated box," I interjected.

"Yes. It says this is important. Weird, it certainly is... but... somehow I don't think we should risk letting it slide."

"Okay," I agreed. "Your call."

"But if we can at least clear this up with the police," she continued, "then... I think we should try to do that. Let me think about who I know.

"How safe is it here? Can I go outside at all?"

"This is a quiet area," I told her. "I deliberately picked it partly for that. It was one of my criteria when I picked out the house. Only ever really see a car out here if someone calls 911. The risk of you being spotted here is very low."

"So," she said, "fairly safe, then? In the meantime, though, I have an idea that doesn't need going out. At least, not yet."

"Go on...?"

"We both know I can't contact anyone at Harris Magnusson myself. But I know other lawyers in the area. They—the Black Hats—can't... *reasonably*... be bugging or watching *all* of them."

I nodded.

"I'm personal friends with one of the partners at Jerison, Whitewell and Lang, and *she's* friends with Edrick Magnusson. But there's no *direct* professional connection between the two firms. Jerison, Whitewell and Lang is a family-law firm."

"Good thinking. You're suggesting a discreet message back-channel?"

"Exactly." She nodded. "Do you think it's... safe?"

I thought about it for a few minutes.

"It should be, if we're careful," I concluded. "That gives us two irons in the fire.

"You should use my phone to contact her." I took out my phone. "Just take it from me for the moment that the chances of anyone we're concerned about being able to trace it are approximately nil."

She looked at the oddly bulky phone, turning it over and over in her hands.

"Why is all the writing on it in Cyrillic?" she asked.

"Let's make that a question for another time, please? The answer is complicated."

"Of *course* it is," she said, with a knowing smile.

"Anyway, we both have calls to make today. You, to your partner at Jerison, Whitewell and Lang, and me to Judson, my contact at, uh...

well, he's at the Smithsonian, but doesn't *work for* the Smithsonian."

"What does that mean?"

"It means the Smithsonian Institution owns a lot of real estate in the suburbs of Washington, D.C., and leases it out on century contracts to various federal agencies. Most of these agencies tell their employees to say they work at the Smithsonian, which is... *technically* true, they're on Smithsonian-owned real estate. It means I'm sure Judson is a spook. I'm not officially certain for which agency, or whether his agency even *publicly* exists. And if I *did* know, I couldn't tell you."

"But he did once tell me he works at the Smithsonian."

Sharon nodded in understanding. Then another thought occurred to her.

"Marilyn will probably want to know where I am and whether I'm safe. What can I tell her?"

I thought a moment.

"Tell her you're in witness protection," I suggested. "That will be totally believable in the present circumstances."

She nodded agreement.

"Good," I said. "We have a plan."

I made the first call. The call went through on the second ring.

"G'day, squire," I said.

"'Allo, guv," he replied. "What's up with you these days?"

"Busy busy. Doing some personal protection. And you?"

"The usual. This shit never ends. So why the call?"

"I need a helping hand, if you can," I asked. "Do this first for background: news articles in the past seventy-two hours referencing Harris Magnusson Partners. You may draw some attention, though; I don't know for *certain* that they *don't* have intelligence assets, but so far I've seen no indication they're operating on that level. The direct action we've witnessed was too... amateurish."

"Wait one." I heard paper shuffling in the background. "Some very scary people have a deniable non-attributable link that's not in use, due to be recycled in six hours. If your... friends... have spooks they'll spend six months figuring out who owned that IP, immediately shit themselves, and spend the next six months running away."

There was a pause.

"Okay, we've got basic counterintelligence cover. Harris Magnusson Partners, you say."

I heard his mechanical keyboard clacking furiously and then fall still.

There was a long pause as he read.

"Uh-huh," he said after a while. "I see. Know what's going on?"

"Only partially. I have speculations, and a few hard facts that haven't been reported yet. Strictly confidential."

"About the Kielic attempted hit?"

"Good guess," I confirmed. "She's alive and safe."

"And with you, right?"

"Now why would you think that?"

"Because I know you, guv. Good man. Also, you said 'we'. So what do you need from me?"

"Intel," I said. "If possible. If you should stumble across anything *unclassified* that relates to Harris Magnusson Partners, and might possibly shed light on *why*. I strongly *suspect*, but don't *know* yet, that this is all about some key document or damaging information that somebody thinks, or knows, that Sharon and/or her boss at Harris Magnusson saw."

"I'll poke around discreetly a little and see if I can find anything. Do I get to meet her?"

"Let's play that one by ear for now, and see how it shakes out."

"Got it. Got to run. You two stay safe, you hear?"

"You got it, brother. Catch you later."

Sharon had of course been sitting by, listening.

"What did he mean when he said 'Because I know you'?" she asked. "Do you make a habit of this or something?"

I chuckled.

"No," I explained, "not at all. What he meant was that under circumstances like these, I wouldn't *tell him* you were safe, unless I *knew* without any doubt that you *were* safe, and if in a situation like this, when reports say your whereabouts are unknown and I'd already mentioned personal protection, I know to *that* degree of confidence that you're safe, it's because you're with me."

She nodded.

"You two really trust each other, don't you?"

"Yup," I agreed. "So when do you want to make your call?"

She checked the time.

"Now would probably work," she said.

"Okay," I replied. "Just a moment. I'm going to disable the outgoing caller ID. Uh... Will she answer an anonymous call?"

"It's a family law practice," she pointed out. "They deal with battered women's shelters all the time. Of *course* they take anonymous calls."

I winced. It was obvious enough, in hindsight, that she shouldn't have had to point it out to me.

"Right," I said, resisting the urge to facepalm. "I should have figured that out without being told." I changed a few settings, and handed her the phone. "Good to go."

She had to look up the number for the firm.

"We get so dependent on our phones to remember everything for us," she muttered, dialing it. "I know her direct extension off of the main office number, though." It rang for a moment, on speaker, then picked up. A woman's voice answered.

"Jerison, Whitewell and Lang. Can I help you?"

"Marilyn? It's Sharon."

"*Sharon!* Oh my *god*, Sharon, are you *all right*? I saw the news! I talked to Edrick yesterday, and he said they'd been trying to locate you, but nobody knew where you were. Thank god you're *alive*! Edrick told me about poor Philip. The police are saying he was tortured before he was murdered. So terrible! Are you *safe*?"

"I'm safe, Marilyn," Sharon said. "I'm safe, and I'm unhurt. But it was a near thing. Someone tried to kill me. A paid hitman."

"Oh god, Sharon! Are you serious? *Why*?"

"We don't know yet. But listen, Marilyn, this is *really important*.

This needs to stay a secret between us. You can't tell *anyone* I'm alive. At least, not anyone I don't tell you is okay to tell."

"Sharon, are you in danger if it's known that you're alive? Where are you?"

She remembered what we'd agreed.

"Marilyn, I'm in witness protection. My... my bodyguard is sitting right beside me right now. And yes, if anyone knows I'm alive, it puts me in more danger."

"Hello?... Thank you for taking care of Sharon. She's a good girl."

"Think nothing of it, ma'am," I said, doing my best Men in Black impression. "I know she is."

"So Sharon," Marilyn continued, "if it's a risk for you to call me, then you must have an important reason. What do you need from me?"

"Marilyn, I need you to talk to Edrick for me. I need to know why someone tried to kill me. But you can't say *anything* to him on the phone, in email, anything that leaves a record, about me being alive. I need you to meet with him in person for some innocent reason."

"I can set up plans to meet him for lunch on Friday," Marilyn agreed after a moment. "That'd be perfectly natural, what with the fire and all. Would that work?"

"That would be great," Sharon agreed. "You can tell him that I'm alive, but he has to keep it secret. I need to know if *anything* had just been assigned to Philip or to me, to work on, or any document *received* for either of us. We are working a theory that this happened because of some crucial incriminating thing that somebody thinks I know, or Philip knew. But we don't know what that thing is. We're trying to figure it out."

"That sounds straightforward enough," Marilyn said. "How will I get back in touch with you if I can find anything out?"

I held up a finger.

"Just a moment, Marilyn," Sharon said. I thought quickly, then scribbled down a URL. Sharon handed me the phone without asking.

"Make a record of this," I told Marilyn. I sent her the URL. "That page will be live in about fifteen minutes. It won't show up in search engines, not even the badly behaved ones. Ignore the page contents, the content is unimportant. You can safely bookmark it, there's nothing *on* the page to hide. It's all about timing. Load the page, let it finish loading, immediately force-reload it *once*, then close the page. Clear your browser's cache, wait five minutes, and do exactly the same thing a second time. That will generate a signal, and we'll know it's time for Miss Kielic to call you again. If we haven't called you within a reasonable period of time, do it again, just in case something went wrong the first time.

"Got all that?"

"Got it," Marilyn confirmed. "Thank you again, Mr...?"

"Agent Cole, ma'am," I said, improvising. "Handing you back to Miss Kielic now."

"Thank you, Agent Cole. Sharon, I don't know when I'll have any news for you. It *might* be as soon as Friday, it might not be until next week. Is that all right?"

"I'll take whatever I can get," Sharon said, "whenever I can get it. Thanks, Marilyn. I need to go now."

"You take care, Sharon," Marilyn replied. "Agent Cole, you look after her, all right? Keep her safe."

"Don't worry, ma'am," I nodded. "Anyone trying to harm Miss Kielic will have to come through me first."

Sharon ended the call and handed the phone back. I returned the outbound caller ID setting to normal.

"So what's on that page?" Sharon asked me.

"Nothing, yet," I said. "It doesn't exist yet. But I'm going to go and create it right now."

I headed downstairs to my office, and she tagged along. She stood behind me as I worked, her hands resting lightly on the back of my chair.

I logged into a remote cloud server that I kept for occasional small things like this, and set to work. I explained as I went along what I was doing.

"There's a robots file on this server that tells web search engines not to index it," I said. "Of course, not all search engines honor robots files —Baidu is particularly ill-behaved, for example—but I block those for bad behavior. The location *itself* is inaccessible by browsing from the top level anyway, there's no direct link to it, so you have to already know where it is. A web search indexer won't be able to find it, because there's no links to it."

I grabbed an existing file to use as a template, deleted all of its content, and replaced it with one call to a script that I quickly pasted together.

"Each time this page is loaded," I explained, "it will call that script, once."

"What does the script do?" Sharon asked.

"What do you *think* it does?" I asked, grinning. "This is the Internet. It loads one random cat picture."

Sharon laughed.

"Of course it does!" she said.

Next, I wrote and activated a quick fail2ban rule.

"This rule makes fail2ban watch Apache's logs for any time the same IP address requests that page I just created, twice within one minute of each other. When that happens, it adds a line to this log file, with the time and the IP address."

I made a copy of another monitoring script and replaced most of its guts with a few lines of code, then set up a cron entry to run it.

"The system timer runs this script once a minute," I continued. "Each time it runs, it looks at the last three lines of that log file. If two of them contain the same IP address and are within no less than four, no more than six, minutes of each other, then it calls *this* script, *then* once the script reports success, it erases everything in the file to avoid duplicate alerts.

"And *that* script sends an SMS alert to my phone."

Sharon looked at me.

"You said you weren't a hacker," she said, accusingly, but smiling.

"And I spoke the truth," I said. "This is just some fairly trivial Unix admin stuff, all built with pre-existing tools. Like building with Legos. All I had to do was snap the pieces together."

"No," she corrected me. "All you had to do was *know how* to snap what pieces together, and in what order."

"I…"

I paused.

"Okay, you're not wrong," I admitted. "But an actual crack, an intrusion, is enormously more complex than what you just watched me do, and I couldn't do it except by following detailed, exact instructions. And if some step along the way didn't work, I probably wouldn't know what to do except try that step again or start over."

She thought about that.

"All I'm saying," she said at last, "is that I think you underestimate how much you know."

I considered that.

"I'm not saying you're necessarily wrong," I replied after a moment. "But on balance, it's a lot safer to underestimate your ability, than to overestimate it. In the famous words of Detective-Inspector Harry Callahan, 'A man's got to know his limitations.'"

Sharon nodded.

"I can see the sense in that," she agreed.

That left us a bit at a loose end, with nothing much that we could usefully do for now. I checked on the webspiders again, but they had still turned up nothing we didn't already know that seemed of any relevance, so I sent them commands to silently terminate themselves. We were both on edge. We tried to distract ourselves with mundane tasks, but it wasn't working very well.

"Hey," Sharon asked after a while. "Are you willing to answer some more questions about the Box?" We were sitting in the living room at the time.

"I'll try," I said. "I haven't had much luck getting answers to direct questions out of it myself."

"No, not like that. Perhaps I should have said, questions about your own experience with the Box."

I shrugged.

"Sure. Shoot. I'll try to answer all I can."

"All right. You said the Box 'just appeared' one day."

"Yup. I got up one morning, a bit more than five years ago—maybe five and a half—came down the stairs, and there it was, in the middle of the floor." I pointed into the hallway. "Right about there. Just... *being* there. Hanging out. Chillin'."

"It was on the floor?"

"Well... no, it was floating *just above* the floor."

"Floating?"

"Maybe an inch off the floor. No visible means of support."

"Did you try to see what was holding it up?"

I nodded. "I tried tossing a plastic coaster under it, and it came straight out the other side. So then I tried a bamboo table mat, and that came straight out too. But when I tried a table knife, it went about a third of the way under and just... stopped. I couldn't push it in any further. But I was able to push it back *out* from the other side with a piece of wood. It wouldn't go through the middle. The harder I pushed, the harder it resisted."

"And then? What did you do then?"

"I walked around it and scratched my head a lot. I tried pushing it, and I found it would move if pushed, but it... was like it didn't *want* to. It resisted. Not pushing back, not heavy, more kind of... sticky."

"And then?"

"Well, after a while, I got out my phone, and I went to take a photo of it. I intended to ask around a bit and ask whether anyone I knew had any idea what the heck it was, and what was going on with it. Not to mention what practical joker somehow put it there without me knowing."

"You say, 'intended'. You didn't?"

"No. Because when I opened the camera app and pointed it at the Box, a message came up on my phone screen instead. It said, 'Please do not do that.'"

Sharon blinked.

"Huh," she said. "Interesting."

"Yeah," I agreed. "I experimented a little, and found that it could display messages on any digital screen within about six feet of it. Even if it wasn't turned on, or even plugged in. Like the little TV downstairs."

"Huh." She paused. "You know, I noticed the TV, but I didn't really pay attention to it not being connected."

"Understandable," I agreed. "You weren't in the clearest state of mind just about then. For very good reasons. And nobody really *expects* a screen that's actively displaying information to not be connected to anything."

She nodded agreement, and shivered slightly.

"So what happened after that?"

"Well, once I'd learned it could communicate, I tried talking to it and asking what was going on, and why it was here."

"Did you get anything out of it?"

"Not really," I replied. "About the most I managed to get out of it then was that it was here because 'It is necessary.' I asked, necessary for what, and it didn't respond. I asked it why it didn't want me to take a photograph of it, and it told me it was not desirable that its presence be announced. That doing so would cause 'difficulties'."

Sharon looked thoughtful.

"Did you ever ask it," she said slowly, "why *you*?"

"Huh," I mused. I hesitated for a moment. "No, I don't think I ever did. It never occurred to me."

"Do you mind if *I* ask it?"

"Be my guest. I'm curious about the answer myself, now that you raise the question."

We got up and went downstairs.

"How did you get it down here, anyway?" Sharon asked, as we descended the stairs.

"Well," I began, "I figured I should get it out of sight, because, you know, awkward questions I couldn't answer. Not that I get a *lot* of visitors, but... there were some. And I mentioned I could push it." She nodded.

"Well, I knew I could push it around, so I pushed it to the stairs. And I was really, really careful about trying to get it down under control. I'd rigged belaying lines and everything.

"None of them were needed. It reached the point where I expected it to tip up, and it didn't. It just slid out on empty air."

"It stayed up on its own?"

I nodded.

"I don't know why I didn't expect it, really. Given that it had already demonstrated an ability to, well, levitate."

"I don't think *I'd* have expected it," Sharon said. "As soon as you don't know what is going on..."

I considered.

"Valid point," I conceded. "But it was... well... in an odd way, *consistent* with the earlier behavior."

"Okay," she nodded, "I can kind of see that. So what did you do then?"

"Well, I took away all of my belays and tackle, once I'd verified I could push it both forwards and back without it falling. And then I pushed it forward again until it was half way over, and it didn't fall." I gestured back towards the stairs, showing her with my hands how far the Box had overhung the stairs by that point. "And then I pushed it forward, little by little, until only a few inches of it was on the top stair. And it *still* didn't fall."

"...And then?" she prompted.

"Then I got brave, and carefully pushed it the *rest* of the way off the top stair. And it just slowly, unhurriedly slid down the stairs, straight down the middle, at a slow walking pace, never tipping. And it got to the bottom, and just... stopped."

"Just stopped," she repeated.

"Yup. And then, well, since I wasn't using that middle room for anything else, I pushed it in there. I had to take the door off to get it in. And some of the frame."

I flipped the light on as we walked into the Box's room again, and she made a slow circuit around the Box, examining it from all sides.

"And the platform?"

"I built that to keep it off the floor, just in case there was a water leak. I didn't know whether getting wet would damage it. I still don't know."

"It looks like you built it pretty solid."

"Well, yeah. I mean, look at the Box. It looks like it *should* weigh hundreds of pounds, at least. Maybe tons. I expected to have to use an engine hoist to lift it onto there."

"But you didn't?"

"No. After I'd already built and leveled the platform, I thought about the experience with the stairs, and I thought, you know, this thing is weird enough, I'd feel really silly if I struggled down here with an engine hoist only to find I didn't need it.

"So... I tried just lifting it."

"And what happened?"

"It... resisted, like it resists all motion. But not a *heavy* resistance. Just a kind of *sticky* resistance. It just slowly came up, with a good steady pull. And then when it was high enough, I just... pushed it onto the top."

"And...?"

"And it settled there and hasn't moved since."

Sharon walked in a complete circle all around the Box again, looking at it.

"This was how long ago, again?"

"Five, maybe five and a half years?"

"What were you doing at the time? For a living, I mean?"

"I was, uh, between jobs. My previous employer had decided they were good with paying somebody in India thirty percent of my salary to do sixty percent of my job, as long as they were satisfied with the other forty percent not getting done."

She winced.

"Sorry."

I shrugged. I was over it.

"It happens. It was happening a lot, around then."

There was a long pause. She turned to face the Box.

"So," she said, "why him?"

Snap, went the little TV, as it turned on.

THERE WAS NO OTHER CHOICE, the Box replied. I blinked.

Sharon pressed for more information.

"No other choice?"

The Box didn't respond.

"Why?"

ANSWERING THAT WOULD BE PROBLEMATIC.

"Why... problematic?"

THAT ANSWER, TOO, IS PROBLEMATIC.

"Problematic for us, or for you?"

YES.

"Can you be more specific?"

NO.

"Let me guess," Sharon said. "It would be problematic."

YES.

"Argh!" She threw her hands up. "This box of yours is *obstinate*. I can see why you haven't been able to get much out of it."

"I... wouldn't say it was mine," I demurred. "I think of it more as a house guest."

She laughed at that.

"Uncle Fester, living in the basement," she said. She turned to the Box. "Shall I call you Uncle Fester?"

IF YOU WISH.

She laughed again. Then she paused, with a thoughtful look.

"Do you understand the reference?"

YES. CULTURAL REFERENCE. THE ADDAMS FAMILY, CREATED BY THE CARTOONIST CHARLES ADDAMS.

She looked at the Box, tapping a finger on her pursed lips.

HE IS NECESSARY.

"What makes him necessary?" she asked.

YOU, TOO, ARE NECESSARY.

"...Wait, what?" She stared at the Box.

THIS IS IMPORTANT. YOU ARE BOTH NECESSARY.

"Wait a minute," I broke in. "'This is important.' That's the second time it's said that."

Sharon looked at me.

"So?" she asked.

"I... don't *think* it's ever done that before. Not even about Syria. Or Avianca Honduras."

I addressed the Box directly.

"Is there something about this assignment," I asked carefully, "that makes it more important than any previous assignment?"

YES.

"And we are *both necessary* to this assignment?"

YES.

"Why?"

NEITHER OF YOU CAN COMPLETE THIS ALONE. YOU MUST SOLVE IT TOGETHER.

Sharon and I exchanged a long look. I thought carefully.

"Did you *know* that, when you sent me to rescue her?"

YES.

"What if I had... failed?" I didn't like to think about it.

THAT OUTCOME WAS NOT CONSIDERED.

"Why not?"

IT WAS NOT POSSIBLE.

Wait, what the fuck?, I thought. I looked at Sharon.

"What do you mean, 'not possible'? Why was it not possible?"

THAT ANSWER IS PROBLEMATIC.

Sharon and I looked at each other.

"*Why* is this assignment so important?" I asked.

THAT ANSWER IS PROBLEMATIC.

"Of course it is," I retorted drily. Sharon, meanwhile, looked as though she was thinking furiously.

"Is the nature of the importance of this assignment," she asked carefully, "such that its importance *itself* inherently poses additional risk or danger *specifically* to Ciárán or to myself?"

Dang, I thought to myself, *that's a legal mind at work.*

There was a long pause.

ONLY INASMUCH AS THE ASSIGNMENT ITSELF IS INHERENTLY DANGEROUS, AND IT IS THE TWO OF YOU WHO MUST COMPLETE IT, the Box replied.

"Well, that's something," Sharon said. She paced, circling the Box again. After a few laps, she stopped and faced the Box.

"You have stated that answering certain questions would be problematic both for you, and for us."

CORRECT.

"Is the problematic nature of the answers such that answering the questions would expose us to additional risk or danger, or jeopardize completion of the assignment?"

CORRECT.

"Which one?"

POSSIBLY BOTH.

"If the assignment is completed, will that *completion* itself expose us to additional risk or danger?"

NO.

"Conversely, if the assignment is NOT completed, will *that* expose us to additional risk or danger?"

YES.

She paused, deep in thought.

"Are there *additional* reasons, not so far stated, why the answers previously referred to are problematic?"

YES.

"Are you able to disclose those reasons?"

NO.

She started to turn away, but then something occurred to her and she looked back at the Box.

"Was Philip Bartholomew deemed necessary?"

NO.

"Is that why you didn't save him? Because he wasn't *necessary*?"

There was another pause.

SINCERE APOLOGIES, said the Box. HE WAS NOT ON THE CRITICAL PATH. THEREFORE IT WAS NOT POSSIBLE TO PREDICT THE ATTACK AGAINST HIM. Then, after another moment, THE LOSS IS NEVERTHELESS REGRETTED.

She turned and looked at me. I looked back.

"Would you have had me save him as well, had you known he was at risk?" I asked, still eye-to-eye with Sharon.

Only if it was feasible for you to save both him and Sharon. The timing would have been... extremely difficult, and would have exposed both Sharon and yourself to much greater risk. By the time you and Sharon left her home, Philip Bartholomew had already been abducted. His location at that time was unknown.

I looked at Sharon. She nodded slowly, after a moment. I cast my mind back to the initial report, mentally doing the math. The accident had apparently been staged some time after midnight. That meant they'd had him for over four hours, maybe five, before they'd finally killed him. I decided not to share that thought with Sharon. She'd already been hurt enough. She didn't need to know the Black Hats had probably spent at least four hours torturing her boss.

"I have one more question," Sharon said to me slowly. "At the moment, that is. The usefulness of the answer is dependent upon whether the Box is being straight with us. But I... don't think there is any actual evasion or deception in its answers. As you said, it is extremely terse and sparing with its answers, but I think it is being strictly truthful. If it's unable to answer, it doesn't lie or dissemble, it just says so."

"All I can tell you," I answered, "is that so far, it has not to my knowledge ever intentionally led me astray. And I have the feeling it is *trying* to tell us as much of what we *need* to know as it actually *can*. It's just... I think maybe not programmed to *volunteer* information without being asked a more or less direct question. And it's very constrained in what it *can* tell us."

That surmise is substantially correct. For most purposes.

"Huh," Sharon said. She thought about it for a moment, one eyebrow raised. Then she nodded, and turned back to the Box.

"Consider again the questions which you have declined to answer on the grounds that answering them is problematic," she instructed the Box. "Without disclosing the answers, is there any information which you are withholding from us by *not* answering those questions, *outside of* any information relating to this current assignment or the completion thereof, the *lack of which* exposes Ciáran or myself to increased risk or danger?"

No. The Box's response was instant.

"Well," I remarked, "it seems pretty sure about that." A thought struck me.

"Can you expand in any way upon that last answer?"

The continued health and well-being of both of you is deemed desirable. It is a secondary objective.

Sharon gave the Box a hard look.

"Does that answer," she asked, "mean that Ciáran's and my continued health is directly, *in and of itself*, in your interest, separate from and in addition to completion of the assignment? Or only in as far as it results in the completion of the assignment?"

The former.

"Well damn," I said. "I don't think we're going to get better than that."

"No further questions," Sharon declared.

═══════════

We went back upstairs and I turned on the Breville to make coffee. On a whim, I went to my liquor cabinet, a lovely piece of 1920s-vintage woodwork, and pulled out a bottle of Balvenie Doublewood.

"Irish?" I asked.

"Sure," Sharon agreed.

It was difficult to talk while making espresso, it's an inherently noisy process, but it doesn't take all that long. Once the machine was warmed up, it was only about ten minutes before we were sitting at the table with our coffees.

"How far away can the Box 'hear'?"

I pondered.

"That's a difficult question," I replied, "and I haven't the faintest idea what the answer is. It clearly has access to intel sources that I can't begin to guess at."

"I meant on a shorter distance scale," Sharon clarified. She paused for a sip at her coffee. "Do you have any other way to communicate with the Box, except by going downstairs and talking to it?"

"Sure," I replied. "It sends me messages on my phone at times."

Sharon gave me a hint of side-eye.

"Somehow I expected something more mysterious," she said.

"Oh, there's mystery to it, don't worry," I assured her. "The messages self-erase, a period of time after I've read them or don't need them any more. And according to the satellite phone service, they don't exist. They... do not show up against my message count. Either transmission or storage. Like they don't exist in the system."

"Well, that raised more questions than it answered," she said ruefully.

"Welcome to my world," I replied with a grin.

"What's with the painting, anyway?" she asked, as we drank our coffee.

"Painting?"

"The one in the room with the Box."

"Ohhh," I said, "*that* painting. I stumbled across that one day in a home-furnishing overstock store, priced at something like sixty bucks, and, well... I mean, just look at it and the Box. Geometric squares, triangles, light toward the middle. I *had* to."

"I can see that," she replied, laughing. "It *does* kind of fit in."

It was getting on toward supper time.

"Sweet and sour glazed pork tenderloin medallions sound good to you?" I asked.

"Sounds great," she agreed. "Want any help?"

"Let me think about that," I said. "There's still rice from yesterday. That'll only take minutes to reheat. Want to make a vegetable side dish to go with the pork? Fresh or frozen, your call. You saw where the freezers are."

"Indeed I did," she agreed. "I'll look."

She checked the refrigerator first.

"How about gingered carrots?" she asked.

"Sounds great to me," I replied. "Did you see where the spices are?" She shook her head. I pointed to a cabinet.

"I'm on it," she said, and set to work.

I wasn't used to having someone else working in my kitchen at the same time, and I don't think Sharon was used to tag-team cookery either, so there was a bit of dancing around as we tried to avoid getting in each other's way. We quickly got the hang of it, though, and fairly quickly we had supper on the table. There was a little left of yesterday's wine, so I poured the last two glasses. I filled water-glasses for us with freshly chilled water from the filter in the fridge. Not Perrier or Evian, perhaps, but it wasn't bad at all.

"Tell me something, if you can," Sharon said as we ate.

"I'll try," I answered, around a mouthful of really tasty gingered carrots. I was glad she'd offered to pitch in. Fancy things with vegetables were not my forté.

"Can you remember what the *first* thing was that the Box asked you to do?"

I had to stop and think hard about that.

"I remember it was something really small and inconsequential," I said at last. "But useful. I don't recall exactly what it was. There were several of those. Getting me used to the idea that it could be helpful, I guess." I paused for a bite of glazed pork.

"Then one day it suggested that I should change my internet service. I asked why, and to who or what. It told me, 'Improved service and operational security.' Then it sent an SMS message to my phone with a link to a specific plan at a provider I'd never heard of. And another link to a specific fiber bridge to buy and install.

"I went to the site and looked at the plan, and it gave me five times the bandwidth I had, and symmetric. Same speed up and down, not fast download, slow upload like typical consumer broadband. And it would be static IP and a dedicated fiber drop, no shared segment that anyone else on could potentially sniff my traffic in and out. But it was a business-only plan, and it cost nearly ten times what I'd been paying."

"Ouch," Sharon said, wincing slightly.

"The Box told me a specific business name and purchase order number to use, all the information to put in."

She pursed her lips, and her eyes narrowed slightly as she contemplated something.

"Penny for your thoughts, Sharon?" I offered.

She shook her head No. "These thoughts aren't steak tartare. They need to marinate and cook for a while. Pass me the ginger carrots."

I did, and she helped herself to almost half of what was left, which was unsurprising. Nothing dresses up vegetables like a subtly sweet and spicy ginger finish. I gave her time both to enjoy the food and to refine her thinking, and was rewarded a minute later.

"What was the business name?"

"I don't remember. I could look it up, but I did that at the time. It wasn't anything memorable. And there was really nothing much I could find about it. It appeared to be a shell corporation located—on *paper* at least—in the Bahamas."

"Interesting. And what happened?"

"The order went through, and a technician came out five days later and installed the fiber drop. I've never seen a bill from it. Just invoices marked paid. The service has a built-in secure VPN that has egress points all over the world.

"Later, it told me I needed a different, more secure phone, too."

"Aha. The Russian phone."

"Exactly," I agreed. "The Russian phone." I reached for my water glass to clear my palate for another pork medallion. There's something cleansing about ice cold water that goes beyond the physical. For a moment, some fey part of my mind wondered whether the French put cold packs and Perrier in their military rations.

"What *is* that phone, anyway? I've never seen one like it."

"Honestly," I said carefully, "neither have I. I hardly know a damned thing about it *except* that it's apparently Russian. Or maybe Ukrainian, I suppose. And I've tried to find out."

"Because of the Cyrillic writing?" Sharon asked, frowning.

"Well, that, but there's more. Here's what I *know*: It's some kind of secure satellite phone, and somehow or other, the Box sourced it, or *arranged* for it to be sourced, presumably from Russia. And the Web doesn't know about it, so it's probably classified."

A thought occurred to me.

"Or maybe," I amended, "sourced from someone who had already *gotten* it from Russia. I don't know the details. It's pure guesswork either way, beyond the visibly obvious, and the Box wouldn't tell me.

"Anyway, part of the reason it's secure is because it doesn't use the ground-based cellular network *at all* to make or receive calls or messages. And that means it can't be tracked—or sniffed, or located, or tapped—by any of the usual cellular surveillance tricks like Stingrays or triangulation from cell towers. Anyone trying to track it would first of all have to know to look for it in the satellite phone system.

"But it goes further than just having to know to look in the satellite phone systems for it. It enters the global phone network in Moscow and looks to the world like it belongs to a Mercedes-Benz dealership there. I *think* the dealership is an FSB front, but for obvious reasons I haven't tried very hard to find out. Right now there's basically no chance of intra-government cooperation between us and them. Someone would have to hack into the system, dodge the FSB minders, read Russian, and unwind the rat's nest of false fronts and shell companies that I'm sure is there, to be able to get back to us.

"But none of that is obvious, because the visible phone number is perfectly ordinary. It just forwards everything transparently to the Russian number. Calls to it don't even get billed as international. Don't ask me how that works, because I don't know."

"Do you think the phone company knows about that part?" Sharon asked.

"I've wondered about that myself," I answered, nodding. "I... wouldn't feel confident betting that they do."

"And we're assuming the Black Hats can't do any of that... right?" She took a sip of her wine.

I nodded.

"Yup. I... could *ask* Judson whether he could do it—for all I know, he already has—but my guess is he couldn't tell me the answer anyway."

"I don't believe for a moment that the Box is Russian," she said.

"Neither do I," I replied. "I'm pretty certain the West couldn't build it, and Russia is a long way behind the West on that front.

"For what it's worth, I asked the Box if it was connected in any way to the Russian government. And the Box said, straight out, No. So then I asked it if it was acting as an agent for any other national government. Including ours. And again, it said No."

"Interesting," she mused. We'd nearly finished eating by now, and we paused our discussion long enough to finish our meal and clean up. I started the dishwasher, and we retired to the living room again. This time, Sharon just went straight to the couch, sat down, grabbed my arm, and pulled me down next to her.

Far be it from me to argue. I put an arm around her shoulders and she snuggled in.

"When did it first give you a real assignment?" she asked.

I thought briefly.

"About six months after it appeared," I said.

"And what was that?"

"It had me connect to a naïvely-insecure cloud storage bucket, download a pile of documents, print them all out, put them in a folder, and mail them to the city public works department."

"And what happened?"

"About five or six weeks later—"

"Wait," she interrupted me, raising a hand. I could see she was thinking hard. "Let me see if I can figure this one out on my own. Six months after it appeared. So, somewhere about four and a half to five years ago, document dump, Public Works." She looked at me. I nodded affirmation.

"That was when the city announced that it was switching to a different contractor for the overpasses on the new bypass, citing breach of contract, because it had come to light that the selected contractor had knowingly grossly underbid and falsified estimates in order to get the contract, planning to make it up in cost overruns and reworks later once the city was committed."

"Ding ding ding!" I said, grinning. "Got it in one."

"What do I win?" she asked, with that brilliant smile.

I couldn't think of anything to offer as a prize. So in a moment of mad impulsiveness, I threw caution to the winds, leaned in, and kissed her gently.

"Will that do?" I asked, when we separated a few moments later.

"...For now," she replied, smiling.

We sat without further words for a little bit.

"Just out of curiosity," I asked slowly, "was Harris Magnusson involved in any way in that change of contract?"

"I doubt it," she replied. "I wasn't with the firm then. I just remember seeing it on the evening news. But the city has its own legal department. It doesn't use outside law firms."

"Hmm. Okay." Then a thought occurred to me. "Wait. What about 440 South Ninth? You told me Harris Magnusson handled that."

"That wasn't a city-initiated suit," she said. "The city was *involved*, and joined the suit, but the suit was filed with Harris Magnusson by and on behalf of all the people who'd bought units in the buildings.

"Anyway, why did you ask? What are you thinking?"

"I just wondered, just for a moment," I mused. "The Box says that *you* are necessary. I was wondering whether it had its eye on *you* that far back."

She looked startled, then pensive.

"You know," she replied after a minute, "that's a... disturbing thought."

"Isn't it?" I agreed.

Her expression became more unsettled.

I thought some more.

"You know," I said after a minute or so, "we could probably ask it. It doesn't seem like a 'problematic' question."

Sharon looked at me, then without a word, jumped up and headed for the stairs down. I hurried after her to keep up.

She walked into the room and stopped in front of the Box.

"Additional question," she said sharply.

Snap went the TV.

"You have stated that I am 'necessary'."

CORRECT.

"How long ago did you determine that I was 'necessary'?"

THREE DAYS.

She hesitated. That hadn't been the timescale she was expecting.

"Prior to that time, had you observed or monitored me in any way? Or anyone else at Harris Magnusson?"

No.

She let out her breath raggedly.

"Thank you. No further questions at this time."

You are welcome, Sharon.

She laughed darkly. I raised an eyebrow.

"It's so *polite*," she said, as she left the room and headed back upstairs. I couldn't quite read the edge in her voice. But it sounded like the moment we'd had was gone.

When I got upstairs, she was curled up in the big overstuffed chair again. I picked the other chair this time.

"I'm... sorry," she apologized after a little bit.

"For what?" I asked.

"That kind of spoiled the mood," she said. "I just... I *really don't like* the idea of being surveilled, spied on. You know what I mean?"

"I don't blame you in the least," I replied. "I imagine most people..." Then I paused. "No, actually, now that I think about it, a surprising number of people seem to be *perfectly fine* with being spied on twenty-four by seven, everything they do. Or they wouldn't use half the online services and social media they do."

"And, well, yeah," she went on, "I guess I'm still... on edge, and I let it get to me. I'm sorry."

"Sharon," I said truthfully, "as far as I'm concerned, you have nothing to apologize for. It was a perfectly normal reaction."

"I still feel kinda guilty, though," she said. "I... it was a *really nice* moment. And I spoiled it."

"I'm the one who brought up the question," I pointed out.

She paused.

"Yeah. I suppose you did." She sighed. "Well, at least now I know the Box *wasn't* watching me, and I don't need to have *that* question festering in the back of my mind."

A thought struck me.

"You know," I mused, "maybe that's exactly it."

Sharon looked at me enquiringly.

"You know I said that it barely gave me enough warning to get there in time?"

She nodded.

"Yeah, you said that... what are you thinking?"

"I'm thinking," I said, "that it gave me so little warning precisely *because* it wasn't watching you. It said it determined three days ago that you were necessary."

I paused. She still looked puzzled. For once, she hadn't put it together yet.

"Sharon, I don't think the Box *knew* you were important, *until the moment the Black Hats moved against you.*"

Light dawned. I practically *saw* the logic connect in her head. Then she took it and ran with it.

"...And the moment it *knew*, it sent *you* out, post-haste, not taking the time to brief you, *just trusting you* to get to me in time and figure it out when you got there," she finished.

Gods. She was probably right. That's why it hadn't briefed me in advance. We stared at each other.

"And you did," she added.

"...Fortunately," I agreed.

"I think I owe your box an apology, don't I?" Sharon said in a small voice.

Before I could figure out an answer to that, she stood up and walked to the top of the stairs.

"I'm sorry I misjudged you," she called down the stairs. Then she turned around and sat back down, on the couch this time.

Bleep! went my phone, a moment later. It was the particular tone I'd assigned to messages from the Box. I pulled out my phone with a grim expression, wondering what shit had just hit which fan, and in what quantity. Sharon saw my expression, and leaned forward, concern on her face.

"Is something wrong?" she asked.

"I don't know yet," I answered. "Checking. We might need to move in a hurry."

I opened the new message, and read it. I started to speak, but then I saw the bottom of the message. I closed my mouth again, trying to suppress the smirk that I knew was spreading across my face, but I couldn't do it. I got up, my face twitching, walked over to the couch as Sharon looked strangely at me, and sat down beside her.

I showed her the phone.

APOLOGY ACCEPTED, BUT UNNECESSARY, the message read.

"Well, that's polite of it," she said. Then I pointed out the signature at the bottom of the message.

It was signed, UNCLE FESTER.

She blinked, stared, her jaw dropped... then she lost it. I couldn't hold it in any longer either. We both *howled* with laughter. She leaned on my shoulder, one arm around my neck, and I put an arm around her, each supporting the other. We laughed until our cheeks were wet.

"Gods," she gasped out at last, "I *needed* that."

I grinned.

"You and me both," I replied, still chuckling myself. "They say laughter is the best medicine."

She turned and looked at me for a long moment, her eyes suddenly serious.

"No," she said. "*This* is the best medicine." Then she threw both arms around my neck and kissed me fiercely. I wrapped my arms around her and held her tight. We kissed for a long, long time.

After a while we came up for air. She looked at me for a long moment, then seemed to come to a decision.

"Ciáran?"

"Yes?"

"Take me to bed. Right now. Please."

She didn't have to ask me twice. I half-rose from the couch, turning towards her, then bent and slipped one arm under her thighs, the other behind her back. I picked her up and cradled her in my arms, and she put her arms back around my neck and kissed me again. Then I carried her up the stairs, to my room. Her eyes never left mine for a moment.

I kicked the door gently closed behind us, then set her down. We slowly undressed each other. She ran her hands up and down me, kissed my shoulder, then nibbled my collarbone. I bent and kissed the angle of her jaw, her throat, her shoulders, her breasts, as her fingers explored me, then I dropped to my knees and kissed my way down her smooth belly. She wound her fingers in my hair, and I kissed the hollow of her groin. I felt her shiver. Yeah, we'd only known each other a few days... but gods, she was an absolutely amazing woman, and I wanted her *so much*.

She took hold of my shoulders, urged me back to my feet, and then pulled me towards my bed. We fell onto the bed together. We crawled up towards the head of the bed until we reached the pillows, then I caught her, rolled onto my back, and pulled her on top of me. She spread herself out on me like a blanket, I wrapped my arms around her, and we kissed again. I caressed her hips, her butt, the small of her back, as she kissed the side of my neck, then she found the scar on my left shoulder.

She traced it with her finger, giving me a questioning look. I nodded. She reached and kissed it, then sat up and traced her fingers down the length of my body, as far as my waist. I put my hands on the beautiful curve of her hips, then slid them slowly up her sides and cupped her lovely breasts, teasing her dark nipples with my thumbs. She gasped. I took hold of her sides and pulled her forward towards me, enough that I could raise my head to reach her breasts. I circled her right nipple with my tongue, then took it into my mouth. She moaned in pleasure, wound her fingers in my hair, pulled my head against her, as I ran my hands over every part of her body I could reach, her firm thighs, her pert butt, her smooth belly, her back.

She adjusted her position, reached down, and guided me inside her. She was warm and soft and—

BIRTH CONTROL, my brain shouted.

"Sharon, wait," I gasped out, "do we need—"

"It's all right," she said urgently, "it's safe, *don't stop now.*"

And then *everything* was warm, and soft, and close, and all our barriers were down, and we just lost ourselves in the miracle of each other.

Afterward, we lay, spent, wrapped around each other, not ready yet to stop exploring the joys and wonders we had found. Her hand traced down my back, and trailed across the scars there. She stopped.

Her fingers followed the extent of the scars, probing.

"This is the one from Syria, isn't it?" she asked softly.

"It is," I agreed.

"Does it ever… still hurt?"

"It aches a little sometimes," I admitted.

"I so nearly lost you there before I even met you," she said. I hugged her tight.

"You said three times," she said after a minute or two.

"Syria," tracing the scars on my back again.

"And this one," as she kissed my shoulder.

"Where's the third?"

I reluctantly moved my right hand from the small of her back, where I was enjoying it being, then took her left hand and gently guided it down to the small, oval scar in the outer part of my right thigh. She traced around it with her fingers as I returned my hand to her lower back.

"How did this one happen?" she asked.

"Personal protection assignment," I told her. "Federal district judge, civil rights case in Arizona. She'd received death threats, but the police didn't believe they were serious. The Box had me contact her and offer protection. She took it. She was scared, and rightly so. Two men followed her home from the courthouse one night and tried to kill her in her driveway. One of them got a hit on me as I was getting out of the car, before I shot him. Managed to get the other one alive. Turned out they'd been hired by one of the defendants who wanted a white man judging his case, not a Hispanic woman."

"And the judge?"

"Unhurt. Police took the threats seriously after that, and gave her an around-the-clock protective detail until after the case was concluded. Guilty on all charges, by the way, *plus* new charges related to murder-for-hire against the judge."

She considered that for a minute.

"So what about the shoulder wound?"

"Ah. *That* one," I said. "Well, you remember I told you that most of the times I've been shot at, I've managed to avoid having to shoot back?" She nodded. "Any time you can avoid a shoot-out is good. If you're forced into an exchange of fire you didn't plan, something's gone badly wrong with the plan.

"This was one of those times when the plan goes to hell. The Box sent me to Mexico, near Tijuana, to extract a journalist abducted by one of the cartels. There's little doubt they intended to kill her. And then probably display her body somewhere public, as a warning to others. Probably dismembered. They do that a lot."

She flinched a little. That might have been too much information. Oops.

"I was able to extract her, but we were spotted during our exit. Just dead unlucky, inadequate prior surveillance on my part, a man I didn't spot who showed up at the exact wrong moment, and it turned into a bit of a shoot-out with three or four cartel *sicarios*—fortunately, *only* three or four, and not at close range—and one of them grazed me before I was able to break contact and disengage, with her still in tow. It was a close thing. I don't think they'd realized yet that I'd gotten away with their captive, or they'd doubtless have chased us a lot harder."

She thought about that for a moment.

"So... did you end up shooting any of them?"

"Probably. Pretty sure I at least *hit* one or two. Taking them out wasn't my first priority—I wasn't there to do that, or I've have gone about it totally differently. Mission priority objective was getting the journalist out alive."

"And the journalist?"

"Safe. She lives in Toronto now. Nice lady."

She looked at me.

"What if you *had* been there to—take them out?"

"I'd have done it from six or eight hundred yards, with a good rifle. I'm not stupid. But I couldn't have guaranteed getting them all *before* they killed her. Getting her out alive meant going in slow and quiet, not raising any alarms, and ideally getting out unseen. The best plan can go to hell in a hurry when lead starts flying. It's a last resort, not a first choice."

She touched the scar on my thigh again, then ran her hand slowly all the way back up to my chest, never lifting the contact. She laid her head on my shoulder.

"My Fenian warrior," she whispered. "I'm so glad Fester introduced us."

I kissed her forehead and held her tight.

Eventually, we both fell asleep.

4: The Fourth Day

I woke before Sharon in the morning. I just lay there and looked at her for a little bit, then I stroked her hair and caressed her exposed shoulder, wondering how the hell this had happened, and whether it would ever happen again.

After a little while, she woke up, shifted her head slightly, and looked at me. Her arms tightened, then she stretched up and kissed me.

"Good morning," she said sleepily.

"It is a very good morning indeed," I agreed.

We lay there for a while and just cuddled.

"I'm in the mood for a run before breakfast," she said after a while. "How about you?"

"Sounds good to me," I replied.

She hesitated.

"Is it safe?" she asked.

"Should be," I said. "There's been no indication whatsoever that anyone is actively looking for you *here*. And nobody—"

I stopped.

"And nobody who's seen anything about me on the news will be looking for me," she finished for me, "because they think I'm dead."

"...Yeah," I said. I squeezed her tightly. "Sorry for bringing that up."

"It's alright," Sharon replied. "*We* know I'm alive. Nobody else needs to right now. It's like a kind of invisibility." She had a point, I reflected.

"Speaking of which, did you come up with anyone who could act as a go-between to the police, so that we can keep you off the suspect list?"

"I have a couple of ideas," she said. "I think I know who I want to call."

"Great," I said. "We can take care of that later. For now, I'll show you my regular running loop. You good for five miles?"

She grinned.

"Lead on, Tiger," she said.

We got up and got dressed, her in her leopard-print joggers and a pale green tank top, me in cargo shorts and a T-shirt. The shirt had a heavily-armed polar bear on the front, wearing a military beret, with a caption that read "Only you can prevent friendly fire."

We went out the front door, and I led the way... well, not exactly *led*; she kept pace right beside me. I wasn't going full out, settling for about seven minutes a mile. If I had to, I could do it in five. From time to time I pointed out turns, when the next turn was to her side.

About three miles in, a big black shape came pell-mell towards us. Mrs. Watkins' dog Sam had gotten out again. He was a big black Labrador. He raced up and circled us, barking in his usual good-natured way. We slowed to a walk for a moment.

"Hi, Sam," I said, reaching out a hand toward him. Of course, he slobbered on it. "This is Sharon. She's good people."

Sharon stopped and held out her hand, and Sam sniffed it, licked it, then jumped up and gave a friendly "Hello" bark, his paws on her waist. Sharon rubbed the back of his head and neck.

"Aren't you a good boy?" she said. He barked again, then he dropped to all fours and started racing in circles around us again. We resumed our run, at a little easier pace for the moment, until we rounded the next corner. Mrs. Watkins was outside by then. She quickly spotted us.

"Sam!" she called. "Here!"

"Hi, Mrs. Watkins," I called, then pointed that way and looked at Sam.

"Go home, Sam," I said, "go home." He danced backwards, turned, gave us one more bark over his shoulder, and pelted for the front door. I gave Mrs. Watkins a friendly wave, and she waved back.

A minute or two later, her house was out of sight, and a bit more than ten minutes after that, we were back home.

"Shower?" Sharon said.

"Sure."

We soaped each other up in the shower, and, well, there was quite a bit of cuddling, but we tried to keep it short. Then we came out, toweled each other off, got dressed, and went downstairs to make breakfast.

This time Sharon made the coffee while I got out eggs, ham, mushrooms and sharp Cheddar cheese, and built a large, fluffy, generously-filled omelet. Sharon glanced into the pan as I worked.

"I haven't seen an omelet made quite like that before," she said.

"I'm not sure how to label my omelet technique," I answered. "I beat my eggs first, like the French method, but unlike a French chef, I don't feel I've committed an unspeakable barbarity if my omelet develops a little color. In fact, I wonder what I've done wrong if it *doesn't*. A French-trained chef would probably consider me a heretic or something."

She smiled and lightly touched my upper arm in approval. She didn't say she was looking forward to it, but the message was clear regardless. When it was done, I halved my fluffy, cheesy creation between us and we sat down for breakfast together.

I did my usual morning news check, but there was nothing much of note in the news. Certainly nothing relevant to us. The top story was the huge climate bill that was still stalled in the House—primarily because a large group of Republican representatives had managed to attach pro-fossil-fuels poison-pill riders to it, that made a cruel mockery of it. Welcome to the American political process.

"Ciáran?" Sharon began, uncertainly, as we ate breakfast.

"What is it?" I asked.

"Ciáran… about last night." She sounded nervous, uncertain.

"Yes," I said, my heart suddenly in my mouth. Of *course* it was too good to be true.

"Um… a bit later…"

She hesitated, then found resolve. She looked at me eye to eye.

"Ciáran, look. I know this is really, really *sudden*. But… well, later… would you help me move that chest of drawers into your room? …If that's okay?"

I let my breath out explosively and looked at her. My heart leapt.

"Sharon," I said, relieved, "that is okay like a giant sequoia is *tall.*" Her face lit up. "I was horribly afraid for a moment there that you were about to say it was a one-time-only thing. A stress release. It was so... sudden. Unexpected."

"If it's one time," she replied fervently, "then that one time had better last *forever.*"

"Forever looks... mighty good from here," I agreed.

"You don't have any doubts?" she asked, hesitating for just a moment.

"Sharon, girl, I already told you two days ago how much I appreciate you. And I meant every word."

Then I reached for her, and she reached for me, and we wrapped our arms around each other and silently held each other. It was a slightly awkward angle, sitting at the table, but we endured. Our half-finished omelet cooled, temporarily forgotten, for a little while... but better a cold breakfast than to interrupt a moment like this.

"Look," she said, as we cuddled, "I wasn't *planning* last night. I *know* it was really sudden. Sudden as hell. I admit it was a spur-of-the-moment decision. And I know we're both under a lot of stress right now, and it'd be easy to think that it was just an unconsidered choice made under pressure, without real thought behind it." She looked up at me. "But it didn't come out of a vacuum. That's *important.* I want you to understand that. You don't talk down to me, you don't dismiss my ideas, and you have no idea how much of a breath of fresh air that is."

She took a deep breath.

"All the time going through college and in law school, professors would make a point, then ask whether anyone had any questions. And if you follow the professor's eyes around the room, his eyes would always be on a girl when he asked if anyone had any questions. There was an unspoken *assumption* that if anyone didn't fully understand, it would be one of the girls. We had to work about a third harder to get the same grades. Probably three out of four professors were more critical of our work, challenged our sources and references more often. Marked us down for mistakes that they let slide for the guys. It felt like we weren't supposed to be there. Weren't *wanted* there.

"But you don't do that. You don't dumb down your answers, you don't disregard my questions, *your default assumption is that I understand.* That my questions are worthwhile and good. Or that I can do what you're asking me to, without being walked through it. Even... that first night. You told me what you needed me to do to keep me alive, and just took it for granted I'd get it done.

"Do you have any idea how uncommon that is? How much it *meant?* How much it helped me get through it?"

I gave that a bunch of long, hard thought. It wasn't something I'd ever really thought about before. At least, not in this much depth, and really hearing it from the female perspective. And I said so.

"I've... just never understood why anyone would do that," I told her. "I mean, I get that some people have a need to feel superior to other people. And I know that a lot of... well, granted, *mostly* men, but sometimes women as well, can be real assholes to people, but especially to women. I just don't understand how anyone can be happy going through life that way. How *broken* does a person need to be, for their deepest need to be having underlings they can abuse, or getting away with treating people badly? Just because they *can?*

"I've never wanted *underlings,* Sharon. I've always wanted an *equal companion.*"

She nodded, and I went on, encouraged, breakfast forgotten for the moment.

"Tuesday night, you'd... just had a hell of a shock, and I was prepared to handle you like eggs if I had to, but I could see that even after that *you had it together,* and I saw no reason to believe you wouldn't *continue* to have it together. So, well, I just kinda assumed you *would.* And you know what?"

She raised her eyebrows enquiringly.

"It was really *nice* to feel I could safely assume that," I continued. "And you didn't disappoint me one bit. Not once. And... truth is, I was even *more* impressed after you told me about, uh, the towel." I felt her tense for a moment, then she nodded quickly, jerkily. "A lot of people would have just lost it and come apart, right there. Completely hysterical.

"You *didn't.* You kept it together and stayed functional. And that's a large part of why we made it out unscathed."

She hugged me a little tighter.

"I don't really know how to explain how much that means," she said slowly. "And, what you said about how much you appreciate me. It *felt...* like it was coming from the heart. Nobody has ever said anything quite like that to me before, and certainly never so obviously meant it. A girl comes to expect that when a man compliments her, it's most likely because he wants into her pants. We can tell. We learn to look out for it. In self-defense. But you're not like that. When you give me a compliment, it *feels* honest. Sincere. And you just... don't seem to have anything at all to prove.

"I stopped going out in the evenings, you know? Because eating dinner at a restaurant alone is just sad, and I got sick of lame pick-up lines in bars. Being hit on by strangers, just because I was a single woman in a bar and they might get lucky.

"You never once tried to hit on me. Even though I saw the way you looked at me sometimes."

I felt suddenly sheepish. I thought I'd hidden it better.

She looked very seriously at me again.

"And sudden or not... well, I decided... I *want* that. I want *you*. I *want* to be treated the way you treat me. Like an equal partner. I don't know if we'll last forever, if it'll work out, but I'm in this for the long run. I *want* it to work out."

I nodded slowly as I listened, thinking carefully about my words. These were pretty heavy thoughts for the breakfast table.

"Sharon," I replied after a moment, "you are one very special lady. I have never met a girl like you. And sudden or not, I think I'd be an idiot not to give this the best shot I can, and hope not to find myself chewing on my own foot too often.

"So... yeah. Come what may, however this ends, I'm in it for the long run too. I won't deny I'm a little—well, okay, a *lot*—scared about it, but... I want us to come out of this together. And then we can figure out everything else later.

"You are precious and wonderful, Sharon, and I'll do anything I can to keep you. For as long as you still want me."

I think after that, we both ran out of words. So I kissed her, and she kissed me back, and we just held and kissed each other for a little bit.

So after we finished our breakfast, we went and moved the dresser. We took all the drawers out, in order, then we carried the dresser into my room and found a good spot for it, then I brought the drawers in and Sharon put them back in, in order.

"There's... another thing," Sharon said afterward. She looked thoughtful.

"What's on your mind?"

"Can I use your computer? I want to do some research. And I want the name of the corporation that pays for your internet service. If that's not a problem."

"I don't have any objections," I said. "Go right ahead. Look at anything you want to."

I logged in on the computer, pulled up the most recent PAID notice on the service, and handed it off to her. She gave me a quick kiss, then sat down to work. I went away and... did domestic things. I put in some laundry, figured out what needed restocking on the next grocery trip, and a few other things. Then I went and checked over the Volvo, checking tire pressures, checking for debris in the tires, checking lights, checking charge level, making sure it didn't need any maintenance tasks.

Sharon reappeared after about four hours, while I was on a mechanic's rollboard checking the underside of the Gray Ghost. She looked both satisfied, and puzzled, but opened the dialogue with "Don't tell me you're an electric vehicle mechanic, too?"

"No," I chuckled, "just looking for obvious problems. Leaking seals, things coming loose. And minor maintenance tasks that I can take care of—low tire pressures, low oil, low washer fluid, loose cables. Worn wiper blades. Rotating the tires. Right now I've got a multitool and a flashlight, and that's all I'm qualified to use on the Ghost's internals. I don't have the specialized equipment or knowledge to do anything major, let alone touch any of its control systems. CAN-BUS is black magic as far as I'm concerned."

She knelt down by the Ghost and I rolled over to poke my head out at her. She smiled at me and ruffled my hair. "So how do you do shop-level maintenance? Just take it to the dealership?"

"I'm... trying to avoid that at the moment," I replied. "And I hope we won't need to. It could be a problem. If, *if*, someone made us at your house, and noticed that this is the Polestar model... well, there's not a lot of them around. I didn't really have a need to stay hidden in mind when I picked it out. I was just thinking about its capabilities."

"Why is that an issue?" she asked.

"Well, *if* we were made... I don't *think* we were, but I could be wrong... then someone might think to ask around the Volvo dealerships in the area, and bribe a clerk to tell them who in the area brings in a gray Polestar for service."

"Oh," she said. She thought for a moment. "I didn't think of that."

"Neither did I," I agreed, "when I bought it. Anyway, Fester tells me what to look out for, and just says that if I spot problems early, 'the issue will be dealt with.' I have no idea what exactly that means. It hasn't come up."

I stretched a little, working my shoulders. Rollboard or no, even with the XC60's higher ground clearance, it was cramped under there. "So, did you find anything?"

"Sort of," she replied. "I traced that corporation. As you thought, it's a shell corporation. It traces back to *another* shell corporation. And I was able to trace *that* shell corporation, in turn, back—indirectly—to something called the Long Now Foundation."

"I've never heard of that," I admitted. "What is it?"

"That's the puzzling part," she replied. "It's a San Francisco-based non-profit founded to encourage thinking about civilization on the scale of tens of thousands of years.

"Now, from what I can find out about their finances, it's... certainly *conceivable* that they could spare the resources to pay for your internet service. But I don't see why they *would*. And the whole setup of all the shell corporations to do it seems... improbable. I can't come up with any plausible normal reason why they would do it that way, even if a relatively small non-profit could spare the time and resources to set them all up.

"And in any case, even if they had the motivation to do so, I can't see *any possible way on earth* they have the resources to get you a secret Russian satellite phone. Let alone come up with the Box."

"I see what you mean," I agreed, after considering it at length. "It's answers that don't actually answer any questions."

"Exactly," she agreed. "We know more, but we're not actually any further forward than we started. The answer is still just as far away."

I thought about that, tried to see these answers as Judson would—and it hit me.

"These answers don't answer *our* questions," I mused. "Maybe that means we're asking the wrong ones. We're asking if Fester's spooks are running the Long Now, or if the Long Now is running Fester's spooks. We're looking for collaboration. But the hallmark of a good, professional intelligence operation is that cells are kept isolated, specifically to foil the kind of digging we're doing.

"So maybe... I mean, I've been wondering for a while if I've become a deniable actor for someone's intelligence operation. I just don't have the first idea *which* agency—or even which *government*—could be behind it. And that *still* poses more questions than it answers.

"The phone is one thing; it seems easily traceable to Russia. But nobody is ever going to convince me that Russia could manage the Box. I have a pretty good idea of what they're technically capable of, and the Box is so far outside that, it's not even funny."

Sharon turned to sit on the cold garage concrete, her back to the Gray Ghost's wheel, her head tilted back.

"It fits," she said slowly. "Could it be corporate, not governmental?"

"Corporate?" I replied. "It feels more like somebody's trying to *stop* a very well-heeled corporate effort. But still... who? I'm still drawing a blank here."

"Yeah." She was silent for a minute. "Is your friend Judson playing us?"

"No. I'm sure of that much. Judson works for people who don't need to rely on people like us. And besides, I'm not enough of a conspiracy theorist to believe the U.S. government has secret tech like this hidden away in Area 51. It just feels too *advanced*. But I can't think of anyone *else* I could believe capable of doing it, either.

"Conan Doyle had Sherlock Holmes say, 'When you have eliminated the impossible, whatever remains, however unlikely, must be the truth.' But where do you turn when *all* of the potential answers look impossible?

"That's perhaps the weirdest part of this. I don't honestly believe there is any power on earth that is capable of producing the Box. So where the hell did it *come* from?

"And yet... so far, it seems to have never steered me wrong."

I rolled out from under the Ghost so that I could sit up, and scratched my head in frustration. But *this* question that wouldn't go away was an itch I just couldn't scratch. Sharon's expression made it clear she was as baffled as I was.

"*Could* we go to Judson?" she asked.

"Not yet. Not unless we want to be under FBI surveillance for a few years, and face some really rude questions about for how long we've been working for a shadowy unknown intelligence service."

She shivered visibly. "We can't go to our own government."

"Not without something to negotiate with. Something that will make it possible for them to forgive and forget. Like figuring out what's going on here.

"And all of this speculation aside, we're still waiting for any clues on what the... assignment actually is."

Sharon nodded slowly in agreement. "I wish there was something we could do," she said. "This waiting around chafes."

"I know exactly what you mean," I agreed.

She thought a moment, then looked at me.

"Ciáran?" she asked slowly. "Would you teach me to use a gun? I really hope I don't *need* to, but..."

"But you're afraid you might *have* to," I finished for her. She nodded silently.

"All right," I agreed. "You want to learn, I'll gladly teach you. Are you good with getting started right now?"

She shrugged.

"Sure," she said. "No time like the present."

"Well, not quite," I replied. "Let's get off this cold concrete first."

<hr>

So we got up, I led her through the storeroom and kitchen, and we sat down at the table.

102

"Right then," I began. "We're going to start at the beginning: with safety. I'm going to introduce you, metaphorically speaking, to Colonel Jeff Cooper, United States Marine Corps."

She gave me a questioning look.

"Safety is the first and perhaps most important thing to know about guns," I told her. "So that you know how to avoid accidents. But most of gun safety that isn't just 'Don't be *fucking stupid*'—like not leaving a loaded gun lying around where unsupervised kids can find it—can all be distilled down into just four rules that were formally stated by Colonel Cooper. I swear, I honestly believe that ninety percent *plus* of all firearms accidents in the US every year could be prevented, if people just *knew and followed* these four rules.

"So before I even have you put hands on an actual gun, I'm going to start by teaching you Cooper's Laws—and my own interpretations of them. His formulations are rather... terse, but I tend to think a little more explanation can help in understanding them. So I'll give you both his versions, and my additional explanation."

"That makes sense," she replied.

"Right, then. First law, per Cooper: 'All guns are always loaded.'"

She gave me a questioning look.

"You mean... always keep guns loaded, even when not using them?" she asked doubtfully. "That sounds unsafe."

"It would be," I said. "Here's what it *means*: Always *treat* any gun as though it is loaded, *until you yourself* have *personally* verified its condition..." I waited to see if she'd pick it up. I fully expected her to.

"...So that you never shoot someone *by accident* with a gun you *thought* was empty," she completed. "Including yourself."

"Precisely," I agreed. "Got it in one. Now think about the words I used. What's the corollary? What does it imply?"

She thought about exactly what I'd said, tapping a fingertip on the table.

"If someone hands you a gun and says it's not loaded," she said, "don't take it on trust, verify it yourself."

"Good. But there's a non-obvious, but crucial, part beyond that. What is it?"

She thought, pursing her lips. Then it came to her.

"You have to *know how to verify*," she declared, sitting up straighter in her chair. "If you *don't know* how a particular gun works, you can't *verify* it's not loaded."

"Perfect!" I replied. She smiled. "And there's another corollary: If you need it to be loaded, don't just *assume* that, either."

She hesitated for a moment, then nodded thoughtfully.

"*Always* check," she said. "Never assume anything."

"Right," I agreed. "Okay, on to the second law: 'Never let the muzzle cover anything you are unwilling to destroy.'"

She nodded.

"That one seems pretty clear and obvious," she replied.

"Uh-huh," I agreed. "It is. But it has a corollary, or extension, as well, that's a part of it but bears stating explicitly: Whenever you're handling a gun, make sure you keep the muzzle pointed in a safe direction at all times... and be aware of what those safe directions are."

She thought about that for a moment, then glanced around the room, looking at the floor, the walls, the window.

"A concrete floor is pretty safe," she said thoughtfully. "But not a wooden one that's someone else's ceiling. And you never know who might be standing on the other side of a sheetrock wall."

"Exactly," I agreed. She was picking this up fast. Not that I'd expected any different at this point. Sharp legal mind and all that. Competence and intelligence are sexy as fuck. Seriously.

"Right, then. Onward," I said. "Third law: 'Always keep your finger off the trigger until you are on target and ready to fire.'"

She nodded again.

"Not much nuance to that one, I think," she said. "Don't put yourself in a position where you might accidentally pull the trigger when you didn't intend to."

"And you'd be right," I agreed. "It's probably the most straightforward of the four. As a friend once rephrased it, 'Keep your booger hook off the bang switch.'"

She laughed.

"And that brings us to law four: 'Always be sure of your target', in Cooper's form."

"Don't shoot at something you haven't identified," she replied immediately.

"Yup," I agreed. "But there's more to this one. It's a big one. I prefer to expand it like this:

"Always be sure of your target, *and* your backstop—that's what's *behind* the target—and anything else that is in, *or might enter*, your line of fire if you miss."

She considered that.

"So it's—safe—to shoot at someone standing in front of a brick wall that would stop the bullet if you miss," she said. "But not if they're standing in front of the window of a busy restaurant. Because if you *miss*, the bullet will go through the glass and maybe hit someone inside."

"Right," I said. "Or if you're shooting down a narrow hallway with doors on either side. Someone could unexpectedly come out or look out of one of those doors at any moment, especially if the shooting panics them."

She nodded. "This kind of overlaps with the second law, doesn't it? Thinking about what might be in your line of fire and what really is a safe direction."

"It does indeed," I agreed.

I hesitated. This might be a... delicate subject. I shuffled uncomfortably in my chair a little.

"At the risk of scraping raw nerves," I said slowly, "I'm going to put that in context with a real-world example. Your bathroom." I paused. "Are you all right with that?" I wanted to be sure. I didn't want to upset her.

She took a deep breath and bit her lip, but nodded. I reached out and took her hand, where it rested on the table in front of her.

"When I took the shot," I said, "the hitman was standing at about a sixty degree angle to me. He had you off the ground, and your head was almost level with his. But he had you in front of him, and since he was standing *mostly* side-on to me, there was nothing behind his head but wall. And I'd already seen the outside of the house was stucco. Above and beyond the bathroom tile."

I paused.

"So you had a clear shot," she said slowly, "because I was out of your exact line of fire, and the outside wall would stop the bullet if you missed."

"And you weren't going to be moving much on your own," I continued, nodding agreement. "It was still risky, if I missed, but he didn't know I was there, and there was very little risk of missing at that range. But if he'd been facing directly away from me..."

"My head would have been in line with his," she broke in, her hand tightening.

"Exactly," I replied. "And so the head shot would have been a big risk. There would be too much chance of a bullet or fragment going through and killing you too." Her hand clenched.

"What would you have done instead?" she asked quietly.

"There would have been no good options. I could have gone for the spine shot. It's more solid than the head, but a more difficult shot, smaller target, greater chance of deflection, maybe a fifty-fifty chance—and fifty-fifty chance of a bullet going through him into you.

"Or a pelvis shot, which is a nice large target, lots of heavy bone that would definitely stop the bullets and would have totally disabled him, but would not kill him instantly. He might have had time for one good hard yank on that garotte before he went down, and that would possibly have killed you anyway." I was about to go into further details, but wisely stopped the thought before it could come out.

"My best chance might have been to shout to startle him, and hope for a clear shot as he turned. But he might have been hardcore enough to *not* turn, until he'd finished you first."

She shuddered, and shifted position uneasily in her chair. I could easily understand her discomfort. Honestly, anything else would have surprised me. She was really remarkably resilient, I'd learned that about her already—but she was still human, and few people can consider their own violent death with equanimity.

"I'm glad it didn't come to that," she said at last.

"So am I," I agreed. Then I remembered something the Box had said.

"You know," I said slowly, "I really wish I knew what the Box meant when it said it was not *possible* for me to fail to save you."

"'Problematic'," Sharon said, with a grimace.

"Yeah," I agreed. "I hope we get answers to some of those 'problematic' questions some day." She nodded agreement.

"I think we need a change of subject. It's practical exam time." I picked up the tablet I'd been using to look up Volvo service check notes from the table, where I'd put it down when we came in, and searched for a specific video clip. It didn't take me long to find it.

"Watch this video," I told her, and handed her the tablet.

She looked at the video, and frowned.

"Wait," she began, "isn't that…"

"Who it is isn't the point," I said. "Focus on the what, not the who."

She nodded and watched the video, then handed the tablet back to me with a questioning look.

"Right," I said. "Now: Which gun safety laws did she violate?"

She thought for a moment.

"Second law," she replied. "She waved the rifle she was displaying all across the audience."

"Good," I agreed. "Anything else?" She thought a bit longer.

"Can I see it again?"

"Sure." I handed it back to her and she watched it again.

"Third law," she said, almost immediately. "I wasn't sure without re-watching. But her finger is on the trigger."

"Very good. Anything else?"

She looked at the screen, which she'd paused.

"I don't think there's a magazine in the rifle," she said uncertainly. "I'm not *seeing* one. But does that mean it's actually *completely* empty?"

I golf-clapped.

"Very good," I agreed. "No, it doesn't. It could still *potentially* have a round in the chamber."

"Potential first law violation, then," she declared. "We don't *know* that she verified it was unloaded, and since we already know she violated laws two and three, it's probably *safer* to assume she didn't."

"Correct," I nodded. "Anything else?"

"Well," she said after a moment, "considering she just waved the rifle across an entire crowded auditorium, I'd say the fourth law is pretty much moot. So second, third, and potential first law violation."

"One hundred percent right," I told her. "Perfect score."

She grinned.

"Does... that sort of thing happen a lot?" she asked.

"Far more than it should," I replied. "Carelessness and ignorance cause probably ninety-nine percent of firearms accidents. You hear a lot about suing manufacturers, and it's true that *some* accidents *are* attributable to manufacturing defects or design mistakes, like the accidental-discharge problem with the SIG P320, but the safe bet with *almost any* gun accident is that it *probably* happened because someone was stupid or careless."

She nodded thoughtfully.

"Right then," I told her. "You just passed gun safety *theory* 101 with flying colors. Want to try for some mechanical familiarity before supper?"

"Sure," she replied.

"Then let's go to the armory."

"*Armory?*" she exclaimed. Then she laughed. "Of *course* my Fenian warrior has an armory!"

<hr>

We went downstairs, and I led her to the third door, the end one, past my office. It was set into a wall that went right across the basement. I put my hand on the biometric lock panel, and the door unlocked.

"Fancy," she remarked. It sounded approving.

"Secure," I replied. "Battery backup will keep the lock powered for several months if the power goes out. After that there's a mechanical backup release method... if you know where it is. It's well hidden."

I pushed the door open and led her in. As she passed through the doorway, she looked at the eight-inch-thick concrete wall.

"Wow, this is... pretty serious," she said.

"Yup." I pointed up at the ceiling, where steel beams ran across the underside of the slab above. "This entire room is a vault."

The walls of the room were mainly unadorned concrete, just painted flat white to keep dust down, as were the ceiling and its steel beams. There were bright LED bay lights mounted to the ceiling between the beams, their electrical conduits running along the concrete.

The floor was flat, rugged office carpet tiles in a neutral dark gray. I had a row of steel cabinets across one long wall, one of them very visibly more robust than the other two, and workbenches along the other. There were three stools, for no better reason than that there were three places I typically sat to work. One of the benches mounted a big blue Dillon progressive loading press.

"What have you *got* in here?" she asked.

"Uh... let me answer that another time," I deflected. "For now, let's just say it's all legal. I have all the correct Federal paperwork for everything that needs it. And a lot is just tools and supplies."

She eyed me, one brow raised.

"That's an interesting answer," she said.

"I'll show you everything another time," I replied. "I promise. But right now, let's focus on the basics and not get distracted."

I sat her down at my main bench, then opened the arms cabinet, took out three pistols from the rack inside it, made certain they were clear, and set them down in a row on the bench in front of her.

"These are the three *fundamental* types of pistols in common use," I told her. "Excluding exotic things like Olympic free pistols, high-power bolt-action hunting pistols, prototype Air Force survival weapons, and stupid rifle-pistol bastardized... *things*... that some idiot 'invented' Because He Could and because other fellow idiots who thought the same way he did would buy it. And when you get into early antique weapons, there's some *really weird* stuff out there. But none of those is our concern today."

I picked them up in turn, starting with the Super Blackhawk. It looked old and new at the same time, almost as though it belonged on the streets of Tombstone or Dodge City, yet with a deep black finish so mirror-like it seemed almost iridescent in the nearly shadowless light. I'd been very careful about exactly how I placed those lights, to get light exactly where I wanted it. You can't do good work without good light.

"This is a single-action revolver," I stated. "A modern take on the classic cowboy gun. We're going to start with it because it is the simplest, mechanically and operationally. There are variations in caliber, number of chambers in the cylinder, and so on, but all single-action revolvers are *fundamentally* like this one. This particular one is a Ruger Super Blackhawk, and it holds six rounds of .44 Remington

Magnum—and it has an extra safety feature that most other single-action revolvers don't.

"It's called single-action because you have to manually cock the hammer for each shot. The trigger does only one thing—it drops the hammer."

She nodded, following along.

"This is called the loading gate." I pointed it out and flipped it open. "If it's open, you can see the back side of the cylinder.

"To clear it, you open the gate and rotate the cylinder, like this," showing her, "until you have seen every chamber. It's better to overdo it and look at some chambers twice, than under-count and miss a chamber." She nodded again. "The cylinder will only rotate in one direction, and *shouldn't* rotate when the hammer is cocked. If it does, the gun has a mechanical problem that makes it unsafe.

"This is the ejector rod." I pointed it out and showed her how it worked. "It's there to eject fired cases, but it will also eject a live round if you find one unexpectedly."

I closed the loading gate and handed it to her.

"Now you do it."

She took the Blackhawk carefully, cradling the frame in her hand as she'd just watched me do, keeping it pointed at the wall. I saw her adjust to the weight. Finger nowhere near the trigger. Good. She found the loading gate and thumbed it open, then rotated the cylinder, looking into each cylinder in turn and counting aloud.

"One... two... three... four... five... six... and seven of six. It's empty."

"Good," I said. "Now we both know it's empty." She nodded. "By convention—think of it as best practice, common jargon to make sure everyone understands—we say it's 'clear'."

She nodded. "Clear," she repeated.

I reached into a box.

"These are called snap caps," I told her, showing her one. "No bullet, no powder charge. But it has a spring-loaded fake primer. These are for safe dry-firing." I handed one to her. "Slide that into one of the cylinders. All the way in. You can see it'll only go in one way."

She nodded and inserted the snap cap. I handed her the other five. She hesitated for a moment, then rotated the cylinder and slipped them in, one after another. When she'd inserted all six, she closed the loading gate and looked at me.

"Good," I nodded. "Hand it back to me a moment." She did.

"I'm going to teach you to shoot two-handed," I explained, "because it's more accurate and easier to control recoil. You're right-handed, right?"

She nodded confirmation.

"Take it in your right hand, like this. Notice my finger is alongside the frame, outside the trigger guard." She nodded again. "Then wrap your left hand around your right, like this. Notice I'm keeping my fingers well away from the cylinder."

I handed it back to her.

"Now you do it."

She took it in her hands, slowly and carefully, just as I'd showed her.

"My hand kind of wants to slip up it," she said.

"Yeah," I agreed, "single-action revolvers aren't great that way. Hold it out and aim towards the end wall." I stood behind her and adjusted the position of her left hand slightly.

"Okay, now take the thumb of either hand, I'd suggest your left thumb but whichever is more comfortable for you, and pull back the hammer all the way until it stops. It'll be stiff. Notice that this particular pistol will click three times as you draw the hammer back, but don't take that for granted on others."

She nodded, then drew the hammer back with her left thumb, all the way until it stopped. Then she put her thumb back down where it was.

"Good," I said. "Now, I want you to put your finger on the trigger—it's not loaded, remember. You want the trigger right *here* on your finger." I showed her on the pad of my own finger.

"That's good. Now firmly, but smoothly, squeeze. Don't jerk it, don't yank it, *press* the trigger straight back."

A moment. Then CLACK, a sharp, assertive metallic sound as the hammer dropped decisively.

She gave just the tiniest little startle reflex, then looked at me.

"Good," I said. "Again."

tick tick tick... pause... CLACK. No startle this time.

"Again."

tick tick tick... pause... CLACK.

"Good. Keep going until it's 'empty'." She dry-fired it three more times, then looked expectantly at me.

"Good. Now clear it."

She laid it into her left hand, opened the loading gate, hesitated, then touched the ejector rod and pulled it back. The snap cap slid mostly out of the chamber. She pulled it the rest of the way out, set it down on the bench, rotated the cylinder, and ejected the next one. She had the feel of it by the third. Shortly she had all six snap caps on the bench in front of her. She rotated the cylinder one more time.

"Clear," she announced, then handed the Blackhawk back to me—correctly, keeping the muzzle away from both of us.

"Great," I said. "Ready for a break?"

"You said it had an extra safety feature," she reminded me. Sharp. I'd forgotten I mentioned it.

"I did," I agreed. I cocked the hammer and had her look into the back of the action.

"See that little round nub?" I asked, pointing it out. She nodded. "That's the end of the firing pin. Now look at the shape of the hammer, and where it meets the frame."

She looked, examining it carefully.

"It... can't reach the firing pin. Can it?"

"Very good," I said. Then I pointed out the transfer bar, and how it rose into position as the trigger was pressed. "The trigger *has to be* all the way back, or the hammer can't strike the firing pin. That means this revolver *can't* go off if you drop the hammer while cocking it—or if the sear fails. Or if something strikes the hammer."

She nodded, understanding.

"Is—or was—that a common problem with other... single-action revolvers?" she asked.

"Common enough," I replied, "that it became very common practice to load only five rounds and carry with an empty chamber under the hammer. So that your gun wouldn't kill you if you dropped it just wrong."

She looked very thoughtful at that.

"Is the other revolver similar?" she asked.

"Conceptually similar," I said, "but there are important differences."

I put the Blackhawk back down on the workbench, and picked up the Smith and Wesson. The Smith was for modern-day *vaqueros*, a study in mirror-bright metal and black rubber grips. Even if you didn't know guns, you could see a genetic link between it and the lean simplicity of the Blackhawk, like some prehistoric bird of prey and a hawk with stainless steel feathers.

"This is a double-action revolver," I began, "and it's called that because the trigger can both cock the hammer and release it. This particular one is a Smith and Wesson Model 657.

"Again, the number of chambers in the cylinder may vary—this one has six again, but they range anywhere from five to nine—and on some revolvers, notably Colts, the cylinder revolves in the opposite direction. But again they're all *fundamentally* similar."

I showed her the cylinder latch and how the cylinder swung out on the crane when it was released, allowing access to and inspection of all six chambers at once, and how the ejector cleared all six chambers at once. We did a little dry-firing, again, so that I could show her the difference between single-action and double-action fire.

"This feels a lot more secure in my hand," she pronounced after a few moments. "It doesn't feel like it's trying to slip around all the time."

"Yeah," I agreed, "most full-size double-action revolvers are a lot better that way. Some of the compact ones, not so much. The classic snub-nose Detective Special or Chief's Special is a bitch to shoot, and a bitch to hit anything with beyond across-the-room range. And modern .357 Magnum variations are even worse, especially the ultra-light ones with scandium-alloy frames. They punish the shooter almost as badly as the target. But the truth is the Chief's Special was intended to be easily concealed in a coat pocket, much more than it was intended for doing any serious shooting with."

By the time we were done with the Smith & Wesson, we were both more than ready for supper. I put the pistols back into the cabinet, Sharon peeking over my shoulder this time.

"Four rifles?" she asked. I nodded.

"This one's a general purpose combat rifle," I said, pointing at the full-size 6.8mm SIG. "Then this next one is a short version of the same rifle, intended for close quarters where the ability to pop around a corner quickly with it outweighs the ability to hit a target four or five hundred yards out." She nodded understanding. "The other two are long-range rifles. That one's Russian, an Orsis, chambered for the 7.62mm NATO rifle round, and the last is an Accuracy International in .338 Lapua for extreme long-range targets."

"You're talking sniping, right?" she queried.

"Well, yes," I agreed. "But also for very long range target shooting. You remember I told you about the *sicarios* and the kidnapped journalist?" She nodded agreement again. "You asked what I would have done if my assignment had been to take out the cartel presence there, not to rescue the journalist. I'd have used one of these. I'd have been able to engage from far enough away they'd never have spotted me."

"*Has* the Box had you do anything like that?" she asked hesitantly.

"No," I said. "It's never sent me out specifically to, well, kill anyone. Every time I've gotten into an exchange of fire on one of its assignments, it's been... an unavoidable consequence, not a goal in itself."

"Why do you have them, then?" she asked. "Just in case?"

"Well, partly," I agreed. "But also because in the words of a man named Townsend Whelen, 'Accurate rifles are interesting.'"

An afterthought occurred to me.

"To be completely honest, if I knew then what I know now, I'd have *preferred* to get you out of your house before the hitters even showed up. But I don't know what on earth I could *possibly* have told you to get you to believe me. I didn't know *myself* what was going on until Thugly showed up and tried to kill you. We'd probably have been arguing about it when they showed up... and that would probably have been very bad. There's a good chance we'd have both wound up dead."

She shuddered a little bit. I couldn't blame her.

I locked the cabinet, and then we closed up the vault and headed back upstairs to make supper.

"Spaghetti?" I suggested, when we got to the kitchen.

"Sure," she agreed.

"You want to handle the noodles while I make the sauce?"

"Sure! Where's your pasta pot? And the spaghetti?"

I pointed.

"Pot in that cabinet, pasta in the pantry, there. Salt is in the spice cabinet, of course."

Then I gathered ingredients and started making a Bolognese sauce, while she boiled water and cooked the spaghetti. In about thirty minutes, we were ready to eat. You *have* to have red wine with Bolognese, there's a law or something, somewhere, probably, and if there isn't, there *ought* to be, so I willingly pulled out another bottle of the Roscato. I liked the Roscato, it wasn't sour and mouth-puckery like too many other red wines. I knew a lot of people thought they were supposed to like that. I wasn't one of them.

We took everything to the table and sat down to eat.

"So this Long Now Foundation," I asked while we ate. "You said it's... not reasonable that they would have the resources to arrange my phone. And the Box is *obviously* beyond the resources of anyone *I* can think of."

She nodded agreement.

"So... a red herring? *Another* cut-out?" I continued.

"I wish I knew," she said. "But... I don't think we're going to find any answers there."

"What do they actually *do*, anyway?" I asked. "You said, thinking about civilization on scales of thousands of years—"

"Tens of thousands," she corrected me.

"Okay, tens of thousands of years, but... what does that actually mean?"

"I'm not really clear," she said. "I didn't dig into their mission in great depth. They have projects to preserve languages in danger of extinction in the next century, projects to try to figure out how to maintain organizational continuity over centuries or millennia, they're supposed to be building a ten-thousand-year clock inside a mountain. Everything seems to be focused on planning for the long term instead of thinking only about *right now.*"

"Huh," I said. Then, "You suppose this Long Now Foundation could still be around in a thousand years? Or ten thousand?"

"I don't know," she replied. "But at least they're trying to think about the problem. That's more than anyone else is doing."

"Yeah," I agreed sadly. "Look at this stalled climate bill. One side's trying to keep the world habitable for humans over the next centuries, and the other is screaming BUT WE WANT MORE PROFITS MORE MONEY NOW NOW NOW."

Sharon nodded.

"Corporate law," she said. "There's always *somebody* trying to find a new way to cheat without getting caught."

We ate in silence for a little bit after that. I refilled our wine glasses.

We finished our supper, cleaned up, and put away the leftovers. It's really hard to make only two portions of Bolognese, so I hadn't tried, but that's fine—it freezes and reheats well.

"Do you want to go on to the semi-automatic now?" I asked. "Or give it a break for a bit?"

"How about tomorrow?" Sharon said. "I want to be sure I absorb all of this first, with everything else that's going on, before I try adding more."

"Fine by me," I agreed. "That's a sound plan."

So we retired to the living room couch with our unfinished wine. We sat there, gently cuddling, and tried to think about whether there was anything we'd missed that might possibly let us crack open the mystery of what was going on.

"Got any music?" Sharon asked after a while. "I need something to get my mind off this hamster wheel."

I knew exactly what she meant, so I got up for a moment and put on some *Within Temptation,* and we sat back and let ourselves get carried away by Sharon den Adel's incredible voice.

"She has the same first name as you," I commented idly.

"Who does?" Sharon asked.

I gestured in the general direction of the speakers.

"Sharon den Adel. Dutch self-taught lyric soprano. This band started out as a death-metal band, before they pivoted to symphonic metal." She looked surprised.

"Well, I prefer this to death metal," she said. "This is... *amazing*."

I agreed wholeheartedly.

When we hadn't come up with anything new after an hour or so, we turned off the music and went upstairs. We took a long, luxurious shower, attentively washing and drying each other, then went to bed. We spent a long time just gently cuddling and caressing each other, not driven by the desperate, urgent *need* of the night before. There was every bit as much passion, we just weren't desperate any more, because we both knew now that it wasn't going to be just one night, that we were in it for the distance.

After a while, we drifted off to sleep in each other's arms.

5: The Fifth Day

Sharon awoke before me the next morning. I woke to her nuzzling my neck.

"Good morning, beautiful," I murmured. She smiled.

"Mmmm. Good morning, my warrior."

We spent a few minutes, you know, twenty or so, cuddling and kissing before we got out of bed.

"Want to run again?" I asked.

"Sure," she agreed.

The weather was good, so we did the five-mile loop again. There was a light early-morning breeze that might have been on the edge of chilly, if running hadn't been keeping us warm. It wasn't full summer yet, but the last gasps of spring were definitely on their way out the door, and the door was swinging closed behind them.

"You make this look pretty easy," Sharon commented, about half-way through. "Are you holding back for me?"

"No," I replied. "Just taking it easy."

"Want to push the pace for a bit?"

"Sure. You go ahead and set the pace."

So she sped up. I let her get a pace or so ahead, let her establish her comfortable speed, and then caught up and paced her. I guessed it at somewhere around a six-minute pace. We did about the next mile and a half at that pace. She was breathing harder now, though clearly not winded yet.

"This is still easy for you, isn't it?" she asked.

"Yeah."

"How fast *can* you run?"

"Over this kind of distance?" We were talking in short bursts between breaths to keep our breathing steady.

"This is a good sustained pace." Breathe. "About six minutes a mile." Breathe. "I can do five minutes for about three miles."

"Damn. Impressive."

"But I'll be wiped by the end." Breathe. "Overheated."

"I don't think I can run *one* five-minute mile."

"This is a respectable pace." Breathe. "Remember I have height and stride on you." Breathe. "But I'll bet you *could* run—a five-minute mile, if you worked at it." Breathe. "You're fit, and in good shape." Breathe. "This six-minute pace isn't—giving you any trouble." Breathe. "If I really push it, I might do—a single mile in four thirty, four forty." Breathe. "I'd have to sustain another—three miles an hour faster again— to break four." Breathe. "That's a *lot* harder than it sounds." Breathe. "Bannister's record is safe from me." Breathe. "And he set that about eighty years ago." Breathe. "Other people have broken it since." Breathe. "I'll never be among them."

We were almost within sight of the house now.

"What about in a flat-out sprint?"

I figured it was about two hundred yards to the house. I scanned around us, ahead and behind. There was no indication of any threats. So by way of answer, I cranked it up all the way into overdrive, giving it everything I had left.

I slowed to a stop and turned around when I got within a few yards of the door. She was about forty yards behind me. I stood there, half bent over, with my chest heaving as my body tried to recoup the oxygen debt I'd just incurred. I was fit, sure, but not a professional athlete by any standard.

She caught up, gasping, a few seconds later.

"Holy mother of god, man," she got out. "You practically *FLEW*." I couldn't steady my breathing enough yet to answer.

I opened the door, and we went in and headed straight for the shower.

"Early humans evolved to be endurance hunters, you know," I remarked in the shower, as Sharon soaped my back.

"How's that work?" she asked.

"We weren't the fastest thing on the plains, and certainly not the strongest. But we just kept right on going. Over a long distance, humans can outrun anything. So we'd go after, say, an antelope, and it would run off, and leave us behind.

"But then as soon as it couldn't see us any more, it'd stop to rest. And then a couple of minutes later, here come the humans again. So it'd run off, a bit further this time, and it'd burn more energy reserves. And then it would stop to rest."

"And the humans caught up again before it was rested," she said.

"Yup. Give me the scrubby now and let me do your back.

"So then after a couple of rounds of this, it'd get freaked out, and it'd run, and run, and run, until it was too overheated to run any further. Use up everything it had left. Until it had to stop because it could barely even stand any more. And then maybe half an hour or so later, while it's still too exhausted to run... here come the damn humans again.

"And they'd just walk right up to it and kill it."

"Huh. So you're saying our survival model was to just be total pains in the ass?"

I laughed.

"Yeah," I agreed, "you could look at it that way."

We got out, dried each other off—much more fun than drying ourselves—and went downstairs to get breakfast.

Sharon made breakfast, this time, while I made coffee. When we sat down to eat, I did a scan of the news headlines, as usual.

This time, there was a hit. "New Developments in Harris Magnusson Case," read the headline. I pulled up the video, and we watched it.

> "There have been further developments today in the Harris Magnusson case. A statement released by police declared that forensic analysis of blood and tissue recovered from the house of Harris Magnusson associate Sharon Kielic, who is still missing at this time, has confirmed that they are definitely *not* hers, and in fact belong to an unknown male, most likely Caucasian, who appears to have been shot in the head in the master bathroom of the house.
>
> "It is not known at this time who he was, who killed him, or who removed his body from the house, but it seems possible there is at least some slim hope that Sharon, wherever she may be, *may* still be alive. All of our hopes here in the Channel Nine

newsroom go out to you, Sharon, wherever you are.

"There is still no known motive for the murder of Harris Magnusson senior partner Philip Bartholomew, or for the arson attack against Harris Magnusson's offices. Police say they have nothing definite to go on at this time, but there is no longer any doubt that all three events are connected.

"This is Andrea Cassey for your News Nine team, and we will bring you more updates on this story as soon as we have them."

"Well, that tells us two things," I commented, "neither of which really helps us a great deal. Again."

"Two?" Sharon asked.

"One, we now know for certain that the *police* know that a person who wasn't you was killed there, and his body removed by parties unknown.

"And two, we can *infer*, from the tone of that report, that you are still not a suspect, which is very good. But we need to keep it that way. Are you ready to call your attorney contact?"

"I think so," she nodded.

We cleaned up from breakfast. Half way through, my phone chimed.

"New message," I said as I pulled it out. I went to my messages and looked to see what the new one was. It was the website knocking signal.

I looked at Sharon.

"You need to call Marilyn," I told her. She nodded understanding. I turned the outgoing caller ID off again and handed her the phone. She quickly found the call history, and redialed.

The phone connected after two rings.

"Hello?"

"Hi Marilyn, it's me, Sharon."

"Sharon! That was quick. Are you still okay?"

"I'm fine. Still safe."

"Good. Listen, Sharon, I talked to Edrick yesterday. I passed on your message."

"Great! Did he have anything?"

"He said there were a group of five commercial real estate contracts that came in on the day before the fire. They were assigned to Philip, and Philip was going to assign them to you in the morning to go over them."

Sharon's expression was intent. She shot me a look, and I nodded.

"Listen, Marilyn," Sharon said, "I *really need* the document numbers on those contracts, any information I can get. Can you get them for me?"

"Way ahead of you, dear," Marilyn replied. "Edrick already said he's going to get them for you. Discreetly. He's going to send them to me, and then we'll arrange a way I can get them to you."

"Thank you, Marilyn! You're wonderful. Did you warn Edrick to be *careful*?"

"I did, but I didn't have to. We already talked about it. He's going to have people he knows retrieve the contracts individually via different sources, none of them connected to the firm, just in case."

"Good," Sharon sighed in relief.

"Sharon," Marilyn said, "you told me you're in witness protection. Is there anything you can safely tell me about... the investigation?"

Sharon looked at me, shook her head slightly. I shook mine in confirmation.

"I'm really sorry, Marilyn," she answered. "I can't say anything."

"I understand, dear," Marilyn replied. "You stay safe now. We'll talk later."

"Okay. 'Bye for now."

She disconnected and handed the phone back, and I reset it to normal. Sharon fist-pumped in the air.

"A lead!" she declared. "We're going to have a lead!"

I grinned and hugged her.

"That's great," I agreed. "Now let's talk to that attorney and see what we can get cleared with the police... can you get hold of him today?"

"I think so. I think he's *usually* in on Saturday mornings."

We finished clearing up from breakfast, then I gave her the phone again, and she made the call.

"Hi," she said, "is Jim Bell available?"

"I believe he should have a few minutes," a male voice replied. "Who can I say is calling?"

"I... need strict confidentiality," she replied. "Can you just tell him that it's an urgent personal call? He knows me."

"All right, just a moment," the voice replied.

There was a brief pause, then the call transferred.

"Good morning, this is Jim Bell. Who am I speaking to?"

"Hello, Jim. This is Sharon Kielic."

"Sharon!" Jim exclaimed. He sounded surprised, in a good way. "The news says you're missing." The briefest pause. "I'm going to take a guess here that you need to talk to me about the recent events at Harris Magnusson." He'd picked that up fast.

"That's exactly it, Jim. Can we meet and talk?"

"Tell me one thing first before you say anything else. Do you need to retain me in your defense?"

"Yes."

The immediate response surprised me. It clearly showed on my face.

"Just a moment, Jim," Sharon said, and turned to me.

"That answer is always 'Yes', Ciáran," she told me. "You and I both know I haven't done anything wrong. But when it comes to convincing the police of that, Jim is the expert. If the question comes up, the answer is 'yes'."

"Someone else is there with you, Sharon." It was a statement, not a question.

"Yes, Mr. Bell," I replied.

"And you are...?"

"My name is Ciáran mac Cool, Mr. Bell, and I am Sharon's personal protection."

"Personal protection," he echoed. "Hmmm."

"Jim, I need your help in talking to the police, in strict confidentiality," Sharon said. "I need a chance to explain that none of what happened was my doing. In fact, they tried to kill me, too."

"Hence the personal protection," Jim stated.

"Yes. But I can't go to them myself. If the people who did this find out where I am, it puts me in deadly danger. Can we meet?"

There was a pause on the line.

"Sharon, I am now representing you. Can you be at my office at eleven? I'll fit you in. Don't tell me anything more until then."

Sharon looked at me.

"We need a better place, Mr. Bell," I said. "With all due respect, a law office is far too publicly visible and I won't risk taking Sharon there."

"I understand entirely," he agreed. "You need to be discreet. How about this: Do you know the New World Taipei Restaurant on North 40th, out toward the airport?"

"I do indeed," I confirmed.

"Can you meet me there at eleven thirty? When you get there, tell them you're meeting with me, by name."

"We'll be there."

<hr>

I'd been to New World Taipei before. It was a big, sprawling building with a slightly strange mixture of modern construction with traditional Chinese decoration, but it all somehow worked. The smaller signage across the front of the marquee read MANDARIN—CANTONESE—SICHUAN—HUNAN—FUJIAN. I'd always thought it odd a place named for Taipei wouldn't offer Taiwanese, but maybe there just wasn't a market for it. I circled through the lot once with my head on a swivel, just to be sure, then parked near to the front door, and we went in.

"Table for two?" asked the petite, ageless-looking woman at the desk inside the door. She was resplendent in heavily embroidered red silk.

"Actually," I said, "we're here to meet with a Mr. Jim Bell."

"You are with Mr. Bell?" she replied, with a big smile. "You wait one minute please." Then she turned and shouted something back into the restaurant. In a moment, one of the servers came up to the desk, a twenty-something young woman in a brilliant blue cheongsam.

"These are Mr. Bell's guests," Red Silk Lady told her. "You take them back."

"Follow me please," the girl said, and led us deeper into the restaurant. I expected to be led to a back room. But to my surprise, we didn't go to a table; instead she led us back into and through the kitchens. Near the back side of the kitchen, within sight of the back doors, was a small room where it was evident the staff ate and took their breaks.

"Mr. Bell, your guests," said Sapphire Girl. Then she left us there.

Jim Bell was a tall, rangy, jovial-looking man with dark skin and a full beard. He looked almost more like a pro basketball player than an attorney.

"Good to see you, Sharon," he said. Then he turned and looked me up and down. "And you would doubtless be Mr. mac Cool."

"I would indeed," I replied. Heard directly instead of over a phone, his voice had a faint accent. Jamaican, I thought. Maybe Haitian. Definitely somewhere Caribbean.

"And your capacity in this matter, again?"

"Personal protection," I repeated. He nodded.

"Okay, first things first," he said. "I've drawn up a representation agreement. Before anything else is said, I'd like you both to sign it."

We signed the paper and handed it back.

"Good," he said. "That's taken care of. Now, take it from the top, please. What happened on Tuesday night?"

Sharon took a deep breath.

"I left work about half past six," she began, "and went straight home, with just a stop on the way to fill up my car. I got home shortly after seven."

"Can anyone corroborate that?" Jim asked.

"Only Ciáran," she said.

"And all I can corroborate is her arrival time," I interjected.

Sharon nodded and continued. "I got in and went straight upstairs to take a shower." Her voice was understandably tense. I discreetly offered my hand, and she took it thankfully.

"A moment after I got out of the shower," she went on, gripping my hand tightly, "I was attacked from behind. Someone bigger and much stronger than me. He started strangling me with, I'm not sure what, some kind of cord. I tried to fight him off, but he was too strong. He'd lifted me off the ground and my vision was going black.

"Then Ciáran shot him."

Jim looked at me.

"There was no time to do anything else," I said. "She had seconds to live. All the signs pointed to murder-for-hire."

"Can I ask why you were there?" he asked me.

"That's personal," Sharon replied.

"He was there at your invitation?"

"...Not exactly. But I'm very glad he was." She paused for a moment. "He has my permission to enter my home at any time." I noticed she didn't mention that I *hadn't* had that permission at the time. I understood why, but I hoped it didn't come back to bite us. I noticed that Jim didn't ask.

"Okay," Jim nodded. "What happened then?"

"With Sharon's consent, I removed her from the house by a back route, and took her to a safe location. What I presume to be a backup team came in the front door right as we were going out the window. There was a vehicle parked in front of her house, blocking her car in, lights off, engine running. Subsequently, it appears the backup team removed the assassin's body, presumably to prevent him being identified."

"You know that last for a fact?"

"Not directly first-hand. We infer it from the fact that the statements released by police stated someone was killed in her bathroom, and the body removed before they saw it, but made no mention of it being a Caucasian male *until* they got DNA results back from Forensics. We know his backup team entered the house. The logical assumption is that they are the ones who removed the body."

Jim nodded.

"That's a fairly logical inference," he agreed. "And since then?"

"Since then, I've been keeping her safe and out of sight while we try to figure out what's going on. To which we don't have any positive clues, *yet*, but we're working on it. We are working from a theory that the entire group of events hinges on some piece of information, presumably incriminating, that Sharon and her boss know, or which persons unknown *think* they know. Or knew."

"And you haven't spoken to the police."

"No. Not up to this point. Though we would both be more comfortable if it were possible to establish that Sharon had nothing to do with the other events, and in fact was a victim of attempted murder herself. But for her safety, her whereabouts must remain unknown to the greatest degree possible."

Jim thought about it all.

"Are you willing to meet with the police?"

"Yes," Sharon said at once.

"Provided it can be done in a way that does not endanger her safety or reveal her whereabouts," I added.

"All right then," Jim replied, with another nod. "I'll run with what you've told me for now. Based on your account, and given what is already known about the *other* Harris Magnusson incidents, there seems little question that it was a justified defensive shooting.

"I'll talk to the Chief and set up a meeting with the two of you, myself, and a police detective. You'll need to give statements. But I don't think there's any doubt we can get you off the hook here.

"Do you need police protection?"

Sharon looked at me.

"Honestly," I said, "the extra attention and visibility would do more harm than good. Sharon's best defense right now is to be invisible."

He nodded.

"Fair enough. How can I get in touch with you?"

Sharon and I exchanged glances.

"There's no connection to either Harris Magnusson or, uh, Marilyn, right?" I asked. She nodded.

"Okay, then," I said. "I'll give you my number. That should be safe."

I wrote the number down and gave it to him. He looked at it, and nodded.

"And this line is safe to call you on?" he confirmed.

"Yeah," I agreed. "It's complicated, but the important part is it's a very secure phone. Tools of the trade, you might say."

Jim nodded. "In your... trade," he observed, "I suppose I can see the value of that."

I nodded in agreement. "Now if you'll excuse us, we need to get Sharon out of sight again."

"Good luck," Jim replied. "I'll get on this as soon as I can. Expect something early next week."

He walked us back out through the kitchen and out the front of the restaurant.

"See you again soon, Mr. Bell!" Red Silk Lady said to him as we passed the desk again.

"Count on it," he replied with a grin.

We went straight home and got some lunch. Then, a little later, we went back to my armory to finish Sharon's hands-on familiarity training. I got out the Browning Hi-Power from the pistol rack in the arms cabinet.

"Yesterday you learned to handle both types of revolvers," I told her. "We started with those because they're simple to operate. This is the third common type of pistol, and in this day and age, the most common, the semi-automatic pistol. Which many people mistakenly call the automatic pistol."

She raised her hand.

"Why 'semi-automatic'?" she asked.

"Good question," I replied. "Each time you fire a shot, the pistol itself *automatically* loads the next round from the magazine into the chamber again. If there is another there to load." She nodded. "But it does *not* also automatically fire it. Each shot requires a distinct, separate pull of the trigger. That is what makes it *semi*-automatic."

"...And if it kept firing as long as you held the trigger back," Sharon asked, "that would be fully automatic?"

"Bingo," I agreed. "Fully automatic machine pistols exist, but automatic fire in a pistol is *extremely* difficult to control. I don't own one, nor see any good reason to. If I need automatic firepower, there are better options."

She nodded.

"This is a typical, older-generation design," I went on, "an FN-Browning GP35 Hi-Power."

"Pretty long name," she commented.

"Oh, that's the *short* form," I told her with a grin. "Its fully expanded, original proper name is the Fabrique National d'Armes de Belgique Pistolet Modele 1935 de Grand Puissance."

"That's a mouthful and a half all right," she chuckled.

"Yup," I agreed. "John M. Browning, who was arguably the greatest gun designer in history, started it, but died before it was complete. His greatest student, Dieudonné Saive, finished it. They were living in Belgium at the time and it shows. Judson would tell you that it looks like jazz on the Seine sounds, has the effortless cool of Alain Deleon, fits in your hand like a lover's thigh, and after you're done capping Nazis with the rest of your Resistance cell you swear even the gunsmoke smells like unfiltered Gauloises Brunes. A weapon perfectly engineered both for killing, and looking good. A true classic of the genre."

"You didn't tell me he was a poet as well as a spook," Sharon said, laughing. I grinned in reply.

"Anyway. It has more controls than a revolver, as you see—though not all semi-automatic pistols have *all* of these controls, some have more, and some of them vary between pistols. This is solid, as reliable as a brick, and safer than some more modern designs. Some call it by its French name, the FN GP35, and others by its American name, the Browning Hi-Power. They differ mostly in what's stamped on the slide.

"It's a nine-millimeter that comes with a thirteen-round magazine, stock, but these are fifteen-round magazines. The magazine release is here." I showed her. "You just press it in, like this, to drop the magazine.

"Now, there's no magazine in it. Is it unloaded?"

"I don't know," she replied. "How do I check?"

Good girl. Exactly the right answer. So I showed her how to press-check it, how to hand-cycle the action, and what all of the controls did, then explained and showed how the action locked closed when in battery, and how recoil unlocked the action after a momentary delay. I got a box of snap caps out of the cabinet behind us and topped an empty magazine with three or four, and we cycled them through slowly so that she could watch the action at work. I had her manipulate the controls and verify she knew how they all worked and what they did. Then we did a little bit of dry firing to get her used to the trigger.

"It has a very light trigger," she remarked. I agreed, and waited.

"...And that's why the third law," she continued after a moment.

"Top marks," I said approvingly. Then I showed her how to field-strip and reassemble it, twice.

"Think you've got that?"

She nodded, fairly confidently. "I think so."

"Good." I handed it to her. "Now you do it."

The first time, she needed a little help. The second time she did it unaided, with just one or two slight fumbles that she corrected herself. The third time was flawless.

"Fantastic," I told her. "You are now ready for the range, and I'll teach you how to actually shoot."

"Today?" she asked. I thought.

"We could probably fit in a range trip this afternoon," I agreed. "Do you want to?" She nodded.

"Okay, then. Barring interruptions, range day it is."

"Is a heavier trigger safer?" she asked a few minutes later, as I put things away.

"Sort of. A heavy trigger reduces the likelihood of an accidental discharge by a poorly trained shooter, but makes it harder to shoot accurately. There exists a nine-and-a-half pound trigger for some Glock pistols. It's called the New York trigger because it was expressly developed by Glock for, and at the specific request of, the New York Police Department."

She thought that through for a moment, then had to stifle an embarrassed laugh behind her hand.

"That's *terrible*," she giggled sheepishly.

"I... can't disagree," I replied. "To be completely fair to NYPD, the actual *intention* was to try to reproduce the trigger feel of the Colt Police Positive double-action revolvers they were used to.

"But anyway, for a trained shooter, a lighter trigger—within reason —is safer. It's hard to shoot straight when it's taking half the strength in your hand just to haul the trigger back. Olympic free pistols, which demand incredible accuracy, tend to have electronic triggers with pulls measured in grams. You barely have to *touch* the trigger."

She nodded in understanding.

In the early afternoon, when nothing further had come up, I packed up a range bag, with two sets of eye and ear protection, the Browning, a .22 SIG, and a few boxes of ammunition for each. Sharon watched as I loaded up the bag. I also put in some .40 for my Laugo, as well. Then we headed out to an indoor range that I liked, about twenty miles away.

═══════════

"Heeey, Mr. mac Cool," the proprietor greeted me as we walked in. "How's it going?"

"Pretty good, Lee," I replied. "Got a new shooter with me today."

"Good day to you, young lady," he said to Sharon. He looked at me. "Of course there's no point in asking *you* whether *your* guest has had safety training, is there?" I grinned. Sharon looked at me curiously, but Lee beat me to the response.

"Did he mention to you that he teaches safety and basic pistol classes here sometimes?" he explained.

"No," Sharon replied, smiling, "but somehow I'm not surprised."

"Anyway," Lee went on, "as a first-time shooter here I'm going to need you to fill out a little bit of paperwork."

"Uh, about that, Lee," I said. "Can we skip the sign-up this time and just let her ride on mine?"

Lee gave me a questioning look over his bifocals.

"She... lost her ID. We haven't been able to recover it yet." All perfectly true. "It's complicated."

He thought for a moment, then shrugged.

"Sure," he said. "No big deal. You'll have the range to yourself anyway, nobody else here this afternoon. Need any ammo?"

"Tell you what, give me another brick of .22 just in case. Oh, and half a dozen bullseye pistol targets."

"Sure thing," he nodded, and grabbed a box of Remington.

"Eighteen bucks for the ammo, ten for the lane fee. Your targets are free."

I paid, and we went to the range door. I stopped Sharon before she could open it.

"Eyes and ears FIRST," I cautioned her. "Gunfire at close quarters without ear protection, especially in an enclosed space, can cause permanent hearing damage. So even if the range is empty, *always* eye and hearing protection *before* you go in."

"To build the habit," she said.

"Yup."

We covered up and went in. There were eight lanes side by side, each lane about four feet wide, the shooting stations separated by heavy plywood dividers nearly two inches thick. A quarter-inch steel plate was just visible in the middle, sandwiched between the two layers of plywood. Each station had a work surface, like a standing desk, at a comfortable height to put guns, magazines, ammunition boxes and the like on while shooting from standing. Overhead target holders on a cable ran down each lane, out to perhaps twenty yards. The walls were concrete, the backstop at the far end a heavy metal deflector that directed bullets downward into a catch bin. I knew Lee emptied it out about once a month and sold the collected lead and copper for recycling. I knew he cleaned regularly, too, but still everything was grubby. Every indoor range was like that. Powder residue got over everything, no matter how much you cleaned. The lanes weren't brightly lit, but enough to clearly see the targets.

I mounted a target in our lane, and ran it seven yards downrange. Then I got out the little SIG .22, showed her it was clear, and loaded a couple of magazines.

"You already know how to hold it," I said. "So take a good grip on it, and line it up on the target." She did as I said. I stood back, looked at her, and guided her into a couple of adjustments.

"Put your left foot slightly ahead," I advised. "Yeah, like that. Lean *into* it just a little, don't lean back. Don't be afraid of it. Push your right hand into your left hand. Just like that, that's great.

"Now the back sight is this notch here, the front sight is this short blade. Focus on the *front* sight. Adjust the angle until the front sight is centered in the back sight notch and at the same height. Got it?"

She tucked her head just slightly to align with the sights. I corrected that.

"Don't drop your head to the sights, adjust your arms to bring the pistol *up* to your sight line."

She raised her head and the pistol.

"Fantastic. Now aim with your entire upper body, to maintain that sight picture, and sit the place where you want to hit right on top of the front sight."

She adjusted her aim. I reached out and cocked the hammer by hand.

"Okay, we're going to do a little dry-fire. Smooth squeeze..."

snap.

"Good. Again." I cocked the hammer for her again. Then the next time I had her cock the hammer with her left thumb.

"Got the feel of the trigger?" She nodded. "Good. Here's a magazine. Insert it, all the way, cycle the action, and let's try it for real."

She took the magazine, pushed it firmly home, racked the slide, took a deep breath, aimed, and squeezed.

Bang.

"On the paper," I said. "Good start. High and right. See it?" She nodded. "Don't try to correct your aim just yet, just try to be consistent." She nodded and fired twice more, taking her time. All three were high and right.

"Okay, I want you to think about pressing the trigger *smoothly* straight back, without pulling it or the gun to one side or the other. Don't jerk the trigger. Just a steady press."

She nodded and tried again, another three shots. This time they were in the black.

"Good. Keep going."

She fired steadily until the slide locked back.

"You're out," I said, and handed her another magazine. She ejected the first, put it down, then took the new magazine and inserted it. She pulled the slide all the way to the rear just like I'd showed her, not just dropping it with the slide stop. Then she resumed fire.

By the time she emptied the second magazine, she was developing a not-bad group about five inches high and two or three right. I handed her a third magazine.

"Okay," I told her, "I want you to adjust your point of aim about four inches down and left. Can you do that?"

"I think so," she said. She tried again. A lot better this time, almost centered and only slightly high. I reeled in the target and posted a new one, then handed her a fresh magazine. I watched her closely as she shot. Good stance, head up, no flinch. She was doing great.

After another thirty rounds of .22 downrange, I stopped her.

"You're doing great so far," I told her. "You have the basics down. Ready to try the nine millimeter?"

"Sure," she said. I cleared the SIG, put it back into the bag, and got out the Browning.

"Now be aware," I cautioned her, "there's going to be more muzzle flash, more noise, and more recoil. Try not to let them distract you. Just keep going the way you have been with the .22 and you'll do fine. Remember that it's a different pistol, and you may need to adjust your aiming point. But you should find it shoots more accurately to point of aim than the little SIG, so you don't need to aim off to compensate."

I handed her the Browning, noting with approval that she immediately checked it, then I posted a fresh target and handed her a loaded magazine. She loaded, resumed her firing position, aimed, and squeezed the trigger.

BANG.

She looked a little startled at the first shot.

"That went off before I was expecting it," she said.

"That's okay," I reassured her. "It was a great first shot. Look." The shot was a little high, but nearly centered. "The shot *should* take you a little by surprise. Means you're not anticipating it and jerking. Keep going."

She did, and she did well. She jumped a little on the first couple of shots, but then got used to the increased flash and recoil. She didn't try to fight it, just recovered it smoothly. She was a fast learner.

We put sixty rounds through the Browning, then I called a stop.

"That's enough for today," I said. "We don't want you getting tired and falling into bad habits." She nodded, and I put away the Browning.

"Can I try *your* gun?" she asked. Then she hesitated. "...Well, I mean, they're *all* yours, but..."

"Sure," I agreed. I pulled out the Laugo and held it out to her, but didn't let go yet. She looked at me.

"Hot gun," I stated distinctly. Sharon nodded in acknowledgment and repeated, "Hot gun. Means it's loaded, right?"

"Loaded *and chambered*," I confirmed. She took it cautiously and looked at it.

"It looks a bit... strange," she said. "What is it?"

"That's because it's a distinctly different design," I explained. "But it works *fundamentally* the same way as the Browning. It's a Czech design, a Laugo Alien in .40 Smith and Wesson. It's... oh, about a third more powerful again than the Browning."

I pointed out the safety lever in the middle of the trigger.

"It doesn't have an external manual safety. This is the safety. It won't fire unless that is depressed into the trigger." She nodded.

"The barrel is so low down," she observed as she examined it.

"Yup," I agreed. "That's a major benefit of the design. Try it."

She turned back to the target, took her firing stance, adjusted her grip, and took aim.

BANG.

"Huh," she said, not in an unhappy way, just slightly surprised. She fired it five more times, not rushing it. Then she lowered it and handed it back to me. All six shots were nicely close to center and actually an inch or two low.

"I'm not sure quite what I was expecting," she remarked. "So I'm not sure whether that was it or not."

I nodded understanding, and then we finished packing up, policed up the fired brass, and left the range.

"See you another day," Lee called cheerfully as we left. "Come back soon, young lady." Sharon and I both turned and waved.

"Your gun *feels* different from the Browning," Sharon said to me as we drove home. "The Browning feels like the .22, just with everything amplified. It jumps more, and harder. But yours has... a *firmer* kick, but jumps less. It's like it pushes nearly straight back instead of trying to flip up."

"Yup," I agreed. "That plus the fact that it has a rigidly fixed barrel, not tilting like the Browning's, makes it *extremely* accurate. Someone I know who owns one in nine-millimeter described it as like using a cheat code."

"And I'm guessing that's why you like it?" she asked. "Because it's accurate?"

"Well, that, plus it's just technically cool as heck. I'm a sucker for innovative engineering." She laughed. "It's also *expensive* as heck. The Browning is a six hundred dollar pistol. The Laugo cost six thousand."

═══════════════

Half an hour later, we were home.

"Right," I said, "now we have one more job to do." I looked at her expectantly.

"...Right," she nodded.

"Clean the guns," we chorused.

So we took the range bag back down to the armory, and I showed her how to clean everything. I pulled out the cleaning gear—brushes, patches, powder residue solvent, gun oil, and more—and laid it out on the middle one of the three benches. We field-stripped the SIG, the Browning and my Laugo, and I showed her how to properly clean them. Brushes first to clean the bore, then cloth patches and solvent to clean out powder residue, dry patches to clean up any excess solvent. She wrinkled her nose at the smell of the solvent.

"I'm sorry," I apologized. "The solvent doesn't smell great."

She shrugged. "It smells strong," she agreed, "but not really *bad* or anything. It's just a strong smell."

After everything was clean, I showed her the couple of spots that should get fresh lubrication—and how much.

"Too much can be as bad as not enough," I said. "In general, if you can easily see it, it's too much."

She nodded understanding, looking curiously at the Laugo's internals as I oiled the couple of spots that needed it.

"That's... *very* different from the Browning, isn't it?"

"It is," I agreed. "It's a completely different design approach from the Browning action plan. It's gas-delayed blowback, instead of a

Browning-style short-recoil locked action, and the fact it has a partial, skeletonized slide helps to even further reduce felt recoil, because there is less reciprocating mass. Which *also* means it cycles faster... though the truth is that doesn't make much difference."

"Why not?" she asked, curiously.

"Because almost any modern semi-automatic pistol already cycles faster than you can reset the trigger," I replied. I pointed out a group of parts above the barrel.

"While the Browning has a recoil spring and guide *below* its barrel, the Laugo instead has a gas system *above*.

"This gas piston assembly bleeds a small amount of gas from the barrel, after the bullet has passed by, to hold the action closed until after the bullet has left the muzzle and chamber pressure has dropped to safe levels. But it's still hammer-fired, unlike most modern designs that tend to be striker-fired, so it's still able to have a very good trigger." I picked up the top strap and pointed into it. "Here's the hammer, up under the top strap, pivoting down where the Browning's pivots up."

Sharon nodded slowly.

"How *many* different internal mechanisms are there in pistols?"

I thought about that for a moment.

"Quite a lot, actually. I couldn't begin to count, especially among early designs when people were trying everything to see what worked. But these days, not more than half a dozen basic plans. The Alien is unique, though. *Nothing* else works quite like it... though the Heckler and Koch P7 has some similarities."

After we finished cleaning and put everything away, we went next door to my office and checked for anything new on the computer. There were no updates. It was getting on for supper time, so we headed back upstairs.

When we reached the foot of the stairs, Sharon stopped. She paused for a moment, then turned.

"Fester," she declared, pointing to the first side door. She turned slightly. "Computer room. Armory."

Then she turned around and pointed to the other end door, only a few feet from the bottom of the stairs.

"What's the fourth door?"

I took three steps forward, opened it, and flipped on the lights as I heard her follow me.

"Dojo," I said. This was the largest room in the basement. The floor was covered with heavy exercise mats. There was a universal gym machine in the far corner, and a rack of martial-arts weapons on one wall—a bo staff, several tonfa, several bokuto. A heavy bag hung in the nearer back corner.

"You do martial arts?" she said, more a statement than a question.

"Several different styles. I use what works for me from each." She nodded understanding. "You're welcome to use it any time you want to. I should have thought to offer it sooner."

"I'll keep it in mind," she said. Then she paused.

"Do you think you could teach me a few things?"

I thought for a moment.

"If you want to learn, I'll gladly try. Though I have to disclose up front that I have never been a martial arts instructor and I'm not really sure how or where to start."

Sharon eyed me measuringly.

"I'm confident you'll come up with something," she said, smiling.

We went back to the stairs and headed up. We decided on Chinese style for supper, so Sharon put rice on while I got out and prepped ingredients for a quick stir-fry, a Szechuan-inspired thing with chicken and shrimp. I put the wok on to heat about fifteen minutes before the rice was done, then cooked everything in the last five minutes. I brought the sizzling wok directly to the table, while Sharon got the rice.

After we ate and cleaned up, we went to relax in the living room as usual.

"So," I asked after a little bit, "how confident do you feel now about your ability to handle and use a pistol?"

Sharon thought about that for a few moments.

"Pretty good," she announced at last. "I'm sure I could benefit a lot from practice—and I *want* more practice—but at least I know basically what I'm doing now. Enough to not do anything really stupid."

I nodded understanding.

"Does that feel better?" I asked.

She thought again.

"...Yes," she said slowly. "Yes, it does. Thank you, Ciáran." Then she stopped, frowning. I could see the play of expressions shifting across her face. She was obviously working through something, so I didn't press her, I just sat and waited for her to process it at her own pace.

Eventually she raised her head and looked directly at me.

"I... I honestly *don't know* whether I'm ready to actually shoot *at someone*," she said at last. "But at least now I'm reasonably confident that if I ever *have* to, I'll know *how*. I won't let myself or someone else get killed *just because I don't know how it works*."

"That's a good place to start," I said approvingly. "And I really hope that you never have to."

"So do I," she agreed fervently. "And before this week I'd never dreamed that I might ever need to." I nodded.

"It's been a hell of a rough week, hasn't it?"

"Yes," she agreed. I moved a little closer, put an arm around her, and we held each other and snuggled.

"What about you?" she asked after a while. I thought for a moment.

"Right now," I said, "my greatest fear is of you getting hurt. The rest, I can handle. But that gives me chills."

We talked about deliberately inconsequential things for a while, listened to music, and just cuddled. Then when it started getting late, we packed up and went to bed.

6: The Game Is Afoot!

On Sunday, we really didn't do very much of anything. We slept in late, ran again—this time, at Sharon's six-minute pace the whole way—came back and showered, got coffee and breakfast. Then we pretty much just took it easy for the rest of the day. Sharon asked if she could practice field-stripping the Browning again, so we went downstairs and did that a few times, then I pulled out a 1911 and showed her what was different between it and the Browning. (Which isn't a tremendous amount, really.) She had a little difficulty with the heavier recoil spring on the 1911. Then, just for contrast, I got out the Laugo again and showed her *in detail* how it worked, and how utterly different it was from either.

"I can see why they call it the Alien," Sharon mused. "Almost nothing in it beyond the magazine catch works the same way."

I agreed. "Also," I pointed out, "it looks a little tiny bit like the alien predator from the film."

She looked at it again.

"Yeah," she chuckled, "I can sort of see that. It does."

We were both a little agitated waiting for the information we'd been promised, but there was nothing we could do about it, so we went out and did a second run before supper.

When Monday came around, we both spent the day impatiently waiting for the signal. There was still nothing of obvious significance on the news. We'd have gone over what we knew again, but there really wasn't anything much to go over.

Finally late Monday afternoon, the signal went off again. I handed Sharon my phone and she called Marilyn.

"Hi, Marilyn. Do you have something for us?" Her tone was hopeful, anticipating.

"I have them," Marilyn replied. "Edrick just met me for coffee and dropped them off in person. Now, how do I get them to you?"

"Just a moment," Sharon said. She looked at me.

"We need to risk going out to meet her, don't we?"

I nodded slowly.

"It is a risk," I agreed. "But it's that, or we bring her here. And if she's followed here… that's a lot *more* risk. If we meet her somewhere fairly public, the presence of witnesses will limit the opposition's options."

Sharon nodded.

"I told you you might have to risk me," she replied. "Marilyn doesn't know you, and you don't know her. But she knows me. I *have* to be the contact."

I couldn't argue with her point. "I don't like it, but I don't see a way to avoid it. Are you okay with it?"

"I… don't see a choice either," she said at last.

I thought for a few moments, then took the phone.

"Do you know where the Shōgun Japanese steakhouse is?" I asked.

"Hello, Agent, uh, Cole," Marilyn said. "Yes, I do."

"I'm going to make a reservation at their sushi bar for 7PM. It'll be in my name. Meet us there. Don't be alarmed if we're ten or fifteen minutes late. I'll be watching to make certain nobody followed you before we come in. If you *don't* see us within thirty minutes, leave and go directly to the nearest police precinct, do *NOT* go straight home, tell them you think you may be in danger related to the Harris Magnusson case. Use your judgment about how much to tell them, but try to avoid disclosing that Miss Kielic is alive.

"Got all that?"

"Yes, I think so, Mr. Cole," she agreed. She sounded a little shaken. "Shōgun sushi bar, 7PM, reservation for Cole, go straight to the nearest police if you're not there in thirty minutes."

"Perfect. We'll see you there."

"Please be careful, Marilyn," Sharon added.

"One more thing," I cautioned Marilyn. "If any stranger *not* accompanied by Miss Kielic accosts or threatens you in the restaurant, *DO NOT* leave the restaurant, stay right there where there are witnesses and call 911. Stay on the line until they arrive. Do you understand?"

"I understand, Agent Cole," Marilyn said. "Thank you."

"Okay," Sharon said, "see you later."

It was 5PM. That gave us a good amount of time. I called Shōgun and made the reservation for a party of three, then we went upstairs to change. Sharon put on her business outfit, with the pale blue jacket over the dark blue dress, and I pulled out my "official business" suit. It was dark gray, conservatively cut, double-breasted, and would conceal the Laugo without noticeably printing through. I wore it over a dark blue dress shirt and a grey silk tie. A pair of lightweight police duty boots passed closely enough for dress shoes.

"Wooooo," Sharon said with a smile, when she saw the completed outfit. "Sharp dressed man."

"Every girl crazy for a sharp dressed man!" I sang. Probably badly. She laughed.

"I'm pretty crazy about you," she declared. "They can't have you. You're *mine*."

"I'm pretty crazy about you, too," I agreed, and kissed her.

I added a shoulder rig and put the Laugo in it, not taking any chances. Then it was time to go. We went downstairs and climbed into the Gray Ghost.

We made our first slow pass by the restaurant about 6:40PM. I scanned the area as we passed. Nobody appeared to be loitering, and there were no obviously suspicious-looking vehicles. We went around a two-block loop that got us back just before 6:50, and I parked in a spot that was near but not too near, from where we could clearly see the approaches to the restaurant. People occasionally went in or came out.

Just before 7PM, a statuesque, dark-haired woman in a smart business dress and a wide hat got out of a Lexus that had just parked almost in front of the restaurant. She walked over to the front of the restaurant, paused, looked around, and went in.

"That's Marilyn," Sharon pointed out.

For the next ten minutes I scanned the area like a hawk, looking for anything out of place. I didn't spot a thing. There was an empty space behind the Lexus, so I pulled out from where we were, pulled in behind the Lexus and parked.

"Don't get out *quite* yet," I told Sharon. I got out and walked around the back of the Volvo, scanning all around as I did. It looked clear. So I stepped up to her side and opened the door. Sharon stepped out, and we walked into the restaurant together.

"Cole, party of three," I told the girl at the desk. "The other guest should already be here."

"Right this way, please," the girl said, and led us back into the sushi area. We spotted Marilyn about halfway there. We went straight to the table.

"Sharon!" Marilyn greeted her. "It's so good to see you!"

We sat down. I made sure to sit where I had line of sight towards the door.

"Hello, Marilyn," Sharon said. "...Agent Cole, this is Marilyn Lang, of Jerison, Whitewell and Lang."

"Pleased to meet you, ma'am," I nodded, putting on my Men In Black face again.

"Please, Agent Cole," Marilyn said, "call me Marilyn."

"As you prefer," I nodded again.

Our waitress showed up about then.

"If you'll permit me," I said. I turned to the waitress and placed a fast order for a large sushi appetizer platter and green tea all round.

"Is everything okay, Sharon?" Marilyn asked. "Aside from the obvious?"

"Yes, really," Sharon answered. "But I'll feel a lot better if we can figure out what's behind all this."

"And you, Agent Cole?" Marilyn asked, turning to me. "The police... clearly don't know Sharon's status, which I find interesting. Can I ask which agency, exactly, you are with?"

Sharp. But we *were* talking about another legal mind here. Very little got past Sharon, and I was sure Marilyn was no different.

"I'm sorry, Ma'a— uh, Marilyn," I replied. The 'slip' was deliberate. "I cannot disclose that information at this time." It wasn't technically a lie, just a deliberate omission. I couldn't disclose my agency because there wasn't one, not because I wasn't allowed to.

Our tea arrived, and I lifted mine and took a sip. It was hot, and good.

"So what do you have for me, Marilyn?" Sharon asked. By way of reply, Marilyn reached down to her other side, picked up a briefcase, passed it across her lap, and set it down next to Sharon. Sharon shot me an excited look.

"Take the whole case," Marilyn told her. "It's from Edrick." Then she looked back at me.

"There *is*, I presume, a parallel official investigation into this?"

I nodded.

"There is," I affirmed. "Our hope is that Miss Kielic will have some unique insight into these specific documents, perhaps some non-obvious special knowledge that made her a threat." I didn't mention that the only 'parallel investigation' we were aware of was the police one that wasn't going anywhere.

Marilyn nodded. Our sushi platter arrived at that moment, and we all dug in.

"The thing I'm curious about," Marilyn continued, "is why you aren't simply sourcing these contracts directly." Yeah, definitely sharp.

"Two reasons... uh, Marilyn," I replied.

"One, there are an unknown number of documents involved, and neither we nor the other team has direct knowledge of which *specific* documents triggered this event. Assuming that theory is even correct. We're still hunting for clues." All perfectly true.

"And two, uh..."

"Chinese wall," Sharon explained over me, saving me from further ad-libbing.

"There's an investigative team that's collecting information all by-the-book, which means slowly, and a protection team that might have to, in the name of my safety, be a little cavalier about the Fourth Amendment. Obviously Agent Cole can't just walk into the offices and ask the investigation team for documents. It would breach the wall and jeopardize any future prosecution. The protection detail has to do their stuff, well, separately."

I nodded confirmation.

"Please don't ask any further questions in that line, Marilyn," I asked. "The more you know, the more *you* are at risk." And *that* was true.

She gave me a questioning look, but seemed to accept it.

"Really," Sharon interjected, "there are a *lot* of questions that we can't answer yet. I wish we *could*, but..."

Marilyn looked back and forth between Sharon and me.

"Sharon," she said slowly, "there's more going on between you and… Agent Cole than just protection detail and protectee, isn't there?"

Sharon blushed slightly, and Marilyn caught it. I thought we were in trouble, but then a big smile slowly spread across her face. It wasn't an "Aha! Busted!" smile, it was a genuinely-happy-for-you smile.

"Well, whatever is going on," she said, smiling, "both with this case and between the two of you, I hope you figure it out and it all works out in the end. Just reassure me of one thing: Promise me you are certain you are on the *right* side of all of this, correct?"

We both nodded.

"I firmly believe so, ma'am," I confirmed. "Uh, Marilyn." It *was* accidental that time.

"And I'm going to take an informed guess here," she continued. "The 'unknown Caucasian male' who was reported killed in your bathroom," looking at Sharon, "was the hitman you previously mentioned to me." She turned to me. "And *you* shot him—completely legally justifiably, in my opinion, I will stipulate on the record if asked— to save her life."

"Yes," Sharon confirmed, before I could form a reply.

"Thank you, Mr. Cole," Marilyn said. "Truly, from the bottom of my heart, *thank you*."

"Marilyn," I replied, "truly, I couldn't have done anything else." I set caution aside for the moment. "And that was before I *knew* Sharon and found out how wonderful she is."

"You're not wrong, Mr. Cole," Marilyn said. "You're not wrong."

"And Marilyn? It's Ciáran."

She held out a hand, and I took it.

"It's a pleasure to meet you, Ciáran," she said. "Please continue to look after our Sharon."

"I promise you I will guard her with my life," I agreed, and meant every word.

We were almost finished with the sushi platter. I beckoned a waiter over and asked for the bill. He was back with it in a moment, and I passed him a black card for it. By the time the bill came back for my signature, we were done.

I signed the slip, pocketed the card and stood up.

"We'll escort you to your car just to be sure," I told Marilyn. We all got up and headed for the door. I went out first just in case, but nothing happened and there was no sign of any threat. We walked Marilyn to her Lexus. She gave Sharon a quick but tight hug, then walked around her car, got in, and drove off. We got into the Volvo and headed for home. I kept a wary eye on everything around us, just in case we'd somehow picked up a tail.

"Marilyn seems like a good person," I remarked, as we drove home.

"She is," Sharon agreed. "I really like her."

It was after nine by the time we got back. We'd had a decent amount of sushi already, so I just put together a light snack to finish us up. After we finished eating, Sharon went straight for the briefcase.

"I'm not going to go through these in detail tonight," she said, "but I do want just a quick skim to see if anything immediately leaps out at me." She pulled out the stack of contracts and started leafing through the first one. I cleared the table, then looked for some peaceful music to put on that wouldn't interrupt her concentration. I went with Beethoven's Pastoral Symphony.

She looked up after a few minutes and smiled at me.

"I love Beethoven," she said. Then she went back to the document.

She read through them, sheet by sheet, for the next couple of hours. Then we packed it in and headed for bed.

7: Private Investigations

We got up the next morning and ran before breakfast again. The routine seemed to set us up on a good start for the day, so we maintained it—and kept with the six-minute pace. There was nothing of evident interest in the morning news check.

After breakfast, Sharon dived straight into the contracts. There really wasn't a lot I could do except wait around in case she needed anything, so mostly I did that. Occasionally I went downstairs and checked to see whether anything new had shaken loose online.

By lunchtime, Sharon had exactingly gone through two of the contracts. I brought her a ham-and-Swiss sandwich and a glass of lemonade, and the same for myself.

"Any insights yet?" I asked, not really expecting anything. She shook her head.

"Nothing is leaping out at me so far," she replied. "These first two are... just ordinary, routine, boring, mundane, pro-forma commercial-space lease contracts. They're not even interesting or unusual properties.

"Maybe some pattern will emerge after I've been through the other three, but so far... I'm drawing a blank. Nothing is out of order, they would both have been utterly routine."

She went back to the contracts after lunch. I put on some Mike Oldfield and Clannad, and tried as much as possible to leave her to it and find things to keep myself busy. I chafed at not being able to do anything to help.

About 2PM, Jim Bell called us.

"Can you come and meet with a detective to make a statement?" he asked. "Same place as last time."

"Sure. When?"

"Can you do 4PM today?"

I looked at Sharon. She nodded.

"We can do that," I replied.

"Right," Jim said. "I'll call back and let Detective Taylor know it's on. See you there."

"Thanks, Jim," Sharon said.

<hr>

We were there a few minutes early. Our guide this time was a young man in green who didn't look over twenty.

"Good to see you back," Jim greeted us. "Any new developments?"

"We've managed to get our hands on copies of the contract tranche," Sharon replied. "But we haven't learned anything new from them yet."

"Did you bring them with you?"

"No. Should we have?"

"No, that's good. But don't be surprised if there's a request to obtain them. Do you have any problem with providing copies to the police?"

"I don't think so," I said. "They might even catch something we're missing."

A few minutes later, the police detective was led in by the same boy who'd brought us back. He was an older man, wiry and weathered, thinning on top.

"Good morning, Mr. Bell," he said. Then, to all of us, "I'm Detective Taylor."

"Detective Taylor," Jim replied, "Sharon Kielic, Ciáran mac Cool."

The detective nodded to both of us.

"Thank you both for coming. I'll be recording your statements." He looked at Jim.

"Mr. Bell? Everyone ready to begin?"

Jim nodded, and so did I.

"I think the best place to start here is for you both to tell Detective Taylor exactly what you told me," Jim told us.

150

So we did exactly that.

"I have a few additional questions," Taylor said, when we were done.

"You said you shot the assailant. We found two recently-fired .40 casings on the bedroom floor. CCI-Speer headstamp. Extractor marks are exotic, not in our database, FBI and ATF haven't gotten back to us with their database. Are those cases yours?"

"I can't vouch for that," I said carefully. "I fired two shots, I didn't get a chance to pick up my brass, and that's my preferred brand, but I can't verify sight unseen that the cases you found are mine."

"Fair enough. You didn't touch or otherwise do anything to the body?"

"Nope. We just got out of there as fast as we could. And it was barely in time."

"Can you describe him?"

I thought briefly.

"Heavily-built man, I'd say late thirties to maybe early forties. About six-one, two hundred plus, maybe two twenty. Dark hair, cut short. Squarish face. Bad suit. No facial hair or obvious visible identifying marks. That's about all I can say. If I had to type-cast him, I'd say stereotyped Mob hitter. Didn't really stop for a close look at him. My primary concern was getting Ms. Kielic out alive and as fast as possible."

"Fair enough. If we can work up a possible match from DNA, are you willing to look at mug shots and see if you can identify him?"

I shrugged.

"Sure. It might give us some clues."

"Ms. Kielic. Had you ever, to your knowledge, seen your attacker anywhere before?"

"No." Sharon shook her head.

"Did you have any reason, anything at all, to expect that you might be attacked at that time?"

"No," Sharon replied shakily. "It was an ordinary working day, I came home, I got in the shower, I stepped out, I reached for a towel... and then there was something around my throat and I was being dragged off my feet. I tried to fight, but he was too strong. I was starting to black out. And then Ciáran shot him."

"You didn't call 911 after the shooting. Why?"

"I stopped her because I suspected he *probably* had backup," I said. "A suspicion which it appears was correct. We couldn't take the risk of waiting for police to arrive. As it was, we barely got out ahead of what I presume to have been the backup team.

"Also, if her phone was tapped or compromised—which we couldn't be certain it *wasn't*—it would tell them she was still alive."

He nodded.

"Makes sense," he agreed. "This is not a normal situation. That's why you left the phone there?"

"Yes. Didn't want anyone using it to track her location." I made a mental note that the police probably had her phone.

"You heard additional persons enter the house, but never actually saw them?"

"Correct."

"About how long between when you fired and when the presumed backup came in?"

"Maybe four minutes," I estimated.

"Your shots didn't draw them immediately?"

"Suppressor," I replied tersely. "All tax-stamped and legal." He gave me a sharp look, but nodded.

"Based on what we know," he said, "it seems the attackers, whoever they are, can be presumed to know by now that Ms. Kielic is still alive."

"They know their hitter didn't get her *there and then*," I corrected. "They know she made it out of the house. They *don't* know who killed their hitter, they don't know it wasn't her, they don't know she wasn't wounded during a struggle, and they don't know she isn't dead from blood loss somewhere. Let's maintain that ambiguity, please. They probably know she *may be* alive, but if they *know* for sure, they may step up their efforts to find her."

"Fair. I understand from Mr. Bell that you are acting in a personal-protection capacity for Ms. Kielic, correct?"

"That is correct, yes," I agreed.

"And you have... experience in this capacity?"

"Again, correct."

"Might I ask further details of that?"

"I'd prefer not to say. Unless you believe the answer particularly germane to this case. I can state it was all legal and above-board."

Taylor pondered that.

"Is it relevant to why you were present at Ms. Kielic's home?"

"Detective, move on, please," Jim interjected.

"Very well. We'll leave that for now.

"What was the state of the house at the time you both left?"

"Untouched and completely normal," I said, "aside from having a dead body in the master bathroom."

"Hmm. Which was removed sometime between when you left on Tuesday night, and when we entered the house on Thursday morning." He thought for a moment.

"Ms. Kielic, it appears whoever removed that body also searched your house. I have to warn you, they were not neat about it. Expect a mess. I'm sorry to have to say that.

"Any idea what they might have been looking for?"

Sharon shook her head mutely.

"Was there anything unusual, or of unusual value, in the house?"

"No," she said, shaking her head. "Only ordinary personal possessions and a lot of copies of old legal case files. Study material. If they expected to find anything important in them, they must have been sadly disappointed. And probably got very bored, finding out."

Taylor chuckled, and turned back to me.

"Mr. mac Cool, you stated there was a vehicle outside that you presumed was the backup team. Did you get a good look at the vehicle?"

"Late-model full-size SUV," I said. "Black or dark colored. Cadillac Escalade, I *think*, but I couldn't swear to it. Couldn't read the plate in the dusk from that distance."

"How far away were you when you saw it?"

I thought.

"About a hundred and twenty yards, maybe a hundred and thirty."

"Engine running, lights off?"

"Check."

"Could you make anyone in the vehicle?"

I shook my head. "Not from that distance, in that light."

"Reasonable. Okay.

"At the time this happened, did you have any reason to suspect it was anything other than an isolated assault?"

"Not a thing," I began. Then I hesitated, and clarified. "That is, there was nothing *at the time* to suggest it was connected to anything else. But it was clear from the very start that it wasn't just that some random weirdo had followed her home."

Taylor nodded apparent approval at the clarification. "At what point *did* you become aware that there had been other attacks against Harris Magnusson and its employees?"

"Local news, the next morning."

Taylor nodded.

"Ms. Kielic, I understand you worked for Philip Bartholomew. Is that correct?"

"Yes," she confirmed.

"Anything more to that? Any other connection between you and him?"

"No," she said. "I mean, we were *all* friends. But—no. Not aside from that."

"And yourself and Mr. mac Cool?"

"We are—very close," she replied.

Taylor nodded again.

"I think we're nearly done," he stated. "Is there anything else either of you haven't told me yet, that you think might be useful or relevant to this case?"

"We really don't know anything else at this time," I said. "Except that whoever it was, was willing to firebomb a law office and murder—or attempt to murder—two people over it."

"And your speculation is that this is about something Ms. Kielic or Mr. Bartholomew knows, or knew."

"Or something the opposition *thinks* one of them knows, or knew,"

I corrected.

"Right, right. Any idea what that might be?"

"We're drawing a complete blank so far," I admitted. "We are totally in the dark. The only thing we have to go on is a *guess* that it *might* be related to a group of contracts received by Harris Magnusson on the day of the... attacks. Which I believe we already mentioned."

"You did," he agreed. "Would you be able to provide us with copies of those contracts?"

"Those will be provided in due course, with appropriate procedure," Jim interjected.

"Thanks," Taylor said. "And you've got nothing yet out of those yourselves?"

"Not one damned thing," Sharon agreed, somewhat bitterly. "There is absolutely nothing interesting or unusual about them. They are boringly routine."

Taylor paused, seemingly thinking.

"Since you're closely involved with this," he said at last, "I'm going to pass on a piece of information that your senior partners already know, but which we have not made public. I'm hoping that this won't cause you further distress, but as you worked closely with Philip Bartholomew, you deserve to know. I'm sorry to have to tell you this, but it does raise an unanswered question.

"The medical examiner concluded from the pattern of Mr. Bartholomew's injuries that he was tortured—presumably for information—before he was killed."

"We'd already figured out that much," I noted, a moment before wondering whether I should have said it. Sharon just nodded, her face pale. Taylor raised an eyebrow at me.

"Oh?" he inquired. "Do you mind telling me how you figured it out?"

"The initial news report," I replied. "The report quoted a statement from the Highway Patrol that his injuries were not consistent with the accident. For the Patrol to mention it, clearly enough that the news report quoted it, they'd have had to be very blatantly inconsistent with the supposed single-vehicle accident. And given what we already knew about the murder attempt against Sharon..."

"Okay," Taylor agreed with a knowing nod, "that was a pretty reasonable deduction under the circumstances." He turned back to Sharon.

"Anyway," he continued, "the point is, this does raise a question of why the opposition—as you put it, Mr. mac Cool—apparently tried to get information from your boss, but not from you. Can you think of any reason why that might be?"

Sharon's hand tightened on mine. After a long moment, she shook her head quickly.

"I'm sorry," she said quietly, her voice tense. "I have no idea."

Taylor nodded again, shifting slightly in his seat. "Again, I'm sorry I had to bring that up. Obviously it must be a painful subject.

"Now, just one last question. To your knowledge, is there anyone besides the two of you who is able to corroborate what you have told me here today?"

Sharon and I exchanged looks. She shook her head slowly.

"Nobody, as far as I am aware," I replied. "Nobody else was in the house, and I took every possible precaution to see that nobody saw us leave. I don't know whether any of Sharon's neighbors happened to see her come home from work, to corroborate when she got home, or how long behind her the bad guys showed up. Which can't have been more than about five to ten minutes. Possibly they followed her. She did mention a fuel stop on the way home; possibly that could corroborate part of the timing.

"Only three people know first-hand what happened in that bathroom. Two of us are here, and the third is dead and isn't talking."

Taylor nodded.

"Okay," he said. "I think we're done here. Thanks for coming to talk to me.

"Now, there's one other thing. Mr. Bell has informed us he already asked you this question, but I'm going to ask it again, because it is quite clear there's something fairly major going on here. This isn't like a mugging or a simple assault."

He turned to Sharon.

"Do you want, or need, police protection?"

I looked at Sharon. She looked back at me and squeezed my hand by way of reply.

"Honestly," I replied, "the only thing a police protective detail would do is, if one of the opposition chanced to pass near to our location, draw attention that there was something there to hide. I think she's safer without, and if nobody but the two of us knows where she is, there's zero possibility of leaks. I *am* going to ask, though, that you be very circumspect about who you let see your report."

"I can understand that," Taylor agreed, with a nod. "You need Ms. Kielic's location to stay unknown." He turned to Sharon.

"Ms. Kielic? You agree?"

"I trust Ciárán with my life," she replied. "If something comes for us that he can't stop, I don't think an officer sitting outside in a car is going to stop it either."

"Fair enough," Taylor nodded. "I had to ask."

"And we appreciate it," I said.

"Can I reach you if further questions come up?" Taylor asked.

I looked at Jim. He nodded.

"Please contact us through Mr. Bell," I said. "If you need anything from us, we'll do our best to assist.

"There is one thing though. You asked about why we left her phone in the house. I infer that you have her phone."

"We do," Taylor confirmed. "It's booked in as evidence. It's pretty thoroughly smashed, I'm afraid."

"That's okay," I said. "The phone's not really the point. We don't want it anywhere near her right now anyway. The question is, do you also have her ID?"

"We do," Taylor confirmed.

"Is there any chance it could be released back to her?"

He thought for a moment. Sharon shot me a grateful smile.

"I don't see a problem with that," he replied. "We have some bank cards and other personal documents, too. I'll see about getting those released to you, Ms. Kielic. We can get them to you by way of Mr. Bell?"

"That would work," Sharon agreed. "Thank you."

And then everything was done. There was a little after-the-fact discussion between us and Jim, after Detective Taylor left, and perhaps twenty minutes later, we were on our way home again.

When we got in, I started making supper, and Sharon went back to comparing the contracts. By supper time, she'd been through all five of the contracts once each.

"There is nothing in the least interesting or odd about any of these contracts," Sharon declared at the supper table. "So far, I'm baffled. Nothing stands out. They're all instances of the same general standard contract, no unusual terms, nothing."

"And yet," I pondered, "something about these specific five contracts *appears to have been* the trigger for an arson attack and two murder attempts.   Unless it was actually something completely unconnected to them, that we know nothing at all about.   And the contracts are just a coincidental red herring."

"I'm starting to lean that way," she agreed darkly. "Which would put us right back to square one. So I'm really hoping there's something I'm missing. I just can't figure out what it *is*.

"I need a break. Any ideas?"

"Movie?" I suggested. "Something light-hearted and non-serious?"

She thought about that for a moment.

"Sure," she agreed, "why not? Got something specific in mind?"

So for the next couple of hours, we cuddled on the couch and watched Marvel superheroes battle the forces of evil. Then we went to bed.

Tuesday mostly followed much the same pattern of no progress. After having ascertained to her satisfaction that there were no significant differences between the contracts, Sharon had me sit down with her and go through one line-by-line, just in case I picked up on anything she had overlooked through familiarity. Needless to say, I didn't spot anything either.

"It would be a lot easier to do this if we could get them in digital form," she remarked eventually.

"Why can't we?" I asked. "We know what the specific contracts *are*, now."

She stared at me, then closed her eyes and smacked the heel of her palm against her forehead, hard.

"Gods above," she muttered despairingly, "I'm an idiot."

She opened her eyes again and looked at me.

"We have the document and deed numbers, now. They're all on record *somewhere*. It's just getting access to the records."

"Where would they be?" I asked.

"Commercial real estate database services. There's a lot of them."

I looked at her. Then I picked up the stack of contracts, stood up and went downstairs. Sharon got up and followed me. I walked into the Box's room.

"I need access to commercial real estate databases containing records on these specific properties and contracts," I told the Box. Then I read off the contract numbers and property addresses.

PLEASE WAIT, the Box replied. ACCESS CREDENTIALS WILL BE PROVIDED ONCE RELEVANT RECORDS HAVE BEEN IDENTIFIED.

I handed the sheaf of contracts back to Sharon.

"Hopefully this'll crack something loose," I said. "Let's take a break."

"Sure," she agreed. "I want a loooong hot shower."

So we went and showered, and we stood under the hot water while I rubbed the tension out of her neck and shoulders. After a time, she turned around and pressed herself against me, then pulled my head down and kissed me. And, well, one thing led to another from there.

By the time we were all done and dried off, it was time for bed, so we went to bed.

═══════════

When we got back into it after breakfast Wednesday, the first thing we did was go to check on the Box. As soon as I walked into the room, the screen lit up.

CREDENTIALS SECURED. READY TO SEND.

"Any time," I said. Immediately, my phone went *Bleep!*

I opened the message to find access credentials to log into three different commercial real-estate databases. I walked next door into the office, Sharon right behind me.

"You know," I commented, "I really need to get a second chair in here." I stopped and ordered one while that thought was fresh in my mind, paying extra for overnight delivery. Then I went and connected to the three databases and started searching for the contracts we had, in electronic form. I had to hit all three databases to get the complete set of five.

"You know, that's odd in itself," Sharon observed thoughtfully.

"What?" I asked.

"These five contracts were all in the same bundle. I'd typically expect we'd be able to get at least four of them in one hit on one database. Having to hit three databases to get five contracts presumed to be in some kind of a group is... strange."

I considered that.

"Like... someone's trying to hide something?" I hazarded.

Sharon got a determined look.

"We're onto something here," she said. "I can feel it. I just don't know *what* yet. I'm going to need some legal programs installed, some standard law-office tools."

"Get whatever you need," I told her. I showed her where I kept the payment information the Box had provided for such purposes. She spent the next couple of hours installing and setting up legal software tools, then we took a break for lunch.

She was excited and animated over lunch, and I could understand why. Finally, we had a lead.

We got back into it right away after lunch. She loaded all five of the contracts we'd retrieved into a program that let her match and compare them side by side, character by character. Then she pored over the results, studying every marked difference.

Then she cradled her chin in her hands and sat there staring at them.

"What are you thinking?" I asked.

"It's not the contracts themselves," she mused. "They differ in no significant ways from each other—OR from a standard boilerplate contract—*except for* the lessors, lessees, amounts, and properties."

She sat upright in decision.

"So if it's not in the contracts, it's got to be something to do with the properties themselves."

She opened another program, connected it to the three real-estate databases we had, and started digging into the details of the properties.

She was at it for hours. Eventually, she came up for air again.

"Want something to drink?" I asked.

"Oh god, yeah," she said, "I'm parched. I hadn't noticed."

"You had your head down in the zone," I pointed out.

"I guess so," she replied sheepishly. We went upstairs and I made a pot of Darjeeling tea.

"So, found anything?" I asked, while the tea brewed.

"Not really," she answered me. "They're all to different lessees, but mostly to the same lessor. None of which is surprising. Both the lessors and the lessees appear to be shell corporations, but these days *that's* not all that surprising either. Two of the properties are very similar, but there's nothing unusual about any of them, so *that's* not really a surprise. They're all up to date on lease and property tax.

"Nothing stands out so far. I have a feeling there's still something I'm missing. I just can't put my finger on it yet. It's like having an itch that I can't scratch."

"Well," I said, "we can have another try at scratching it after dinner if you want. What do you feel like for dinner?"

She thought for a moment.

"You're going to laugh," she said.

"Try me."

"At every opportunity, mister," she replied, with a huge grin. "But seriously: Pizza. Please."

"Pizza?" I repeated.

She nodded.

"Okay... we can manage that. We'd probably better get the oven started pre-heating now. But I'll warn you, my pizza crust skills are... *not* top tier. And don't expect me to toss the crust, unless you really want to see me wearing it." She laughed.

I turned the oven up to 500°F and let it start heating up, then I looked up a pizza crust recipe, got out flour and the other essential ingredients, and started putting together a ball of pizza dough. Once I had it together, I set it aside to proof while I collected topping ingredients. I sliced mushrooms, cut up a few slices of ham, thawed some salad shrimp, opened a can of pineapple chunks and started quartering some of them into tidbits.

"Do you like anchovies on pizza?" She held out a hand and waggled it, so-so.

"Okay then," I said, "half and half."

Then I realized I hadn't started sauce yet, so I got out diced tomatoes and tomato paste, blitzed them together, and put them in a pan over low heat. I added a splash of red wine and a spoonful of herbs. Then it was up to the dough proofing.

When the dough was ready, I pulled it out, punched it down a little, then spread a little flour on the counter.

"This is the part I warned you about," I said, "where I bravely DON'T attempt to toss the crust." Instead I just rolled it out into a rough circle, then flipped it over onto a copper baking sheet. I set it aside to rise a little more while the sauce finished up.

When the sauce seemed thick enough, I spread it over my crust, gave it a good layer of Italian six-cheese blend out of a bag, spread the toppings out, then added just a bit more cheese on top. Then I got out the jar of anchovies and spread a few out across one side of the pizza, and into the oven it went. I set a twelve minute timer, then did some quick clean-up and put a wood cutting board onto the table.

When the timer went off, I grabbed a pair of heat-resistant oven mitts and checked the pizza. The cheese was golden and bubbling, just how I wanted it. Maybe a little scorched around the edge, but hey, I'm not a pizza expert, and I didn't have a proper pizza oven to work with anyway. I turned the oven off, slid a wooden peel under the baking sheet and lifted out the pizza, took it to the table, and with very little encouragement it slid straight off onto the cutting board.

"If Madame requests pizza," I declaimed, "then perforce, Madame shall have pizza."

Sharon laughed again, and I took the pan and gloves back to the kitchen, then grabbed a couple of plates and a pizza cutter. The oversized-demilune kind, not the wheel kind. When I got back to the table with them, she grabbed me and kissed me. Then we sat down and ate pizza for supper.

"I warned you it wasn't going to be the world's greatest pizza," I said.

"Nonsense," she retorted. "...Okay, maybe this pizza isn't foodie-magazine picture perfect, but it was made with the most important ingredient in the world."

"What's that?" I asked. She looked me straight in the eye.

"Love," she told me.

"You want to go back and look at the properties again?" I asked after we were done.

"No," she demurred, "I'll sleep on it. I need a break."

So we sat and we watched *Crouching Tiger, Hidden Dragon*. Ridiculous escapist fun, but oh, the cinematography and the wire work.

We sat up for a while after the movie, just enjoying each other's presence, and then it occurred to us that we could enjoy it even more in bed. So we went to bed.

=====

Thursday rolled around, and after our run and breakfast, it was back to looking at the commercial properties. Along about eleven in the morning, the new chair arrived. I took it straight downstairs and set it up, and from then on it was a bit easier to work together, because we could both sit down at the same time and just pass the keyboard back and forth.

"I'm not seeing anything about any of these properties that's obviously off," Sharon said after another while. "And nothing's leaping out at me about the differences between them. We need a different way to look at them."

I was shooting blanks too.

"How about geographically?" I asked. "Maybe looking at where they are will give us a clue?"

"Worth a try," Sharon agreed. "If I give you all the property addresses, can you highlight them on a map?"

"Sure. Let me see the addresses again."

I pulled up some mapping software and stuck the five addresses into an API call that would mark and highlight them on the map.

"There you go," I announced, expanding the map to full screen.

Sharon scanned the map.

"Wait a minute," she objected, "you missed one."

"No I didn't," I said. "I entered all five."

"Look at the map," she told me. I looked. Only four locations were highlighted.

"Huuuuuh," I said slowly. "That's funny..."

I double-checked the API call. The result said it had highlighted five addresses. I looked at the map again. Four.

"Hold on a moment," I said. I told it to blink the first location marker. One of the highlights obediently started blinking. So I stopped that blink and told it to blink the next address. A second location blinked. Then I told it to blink the third, and the third location blinked merrily at us. So I told it to blink the fourth.

The second blinked again.

"Wait a minute," Sharon said. "That's the same one."

I looked at her, and she looked at me. Then I saw the light go on.

She pulled up the two contracts, and zoomed in on the map, and looked at the property addresses.

"*Got you!*" she declared intently. I gave her a questioning look.

She pointed at the two contracts.

"I thought these were leases for two very similar properties," she explained. "They're not. They are two concurrent commercial leases, with a different lessor and a different lessee, of the same commercial property, with its address stated in two different ways that describe it as being on two different enclosing streets—one address on Tenth Street, the other on the cross-street, Acacia—to make it *look like* two different properties.

"The question," she mused, "is *why*."

Right then, my phone rang. It was Jim Bell. I handed the phone to Sharon.

"Hi, Sharon," he said. "Detective Taylor just stopped by my office and dropped off your ID and bank cards. How do you want to handle getting them back?"

"Can we meet?" she asked. Then she looked at me. "But perhaps a different place this time? I'm guessing Ciáran would say we don't want to become predictable." I grinned.

"He probably has a point," Jim agreed. "Do you want to suggest a location this time?"

Sharon looked at me.

"For just a quick hand-off?" I thought for a moment. "How about the Five Guys burger place at the outlet mall? We don't even have to sit down. If we coordinate timing, we can just do a hand-off in the line." I looked at Sharon.

"And if we want to be really cautious, you don't even need to be there. Jim and I know each other on sight now. But it's your call."

Sharon nodded slowly.

"That's... probably wise," she pondered. "No point being seen in public if I don't have to. But damn it, I *HATE* having to hide."

"I understand," I agreed. "It sucks that it's not *them* having to hide." She nodded.

"Okay, is that the plan?" Jim asked. "I can be there in about forty minutes."

"Let's make it fifteen thirty sharp," I said, "and we can just hand off in line."

"All right," Jim said. "I'll be there." And he hung up.

"I kind of want to go with you," Sharon said. "But I probably shouldn't."

"It's six of one, half a dozen of the other," I replied. "Risk being randomly spotted in public, vs. I leave you here unprotected for an hour."

Sharon thought briefly.

"If you put it that way, I'm coming with you."

I grinned.

"Glad to have the company," I told her. "I'd hate to get back and find the house open and you gone."

═══════════

We left the house just after three. Sharon had borrowed a boonie hat of mine and tucked her hair up under it. It was actually three twenty-five when we reached the outlets, so I killed a couple of minutes by going in the far side of the parking lot past the Old Navy and looping around. That put us in front of Five Guys at three twenty eight. I pulled into a space opposite, and waited. At three twenty nine, a dark maroon Infiniti went past behind us and pulled in right in front. The driver looked familiar.

"We're up," I said. We got out, walked across the lane, and headed inside without looking around. Out of the corner of my eye I saw Jim get out of his car. He came in about fifteen seconds behind us and joined the end of the short line. The place was mostly empty, with only one person ahead of us.

"Hey, miss," Jim said, "I saw you drop this outside the door." He held out a rather worn nylon wallet. Sharon turned around.

"Oh, thank you," she answered, taking it. She quickly opened it and peeked inside. The relief on her face was genuine.

"Thanks, Mr...?" I asked, holding out a hand.

"Bell," Jim replied. "Jim Bell." We shook briefly as though we'd never met.

"*Thank* you, Mr. Bell," Sharon said. "I'd hate to have lost this." Jim nodded.

"Any time, young lady," he told her. Then the person in front of us was done ordering, and it was our turn. We looked up at the extensive menu of add-ons and ordered our burgers. "To go, please." The counterman handed us a slip, we took it and went to a table, and Jim stepped up behind us to order. He took his time ordering, then paused as he passed by us.

"New around here?" he asked. It was a clever gambit. I realized immediately he was giving us a lead to lay a false trail.

"Just passing through," I demurred. "Headed up to Montreal for a vacation."

"It would have really sucked to not find out until we got to the border that I'd lost my wallet," Sharon ad-libbed. "Thank you *so* much."

"You're welcome," Jim nodded. "Enjoy your vacation." Then he took a seat at a nearby table.

"Thanks," I replied, "we'll enjoy it a lot more without a lost wallet."

A couple of minutes later they called our number. We got up, took our burgers, and left. Sharon checked through the wallet on the way home. Her ID was there, her medical card, and almost all of her other cards. She pronounced a couple of less important items missing.

"Of course, I don't dare *use* any of these, do I?" she said. But I could tell she already knew the answer.

"If I were you," I confirmed, "I'd use them only in case of emergency."

"I thought so," she agreed, nodding.

———————————

Twenty minutes later, we were back home. We unpacked our order and sat down to eat. They were pretty good burgers, really.

"We need more information about these leases," I said after a little while. "We need to know if there's more."

"Yeah," Sharon agreed. "But I think now we know what to look for. How much data can you get out of that mapping system?"

"A lot. Practically anything that's in it. It's an open API."

"Can you pull out a list of every commercial property in the US whose street address can be described or written in more than one way?"

"Uh," I said, thinking, "I'm not sure about that precisely. That's a huge amount of data to search. The number of permutations increases exponentially. But if we can start with a restricted list of possible addresses to work from, I think I can figure out a way to build a sub-list out of it of every set of different street addresses *from that list* that resolve to the same location. I'll need to write some code."

"Can you cross-reference that with the commercial real-estate databases?"

"Yup. Especially if I cache the necessary data, the set of business addresses, in a local database here. That's where I was figuring on getting our possible-address list."

"Do that, please," she said. Then she stood up and marched out of the room.

"Fester!" I heard her call before she even got into the Box's room. "We're going to need access to more commercial real estate databases."

There was a short pause. I couldn't see the Box's response, from here.

"*All* of them," Sharon said.

<hr>

By Friday morning, the Box delivered access credentials to every major commercial real-estate database service covering the US, and by Friday evening I'd built a simple database schema and written some code that would populate it with every unique commercial property listing in all of the real-estate databases, and every matching "multi-homed" physical address I could pull out of the mapping software— every location in the databases that could be described by more than one distinct recognized address, Post Office "official" or not, that was also in the databases. I didn't bother storing the complete lease contracts; aside from the lessees, lessors and addresses, we'd already figured out that the text of the contracts was uninteresting. But I stored all of the metadata, every available piece of information *about* the contracts.

I did a couple of short trial runs to be certain it was working properly, found and fixed a couple of minor bugs, cleared the database, and ran a few more test runs. Then once I was satisfied it was working as designed, I kicked it off and just let it run.

The collector program was deliberately throttled so as not to generate excessive load anywhere or do anything I couldn't avoid that might attract unwanted attention, including distributing retrieval requests for properties across different databases and pulling them in randomized order so as not to show a continuous scan. It took a couple of days to run. Finally it finished up around mid-afternoon on Monday. I'd never have had space locally to store all of the contracts and all of the property details, but I could store all of the metadata. And that was all we really *needed* anyway.

"This is looking good," I said, when I'd run a few quick queries against our new database. "I'm finding about twenty-three hundred listed commercial properties in the US that can be identified using more than one unique address. Some of them are simply so *large* that they have multiple entrances on different blocks. Large factory premises and the like. I think we can ignore those.

"The interesting ones are all smaller properties that can be referenced by addresses on different crossing streets that enclose them. There's a few hundred of those.

"Sixty-seven of those have multiple active leases on them using different addresses. I'm giving you that list now."

Sharon started going through the list.

"There only seem to be about a dozen distinct lessors here so far," she said after an hour or so. "And more interestingly, only about forty distinct lessees. On average they're leasing five or six properties each. No real pattern that I can see. I'm willing to accept that they are more or less random. There isn't even really any noticeable..."

She paused, struck by a thought, or an insight.

"...No, actually, I take that back.   There is a curious *lack* of geographic grouping. And..." She groped for words.

"The... distributions of the properties leased by each corporation. They're too *uniform*. It's as though they were all stamped out from a template.

"If these were *real* business property leases, you'd expect at least *some* of them to be clustered, the same entity leasing a group of properties in the same general area.   But that kind of grouping is conspicuous by its *absence*. I've only found one such group so far. And it appears to be the oldest. It might have been the first time they tried it."

"A proof of concept?"

"Maybe.   And also you'd expect different businesses to have different patterns of where they put their business operations. But, aside from that first exception, they don't.   It's like... they're Stepford corporations. You'd never notice it if you looked at just one of them. But look at ten or twenty of them side by side, and a clear pattern emerges, a pattern that doesn't look real.

"But there's something else."

She picked a random lease and pointed out the law firm that had handled it.

"I'm not all the way through the list yet," she continued. "But so far... they were clever. They took pains to cover their tracks. They've distributed all of these across a large list of law firms so that none of these multiple leases will show up as recorded by their own lawyers." She hesitated. "I'm *assuming* they have their own lawyers. This is a big operation. It's not four wiseguys in a smoke-filled back room.

"I have not yet found a single case where two leases for the same aliased property were contracted out to the same law firm."

She picked up two folders from the five on the desk, the five we'd gotten from Edrick, the five that were sent to Harris Magnusson, and looked me right in the eye.

"Except for these two."

I looked back at her. Suddenly I knew what had happened.

"Somebody fucked up," I said slowly. "Somebody, somewhere, *accidentally* assigned two contracts for the same location to the same law firm for recording and management. Harris Magnusson. And when they realized they'd done it, that somebody panicked and tried to cover their ass."

"And that's why they hit us," Sharon replied quietly. I nodded.

She sat silently thinking.

"And the bitter irony is," she mused, "it's so subtle that if they hadn't panicked, we would almost certainly *never have noticed*. We were actively *looking* for something we'd *already figured out* had to be wrong, and it's still taken us a week to figure out *what* was wrong with them. The only reason we found it is because you had the idea to look at them geographically, and had the skills to do it."

"And because you noticed the anomaly in it," I said. "If we'd been looking at a thousand locations we wouldn't have seen it. But four, when there should have been five..."

Sharon looked at me. There were tears in her eyes.

"Philip *died*—and I *almost* died—because somebody made a mistake. And then panicked when they realized it."

I reached across and held her.

"We're onto them now," I told her. "We will hunt the bastards down, and figure out who they are. And then we will make them pay."

Sharon hugged me tightly.

8: The Hunting of the Snark

"So how do we use *this*," I asked, waving my hand generally at the computer screen and all of the data we'd collected, "to figure out who the Black Hats are?"

Sharon wiped her eyes and looked at me.

"First," she replied, "we need to trace all of these shell corporations. Both the lessors and the lessees. That's going to take some time."

"Does any of this data give us any clue as to *why* they're doing all this?"

She thought about that.

"On average," she said after a while, "there's around three leases on each of these properties. That's three sets of cash flow. But only one set of overhead costs.   And there's another thing: at least the ones I've looked at more closely so far don't appear to actually *produce* anything. They just move money around.

"I think it's an elaborate, large-scale money-laundering scheme."

"How much money are we talking about?" I asked.

"Across all of these leases?" Sharon replied.   "Millions a month, easily. Maybe into tens of millions."

"Where's all the money coming from?" I wondered. "And where's it going? And why—and I don't mean to minimize anything—why is this specific scheme *so important?*"

Sharon glanced significantly at the wall between us and the Box, then looked back at me. I nodded. She'd clearly picked up what I meant.

"I don't know, yet," she declared, determination in her voice. "But I'm going to find out."

She pulled up the first of the shell corporations, and started digging.

It took days. She buried herself in the task, and I helped where I could and kept her fed and hydrated. We made certain never to miss our morning runs or any of our other "us time". Neither of us was willing to risk what we had. I thawed some frozen salmon steaks and made the lohikeitto I'd promised her, and she agreed that it was wonderful and fully deserving of a top-eight place.

I got a call mid-morning on Wednesday. It was Judson.

"'Allo, guv."

"G'day, squire. What's up?"

"Nothing, in a manner of speaking."

"Oh?"

"I poked around a little and sniffed the ground. I'm unable to find anything related to Harris Magnusson that you don't probably already know."

"Including the dark side of the street sources? The secret-squirrel world?"

"Any assumptions you make about where I looked are your problem, not mine." That was as close as Judson could legally come to saying yes, and I was surprised he'd say it that clearly. I was expecting his usual flat no-comment.

"I hope that's good news."

"Thanks. I... think it is. I appreciate that. That lines up with what we know so far."

"Turned up anything interesting on your end?"

I told him about the money-laundering scheme we'd uncovered, and the discovery of what had apparently triggered the attacks.

"Clever. I'd be... interested to hear what else you're able to develop from that. And, no promises, but depending on what you uncover, it's possible that an agency might take official interest."

He paused.

"Are you sure you don't want to just turn what you have over to Treasury, now?"

I thought about that.

"Not yet. We don't have nearly enough yet. We have a broad pattern of suspicious behavior, but no provable connection from it to anything actually illegal, and no smoking gun. But tell you what. Let me send you a backup copy of all the key data. Just in case. Now that I've explained how the scheme *works*, you'll know what you're looking at. If, uh, anything happens to us."

"Including the shell corporations?"

"Yeah. We're still working on tracing them. Sharon's the one who figured it all out, by the way."

"Smart girl. Okay, I'll see if I can cross-reference any of that to anything. With the usual caveats."

"Thanks."

"Later, guv."

I exported all of the *interesting* properties and contracts, together with the list of first-tier shell corporations on both the lessee and lessor sides, packaged it up into an archive file, and sent it off. I received acknowledgment a few minutes later.

Eventually, Sharon had a group of four top-level shell corporations on the lessor side, and a full list of all the lessees. It took until Thursday afternoon. We hadn't figured out yet where the money was coming from on the input side. From the top level, it appeared *highly likely* the output was being funneled into offshore banks—but we didn't have any proof of that, either. And we didn't know yet where it went after that. We hadn't figured out yet whether there were similar hidden connections between the lessees. And we still didn't have a motive.

So now we had two more problems to solve. Neither of them was going to be easy. But at least now, we were on the trail.

"The only way we're going to be able to figure out where that money is going," I told Sharon as we sat in the computer room downstairs, "is to trace it through the banks. And I don't see how we're going to do that without a US government subpoena. They're certainly not going to just *tell* us."

Sharon looked at me levelly.

"Can you hack into the banks?" she asked.

I blinked. Hard.

"I told you," I protested, "I'm not a hacker. I don't know what I'm doing in that arena. I know just enough to know I'm a babe in the woods."

"But Uncle Fester walked you through hacking DFW. Right?"

"That was a lightly-secured airport security system that I really only needed one known vulnerability to get into. This is a BANK we're talking about. Maybe multiple banks. They'll be locked up like Fort Knox. If I made a mistake at DFW I could probably just try again. Odds are they wouldn't even notice. One mistake trying to crack into banks, and we're blown. The FBI has no sense of humor about bank cracking at all. We need another way."

We exchanged looks.

"Okay," Sharon agreed. "Let's consider that a last resort."

═══════════

We moved up to the living room, side-by-side on the couch, and put on a little music to listen to, to help us relax. She'd picked out some Vivaldi. It was a good choice. It was light and pleasant, but not dramatic enough to break our train of thought as we talked.

"What your friend Judson said," Sharon asked, "about going to the Treasury Department with what we have."

I nodded acknowledgment.

"...*Should* we?" she asked.

I thought about it.

"I don't see that we can, really. Not yet. We don't have *enough*. It's suggestive, but not damning. Yes, we've got a large-scale pattern of very strange behavior that looks like money laundering. But... we can't *prove* it is. I'm not aware of any laws it actually breaks. That's the whole *point* of money laundering, isn't it? To move money around in *ostensibly legal* ways that hide its origin, potentially making it *look* legal even if it originally wasn't?"

She pursed her lips.

"You have a point. But what about the... attacks?"

I winced.

"You know how much I want to nail these bastards to the wall for

176

that. They almost took you away from me before we even met."

She nodded.

"But we have only *circumstantial* evidence that there's a connection," I went on. "Nothing provable. Ultimately, I don't think we can take any of this to the Treasury, or any other agency of the government, until and unless we have tangible proof that a serious crime has been committed. And so far, while we know damned well that there *were* crimes—a murder, an attempted murder, and an arson fire— we can't provably tie them to this scheme."

She nodded reluctantly.

"You're right." She sighed. "In fact, on reflection, that's the same thing I'd be telling *you* if you brought it to me as-is. We have no solid *proof*, and nothing we know so far about the multi-leasing scheme is actually criminal. *Weird*, maybe, but not criminal." She pounded a fist on the desk in frustration. "Unless, say, it was done as some kind of tax evasion scheme... which we *also* can't prove. Because we don't have the authority to access their tax records. And I don't doubt that if it were that, then they'd be keeping two different sets of books anyway."

"Are you speculating that there *is* tax evasion?" I asked.

She thought for a moment.

"Possibly," she replied. "But if there was, we still couldn't prove it without subpoenas and search warrants. So it's a useless speculation at this point."

"And there's another reason, separate from legalities," I said.

She raised an eyebrow.

"The B... uh, Uncle Fester strongly implied that *we* have to solve this, ourselves. I don't know *why* that's so important. But apparently it is. And I don't know how much outside help we're allowed to pull in. So I want to save it until we really need it."

"I just hope it tells us *why* some day," she replied fervently. I agreed wholeheartedly. This was the seventeenth day since the Box had sent me to intercept Sharon's would-be killer, and we still had only a fragment of a picture of what was going on.

"I think we need to tackle the sources first," I said. "Follow the money. Track it back to where it's coming *from*. If they're laundering it in the first place, odds are there's at least *something* sketchy in the source."

Sharon nodded agreement.

"Either the source, or the destination," she agreed. "Or there's no reason to do it at all. The question is how we trace them."

I nodded and kept thinking.

"We probably don't have to be able to source *all* of them," she mused after a little. "Just enough to establish a pattern."

"That at least reduces the scope of the problem," I agreed, pondering. "Tax records would tie the shell corporations to banking accounts..."

"...If tax records were public," Sharon finished for me. I nodded.

"Yeah, exactly. We already agreed that's a bust."

I thought about the problem a bit more, thinking about different angles on it.

"A shell corporation still has to have a board, officers, right?" I asked. "Can we find out who those are?"

"They do, but the information doesn't *have* to be public if it's a Delaware corporation. And all of these are. Two thirds of the corporations in the US are Delaware corporations."

"Well, damn."

"There has to be a registered agent, but, well, that doesn't really help us at all."

"Why not?"

"Because they can be third parties and will be under no obligation to answer any questions we can ask them."

"Point. Also, it'd let the cat out of the bag. They'd know we were onto them."

"It gets worse. A Delaware corporation really only needs to have one officer, one board member, and one shareholder. And they can all be the same person."

"So what you're telling me is, all of these shell corporations *could* be one-man shows thrown up by, say, Oprah Winfrey, and we'd never know."

She considered that.

"That would be pretty *weird*," she said, "but, yes, perfectly possible." A pause. "I think we can safely rule out Oprah Winfrey though."

"Heh, yeah," I agreed. "Same here. And probably John Oliver—I *think*; and…"

She poked me. Hard. I broke off, chuckling.

"Anyway, we can look," I continued. "The worst case is we don't find anything there."

So with no other ideas, we started digging into the shell corporations and their Boards. It was the best shot we had. Without access to their banks or financial records, we couldn't tell where the money was coming from. But perhaps something about the people who controlled the corporations would give us some clue.

<hr>

Strangely, the board appointments *were* public. All of them.

"Now why do you suppose they did that?" I wondered. "When they could so easily have hidden the information?"

"Hiding in plain sight," Sharon suggested. "Nothing to see here, nothing to hide, pay no attention to the man behind the curtain. Don't be the nail that's sticking up."

I realized immediately she was probably right. That was going to make this a lot easier, but it would still be a lot of work.

We looked up the corporations one at a time, finding their public filings, and we built a list—or rather, a set of tables—of all the board members and corporations, working side by side in the computer room, passing the keyboard back and forth. She identified the board members, and I inserted the data into the tables. We tracked them by number in alphabetic order, instead of trying to memorize the list of names.

"You noticing anything about these?" I asked, after we'd gotten the first eight boards recorded.

"Yeah," Sharon answered. "All five-man boards."

I nodded. There was nothing wrong with a five-seat board. Odd numbers were good for things like this, they prevented deadlocks. And few small corporations really needed more than five on their board, unless there was a lot of oversight on board. And if our suspicions were correct, oversight was the *last* thing these shell corporations would want.

But for eight random corporations in a row to have exactly five board members was still stretching coincidence.

Of course, these *weren't* random corporations, were they?

We kept going. The pattern continued... and continued. Every single one of the lessee shell corporations had a five-seat board. And there was a lot of overlap. We eventually ended up with a list of about sixty names.

"Kind of a suspiciously low number, don't you think?" Sharon mused.

"Only kind of?" I asked, with a grin. She mirrored it. Everything we were finding kept displaying the same pattern: Very suspiciously NON-random data patterns that you would never notice if you happened to just randomly glance at one or two of the set. Things you would only notice if you already knew the right set of things to look at, and looked at that set as a whole, in isolation, and already suspected something was off.

"Hang on a minute," I said. "Let me crunch some numbers here. Sixty is too many people to be directly involved in this level of a plot. I'll bet most of these board members are chumps. Patsies."

I collated the data and did a few quick calculations—well, okay, actually I made my database do most of them; it only took a few minutes to frame the queries—and then we looked over my results.

"Hmm," I mused, as we read through the data. "There's about five and a half million order-independent ways of picking five out of sixty. So it's no surprise that no two of these boards are the same. With a total of two hundred board seats and sixty individuals, you would expect that on average, each one would sit on just over three boards... if they were chosen randomly."

"And...?" Sharon asked.

"As I doubt you're surprised, that's not what's happening... well, okay, it *is*, except that they're really heavily skewed *off* the average. The standard deviation stinks to high heaven. There's a massive hole in the middle of the distribution. It's closer to a power law than to a bell curve."

I pointed at a sorted version of the list.

"These fifty-five people sit on an average of a fraction less than three boards each. They account for a hundred and sixty of the two hundred board seats. In round numbers. But they're not the interesting ones."

I pointed to the last five in the list.

"The interesting ones are *these* five. They all sit on either eight or nine boards each, three times as many as the other fifty-five, and no two of them are ever on the same board. Meaning..." I left it to her to finish.

"...That between the five of them, they hold seats on every board," she completed. "What'll you bet me they hold a couple of proxies on each, as well?"

"No bet," I declined. "The rest of each board are sock puppets. They're probably paid a stipend to do little more than read a—probably very deceptive—annual report. Generous enough to discourage them from asking too many questions, but not enough to *raise* questions. Probably attend one or two dog-and-pony-show board meetings a year, staged for their benefit, where non-existent business is lied about.

"These five are the movers. They control the shell corps. Count on it.

"Now, how and where do they coordinate, and who do they report to..."

Sharon studied the table.

"We need to know more about them," she said.

"We do," I agreed. "We need to know where these five go and who they talk to. Phone records. Credit card usage. I'll bet we can find a lot of those in existing breaches. The security on that kind of data is often lousy, phone records especially. Not like banks. Some of these exploits go unpatched for *years*."

"And... this is where we call on Uncle Fester?"

"You betcha," I nodded.

We went next door.

"Fester!" I said.

GOMEZ!, the Box replied.

We cracked up.

"Fester," I said again, when we stopped laughing, "we need as much information as you can get—phone activity, credit cards, anything else you can find—about the activities of the top five people on the list of directors that we built." I'd learned by now that all I needed to do was tell the Box by reference what data I wanted it to look at, and it would pull it out on its own. I won't pretend it wasn't an unsettling capability in some ways, but, well... it saved me some work, and the Box had never to my knowledge abused its ability. "There's good odds a lot of it can be found in pre-existing breaches, but any means that's not traceable back to us is good. I could do it myself, but it'll take a long time. I suspect you can do it a lot faster.

"Can you help with that?"

THE TASK IS FEASIBLE, the Box confirmed. SOME EXPENSE MAY BE INCURRED. WHAT YOU CALL THE DARK WEB CONTAINS MANY SUCH DATASETS AVAILABLE FOR SALE. MANY INCLUDE CREDENTIALS. MOST, IF NOT ALL, OF THEM CAN BE PRESUMED TO HAVE BEEN ILLEGALLY OBTAINED. WILL THAT BE A PROBLEM?

"As long as we're good for the money," I said. "I won't say I'm overjoyed about using illegal sources, but we don't have a lot of options open to us."

INITIATING SEARCH. DATA WILL BE PROVIDED ONCE OBTAINED.

There was nothing further we could do until we got that. And that meant we had some time to ourselves.

We spent it well. With a considerably reduced need to avoid being sighted by police, we judged it safe to return to the outlets for a few things Sharon had missed the first time around. This time, we weren't *play-acting* at being a couple. Sharon bought a few more of the silky shirts she liked, and some nightwear that she wouldn't let me see in the store. I picked up a thing or two for the kitchen, and I bought a kimono-style robe in black with red embroidered dragons that Sharon insisted on. We got home in time to put the new purchases in the wash. Then we dressed up and went out to dinner at one of my favorite semi-secret restaurants.

We went north, away from the city, not south towards it. MacNamara's was a family-run restaurant with a top-class chef who did a magnificent whiskey chicken and a great rack of lamb. It was far enough out of town that I figured the chances of being spotted by anyone we didn't want seeing us were very low.

We had a quiet, casual, relaxed dinner that we didn't have to cook for ourselves, and for once we tried to pretend that everything was normal. And it even mostly worked.

When we came home, we opened a bottle of wine and curled up on the couch in front of the mostly-restored director's cut of *The Abyss*, me in the new black dragon robe, while Sharon surprised me with a satiny iridescent-green nightgown. She cuddled in my lap and we just focused on each other, and left the outside world to its own devices.

It was a really *nice* evening.

———

The Box didn't have anything for us yet the next day, by the time we'd done our morning run and made and cleaned up breakfast. So Sharon asked if we could go out to the range again. This time we left the .22 in the cabinet, and took the Hi-Power and the Smith & Wesson 657, at her request, so that she could get some hands-on experience with a revolver.

———

"Hi, Ciáran," Lee said when we walked in to sign up. Then he turned casually to Sharon. "Any luck recovering your ID, young lady?"

I looked around. I could hear at least one lane was in use, but there was only one customer out in front, and he was two counters over looking at the consignment case.

"Hand me your ID a moment?" I asked Sharon quietly. She passed her driving license over, with a questioning look.

"Look at this, but don't say anything," I told Lee. Then I passed it over, face down.

He took the license and glanced at it, then looked at Sharon. Then he looked at the license again, hard, then back at Sharon. Then he looked at me. Without moving his head, his eyes flicked up to the flatscreen TV mounted high on the side wall, and back at me. I nodded slightly.

He turned the license face down, and looked back at Sharon again.

"I have you down as Ciáran's guest until further notice," he said, discreetly handing her license back to her. Sharon smiled gratefully. "Just let me know when you have your own ID back. Must be a proper pain in the ass."

"Oh, you don't know the *half* of it," Sharon replied fervently. Lee just nodded.

"Not my business," he said. "Ciáran's vouched for you. That's all I need to know."

There were two other lanes in use on the range this time, one shooter with a Glock 20, the other shooting rapid-fire with a heavily customized 1911 racegun. I thought it was a Strayer-Tripp, but I wasn't certain. It wasn't important enough to ask.

We started out with the Hi-Power to let her get some practice in. I pushed the target out from seven yards to ten this time. Her group size opened up a little at first, which was no surprise, but started tightening up again as she practiced. The additional distance didn't give her any trouble to speak of. I loaded magazines for her while she shot, and she did fine.

After putting eight magazines through the Hi-Power, she was starting to tire, so we put it away and sat down for a break. I took the opportunity to set expectations for the big Smith & Wesson and show her how speedloaders worked.

"The ammunition is a lot bigger," she said, comparing the two rounds I'd handed her, one nine-millimeter and one .41 Magnum.

"It is," I agreed, "and it's got a lot more power. This was originally designed as a dual-purpose round for police and hunting, but Remington loaded the police version too hot—more power than originally planned—and it never caught on for law enforcement as a result. Police departments considered the hotter load too difficult to control.

"So what does that tell you?"

Sharon thought for a moment.

"I should be prepared for it to kick, and not under-estimate it."

"Yup," I agreed. "Expect it to kick about twice to three times as much as the Browning. Maybe more. You good to give it a try?"

"This isn't going to be like one of those humiliating YouTube 'girls fail' videos, is it?"

"Sharon," I assured her, rolling my eyes, "I swear, I will *never ever* pull that kind of *stupid juvenile shit* on you. If I thought this was going to be too much for you to handle, I'd advise you—firmly—against it."

"Oh, I never for a moment thought you *would*, silly," she replied, with a smile. "I'm just a little uncertain what to expect."

"You don't need to be afraid of it," I reassured her. "It's not a rhino-roller. Just treat it with proper caution and respect, keep a firm grip on it, and you'll be fine."

She stepped back up to the firing station and I handed her a speedloader. She loaded just like I'd showed her, closed the cylinder, and took a firing position.

"Lean into it just a little more," I advised, and she did.

"Okay. Now try it single-action to start with."

She cocked the hammer, took careful aim, and squeezed the trigger. The big revolver **BOOM**ed and jumped in her hands.

"...Wow," she said after a moment. "Yeah, that's... pretty emphatic, isn't it?"

Then with only a moment's pause, she adjusted her grip, brought it back on target, and cocked the hammer again. This time she was expecting the kick, and handled it better. She fired all six, then cleared it, set it down, and shook out her hands. I was gratified to see that while her group was a bit looser than she'd been shooting with the Browning, all six were well in the black.

"So how do you feel about it?" I asked.

"I can *manage* it," she said slowly. "But it's not comfortable. Especially when I'm already a little tired. I think it's too much for me to really be comfortable with. It jumps so much it takes me longer to bring it back on target."

"That sounds like good judgment at work, to me," I replied. "Ready to pack up and go home?"

"Sure," she agreed. "Thanks for letting me try it."

So we packed up and left.

"Is the other revolver about the same," she asked as we drove home, "or harder?"

"Definitely harder," I answered. "It's lighter, substantially more powerful *again*, and working with the single-action grip shape takes a little getting used to. My preferred load for .44 throws a bullet only ten percent heavier than my .41 load for the Model 657 does, but throws it a good two hundred and fifty feet per second faster, maybe three hundred. Its trajectory is nearly as flat as some rifles out to a hundred yards or so, but the recoil is not trivial.

"Honestly, I would probably advise you not to try it right now. If the Model 657 is uncomfortable for you, then the Super Blackhawk will *hurt*. I don't want to teach you to flinch."

"I'm good with taking that advice for now," she agreed.

When we got home, we went downstairs and cleaned the guns, then we went upstairs to the shower and cleaned *us*, washing off the powder smoke. We took some extra time in the shower for ourselves, then put clean clothes on and made a late lunch. We tried to relax and be patient, but it can be really hard to relax when you're waiting for a lead on why someone tried to murder you—or the woman whom you've fallen deeply in love with. There were a huge number of existing breaches out there, some of them gigantic, but finding the people we were interested in was a needle in a haystack.

Late that afternoon, the Box turned up the first hit. Account credentials from a past breach at T-Mobile gave us access to the mobile phone records of two of our five Persons of Interest, the two directors we had designated C and E. (We'd labeled them A through E for convenience.) We were able to pull out eight to nine months of phone records for both. I spent the rest of the afternoon and evening building data structures to hold the records so that we could search them, manipulate them and cross-correlate them.

Sharon cooked supper while I was working, boiled baby potatoes and grilled pork chops with an onion white wine sauce she'd built around a bottle of Liebfraumilch out of our stores, and steamed green beans on the side. It was excellent. I considered my good fortune again as we ate.

I loaded the phone records into the tables when I was satisfied the database design was correct, but it was too late by then to do anything of substance with it. So we sat in the living room and finished up the bottle of Liebfraumilch between us, and then went to bed early and cuddled until we fell asleep.

The next morning the Box had turned up a year of credit card records for a Mastercard belonging to the director we'd designated POI B, a Jack Higgins, thanks to information from a department store breach. So after our run and breakfast, I spent the morning building tables for credit card data, and loaded that in. We skimmed it quickly, but nothing really stood out yet in isolation.

After lunch, we went through the phone records from directors C and E. Again, nothing jumped out at us, yet. But we had measurable progress, even if we didn't have any further solid results yet.

I decided there wasn't much point in examining partial data sets; it probably wasn't going to tell us anything useful, and it might lead us to overlook relationships in the full data set because "We already looked at that." So we put any further analysis on the back burner until the Box told us the search I'd asked it to perform was complete.

In the meantime, I ordered in a second monitor, and pulled out a spare keyboard and mouse. It didn't take me terribly long to set things up so that Sharon and I could both log in at once and work independently side-by-side, and it kept me busy and occupied for a day or so. I also hung a cheap flat-screen TV on the office wall closest to the Box. As I'd hoped, it was just within range for the Box to display messages on. That made things a little more convenient for us to work.

In the end, the Box took five days before it declared search completion. It seemed like a pretty good time saving. I was pretty sure it would have taken me at least weeks, if not months.

We put the downtime to good use. Sharon had asked me once if I could teach her anything about martial arts and unarmed combat, so I introduced her to my dojo and started her on some basic stretching and strengthening exercises. We went on from there to some simple defensive stuff, like blocks and breaking naïve control holds.

It went pretty well. We had enough trust between us that she knew I wasn't going to intentionally hurt her, and that let her focus on the things she was trying to learn instead of worrying about not getting hurt.

"How many, uh, styles do you know?" she asked, during one of our breaks.

"*Know?*" I hesitated for a moment. "I wouldn't say I *know* any. I've *studied* about half a dozen. Korean tang-soo-do, Okinawan Gojo-ryu, Shaolin bok-fu, Israeli krav maga, a couple of others."

"Why so many?" she inquired curiously.

"Curiosity. And synthesis. I keep trying different styles depending what I can find to study in different places, and then I end up taking what works for me from each one. The same things that work for me won't necessarily work for you. We should probably be focusing more on agility styles and less on power styles, for you. Gojo-ryu and bok-fu are both good on that front. We'll try to figure it out as we go along."

"Can you break boards?"

I shrugged.

"I can, but don't be impressed by that. It's not actually as hard as some people make it sound. It's more an exercise for learning the right kind of mental and physical focus than it is any kind of feat of power or skill.   And the boards are specially prepared.   They're *supposed* to break."

"What about bricks?"

"Dunno." I shrugged again. "Never been attacked by a brick."

She laughed.

When the Box declared itself done, we ended up with phone records for all of the five we were interested in, going back anywhere from five months to a year and a half, and at least one set of credit card records for each, up to three different cards for one of them, some going back as much as two years.

I set up a batch data load into the database, and then we started looking for patterns in the data.

Of course, the vast majority of it was completely uninteresting and didn't correlate to anything useful. Once we had all the phone records, however, it didn't take long at all to confirm that all five were in regular phone communication with each other. We'd expected that, so it didn't really tell us anything new, just verified what we already suspected.

What was more interesting was that two of our top five shared another contact whom they regularly communicated with, almost as often as they talked to the other top-fives. It was an unlisted Los Angeles mobile number. We couldn't get more than that from it, though. Probably a burner phone. We designated this unknown person Contact X.

But where we really hit pay dirt was the credit card numbers.

We filtered out all the really uninteresting stuff first. Utility bills, store purchases, scheduled payments. And then we looked at what was left. And a pattern emerged.

Either director B or E would talk to X. Then, the next day, they would talk to each of the other four A-list directors. And then, over the next day or two, all five would book return flights, on the same day about a week later, to Albuquerque, New Mexico. B and E *also* took regular trips, almost always *also* on the same day as each other, to Cheyenne, Wyoming, but we couldn't see what triggered those trips, and they didn't seem to correlate well to the Albuquerque meetings.

"Almost as though there's two separate sets of overseers," I mused.

"This," Sharon declared flatly, "looks very, very fishy." And I couldn't disagree.

"We have a new problem now," I said. "We have a trail leading two different places. Albuquerque, and Cheyenne. But we need to know what *happens* there.

"I think it's a foregone conclusion they're traveling for in-person meetings, that much seems clear."

Sharon nodded.

"But who are they meeting with?" she asked. "And what about? And who is Contact X?"

"Yeah," I agreed. "We need answers to those questions. And I only have one idea about how to get the answers."

She looked at me uneasily.

"You mean...?"

"Yeah," I nodded. "I think somebody's going to have to follow them and see where they go."

"Somebody? You?"

"I don't know," I replied. "I have no experience at this. Covert infiltration? Sure, with some help from the Box. But the Box can't make me an overnight expert in that kind of surveillance fieldcraft."

We both thought about it for a few minutes. Sharon spoke first.

"Your friend at the... Smithsonian. Could he help?"

"Judson? I don't know," I replied slowly. "I'd been thinking about that myself. I don't know whether he'd be *allowed* to. But I don't have a better idea of who to ask for advice on our next steps."

"How much would we have to tell him?"

"He already knows about the money laundering scheme," I mused. "And we already sent him the list of properties and the shell corporations. It wouldn't be a bad idea to update him with what we've figured out about the directors, even if only as a backup."

"How about we start with that?" she suggested. "Just as... insurance?"

"Yeah," I agreed. "Let's do that."

So I built an archive of all of the salient points of our new findings, encrypted it, and mailed it off to Judson. Then I called him to explain what I'd just sent him.

It rang through to voice mail.

"Judson," I said, "Ciáran here. Just sent you an update package. Call me back when you can and I'll explain the contents. Hoping for advice on following some trails on foot."

"Well, I left him a message," I told Sharon. "But I think we'd better prepare as best we can for me to go myself, in case he doesn't get back to us or can't help. I doubt I need to explain why it'd have to be me if it comes down to the two of us."

Sharon nodded.

"Even if I had any idea how to go about it," she said, "with no ID I dare use, I can't fly."

"And I wouldn't risk you on something like that anyway," I told her. "But I'd prefer not to leave you alone here unprotected either."

Then an idea went off in my head like a cartoon flash-bulb.

"But maybe there's another way," I mused aloud. "Let's look through that credit card data again."

We pulled up the data and went fishing. I was looking for something specific, and it wasn't very long before I found it.

"So look," I said. "Here's the last three times Director D flew to Albuquerque. He likes United, and he flies business class. Notice anything else?"

Sharon looked at the records I'd pulled up.

"...He always rents a car," she said. "So we need to be ready to follow a car."

"That's exactly the point," I declared with a grin. "No, we *don't* have to follow the car he rents. Hertz will *tell us* where he goes. Ever heard of LoJack?"

She thought for a moment.

"Isn't that an anti-theft device?"

"Originally, yes. But it's also a vehicle *location* device. Which makes it a vehicle *tracking* device. Every major car rental company knows exactly where every last one of their cars is at any given moment —or has the ability to know. All they have to do is ask the LoJack system."

"...And if *they* know, than *we* can find out," Sharon finished. "If we can get into Hertz's systems."

"Exactly," I agreed. "We need to watch for the next meeting to happen, then watch for him to pick up his rental, and watch to see where it goes. And then we know where the meetings happen. And if we're really lucky, it's a rented conference room or something—and then we find out who rented it."

"And then we're one step further along the trail," she replied. "And if we can monitor B's and E's phone activity, we'll know when the next meeting is coming up."

I nodded.

"Pretty lady, I believe we have a plan." Her grin answered mine.

I went next door to talk to the Box.

"Fester, do the breaches you found for the telephone companies give you *continuing* access to the phone records of our Persons of Interest?"

UNTIL THEY FIX THE VULNERABILITIES OR REVOKE THE CREDENTIALS, YES.

"And you are aware of the tags we have assigned as Directors A through E and Contact X?"

YES.

"Can you monitor those phone records on at least a once-daily basis? We need to know whenever any of those six contacts call each other."

THAT IS FEASIBLE. PROBABILITY OF DETECTION IS LOW.

"Please do it. Inform us whenever you find anything."

MONITORING INITIATED.

"I'm guessing you don't have *ongoing* access to the credit card information? Only existing breaches?"

CORRECT, AS A RULE. NOT WITHOUT ATTEMPTING TO BREACH THE ISSUING BANKS.

"Which we want to avoid, too much chance of being detected ourselves."

I thought for a moment.

"What's the security like on the airline reservation systems and car rental services?"

YOU WOULD PROBABLY CLASSIFY IT AS POOR. WEAKER THAN THE SYSTEMS AT DALLAS-FORT WORTH AIRPORT WHICH YOU ALREADY ENTERED.

"Can you monitor the airlines and car rental services that our targets have used in the past when traveling to Albuquerque or Cheyenne, and alert us when a flight is booked or a car reserved using any of those known cards?"

YES. THAT IS RELATIVELY TRIVIAL.

"Do it, please. Begin monitoring flights and car rentals as soon as there is phone activity."

STANDING BY.

"Thank you, Fester."

9: Every Move You Make…

There wasn't much we could do until we got a hit on the activity monitoring. We did our best to decompress and relax, watched some movies, spent time working out in the dojo and working on her self-defense skills, even went out to the range a couple of times. We made a point of Sharon shooting the Laugo enough to be familiar with it as well as with the Browning, in case she ever had to pick it up while I was incapacitated. She applied herself quite determinedly to improving her skills, and was getting to be pretty proficient. I guess a near-death experience can motivate a person that way. As the saying goes, there are no atheists in foxholes. I mean, the saying's not *literally true*, but the *principle* is sound.

We also did some more cooking together. Nothing super fancy, yet, but we worked together on dinners, figuring out meal plans that could be split into two parts, with one of us working on each without getting in each other's way. It was a really nice feeling.

The second day, we got a call from Jim Bell.

"Sharon, Ciáran," he said. "Detective Taylor just called me. He'd like you to take a look at some mugshots. Are you free?"

"Today?" I asked. "Sure, we're not busy. Same place?"

"If you're okay with that. Two hours?"

"We'll be there."

"Ms. Kielic, Mr. mac Cool," Taylor greeted us. "Forensics was able to pull up some possible matches from, uh," he glanced at Sharon, "tissue samples recovered from the crime scene. I have two mugshots for the two most likely matches for you to look at, if you wouldn't mind. And two long shots."

"Sure," I nodded. "Let's see them."

He took out a short stack of photos, shuffled them in his hands, then handed me the first photo. I looked at it, but... no. This guy was older, thinner-faced, balding a little. Not our man. I shook my head.

"Sorry," I shook my head, "not this one. Too old, too thin. Not just a fat issue. Facial bone structure is wrong. Couldn't be him, even disguised."

Taylor nodded thoughtfully for a moment and handed me the second mugshot.

"How about this one?"

I took one look and knew the face instantly.

"That's him. I last saw him over my front sight."

"You sure?"

"Positive."

"Sure you don't want to take a look at the other two as well?"

I thought about the question.

"I'll look at them if you want me to, for peace of mind, but I'm certain. I got a fairly good look at him. This is him."

"Ms. Kielic. Did you get a look at his face?"

"No," Sharon said. "I... I'm sorry, I didn't want to look closely. There was blood everywhere." She shuddered at the memory.

"Fair enough," Taylor said. He took the photo back, and handed me the other two. I looked at them.

"No. Neither of these." I shook my head again. "This one's too old, too heavy-set. And this one... he might look like our man in ten years. But not today."

Taylor nodded and took them back, then picked up the one I'd matched again.

"Well, well," he mused. "So this is—was—Nicolas Carravini. Age forty-one. Did ten years for armed robbery, three for assault and battery, known associate of the de Garofolo crime family. Nasty piece of work. Heavily tied up with oil money, much of it dirty. Last released two and a half years ago. And evidently went right back to his old ways.

"Took the wrong job this time, didn't you, Nicolas?" There was a note of satisfaction in his voice. I thought I probably understood.

Taylor looked at Sharon. I sensed the question coming, and reached for her hand. But she got her own question in first.

"Does this get you closer to finding out who killed Philip?" she asked intently.

Taylor nodded slowly.

"I believe it does," he agreed. "At the least, it gives us a better idea where to focus our investigations. And the Escalade fits into that picture."

"*Good,*" Sharon declared.

"I was about to ask, Ms. Kielic," he continued, "do you have any idea why oil interests might want you dead?"

Sharon thought for a moment.

"Not *yet*, Detective," she answered. "But... it raises interesting questions."

Taylor nodded.

"Okay. Well, send me a message via Mr. Bell if you figure anything out," he said. "I think we're done here for today. Thanks for coming." He offered a hand, and I took it.

"Any time, Detective," I agreed. And then we all left.

We had a new clue. A small one, perhaps, and we weren't sure yet how it connected to anything else, but it was a clue.

<hr>

We got three more days off before we got an alert. Then, the next Monday, Contact X called Director B. There would be a Albuquerque meeting coming up some time in the next five to seven days. When the directors started booking their flights, we'd know which day the meeting was. I was guessing probably Thursday or Friday. We'd been at this nearly a month already. Tomorrow would be the fourth Tuesday since I'd rescued Sharon.

It turned out my hunch was right. When the directors started booking their flights, they booked them for Friday. All same-day return flights. Nobody books a same-day-return flight to New Mexico on a Friday for anything but business.

"Fester," I told the Box, "on Thursday night, I want a check on Hertz to see whether a car has been reserved on Friday in Albuquerque using Director D's card, or any of the cards belonging to the other five key directors. And then on Friday I'll be needing access to Hertz's rental vehicle tracking data."

Understood, replied the Box.

"Should we check other rental agencies as well?" Sharon asked from behind me.

I considered that.

"Probably not," I said after a few moments. "Unless we don't get any hits at all from Hertz. But I'm hoping we'll have more than one Hertz car to track already. Tracking multiple Hertz rentals instead of one should be straightforward. Multiple rentals from multiple agencies would add complexity, and I don't think it'll tell us enough additional information to be worth the trouble."

She nodded.

"But we're hoping for two, I presume?"

"Or more, yeah. But I'll be happy if we can get tracking on two. Two or more should pretty much rule out a decoy."

Sharon frowned.

"Why would they set up a decoy? Unless you think they might have an idea someone is onto them?"

"I don't think they have any idea. But it never hurts to be cautious."

"True."

═══════════════

We kept ourselves occupied as best we could for the next couple of days. Early Thursday evening, just after we finished dinner, the Box advised us that no less than three of the target directors had booked cars with Hertz using cards known to us. We went downstairs to the Box's room.

"I want a quick live test, Fester. Please access the Hertz vehicle tracking data, pick a random currently-rented vehicle, and tell me its current location."

CHECKING, came the reply. PLEASE WAIT.

There was a brief pause.

VEHICLE SELECTED. VEHICLE IS A NISSAN ROGUE SUV, COLOR RED. VEHICLE WAS RENTED TWO DAYS AGO, AND IS CURRENTLY LOCATED IN THE MAIN PARKING LOT AT THE GEORGIA O'KEEFE MUSEUM.

I looked at Sharon, and she looked back at me. We nodded.

"We're all set," I said. "What time do the first and last flights land?"

"Okay. Let's be ready to start tracking by ten forty-five Albuquerque time tomorrow. That's twelve forty-five here."

UNDERSTOOD.

We got lunch early on Friday to be sure we had plenty of time, then went downstairs to the computer room. We were in the tracking systems and watching before the first plane landed.

"What's the status, Fester?"

SOUTHWEST FLIGHT WN3097 FROM LOS ANGELES, A BOEING 737-700, IS TWO MINUTES AHEAD OF SCHEDULE. IT SHOULD LAND AT 10:58 LOCAL TIME.

"Do we have a car reservation associated with this flight?"

NO.

"Skip it. What's the first one with a car associated?"

UNITED AIRLINES 1599 FROM WASHINGTON DULLES, A 737 MAX8, SCHEDULED 11:25 LOCAL TIME.

"Let us know when it's on the ground. Figure five minutes taxiing, five minutes coupling up, fifteen minutes to get through arrivals... should be picking up his car sometime between eleven fifty and noon."

"When's the next arrival after that with an associated rental?"

UNITED AIRLINES 1888 FROM CHICAGO, AN AIRBUS A319, SCHEDULED AT 11:41.

"Okay, plenty of time between those."

We sat and waited. At 13:28 our time, the Box informed us UA 1599 was on the ground and taxiing. UA 1888 was right on time at 13:41.

At 13:57, our first target was assigned his car.

THE VEHICLE IS A BMW 530, the Box told us. It left the airport at 14:03, our time. We both watched on the map.

"Target two is probably through arrivals by now," I speculated. "Any activity on that reservation?"

NOT YET.

We waited. At fourteen twelve, the second rental was checked out.

At fourteen twenty, the second vehicle left the rental garage and headed into Albuquerque.

"When is the third flight with a reservation coming in?" I asked.

"Not much likely to happen for the next hour or so, then. Let's see where the first two go."

A little while later, car one, the BMW, stopped on the nine hundred block of Rio Grande Boulevard Northwest.

"Let's see, what's there," Sharon mused, zooming in on the map.

"...Hmm. What's this... D.H. Lescombe's Winery and Bistro. Bet he's stopped for lunch."

"Sounds like a reasonable assumption to me," I agreed. "Car Two is still on the move."

Car Two, the Audi, ended up stopping at the Sandia Resort and Casino.

"Something tells me that's not just a lunch stop," I said. "A casino would be a good deniable cover story."

Sharon nodded agreement.

"Hold on a moment," she told me. "Let me check..."

She pulled up information on the Sandia and clicked quickly through pages.

"Aha! I thought so!"

I raised a questioning eyebrow.

"The Sandia has eight bookable meeting rooms. Meeting place and deniability in one handy package."

I nodded.

"Is there an availability calendar posted for those?"

"There should be." She clicked on a little further. "Three rooms are unavailable this evening, one starting at seven PM for three hours, the other two at eight PM, also for three hours. And more interesting, one of the smaller rooms is booked for two hours starting at two thirty PM local time."

"Bet you that's our meeting," I nodded. "Let's see what happens when tracking target three lands."

We waited.

Shortly after fifteen hundred our time, thirteen hundred in Albuquerque, car one started moving again.

"Activity on Car One," I pointed out. "Guess he finished his lunch. Let's see where he goes."

The BMW took a meandering route through Albuquerque for some time, with no evident destination. It seemed he was just killing time.

ALASKA AIRLINES FLIGHT AS650 FROM SEATTLE HAS LANDED THREE MINUTES EARLY, the Box reported. IT IS TAXIING TO THE GATE.

With any luck," I said, "we should have our third car ID'd in about twenty minutes."

It was actually closer to twenty-five before another location marker popped up at the airport.

CAR THREE HAS BEEN ASSIGNED. IT IS A MERCEDES GL450.

"And that's three," I declared. "Let's see where he goes."

Car three left the airport about ten minutes later, about thirteen fifty-five local time, while car one continued to drive around semi-randomly. Car three headed generally towards the Sandia. It was about half-way there when the BMW stopped meandering aimlessly around and also started heading towards the Sandia.

"I think we're three for three," Sharon said intently.

"Yeah. I think so too. Fester? I think that fourteen thirty reservation is our meeting. Can you determine from the hotel's booking system who booked that room?"

PLEASE WAIT, CAME THE REPLY.

About the time cars one and three arrived at the Sandia, we had our answer.

THE RESERVATION IS IN THE NAME OF P.J. ROBERTSON, said the Box.

"Anything else you can determine?" I asked.

THE RESERVATION FEE WAS PAID USING AN AMERICAN EXPRESS CARD.

"Amex? Does that mean we now have a card number attached to his name?"

THE CARD IS NOT IN HIS NAME.

"...Wait, he paid with—Wait. Is it a corporate card?"

THAT APPEARS TO BE THE CASE.

"Can you determine who owns it?"

PLEASE WAIT.

"I wish we could listen in on that meeting," I mused.

"So do I," Sharon replied. "Fester? There should be a teleconferencing system in that meeting room. Can we tap into it?"

THERE IS, replied the Box. HOWEVER, IT IS NOT ACTIVE AND I CANNOT ACCESS IT.

She sighed.

"Well, so much for that idea."

"Wait a minute," I interjected. "Don't write that thought off yet. Let me think." I sat pondering for a few minutes. Then I fired off a couple of searches. It took me about twenty minutes to track down what I thought I'd recalled reading about.

"Fester," I began, "we know the mobile phone accounts of four of these five directors, right?"

CORRECT.

"Are any of the phones iPhones?"

TWO OF THE FOUR PHONES WE KNOW FOR THIS GROUP ARE IPHONES.

"Fester, I want you to look at this CVE, a clickless remote code execution in iMessage." I highlighted a vulnerability report. "And this one, PAC bypass... and this one, local privilege escalation in the XNU kernel... and this one."

There was a brief pause.

INTERESTING.

"Correct me if I'm wrong, but here's what I'm thinking:

"If we construct an instant message to one of those iPhones, containing a HEIC-format image with a properly crafted URL embedded in the metadata, the iMessage app on the phone will automatically open that URL without any action by the user, as long as the phone isn't patched for that first CVE. And if it's *also* unpatched for at least one of those last two, then we can daisy-chain those together to compromise OS privilege separation and make that crafted URL execute a command to remotely turn on the microphone.

"Does that seem like it would work?"

The logic seems sound. I believe it should work, provided the first vulnerability and at least one of the last two is unpatched. Trying both exploit chain variations against both phones gives four chances at success.

Sharon was looking at me, smiling.

"What?" I asked.

"'Not a hacker'," she quoted, in a fake-accusing tone. I grinned sheepishly.

"I'm just putting together pieces somebody else found," I said. "But the part I'm missing here is how we get the audio out."

"Can you make it execute *two* commands?" Sharon asked.

I thought about that.

"Not in a single attack, I think. Right, Fester?"

Correct. The attack would allow execution of only a single command.

"...Could you attack it *twice*?" Sharon asked.

"With two different commands?... I don't see why not," I agreed. "If it works once, it ought to work a second time against the same phone." Then I thought about it more.

"Not sure what the second command should be, though."

"You could make the remote command download a file, right?" Sharon said.

"Sure. But I don't see how that helps us in this case. We don't have time to build an exfiltration applet. And even if we did, it might well be flagged as suspicious by antivirus tools."

"Could it *upload* one?"

"Sure. But what file?"

"Could it create it as it goes, from the microphone?"

"...Upload an audio *STREAM*. Sharon, you're brilliant, and I love you. Fester, help me out here. Let's put these pieces together."

Thirty minutes later, we were ready to deploy.

"None of the cars have left yet," I observed. "I hope they're still at it. Fire when ready, Gridley."

WHAT SHOULD THE IMAGE CONTAINING THE PAYLOAD BE?

"Cat pictures, of course," Sharon said, with a grin.

"Falsify the sender to be Bill Gates," I added. Sharon laughed.

EXECUTING, said the Box.

TARGET ONE, FIRST PASS, VARIANT ONE.

TARGET TWO, FIRST PASS, VARIANT ONE.

TARGET ONE, FIRST PASS, VARIANT TWO.

TARGET TWO, FIRST PASS, VARIANT TWO.

TARGET ONE, SECOND PASS, VARIANT ONE.

TARGET TWO, SECOND PASS, VARIANT ONE.

TARGET ONE, SECOND PASS, VARIANT TWO.

TARGET TWO, SECOND PASS, VARIANT TWO.

ALL PAYLOADS SENT. MESSAGE DELIVERY MAY BE ASYNCHRONOUS.

We waited, and I watched the incoming file bucket.

One minute passed.

Two minutes.

Three minutes.

A file appeared. I checked its size. It was growing rapidly.

"We have incoming data!" I declared.

"YES!" Sharon whooped. She grabbed me and kissed me, hard. Then we sat and held hands and watched the audio stream in.

"Don't get too excited yet though," I cautioned. "This phone is probably in someone's pocket. We don't know how much we're going to get, or what we're going to be able to make out from it."

In the end, the stream stopped after about forty-five minutes. I waited a couple more minutes to be sure, then downloaded it, then deleted that entire virtual server. Just in case anyone smelled a rat and came sniffing, I wanted to make sure there was nothing there to find.

Then we opened it up and started listening.

The audio was, as expected, muffled, often faint, and interrupted by movement sounds as the phone's owner shifted position. We could hear people talking, but not clearly make out words.

When we *did* get something, a minute or two in, it started out with a bang, though. The speaker seemed to be fairly near the phone, next seat perhaps, and had a Texas drawl.

> "I don't *care*. Not only did you *not need to do it*, the people you used *fucked it up*. You could have blown open the whole scheme. The only saving grace is that whatever happened there, the news reports sound like the girl most likely didn't make it, missing and presumed dead, and nobody's sure what happened. And the backup team got their man's body out, so nothing can be traced back to us. Hopefully.
>
> "Do not send ANY more contracts through that firm, EVER. They're off the filing list. Permanently. All you had to do was *shut the fuck up* and not do or say *anything*, it's a thousand to one they'd never have noticed a thing."

The previous voice spoke again, muffled, unclear. I looked at Sharon, and she looked straight back at me. Her face was pale. I reached out and took her hand.

> "Anyway, it looks like we got away with that one, barely. But there has to be absolutely no more mistakes. If you fu—"

The next words were lost as the phone's owner shifted in his seat. By the time our unwitting leak settled down and stopped moving, someone else was speaking. This voice was further away and we strained to make out anything.

> "We'll cross that bridge when we come to it," Texas said.

The conversation turned into some discussion at a distance. Other end of the table, perhaps? We couldn't really make any of it out.

After a while, someone else spoke, closer, a new voice.

"We've got a couple of new players coming on board. Also, Hanlon's getting greedy again. So we need to increase..."

The voice faded into indecipherability.

"...at the end of the fiscal quarter, and bringing up four additional sites. We've identified a group of suitable properties in Mobile, Alabama. Together, they'll give us fourteen new lines. We'll let you know the new details when they're allocated."

Conversation shifted away again, for a while.

"...greedy bastard. Doesn't he know we have him over a barrel?"

"Yeah," Texas retorted, "the exact same barrel they have us over. Neither of us can rat the other out without being in hot water ourselves. We know that, they know that. Think of it as a balance of power."

Something we couldn't make out from the other end of the table.

"Well at that point, we won't need them any more. We wrap it up, walk away, scorch the earth behind us, and deny everything."

More indistinct voices from the far end. Then, after a while:

"Well, I guess that wraps things up then. See all y'all next time. And no more fuck-ups. I'm serious."

There was a general shuffling of chairs and movement for several minutes as the meeting broke up. Then after a minute or two, the acoustics changed. Less echoey, less meeting-room, more outdoor.

"Hey, John, you want to get some dinner while we're here? I've got four hours before my return flight."

"Sure, why not? I have a few hours to kill."

That last voice seemed to be the phone's owner.

"You should invite that pretty little side piece of yours, and her friend Rosa. We can party a little."

"Heh, sure, why not? Lemme call her and see if she's available."

There was a rustle and a burst of noise, then the voice became clearer.

"One second, need to check this... the fuck?"

"What's up?"

"Ha. Some joker claiming to be Bill Gates sent me a bunch of cat pics. Fuck if I know why."

"There's probably a virus in them. Don't open them."

"Do I *look* stupid? There, deleted 'em. Now lemme call Angel... Oh come on... what the fuck now?"

"Something wrong?"

"Can't dial. Says system resources are busy. Stupid phone. Hang on a minute, I'm gonna restart—"

And the stream ended.

═══════════

I took a deep breath.

"Well," I said, "I think that first bit pretty firmly ties them to the attacks."

"Enough to confirm it for *us*," Sharon agreed, frustrated. "But not enough to convict anyone in a court. Pretty incriminating in context, but on its own, only circumstantial, at best. To present it as evidence in a trial, or even to justify a search warrant, we'd need to have heard them directly talk about the attacks *and* mention Harris Magnusson *by name* in that discussion."

Then she thought for a bit.

"'New players' sounds like they're expanding the scheme," she suggested.

"Yeah, it does... any guesses who Hanlon might be?"

She shook her head.

"No idea. There's got to be thousands of people named Hanlon. There's even a *Senator* Hanlon, for that matter."

"...Yeah, you're right," I agreed. "It's not enough information. So we haven't learned very much useful."

WE HAVE LEARNED SOMETHING.

"Go on?"

THE PERSON NAMED P.J. ROBERTSON.

"Right. You said he paid for the meeting room reservation with a corporate Amex card. Were you able to find out anything more about it?"

IT APPEARS TO BELONG TO CONOCO PHILLIPS.

"Well, well." I looked at Sharon. "That actually sounds like a step closer to the end of this trail."

She nodded. Then a connection clicked in my head.

"...Wait a minute," I said. "Oil money."

Sharon looked intently at me for several seconds. Then she got it too.

"*Bastards*," she swore.

"Also," I added, "at least *they didn't* learn anything, thanks to their guy helpfully deleting all the traces we left." She grinned.

THERE ARE STILL TRACES ON THE OTHER PHONE, the Box observed.

"True," I agreed. "If we're lucky the other phone owner will give them no more thought than this one did. And on the other phone, the exploits apparently didn't work, so there should be no suspicious activity beyond the unexpected messages."

There was a pause.

AGREED. PROBABILITY OF DISCOVERY IS EXTREMELY LOW, ESPECIALLY GIVEN THE OBSERVED POOR SECURITY AWARENESS.

"So what now?" Sharon asked.

"I don't know. We need to figure out our next step."

She nodded, then wrapped her arms around herself and shivered slightly.

"It can wait a bit. Come and get a shower with me first. I feel... *unclean* after listening to them."

I nodded agreement, and followed her out and up the stairs.

10: Location Is Everything

"We know we're on their trail now," I said the next morning, over breakfast. "But we need to know more. And I think the first step for that is to see if I can get a look at one of these business properties. See what —if anything—is actually happening there. There's got to be a lot of paperwork and such associated with running even a shell corporation, if it holds physical assets and moves money, and they're surely not going to be doing it in head office. It's going to be hidden somewhere out of the way."

"And you think that means at one or more of the commercial rental properties?" Sharon asked.

"I don't know," I hedged. "But I want to take a look at one or two anyway. To get a more complete picture. Let's figure out the closest two or three and decide which one—or more—to take a peek at."

"Outside first?" Sharon asked. "Just a drive-past?"

"Outside first," I agreed.

We went and found the nearest few properties, and pulled them up on a map. Sharon went into Street View and took a virtual look around the area.

"Do you ever buy nuts and bolts?" she asked me.

"Sure," I asked, puzzled. "Why?"

She pointed me at one of the properties. "This one's about an hour away and has a Fastenal right across the street from it. Great excuse to loiter for a few minutes in a nearby parking lot without looking the least bit out of place."

I grinned.

"Good thinking," I nodded. "Let's do it."

"Give me the keys," Sharon told me. "I'm driving."

"Okay," I agreed, without hesitation. "Any particular reason?"

"Two of them. First, you can have all your attention on observing while we loop around the property both on the way in and on the way out, instead of needing to divide it between observing and driving. And second, I want to get a feel for how your hopped-up Volvo drives."

I nodded. It made perfect sense. Not that I was expecting any differently, at this point.

So, we went and did just that. We did a little routine shopping along the way, and then we looped around three sides of the target we'd picked out of the commercial properties, about five below the speed limit, while I studied it for anything of any possible interest or utility to us. There was a bored-looking security guard in a booth at one of the two gates onto the property; the other was chained. I spotted security cameras over the front doors and several of the other outside doors. There probably wasn't any sneaking in unseen.

However, I *also* spotted a dumpster placed almost right next to a set of rear exit doors. We were almost at Fastenal's lot by then. We pulled in and parked, went inside, and I bought a box of two dozen M8 by 125mm twelve-point grade-eight machine bolts, with nuts. They were nearly four dollars each. The fact that I didn't have any actual need for them was irrelevant. It was a specialty fastener that I'd *have* to come to a specialty supplier for if I actually *did* need them, because the local hardware store or big-box home improvement store *absolutely was not* going to have them on the shelf, period. And *that* meant that in the miniscule chance of us finding ourselves in a situation of explaining why we were there, all I needed to do was point at the Fastenal sign and show off my box of exotic high-spec bolts.

After we left the store, we stood outside for a little while next to the Volvo, casually chatting about... well, actually, discussing observations on the commercial property across the street.

"I'm not sure if you can see it well enough from this angle," I said, "but do you see that dumpster about half way along the back wall?" Sharon glanced quickly that way, then turned back to me and nodded. "It's only maybe a foot from the exit door next to it. And I'll bet that's a fire door, and I'll bet *that's* a technical fire code violation."

"How does that help us?" Sharon asked.

"Well, if I can arrange for the fire chief to order a fire safety inspection, then with a little luck, I can manage to get attached to the inspection team and get a look around. I know *our* local fire chief, and may be able to ask a favor. And that'll tell us whether there's anything in any of these worth, uh... entering in a more covert manner for a more detailed look."

Sharon gave me a serious look.

"You do understand you're now talking about breaking and

entering," she said.

"Well, hopefully a minimum of any actual *breaking*," I hedged. "And I'm hoping to avoid that altogether."

"All I'm saying," she told me, "is if we have to take that risk, be *sure*."

I nodded. We got back into the car, pulled out, looped around the building a second time, and drove away. I didn't spot anything else. But maybe that misplaced dumpster gave us something we could use.

"So do you have a plan for that?" Sharon asked, on the way home. "For getting an inspection, and for getting on the inspection team?"

"Well, I don't know anyone in *that* fire department. But I *do* know about half of our *local* VFD, including the Chief. I've lent them a hand a few times. So perhaps I might be able to ask a favor."

Sharon nodded thoughtfully.

"Never underestimate the value of connections," she agreed.

<hr>

We got home, unloaded and put away all of the shopping, and made lunch. Then I called Chief McPherson at our volunteer fire department.

"Hey, Bill," I opened. "Got a minute?"

"Hey, Ciáran. No calls out right now, so sure. What's on your mind?"

"I was wondering if you could help me out with something. Call it personal research."

"With what?" Bill replied thoughtfully. "Go on."

"Okay. Do you happen to know anyone in Centerville Fire Department?"

"Sure," he replied. "We send people over to Centerville every now and then to train in their burn house. I know Chief Roberts pretty well. Why?"

"Well," I explained, "for reasons I'm not going to go into right now, I kinda want to know some things about how a fire code inspection is done. It'd be a complicated and mostly boring story that I don't need to waste your time with in the middle of the day."

"Anything to do with some of your, uh, special installations?" Bill asked, chuckling.

"Not directly," I replied.. "But anyway, I was doing some hardware shopping today over in Centerville, and I happened to notice a pretty empty-looking commercial property across the street from the Fastenal that had a dumpster partially obstructing what looks like a fire door. That'd be a clear fire code violation, right?"

"It sure would," Bill agreed. "But it's outside my... Ah. That's why you asked about Centerville FD."

"Exactly," I said. "Could I persuade you to pass along the tip to Chief—Roberts, you said, right?—and ask whether, if he chooses to follow up on it, I could go in with the inspection as a ride-along?"

Bill thought about that for a moment.

"Sure," he replied, after a few seconds. "I'll pass the tip along, and I'll ask him if he'd be willing to have one or two of our people go along on the inspection for training purposes. We've done similar things before, and it's not like you've never helped us out. I'll give him a call later today. Across from Fastenal, you said?"

"Yup," I confirmed. And I gave him one of the street addresses for the property.

"Okay," he replied. "I'll get back to you and let you know if I can set it up for you."

"Thanks, Bill. I owe you one."

"Eh, don't worry about it. You've helped us out plenty of times. You coming to the annual barbecue this year?"

"Planning on it," I agreed. "Unless something urgent comes up."

It ended up being the next day before Bill called back.

"Hey, Ciáran," he told me cheerily, "I talked to Chief Roberts and it's all set up. The inspection will happen Thursday afternoon, and we're sending you and Jay Waters, one of our recent new volunteers, along as a training exercise. You can meet up here in the morning at the station, and ride over with Jay."

"Fantastic," I declared, relieved. I stretched, as one more little bit of tension slipped away, one more obstacle probably solved. "I'll be there."

On Thursday, with little choice in the matter, I left Sharon at home for a couple of hours and went over to the volunteer fire department. It was that or take her over to the fire department and leave her there, and she'd be more likely to be seen there. It would also create a need for awkward and not-really-convincing explanations.

Jay was a tall, wiry, sandy-haired string-bean with a lot of laugh lines and a Donald Sutherland mustache. He offered a hand, and we shook.

"Come on inside," he told me, " and let's get you kitted out with some gear."

I followed him in, and half an hour later, I had a loaner set of fire department togs.

"We really need this?" I asked. "To do an inspection?"

"Safety first," he said, nodding. "Bill said you're doing this for personal research?"

"Yeah," I agreed. "But it's confidential at the moment, and I'd prefer not to say too much right now."

Jay nodded.

"Fair enough," he said. "Let's get underway."

An hour later, we were in Centerville, and climbing into a Fire Chief marked truck with Centerville deputy chief Thad Micklenburg. Twenty minutes after that, we pulled up in front of what I was thinking of as Site A.

"Sorry," the security guard told us, "building is closed, private property, I can't let you in."

"I don't care whether it's private," said Thad. "We have reports of fire code violations on a commercial property. You can either let us in to do a code inspection, as required by law, or I can call the sheriff, and fifteen minutes from now you can explain to him why you're not letting us do our job."

The security guard folded, and let us in. Thad had him unlock the front door for us. He followed us around as we walked the entire building, Thad taking notes as we went.

"Check the gauge on that extinguisher," Thad told me, at the first wall-mounted extinguisher we came to. I looked. It was maybe a tenth down from the top end of the green zone.

"Looks good," I reported. "I'd call it ninety percent pressure, maybe a little over."

Thad noted it down. We inspected alarm panels, fire extinguishers, electrical panels, interior and outside fire doors, making sure that every fire door opened when the bar was pushed and checking whether they re-latched when they closed.

There was clearly no work being done here. Various office furniture and bric-a-brac was scattered about in a semblance of a working layout. But it wasn't convincing. It looked abandoned.

"Does anyone actually *work* here?" Jay asked the security guard.

"I think they're in the middle of a re-organization or something," the guard replied. "At least, that's what I was told." Good excuse, as long as you only heard it once.

It took about an hour to go through the entire building. When we got to the western end of the building, the fire door at the top of the stairwell wouldn't open. Jay had to haul off and kick the door bar hard, twice, before it would unlatch. Thad looked unhappy about that. So did our security escort. He muttered something I didn't catch.

Finally, we wrapped up. Thad finished up his notes as we prepared to leave.

"Is everything else up to scratch in there?" the guard asked. "Besides that stuck door, of course?"

"There's fifteen extinguishers in that building," Thad told him. "Four of them need to be recharged. The dumpster at the back of the building is too close to a fire door, it needs to be *at least* fifteen feet away. And that fire door at the top of the western stairwell absolutely needs to get fixed before anyone returns to work there. It could trap people on the upper floor, if they're blocked from reaching the eastern stairwell by a fire or some other problem.

"None of these are your problem, we'll send the report to the company with an order to remediate. But be aware of those things if you have to go inside for any reason, all right?"

The guard nodded.

"Thanks for the heads-up," he said. "I'll pass the word around to watch out for that top door until it's fixed."

Thad nodded approvingly. It had been a bit of a rocky start, but the guard had shown he was willing to listen, and it was obvious he wasn't any happier about that door than the three of us were.

We got back into Thad's truck and left. On the way back, Thad quizzed us both about details of the inspection, and whether we knew why certain things were checked. We both got it all correct. He pretty clearly approved of that, too.

<hr>

Bill McPherson was waiting for us when we got back.

"How'd it go, guys?" he asked. "Chief Roberts says you guys did good."

"Pretty good trip," Jay answered. "Learned some useful things."

"Reckon you could do a commercial inspection on your own now?"

"With a *partner*, sure," Jay said. "We ran into a jammed fire door. Woulda sucked to get stuck on the wrong side of it."

Bill nodded.

"Good call," he agreed. "And that's why we don't ever do commercial inspections solo." He turned to me.

"How about you, Ciáran? Learn everything you wanted to?"

"Yup," I agreed. "It was very informative and educational. Thanks a lot."

"Glad I could help," Bill said. "Have a good one."

I returned my borrowed gear, and went home to Sharon.

<hr>

Sharon greeted me eagerly as soon as I got in, and we stood and just hugged for a couple of minutes.

"So, how did it go?" she asked. "Did we learn anything useful?"

"Yeah, I think we did," I replied. "The place looked... like it was stage-dressed as an operating company, but nobody was ever actually there. Lots of little things wrong, like phones placed on desks but the lines just tucked under the desk, not actually plugged in. Not enough chair wheel tracks or footprints. The break-room refrigerator was completely empty and smelled stale. Microwave was too clean. No stains at all. The security guard was told a story about re-organization in progress. I suspect the only people who ever actually go into that building are occasional cleaners and the security guards.

"And tellingly, there was not a single *operating* piece of computer gear in the place. Some desktop PCs on desks, but not plugged into a network, and no servers anywhere. I saw monitors not connected. Even what desktop clutter there was looked artfully staged. It's all fake. Wherever the operations of the shell corps are happening, it's not there.

"Now it *could* be that we just got unlucky and picked the one atypical one. But that would be stretching coincidence. The smart money says they're all like this."

Sharon nodded agreement.

"Where does that get us?" she asked. "Where do we go from here?"

I thought about that while I made us some coffee.

"Well," I mused, "all of these corporations, *somewhere*, have digital infrastructure where all of their 'management' happens. All of their financial operations. Where documents get filed from, et cetera. And now we know that it's not happening on the individual rental properties.

"I'm going to hazard a guess that they don't want it in their main corporate operations centers where somebody not in the know—or someone auditing them—might see it and ask awkward questions. So it's going to be hidden somewhere out of sight, but not *suspiciously* so— just like all the Delaware corporations. Probably either in a small colo somewhere, or in a cloud service."

"Colo?"

"Sorry. Rented servers in a co-location data-center. Commercial hosting. Something of that nature."

Sharon nodded understanding again, then rested her chin in her hand, pondering.

"There's two major things we still need to figure out before we can get any further," she mused. "Where exactly the money is coming *from*, which may turn out to be difficult to prove. And where it's going *to*."

I nodded agreement.

"Does what you found out today help us get there?"

"I... think I have an idea about the latter," I answered. "And if we're REALLY lucky, it just might get us both."

She shot a curious look at me.

"What do you have in mind?" she asked.

"I want to repeat the Syrian gambit."

"Syria II, Covert Boogaloo?" Sharon asked, giving me a very unhappy look. "This is the part where you reassure me *very seriously* that you're not planning something that's likely to get you shot again."

"I certainly hope not," I replied. "Here's what I'm thinking. If their infra is in the cloud, it's going to be very difficult to get to, just by the nature of the beast. But they might not want to do that, because either they'll have all of the corps hosted under a small group of accounts, which might arouse curious interest if anyone happens to notice it, and would mean a breach of one probably becomes a breach of all; or they'll have a whole slew of identical cookie-cutter accounts, which also might attract curious eyes. And bad actors are *constantly* scanning all of the major cloud hosting services for misconfigured services, accidentally exposed keys, any kind of vulnerability that can be attacked—because it's the low-hanging fruit, simply because *so many* cloud servers and services *are* poorly secured. Because a lot of them are thrown up quickly by people who don't actually understand what they're doing and don't know how to secure them, and it turns out it's actually really difficult to *automatically* prevent people from making stupid security mistakes out of ignorance.

"And that goes double if the security measures get in the way of people who don't know any better managing their cloud environments. LOTS of breaches, and quite a few outright *failures*, happen because somebody disabled or bypassed a security mechanism because it was *inconvenient*."

Sharon nodded in understanding.

"So if they're trying to avoid attention," I continued, "then they might consider it safer to go for a private physical colo somewhere out-of-the-way. And if it's a small colo, then it's potentially physically accessible. And for plausible deniability and isolation, they're not going to be managing it at all via their own corporate IT. It's going to be sub-contracted out so that they can hide who actually owns it."

"Okay," Sharon nodded, following along.

"And I'll bet that *somewhere*, something in it is vulnerable to at least some kind of attack or disruption," I went on.

"So... we're going to hack them?" Sharon asked.

"Not exactly," I said, shaking my head. "A hack from outside, unless it's very subtle, is likely to raise alarms and be found and fixed."

She nodded in acknowledgment.

"So what we need," I went on, "is something that's 'supposed' to be there."

She looked puzzled, but kept listening, with a thoughtful expression.

"So we find out who they've subcontracted it to," I continued. "And then we find, or if necessary create, a problem..."

"Then we intercept the repair order," she picked up, "and *YOU* go in and 'fix' it."

I grinned.

"That's exactly what I have in mind," I agreed. "Perhaps even *create* a repair ticket out of whole cloth. And while I'm 'fixing' it, I install a little something extra. Almost no matter what software security is in place, if you can gain physical access to the hardware, it's game over. And then we make *their own infrastructure* tell us where the money is coming from, and where it's going."

Sharon grinned back.

"I love it!" she said. "What do we need to put it into action?"

"Three things," I replied. "...No, four." I counted off on my fingers. "We need to find out where their infrastructure is hosted. We need to find out who they outsource their IT to. We need to find a problem that we can create. And we need a way to intercept the repair order."

"I'm betting Fester can help with at least the last of those," Sharon guessed.

"So am I," I agreed. "He's done it before—and that was with a defense contractor. This ought to be *much* easier. As long as it's in a colo."

So we went downstairs and talked to Fester.

═══════════

"We have a search task to be accomplished," I began. "It's probably a bit of a needle in a haystack. You already have the list of all of the fake shell corporations."

YES.

"I need you to look for domains for IT infrastructure associated with those corporations, and I need you to track it down, find out where it is located, whether it's in a cloud service or a physical colocation datacenter, and if the latter, then I need to know who manages it. If it's cloud-hosted, we'll need to think again and revise our plan. We'll need a different approach.

"Can you do that for us?"

THE TASK IS FEASIBLE. IT MAY TAKE SOME TIME. THE MOST IMMEDIATELY OBVIOUS DOMAIN NAMES BASED UPON THE VARIOUS BUSINESS NAMES OF THE FICTITIOUS SHELL CORPORATIONS DO NOT RESOLVE. OTHER MEANS WILL BE NECESSARY TO IDENTIFY THEM. THEY MAY BE INTENTIONALLY ANONYMIZED.

That meant more waiting, of course. But, we really hadn't expected any differently, so it didn't come as any surprise. We had plenty of ways by now to fill the time productively.

It took Fester three days to find them. They turned out to be clustered in a business called Tenth Avenue Digital Hosting, a small, out-of-the-way independent colo in, of all places, Asbury Park, New Jersey, spread across six different fictitious 'owners'. The hosting contracts were quite possibly a big chunk of what was keeping the place afloat. I felt a little guilty about that. If we managed to tear this scheme down, it was going to be a major blow to Tenth Avenue Digital, who most likely didn't have any idea what it was that they were hosting. But then, if the conspirators' plan was to burn everything down once they were finished with it and leave only scorched earth behind them, then the colo would probably go under anyway, if they were as heavily dependent as I suspected they were on the revenue from hosting the scheme. Which they probably had no reason to suspect was anything illegal.

The 'owners' of the obscurely named domains were shell corporations that were owned by guess which four *other* shell corporations? Yup, the ones who owned the properties. That was a pretty solid connection. It was vanishingly unlikely to be a false trail.

We started figuring out what kind of attack surface there was. Given their very narrow and limited purpose, naturally there wasn't a content delivery network in the way. That made life simpler. It meant we could see the hardware more or less directly.

Pretty much the entire internet runs on a pair of signaling protocols collectively known as TCP/IP—which stands for Transport Control Protocol and Internet Protocol. There are strictly defined standards for every detail of every interaction; but there can be subtle variations in precisely how different vendors' protocol stacks, and even hardware, *implement* those standards. And if you can observe and test a large set of those little quirks, then you can usually come up with a very good guess about what network hardware is running—unless someone has taken certain deliberate steps to tweak some of those quirks, in order to harden the system by altering the behavior of the hardware to mislead attackers. And knowing what the hardware *is*, narrows down what particular vulnerabilities *might* be present.

Some patient stealth scanning, some packet fingerprinting, and in a few hours of patient work in the office, we had a pretty good idea of what kind of network hardware they were running, and even some inferences about their probable internal network topology.

I looked at what we had, and I started to formulate an attack plan, bouncing my thoughts off of Sharon. She didn't have any expertise in this field, but she was sharp, smart, and attentive, and that made her a great rubber-duck.

"All of the network hardware seems to be Juniper Networks gear," I started off. "It's good gear, but like any piece of equipment, occasionally people discover vulnerabilities in the software that runs it. That's not calling blame, it's just a fact of life. There's no such thing as perfect error-free code. With certain exceptions." Sharon nodded.

"Exceptions?" she queried.

"Well," I hedged, "I know of at least one special case offhand. The UK's Royal Signals Research Establishment came up with a custom microprocessor called VIPER, during the late 1980s, for mission-critical defense applications. It wasn't a particularly *powerful* processor, by modern standards; it was about the same performance level as maybe an early Intel 80386." She nodded, following along. "Which, to be fair, wasn't bad at all, for its time.

"Anyway, the important thing about the VIPER was that it was intentionally a straightforward-enough design that it was possible to mathematically *prove* that the design of the processor architecture itself was correct."

"...Which meant it couldn't have any bugs?" she asked.

"Which meant that it could be known that *the hardware itself* didn't have any bugs," I corrected slightly. "That doesn't mean the *software* couldn't contain bugs. Or that the hardware couldn't have *defects—* although most possible defects could be tested for.

"Anyway, when vulnerabilities are found, Juniper issues patches and updates to fix them. They're conscientious about it. More so than quite a few other vendors I could name, actually."

"Which actually works against us, here?" she asked.

"Well, sort of," I answered. "It means that especially in a small operation like this, in a customer deployment that probably doesn't have hands on it every day, there's a good chance that at least some of the equipment is a rev or two behind on its firmware. Maybe several. And that means it *may* have unpatched vulnerabilities. If we can figure out what exact versions of firmware they're running, we'll know what they are."

"So how do you find that out?" Sharon asked. "I don't imagine you can tell by looking at the network traffic. That sounds a bit like, oh... trying to tell a car's VIN number by looking at its tire tracks. Right?"

"Absolutely right," I agreed. "In most cases. Sometimes there are distinctive patterns that tell you the device is running *at least* some particular known firmware version. So what we can do now is start *trying* different remote access vulnerabilities—even default passwords— to see if any of them gets us a shell. Even an unprivileged one will tell us the firmware version."

I built a list of documented known remote-access vulnerabilities for Juniper gear, and started trying them, one after another, not too quickly so as not to attract attention. Try one, wait a while, try another, wait, try another. Sharon disappeared for a while and came back with two coffees and a plate of grilled ham-and-Swiss sandwiches, both of which were welcome.

The eleventh try got me an unprivileged login on one of the core switches.

"We've got them," I declared. I pointed out the firmware version string in the banner. "Now we know *exactly* what firmware revision they're running. They're on JunOS 26.3.1 right now. And that means we can get a list of all of the reported vulnerabilities from this version forward to the current release, which is... let me see... 26.3.3."

Sharon nodded.

"And that'll tell us something that we can use to generate a plausible repair ticket," she said.

"Yeah," I agreed. Then I thought some more.

"We may not even have to *actually* perform a real attack. We might be able to gin up a *preventive maintenance* ticket to upgrade the firmware to the latest release. Or possibly, they might do a priority patch if a new high-severity vulnerability is disclosed."

"Which would close the vulnerabilities," Sharon mused. "But would also shut us out, because it would close the vulnerabilities you got in with."

"Well, yeah," I admitted. "That is a drawback of that approach. We could add the access rules we'd need while updating the firmware... but that might be spotted, if we get unlucky and someone happens to do an access review."

"Could you... modify the new firmware to build the rules we need right *into* it?"

"That is *precisely* what I had in mind," I replied, with a grin. "And if we're very careful about it, with some help from Fester, we can possibly make the checksums match the original, so that the insertion won't be readily detected."

"If it helps," she commented as she browsed, "I think I've found who they contract out the administration of the systems to. Looks like they all use the same company, and it looks like a false front. I'm betting it traces back eventually to the backers."

She showed me.

"Hmmm," I thought. "I've never heard of them. You're probably right, it's probably a front. That... makes it risky. It also makes it difficult—and, again, risky—to impersonate one of their people."

"...Because they're an unknown quantity?"

"Exactly. There's almost certainly no way I can manipulate them into 'hiring' me. And without having seen any of their ID documents, we can't fake a set."

She thought about that.

"You said that we have access to their network switches," she mused.

"Yes," I agreed.

"Not to their actual servers."

"Right. We could try to breach the servers, but it's much more likely to be noticed. If we can sniff all of the network traffic going in and out, though, we don't *necessarily* need to... and we might even be able to capture login credentials, if they've been careless and send them in clear. But even so, going in that way, we'd still leave traces in the logs that we'd need to hide. 'Oh, what a tangled web we weave, When first we practice to deceive.'"

"So if what needs to be done doesn't affect their *servers*, just their network equipment, which you said is, uh, Juniper... would they necessarily fix that *themselves*? Or would they put in a service call to Juniper? Corporate procedures die hard."

I sat back for a moment. It was a good idea.

"I think you're onto something," I agreed. "They might *very well* do that. Not Juniper *itself*, but an authorized third-party Juniper Networks service technician."

"Could you *impersonate* a Juniper authorized technician?"

"...Yes," I replied, after a moment. I started to grin. "Yes, I could. And it shouldn't be too terribly difficult to create a convincing Juniper authorized service work order. There's lots of examples to work from. Sharon, I love you."

She pouted theatrically.

"I thought you loved me *already*," she said, but she was smiling.

"Deeply, passionately, and helplessly," I agreed. The smile got bigger. I loved to see her smile.

It took less than an hour to locate the closest authorized Juniper Networks service business, an outfit called Network Gurus. With a little more work, we were able to find evidence that the cabal had used them previously to service their network equipment. Whether by design or whether by oversight, billing records of their past jobs were publicly readable through a site apparently intended to allow customers to check up on completion of their contracted tasks.

By the end of the day, I had a falsified Network Gurus ID. It ought to be pretty simple to create a cloned Network Gurus work order that listed my new false identity as the technician who would go in and perform a routine firmware update on each of the six 'owner' corporations' core routers.

That meant the next step was to build the modified firmware, and make its checksums match the original. I knew I'd need Fester's help for that. Patching the firmware to trojan it and insert the hard-coded hidden rules we wanted would be relatively straightforward. Subtly fuzzing the code to do that and make the checksums come out correct... *that* was beyond me, I knew. Generating a hash collision with modern checksum algorithms is an extremely computationally intensive task that takes a lot of processing power and a lot of time, and often no small amount of sheer luck as well.

Or maybe, a weird-shit fractal box with opinions. I had a strong suspicion Fester could do it.

In the meantime, there were things Sharon and I needed to talk about.

"There's an elephant in the middle of the room with this plan," I told Sharon.

She nodded, her expression serious. "It would be far too dangerous for you to take me with you," she said. "But you're not really comfortable with the idea of leaving me here alone."

"That's it exactly," I agreed. "I'm not wild about the idea of leaving you alone here unprotected for that long. It'd be amazingly improbable bad luck at this point for the Black Hats to randomly stumble across you while I wasn't here. But bad luck happens at the worst of times. Centerville was a risk, but it was only a couple of hours. This would be a much bigger one. It'll take me close to two full days to get there, do the work, and get back."

"So what do we do?" she asked. "We can't just—do nothing."

"I know," I agreed. "We need to come up with something."

"Could you do it remotely?" Sharon asked.

"It... depends," I hedged. "The consequences of a compromise of core networking equipment are potentially severe enough that it's almost universal practice to lock networking stacks down so that the firmware can only be updated from *inside* the managed network, and in small datacenters it's not unusual to allow it only from the physical management port. Which means someone needs to stand in front of it in person and plug a cable into it.

"Also, if you do it that way, and you make some dumb mistake that breaks network routing completely, it's still possible to fix your mistake. If you're relying on a network connection through the router you just broke to be able to fix the router, you're pretty much screwed."

Sharon nodded.

"That makes sense," she agreed.

"Anyway, we've got job tickets from Network Gurus showing that the cabal uses them to do these updates on-site at fairly regular intervals. And that in itself strongly argues that they have the network stack locked down to in-person physical access only."

"Oh, well," Sharon said. She sounded disappointed. "It was a thought."

"And it was a good one," I agreed. "But unfortunately I'm pretty sure it wouldn't work."

"Well, at any rate, I know what our next priority should be," Sharon declared.

"Oh?" I asked.

"Supper."

She had a point.

The next day, we poked into Network Gurus' job records again and figured out the probable timing of the next scheduled networking maintenance. It would be better to switch in and take over a legitimate, scheduled maintenance update job than to create one out of whole cloth. That had the possible risk of omitting some not-externally-visible step in their process that might raise alarm bells.

It looked like it was probably going to be four to five weeks out, but wasn't actually created in the system yet.

"That's a pretty long time to wait," Sharon said unhappily. I agreed.

"Could we insert a job of our own?"

"It would probably raise questions," I replied.

Sharon frowned, pondering. Then she got a thoughtful expression.

"What might induce them to add an unscheduled update themselves?"

It was a good question. I thought about it for a moment.

"A critical-severity remote-compromise CVE against the Juniper firmware revision running on those routers would probably do it," I said. "None of the ones in the most recent Juniper maintenance bulletin are severe enough to trigger emergency action."

"But we can't just create one of those on the fly, can we?" she continued. It wasn't really a question.

"Almost certainly not," I replied. "And it would be deeply irresponsible in any case, even if we could."

She looked at me, her expression intent. I could see that she was still thinking hard.

"Could we make just Network Gurus *believe* that there is one?" she asked.

I pondered that. I pulled up the Network Gurus job records again, and looked back in their history. Yeah, they occasionally did out-of-band emergency updates. The last one had been seventeen months ago.

Then I slapped myself on the forehead. Sharon gave me a strange look.

"We're overthinking this," I explained. "We've slipped into treating this as a problem of fooling Network Gurus. But we don't need to do that. We only need to use the faked Network Gurus documents to fool Tenth Avenue Digital."

Light dawned. She looked sheepish too.

"You're right," she agreed. "We were *both* overthinking it. We might have had our heads down on this a bit too long. We need a break to depressurize."

I nodded.

"Let's take the rest of the day off," I suggested. "We can spend an hour or so in the dojo working the kinks out, get a shower, then go out to dinner. MacNamara's again?"

Sharon grinned. "I like the way you think," she told me.

So that's exactly what we did.

11: Greetings From Asbury Park

It turned out I was right about Fester being able to tweak our trojaned firmware to generate the required hash collisions to get the right checksums, though it took an entire two days to accomplish it. The file sizes were different, of course. But not only was the byte count of the firmware not readily visible once installed, it was incredibly unlikely that anyone would even look at the byte count unless the checksums didn't match... and almost certainly, the only person who was going to actually see and compare this specific set of checksums would be me.

Still, it didn't pay to be careless. Someone *MIGHT* check it... so get it right in the first place.

"There's a vital issue we still have to solve," I told Sharon. "I'm *not* going to risk leaving you alone here unprotected for that long. *Just in case* someone has eyes on us and is waiting patiently to catch you unprotected—although I'd think they'd have made *some kind* of move by now. They haven't particularly shown a trend for careful, considered action so far. And I can't take you with me without running into the same problem—except without the security of being here. And I can't bullshit you into the datacenter with me."

Sharon nodded.

"I'm going to guess you have at least a tentative plan for that," she guessed.

I nodded.

"I do. I *hope*. Let's see if Judson can help us out. I trust him with my life or yours, and I happen to know he has some very scary friends who he can call on if things turn unpleasant."

So I called Judson Ritter.

— *Judson* —

He thinks my name is Judson Ritter, and at this point it would be too much of a headache to tell him that was my cover when we first met. I have others now, and it's been so long since I've heard my birth name that I don't react to it any more. It unsettles my parents.

Yeah, I'm the Judson that Ciáran's been talking about. I wish he wouldn't. So long as he does I'm going to keep my cover, thank you kindly. I work at, not for, the Smithsonian in Washington, the city not the state. From time to time Ciáran has been incredibly useful in ways he doesn't know about, and won't. Management thinks of me as Ciáran's handler, my supervisor thinks of me as his facilitator, and I think of myself as his enabler and janitor. Don't get me wrong, his heart's in the right place and he shows good judgment in when to pull the trigger and when to run, but the man needs someone with a mop following close behind.

I'm ninety-nine percent sure he's an asset for some foreign power. Which power, though, is an open question and a high-priority long-term goal. We've been able to exclude the usual suspects, which just leaves the unusuals. Some group new on the board, that's as much as I know so far.

That sets my teeth on edge, along with the teeth of everyone else working at the Smithsonian. So far his Management's goals seem to have been broadly compatible with mine, so we haven't dropped a FISA warrant on him yet. The warrant application is written, though, and so meticulous a tear of pride rolls down the cheek of Allan Kornblum's ghost. It sits in my desk, unsigned and undated.

God, I hope this isn't the day I file it.

So, Ciáran called me up about five weeks ago to ask some questions about Harrison Bergeron & Partners in Crime. Okay, fine, Harris Magnusson Partners, but this is my internal dialogue and I get to mock biglaw firms how I like. I answered him to the extent I could, then immediately made an appointment with two levels of management, a rep from the office of legal counsel, and the anonymous personal representative (the "left hand") of my agency's deputy director for operations—a nice woman whose name I didn't ask, didn't receive, and don't want to know. I try to avoid coming to the attention of people who scare me.

We debated whether we could investigate Harrison Bergeron & Partners in Crime, and no, we couldn't. Our only lead was Ciáran was concerned about them, but given his compromised loyalties, it didn't rise to the level of opening a file. We discussed filing that FISA warrant application, opening a formal counterintelligence investigation into Ciáran, and using that to justify looking into this law firm. I strenuously argued against it: one, we had no idea what his backer's counter-counterintelligence capabilities might be, and two, when he discovered it we'd lose collaboration opportunities forever. Two levels of management disagreed with me, the left hand weakly agreed with me, and suddenly two levels of management were championing my wisdom.

I love office politics. It's why I jump at any chance to get out. So when Ciáran called me at the office, I was already thinking of how to turn this into a field assignment before he'd so much as finished two words.

"Judson, I need your help, if you can. It's important. REALLY important." A heartbeat later he spoke the magic words: "I think national security may be implicated. MAY. I don't know for certain. Not yet. But that's how my nose is twitching."

He talks like that. Capital letters. They're audible. He's very distinctive.

"Then let's not talk on an unsecure line," I told him. "Still have that list of burners I gave you?"

"Of course."

I opened my desk and pulled out the Ciáran mac Cool file. All promises I made him were on page one (it was conspicuously blank), and contact information was on page two. We'd gone through some burners before so I picked an unused one. "Burner E, E as in Echo. Give me a Signal call in ten minutes and let's talk. Copy?"

"Echo in ten mike. Five by five." He hung up.

He was stressed out. Normally he avoided military communications shorthand. I grabbed from my desk drawer a small Faraday bag labeled "mac Cool / Echo / Unused" and took a walk out of the building.

Ten minutes later I was in the parking lot and the burner was plugged into my car charger. It had been in my desk for months and the battery was predictably dead. I answered Ciáran's call when it came in.

"I have to remind you, if you're going to do crimes I'm going to have to stop you. Respect the law, Ciáran."

"Keeping your hands clean?"

"I'm not going to comment on my motives."

"Right," he said. I liked Ciáran: he understood how to parse sentences deliberately designed to obscure things. So long as he was a free agent and not working on behalf of the United States government, he could break the law and we could still use whatever he turned up. If a judge or defense attorney ever asked if he was a de-facto agent I could honestly say no, and that I had reminded him to obey the law.

"So, here's the problem I need help with," he continued. "Well, no, she's not a problem, but she HAS a very big problem—"

I made a mental note: whomever she was, and I had a good guess, he was either sleeping with her or hoping to, and she was probably in the room listening. Ciáran's normally not that conspicuously conscious of his word choices.

"—and I need to spend a few hours looking under rocks without her. I can't rule out the possibility there's still a goon squad looking for her. Her safety needs to be addressed."

"Put me on speaker so I can talk to her."

He did so and I caught the tail end of her sentence. "—did he know that?" Nice voice, mezzo-soprano, sounded educated.

"Because he's Judson Ritter," Ciáran explained.

"Ma'am—"

"—Sharon. Please, call me Sharon."

Now was not the time to give her, or anyone else, a crash course in not using your real name. "Sharon, I'm glad to make your acquaintance. I'm looking at a police file right now on one Sharon Victoria Kielic and her all-but-disappearance." That was a lie, kind of, but over the last five weeks I'd read that file enough to have it memorized. Everything about it screamed Ciáran. There are six Laugo Alien pistols in .40 S&W that have been imported to the United States. The shell casings and bullet striations announced his involvement as if he was saying it himself in ALL CAPS. FBI and ATF may not have gotten back to the locals with forensics results yet, but my outfit's Tool & Mark nerds get answers faster than Carnac the Magnificent.

"That's me. But nobody calls me Victoria. I don't like it."

"Won't use it, then. Ciáran, where are you right now? Still at your stomping grounds?"

He sounded slightly relieved. I hadn't yet confirmed I'd help, but he was aware enough to see it on the horizon.

"Yes," he confirmed, "still on the old playground hanging out at the monkey bars."

"Help is thirty-six hours out."

"That much?" Sharon asked, concern raising her vocal tone.

"I wouldn't be ready to go for at least thirty hours anyway, I'm waiting on some deliveries." That sounded like it was aimed at Sharon. "She's going to need twenty-four hours of security, a bit more, maybe. How do we proceed?"

"Sharon, do you have a notebook handy? Like, an actual paper notebook, not a laptop computer?"

"Uh, just a moment. Ciáran?"

"Hold on... use this."

"Yes. I do now."

"Okay. I need you and Ciáran to visit Goodwill and buy some cheap clothes. Not bad ones, just common ones. Also two pair of ballet flats. I want you wearing shoes you can run in, and ballet flats are cheap. Pack a bag, specifically a backpack, for three days. You're not going to like the safe house I'm arranging but it's going to be safe, and that counts for a lot. No technology, none. No cell phone, no smartwatch, no fitness tracker, nothing. If it's more complicated than a frying pan I want you to leave it behind. Do you have all that?"

I could hear a stylus of some kind scritching over paper. "Yes. Yes, I have it. I don't have any electronic devices right now anyway. Ciáran already told me not to. We left my house with the clothes on my back."

"Ciáran, the duress code is anything by Burns, the all-clear is Yeats." I could hear him chuckle.

"You're assuming I know them."

"You know them."

"Well, yes. All right."

Sharon spoke up. "Why Yeats and Burns?"

"Yeats is an Irishman, Burns a Scot," Ciáran replied. "If I'm quoting 'Scots Wha Hae' or 'Parcel of Rogues', clearly things have gone wrong."

"Oh."

I spoke.

"Sharon, your life's on the line, but we're allowed to have a little fun here and there. Lean into it. It helps. Ciáran, name a rally point and I'll be there in thirty-six hours."

"Fiddler's Crown." I knew the place: Ciáran and I had drinks there a couple of years ago. Nice faux-Irish bar, which means it was owned by a Taiwanese guy who practiced Irish hospitality better than most Irish. "You're handling this yourself?" He sounded surprised, and not without cause.

"Don't flatter yourself," I said. "I'm scheduled to be the designated victim cleaning out the break room fridge tomorrow. Some of the things growing in there are demanding U.N. representation. I'll take any opportunity to get out of the office right now."

It was all a horrible lie, of course—we had the college interns do crap jobs like that—but Sharon laughed, and I got the idea it had been a while for her.

— *Ciáran* —

"Well," I told Sharon, "that's a relief. We can work with thirty-six hours. That timing will work for me to head for Asbury Park. I can drive overnight and be there bright and early in the morning.

"I can loan you a pack that'll hold three days of clothes. You've probably already got about half the serviceable clothes you'll need, and there's still time to run out today and get the rest." I thought a moment more. "Though let's play safe and make certain you have *all* clothes nobody's seen you in before, and not obviously new. Judson wouldn't have specified a thrift store if he didn't think that was important."

Sharon nodded.

"Does it have to be ballet flats? I hate them. They never feel steady."

"Deck shoes or running shoes ought to be fine, I'm sure. He specifically stated shoes you can run in. If that rules out flats for you, then it rules out flats."

"Okay."

I had to look up where the nearest Goodwill was. An hour later, we were there.

"So I'm looking for three days' worth of comfortable, casual clothes that won't stand out or draw attention, not too new, not too worn, and two pairs of shoes I can run in, that will fit in with the clothes."

"Perfect."

She was quick about it. It took her about half an hour to pick out the clothes she would need. They all looked as though they would work. We checked out, I topped up the XC60 on the way back, and then we were prepared, with a day to kill. We'd be meeting Judson tomorrow evening.

For now, with nothing else to usefully do, we took a trip to the range, then came back and cleaned the guns. Then we spent some time in my dojo. Sharon was getting quite good by now at blocks and the simpler hold breaks. I deliberately hadn't taught her much of anything in the way of offensive techniques, because if it came down to a fight that would probably be against people who made their living hurting people, I wanted her running, not trying to stand and fight, and I'd done my best to make sure she understood that. She wasn't going to win a fight against professional muscle, but she might be able to outrun him. I already knew she was a pretty fair runner. She could do five miles in under thirty minutes, and that wasn't bad.

We made supper together, cleaned up, then went to bed early. We were both going to need to be well rested.

The next day, we followed pretty much the same plan. Morning run, then range, then dojo, then clean up, then early dinner. Then we spot-checked Sharon's go-bag one last time, I made sure I had all of my documents to show the colo, including my falsified ID and work order, and then we headed out for Fiddler's Crown.

It was time for Sharon to meet Judson.

========================

I didn't see his Mustang when we got there. Nor did I expect to. It was fast, but it was also distinctive and not the best vehicle for avoiding attention, Hollywood action movies notwithstanding. If I knew Judson half as well as I thought I did—which, if I'm honest, was something I was never a *hundred* percent certain of; I was very well aware that he was a professional in a field that I knew I was an amateur at—he was probably going to make an SDR.

(Sometimes I wondered whether I knew who Judson really was. Sometimes I wondered whether *Judson* knew who Judson really was. But right now, that was neither here nor there.)

We went inside, ordered two ciders, found a table, and sat down to wait.

— *Judson* —

Fiddler's Crown was a great place to meet, and not just because of draft Guinness. It had two access points, a front door everyone used, and a rear exit which served as emergency egress and a loading dock for the kitchen. Most importantly there was a parking ramp across the street. Not only did it make for easy access, when Ciáran and Sharon entered they had no idea I was standing three floors above street level taking photographs with a digital camera.

Ten minutes later I walked inside and nodded to Gary Tsieh, the owner of the place. He smiled back at me in the welcoming but vague way restaurant staff give to people they don't know. I was reassured. It's nice to not be known. I hadn't been here in two years, but Gary struck me as a top-flight barman, and those can be some of the most annoying witnesses. They remember everybody.

"Ciáran?" I asked. Gary nodded towards a corner. "Guinness, please." I waited for my stout, then walked to where Ciáran and Sharon sat. I set my stout on the table, slung my satchel into the booth, and joined them.

First things first: I reached into my satchel and pulled out a cheap clunky tablet. I was planning on tossing it in a few minutes, so there was no point in springing for high-end tech.

"Any of these people look familiar?" I asked as I opened up its photo gallery app and slid it over towards them.

Ciáran shared it with Sharon and they immediately contradicted each other. "No," he said; "Yes," she said. She gestured vaguely off in the direction of another table and whispered, "I think he's sitting over there."

I lifted my hands, palms-out, and smiled.

"My bad. Have you seen them before just now?"

"Oh. In that case, no," she amended.

"These are the people who came in after you for about ten minutes. Anyone who wants to follow you has to come in through the front doors. The rear entrance goes through a commercial kitchen, and there are angry chefs with knives there who don't like strangers coming through. So we probably aren't being watched right now."

"SDRs," Ciáran volunteered. "Surveillance detection routines. He's looking out for us already."

Sharon looked over at me for confirmation. "SDR just means SDR," I explained. "People have lots of different expansions for that acronym. It just refers to the tradecraft of noticing and breaking tails."

She nodded cautiously. I didn't blame her. She'd seen Ciáran shoot at least one person, and likely thought I was a gunfighter, too. Few women relish the idea of spending twenty-four hours in an unknown location with an untrusted gunfighter. I was no gunfighter, but she didn't know that. I could do something about the trust, though.

"Sorry it took me so long to get here. Traffic was hell."

"You didn't fly?" She sounded surprised.

I grinned, reached into my satchel, and pulled out a paper map of bus routes. "I left Union Station in Washington. I bought three bus tickets: to Philly, to Dayton, to Richmond. I hopped on the Dayton route. When my other rides arrived, I used a VPN to fool the internet into thinking I was in Philly, or Richmond. I booked three tickets to points more distant from each of them. Someone watching my card purchases—and it's a prepaid card, hard to track, not associated with my name—now has to have their goons hopping nine different buses. Except in Dayton I hooked up with a cash-and-carry intercity bus to Cleveland, and repeated the process. Finally I wound up in Des Moines —"

"—but that's too far by at least two hours!"

"—so I could turn around and head back. If I was being followed, whoever was following me had to turn around, too. Just before leaving the bus in Des Moines I took a selfie and made sure to catch the whole bus in the picture. On boarding the bus to come back I compared the selfie against the passengers. And that's when I was sure I could make the meet without endangering you. Thirty-six hours."

She shivered. "I would call that paranoid, but with the few weeks I've... we've had..." She let it trail off. "Do we need the map? Are we going to be taking a bus somewhere?"

"This?" I shook my head no and handed it to Ciáran. "Be a mensch and draw routes from Manchester to Boston to wherever it is you're going." He nodded, unfolded the map, and using the tablet, started looking up departures and arrivals and prices. While he was doing that I reached into my satchel again, pulling out a quart-sized freezer bag with various bits of trash therein.

I tossed it down onto the map. Ciáran looked at it, nodded, and went back to what he was doing.

"What's that?" Sharon asked.

"Pocket litter. There's a receipt from a bus terminal in Boston showing Ciáran bought a ham sandwich, a soda, and a candy bar. There's also a candy bar wrapper and two scratch-off lottery tickets, losers, showing he was there for a while and got bored. A burner phone with a call history—all the numbers belong to now-disconnected spammers, but if somebody's got a burner with a call history of disconnected numbers, most people think it's a network that's gone to ground." Then, to Ciáran, "The phone's unlock code is 1764."

He snorted with brief delight as he continued to annotate the map. "Forty-two squared. Easy to remember."

"The Ultimate Answer times the Ultimate Answer," I agreed.

Sharon looked even more confused, which was normal. "I don't understand any of this. Why is Ciáran carrying around trash?"

I didn't want to explain this one and Ciáran didn't, either. It took about ten seconds for him to speak. "If this goes wrong..."

He sighed, then put down his pen and looked over at Sharon. "I have a finite pain tolerance," he finally stated, calmly, quietly. "If I make a fatal mistake, if something goes horribly wrong and I die doing this, all the evidence points to you being in Manchester, and me being in touch with a lot of scary people who all vanished simultaneously into the wind. That's deeply scary because they don't know who's in their blind spot, only how many. They'll spend hours trying to track down these numbers and sending search teams to Manchester, giving Judson enough time to exfiltrate you out."

Sharon looked over at me sharply. "You're planning for him to die?", and her question was sharper than the look.

"I'm making plans if he dies. Or if he's tortured," I answered honestly.

That broke her. The stress of living on the run for five weeks, with only one person filling all her social needs, from food to sex to making awful puns, caught up to her all at once. Add in the strong possibility that her one source of all human contact was going to be tortured to death in the next few hours, and… it's hard not to empathize with her.

But that's the discipline in my business. Know when to empathize, when to fake it, and when to shut it off completely.

Ciáran, you wretched son of a bitch, you knew better than to start sleeping with her. You had to have known a moment like this would come. What was it? Arrogance? Pride? Foolishness? Whatever it was, you're calling it love, but it's really a fantasy of justification.

I expected better of you, man.

I didn't let any of that show on my face. "Sharon." I repeated her name a few times until she looked up at me with a tear-stained face and blinked her eyes clear. "Sharon, this is how the game is played by professionals. I didn't read all this on the back of a box of kids' cereal, and I don't own a copy of *The Poor Man's James Bond.* I have been doing this, for reals, in places where the local cops shoot people in the head on the mere suspicion of spying. I have an excellent track record and I'm telling you: our odds are genuinely good. If Ciáran thought he needed help in whatever skulduggery he has planned, he would've asked for it. He didn't, so I'm going to trust his track record with his flavor of spooky stuff. He needs you looked after. He called me because I'm the best person he knows at this.

"Yes, it's a highwire act. You think there's no net, but professionals build their own nets. Things are a lot better than they feel right now, and I think you know it. Lean into what you know."

She looked over at Ciáran, still blinking, pleading silently with him for some certainty or assurance. "He's done this before, love," he said, reaching a hand to cover hers. "He's a pro player at this game." She looked back over at me, wordlessly asking for confirmation.

"Every situation is unique, so no, I've never done precisely this before," I told her calmly, honestly. "But I've done harder things before. To you this is a once in a lifetime stress. To me it's another Tuesday in a twelve-year career." I paused to let it sink in, then drained my Guinness in a single long pull. "You can have a few minutes for goodbyes," I said as I grabbed my satchel and tablet, and rose from the booth. "After that, for the next twenty-four hours, you're a ghost."

I turned and walked to the door. I didn't wait for her to thank me.

That would have been really awkward.

— Ciáran —

I held Sharon's hand tightly as Judson got up.

"It's a really, really long-shot contingency," I reassured her. "I about ninety-eight percent expect to walk in there, social-engineer the colo staff into walking me in, do what I need to do, and leave with nobody the wiser. And then come back safely.

"But there's always that other two percent. There's *already* a Network Gurus engineer there when I get there, he says he's never seen me before and demands to know who I am, the police get called. Or someone from the opposition is there, and *they* know there shouldn't be any such work order, they call Network Gurus and NG denies all knowledge, and the oppo snatches me on my way out. I can't risk being stopped while armed in New Jersey, so my options for resistance will be very limited. I might win a surprise brawl against one opponent. Maybe escape from two. Three or four who know what they're doing and are waiting for me, and I'm toast. Or one shot at close range from behind, before I have any warning. I'm not a Hollywood action hero."

She was looking at me, her face pale, clearly badly shaken. In hindsight... this is a talk we should probably have had sooner. I didn't feel good about myself for that. I kicked myself for letting myself get involved with her on an emotional level. But right about then, well, truth was we *both* badly needed the release. And... then the attachment had come knocking. Loudly.

But this wasn't the time to be woolgathering about that. We were on the clock.

"Listen. I *really hope* it doesn't come to this, but if the worst happens... *tell Judson everything. EVERYTHING.* Including about the Box. That is your best shot.

"I don't know whether... he *is able to* complete the mission that the Box has for us. Or help you to complete it. Whether there's some special reason it *has* to be us, and if either of us dies, it fails. But he will keep you alive. And I can't think of anyone better whom I know to follow up on the information we've managed to collect. Most of which, you recall, he already has an archive of."

She nodded. She was starting to calm down. That was good.

"Are you okay with going with Judson? I promise you you can trust him, as far as you can trust anyone."

She nodded slowly.

"I'm okay," she replied, a little shakily. "I'd... just forgotten the stakes for a bit." She took a deep breath and shook herself.

"Just trust him, whatever he tells you to do, like you trusted me that first night. And keep it together. Like you did then. I know you can do this. You've done it before. Follow his lead and it'll be all right."

She took a deep breath, and nodded agreement.

"Good. Now we both need to go."

Our ciders weren't finished. Oh, well. Leaving them unfinished, we got up and I walked her to the door, and outside. I spotted Judson standing a little way off. I nodded my head in that direction. She looked, and saw him too.

"Your ride's waiting, love," I told her. "See you on the other side." Then I squeezed her hand, gave her one more fast hug, and turned to walk back to the Gray Ghost. I had an appointment in Asbury Park, New Jersey.

— *Judson* —

Back in the parking ramp I introduced her to my mighty steed: a 2002 Honda Civic, with just over a light-second on the odometer and a moderate case of corrosion. She was trying to understand that and failing, so I had some mercy.

"It's one of the most common cars in the country. You can find them for private sale anywhere on no notice. It's too old for modern electronics. When World War Three happens, the only two things to not notice will be cockroaches and Civics."

She didn't respond except to say, "Pop the trunk."

"Can't."

She gave me a look that bordered on a scowl—good, that was probably genuine emotion, it's an indicator of trust.

"Let me guess. You threw away the access fob because it wasn't a frying pan."

"Well, yes," I answered as I unlocked the driver's door with a key. "But your backpack goes behind the driver's seat. If we have to abandon the car in a hurry you want your bag in easy reach, not in the trunk. And the trunk's full, anyway."

I climbed in, tapped the power locks, and a moment later she was seated beside me stuffing her backpack where I said. It was covered in stickers of some anime series, a total Goodwill find—it made her look like she was the mother of a seven-year-old, and it was gloriously perfect. "Various and sundry stuff for the journey. Jerrycans of fuel, a go-bag, stuff like that."

I didn't tell her about the Austrian *Sturmgewehr-77* rifle in the trunk. That was something best avoided. Legal, of course, but best avoided. (Why an expensive Austrian import instead of an American-built rifle? Because in my business you don't get caught wearing American clothing or handling American guns. Why don't I call it a Steyr AUG? Because if and when I need it, I want it to remember I'm the guy who speaks its language.)

"And the... is that a paramedic's jump pack?"

"It is."

"Why is it belted in?"

"Car wrecks. Your bag's filled with clothes: it might bruise us but it won't hurt us. If that heavy, hard jump pack turns into a missile, we could get messed up."

She bit her lip a moment as I started the car and began to pull out.

"You know, I keep asking these questions because I feel like if I only know more, I'll have some sense of control, you know? But it really doesn't seem to be working out that way. The more I ask, the more out of control I feel."

I had to give her points for self-awareness. I've had protectees who spent days realizing they were happier not asking questions.

"If you ask me things I'll answer as honestly as I can," I told her, "but I'm also not going to volunteer anything. For exactly that reason."

"If I tell you to stop the car and let me out, will you?"

"Kidnapping's a major felony."

"That's not an answer."

"Sharon, I'm an employee of the United States government. The best, and sometimes only, protection we Americans have from our government is employee unwillingness to break the law. If you want out, I'll stop the car and let you go your way. I don't break the law. Not even when I can get away with it."

She was still for a bit.

"*We* Americans. *Our* government."

"Yeah."

She sighed.

"I'm being a bitch, I'm sorry. It's just really easy to see you as another flavor of boogieman, you know?" She was understandably right, so I said nothing. "So how does this work?"

"In a few minutes you start baring your soul to me. You're scared, you're adjusting to a new protector-figure, you want to form some kind of emotional connection." I looked over at her then, warningly. "Don't do that. I'm not your therapist, you don't want me to know your secrets, and thirty seconds after I'm out of your life you'll offer a prayer to God you never see me again. I'm happy to tell you funny stories or argue about politics or any other thing to help you take your mind off this crushing stress, but I'm telling you that you'll regret turning this into a heart-to-heart. You'll bare your soul, and I will lie shamelessly to you in return. You deserve better. So don't do that, okay?"

"'My boy, we are pilgrims in an unholy land.'"

It took me a moment to get the reference.

"*Indiana Jones.* And yes. Basically. Unfortunately."

She was quiet for the better part of five minutes. Finally, "Thank you for being honest about all this dishonesty."

I wasn't about to answer that and open the door to a touchy-feely on the subject of integrity.

"'Truth is so precious she should always be attended by a bodyguard of lies,'" I deliberately misquoted slightly.

"That's not what Churchill said," she corrected me. "You left off the, 'in wartime'."

"Wartime, peacetime. Can you tell the difference any longer?"

She nodded thoughtfully, seeming to consider the question. It was probably a lot darker than she was used to, but then again, none of the last five weeks had been what she was used to. I'd been there before, more than once. Every time it had been a rude awakening for me. She was probably no different.

"Up until five weeks ago I thought I could, but maybe I actually knew and was just being dishonest with myself."

The problem with avoiding therapy sessions is under stress most people gravitate towards them. I changed the subject completely to make a clean break.

"If you want music, we've got FM and AM stations, and I talked the prior owner into leaving a CD in the player. Allman Brothers Band, I think."

She silently tapped some buttons on the console and soon *The High Cost of Low Living* came through. As far as omens went it wasn't great.

"You're right," she agreed a few minutes later as the song ended. "No more therapy. But for the record, I'm okay with as many funny stories as you feel like telling. God knows there's been little enough to laugh about lately."

— Ciáran —

There was nothing too difficult about getting to New Jersey. I would be passing through most of the worst heavy-traffic areas before the heavy traffic got there.

That meant I didn't have to focus fully on my driving. That wasn't really a good thing, because it meant that my mind could wander to whether Sharon would be safe with Judson. Especially if something *did* go wrong.

There was no point in mind-gaming it, I reminded myself. Just focus on the plan. Stick to the plan.

I drove onward through the night.

Sharon is safe, I told myself. Focus on the plan.

— Judson —

It took her ninety minutes to ask, "Can you find out how Ciáran's doing?"

"He's barely out of the state. He's got a long ways to go yet."

"Asbury Park isn't all that far."

"I hope that was a lie."

Out the corner of my eye I saw her turn to study me. "It wasn't."

"Then that really had better be one."

She watched me like I was some Sphinx to be understood, an oracle to be deciphered. It annoyed me but I didn't show it. I tell the lies I have to, but outside of those I try to be a straightforward, plain-dealing guy. I understand people suspecting me of being unnecessarily opaque, but those suspicions always leave me in a sour mood.

"I get it," she pronounced at last. "I'm thinking about Ciáran being caught and them using him to find out where we are. But if Ciáran's worried about people—"

"—Goons," I interjected. "They're kind of the opposite of people."

"You're not a goon."

"I'm a spook. We're definitely the opposite of people."

Sharon smiled slightly at that.

"If he's worried about goons," she resumed, "so much so he's arranged for a guardian spook, then my guardian spook's thinking, 'are the goons after her in order to find out where Ciáran's off to?' Which is why you don't want me to talk about where he's going or what he's doing. Because your pain tolerance is just as finite as his is."

"Oh, but I bullshit better," I replied. "I could fertilize the Sahara."

"You bullshit so much because it's a perishable skill," she countered, "and sometimes it's the only way to keep people alive, so you had better be ready when it happens. Like my Ciáran putting in his range time. It's a way of life."

"You're doing it again," I cautioned her. "Therapy sessions. If you can't form an emotional connection by baring your soul, you fall back to trying to discover mine. It's okay, I get it, that's a perfectly natural human reaction, but I want you to hear me clearly: it is counterproductive as fuck to distract me like this when I'm trying to keep you alive, and on a personal level, being psychoanalyzed without my consent is fucking offensive, okay? Only warning: knock it off. If you get captured, Ciáran is dead. The more I get distracted with these therapy sessions, the more likely it is you get captured, the more likely it is he's found tomorrow in a drainage ditch."

She shivered so hard her seat belt buckle rattled.

I didn't sigh. I didn't have pity on her, either. But I did do what I was trained to do: give her enough something to attach to, but not enough something to compromise things.

"I have a therapist," I told her as I pulled the Civic into a gas station. "She's an intelligence community employee, holds an even higher security clearance than I do. Well, more compartments, I mean. I see her once every two weeks. It's a condition of my employment. The government's dropped an insane amount of money into training me, and the government wants to make sure I don't become a psychological casualty. We talk about how to manage truths and lies, strategies to bring genuine meaning into relationships where I might have to routinely deceive, stuff like that. Sometimes couples counseling." By the time I finished we were pulling out of the gas station.

"You have a girlfriend?—I'm sorry, I didn't mean to sound so surprised, you're just... kind of prickly."

"You're not seeing me at my best. And no, not right now, but I haven't had just James Bond one-night stands for the last twelve years, either. I've had a couple of good relationships in that time. Did you know most of the nation's intelligence agencies run their own dating services? No kidding."

She couldn't help but chuckle, and I was glad for it. "It makes sense. It must be nice to have someone you can talk about work with."

"Nah, we never talk about work. Even if she has the clearances and accesses to hear about my day, the nation doesn't need her to know about my day. That's what 'need to know' means. The nation's need, not mine, not hers. Relationships between spooks are weirdly healthy. We know the other has to tell us lies, so we ask no questions, seek no answers. That frees us to discover each other. I like that. It's much more reliable than talking."

She furrowed her brow slightly. "How is that possible?"

"How many times in a relationship have you lied to somebody by giving the same bullshit you've fed yourself so many times that you've come to believe it?"

She fell silent for so long I thought she'd abruptly abandoned the conversation. She rejoined it with, "Well, that's disquieting."

"What? My keen insight into human nature?"

"No," she said in a tone of distinct annoyance. "That white Audi A8 behind us followed us into the gas station, and followed us out even though we didn't stop for gas and neither did they, and they're still there. I count four in the car, all men, none of them overweight."

I couldn't help it. I broke out laughing.

"Clever girl," I said in my best *Jurassic Park* imitation. "That's not a surveillance crew, that's a kidnap crew. Want to learn how to break a tail?"

"I want some more," she *Interview with the Vampire*d.

"You want some coffee?" I asked next, still smiling. "You want coffee. Nothing goes with fucking up somebody's whole day like coffee. There's a drive-through coffee joint ahead. Let's get coffee. You want to know the real me? The real me loves a good latte with fucking goons up."

Five minutes later we were in the drive-through line at one of those Pacific Northwest coffee franchises. True to form, there were a number of cars ahead of us, and as expected, a white Audi A8 behind us. I had the window down, and from somewhere ahead I heard someone argue with the intercom barista about why they couldn't get a competitor's signature flavor at this particular franchise.

Every time I hate my job, I remember I at least occasionally get to kill the people who annoy me. Baristas are some of the most luckless bastards on the planet.

"They've got an off-list menu, drinks they don't publicize," I told Sharon as we waited to creep up to the intercom. "Like their hot spiced apple cider, which is technically nonalcoholic but ought to be on DEA's Schedule I, highly addictive with no medical use."

"Sure," and she sounded so absent it was obvious she was thinking about the Audi.

"Don't look back, don't look back, don't let on you made them, now would be a bad time, in just a few minutes you can laugh at them all you want." The car ahead of us finally moved on from the intercom, and I rolled us up in its place. "Hello?"

"Hello, and welcome to—"

"—Not That Other Franchise And No We Don't Offer Their Signature Flavor?" The barista, a woman by the sound of it, laughed. "Ma'am, you have the patience of a saint, God bless you. You handled it just right. Now, I'm Gary Owen, and I've got a little bit of a special request. Not a bad one, just special."

She laughed again, and I was genuinely glad I could improve her day while she was saving our lives. When the scales are completely unbalanced, I worry about my soul.

"How can we help you, Mr. Owen?"

"Well, driving by, I saw my buddy's ride parked out front. I'd like to buy him an espresso, one shot. His name's Miguel. He might go by Martillo, that's his nickname. Can you do that?"

"Are you sure he's here? We can't give refunds."

"Yes ma'am, his ride's here so he's inside. Don't be scared of him, he's really nice, nicer than me."

"One shot of espresso for Miguel. That's all?"

"Plus, the car behind me, they're friends, I want to pay for their drinks. Whatever they order, I want to pay for it. Can I do that at the window?"

"Sure."

"And two spiced ciders."

"You mean our Cinnanutmeg Honeyspice?"

"No, I mean the one that's not on the menu, the version you baristas make for yourselves."

"Oh, the good shit!—wait, I'm sorry, I shouldn't have said—"

"Two of the good shit," I agreed cheerfully. "Big as you can make 'em."

"You know you can make that at home and save yourself a lot of money, right?" she asked conspiratorially.

"You don't say."

"You seem nice, so... I'll put the recipe on the back of your receipt, okay? Just don't tell people I did it."

"How could I, ma'am? I don't even know your name."

The car ahead of us moved forward, and I pulled us away from the intercom.

"Who's Miguel?" Sharon asked once we'd advanced another car length.

"A friend. He and his buddies like to get together and ride Harleys."

"A biker gang?"

"Those are groups of criminals. The Malcontents are a proper motorcycle club. Admission requirements are strict. You have to pass a criminal background check. They work with the local cops providing courtroom protection and companionship for minor children in abuse cases, or if they have to testify in a criminal matter. Even MS-13 thinks twice before trying to intimidate some little girl in Malcontents colors surrounded by Tio Lobo, Tio Oso, and Tio Martillo."

"So these Malcontents are... they're good bikers."

"*Most* bikers are good bikers. The Malcs are like the Knuckle Draggerz or Warrior Brotherhood. No territory, no agenda, no crimes. They're the best bikers."

"So you sent a signal to your friend Mig, who rides as 'Martillo', which means..."

"'Hammer' *en español.*"

"...who's been in there all day waiting just in case he's needed. The drink and shot count is the code."

"Espresso is 'interdict', and one shot means 'the first car behind me.'"

"What's he do for a living?"

"Teaches high school history. He has a Master's in the subject and wrote a great YA translation of Xenophon's *Anabasis*. Received some awards for it, too. Guy loves kids. Total teddybear. Genuinely nice human being."

We pulled up to the window at last. The barista, a perfectly lovely and kind of cute young thing, tried to give me change for the cash I gave her but I wouldn't permit it. I told her it was the least I could do for that recipe. She laughed, scribbled it down on the receipt, and handed over three of those delightful spiced ciders. Out in front of the coffee shop I could hear Harleys come to life, and I took that as my cue to pull ahead out of the drive-through.

Behind us the Audi tried to surge past the barista window, but a flood of Malcontents in their full colors rode directly in front of them and stayed there, all the Harleys making a riotous noise as they encircled the white car. One particular Malc, a Hispanic fellow in his mid-forties, approached my window carrying two cups of something.

"Who are you this week?" Mig asked, setting his drinks down on the Civic's roof.

"Barista thinks I'm some guy named Gary Owen."

Mig laughed, and it was exactly how you'd expect a high school history teacher to laugh. It was warm, affectionate, and about as threatening as your favorite pair of sneakers. "You and the Seventh Cav." He looked into the car and nodded to Sharon in greeting. "I'm Mig. Don't say anything yet." He reached past me to extend a hand, and Sharon shook it enthusiastically.

"Yes, she has a name, no, you don't get to know what it is, yes, I'm operating domestically, no, except I have no legal authorization whatsoever."

Mig nodded and looked back over to Sharon.

"Genuine pleasure, ma'am." He reached into his kutte's pocket to pull out a small Faraday bag containing something small, flat, and rectangular. I took it, of course. "Fresh burner, standard unlock code, plus a grand of mixed bills. How far you want us to take it with these guys?"

"Mig, we have no legal authorization whatsoever," I repeated. "If they want to go, you have to let them go."

He nodded. "We'll keep them angry enough they won't want to go. You have any intel on these assholes?"

"Driver's name is Patrick. Maybe. It's what he gave the barista." I held up the receipt, which had two tickets: one for "Gary O." and one for "Patrick". "Can you use that to get in his head?"

"Brother, I work with teenagers. I am getting a postgraduate education in how to be a little shitweasel. Oh, yeah, before I forget." He grabbed the two cups from atop the Civic and reached past me to give them to Sharon. "They've got this awesome off-list spiced cider you've just got to try."

He straightened up and gave the Civic's roof a pair of hearty thumps, no doubt signaling to his people that we were leaving their area of operations. He then turned to walk back to his friends and the Audi, except he didn't walk.

He sashayed like Johnny Depp in a Disney film. He was equal parts David Bowie and Pepé Le Pew mixed with the self-confidence of Keith Richards studying a cowboy boot full of cocaine, the total self-assurance of an expert doing what could easily kill lesser mortals. I thought briefly of Hunter S. Thompson: he was truly one of God's own prototypes, a high-powered mutant never even considered for mass production, too weird to live, too rare to die.

"Pat-tycake Pat-tycake the Baker's Man," he sing-songed as he approached the Audi and the driver named Patrick, hands on his hips, swaying as he strode like a Vegas showgirl.

I tore my eyes away from the performance and looked over to Sharon, who was turned around to watch the taunting. Her jaw hung open from the sheer majesty of this Frank-N-Furter-esque show. "Now's the time you can wave to them and mock them," I told her.

"Somehow, I just wouldn't feel right interrupting the master at his work," she said without looking away. "Where did you *find* this guy?"

"Sadr City, Iraq, back when he was a master sergeant with Delta Force." I paused a moment before adding, "Squirrelly guy, Mig."

"Oh my God, he's twerking his bare ass on the windshield. You have to get us out of here. I can't look away."

"And that, Sharon, is a surveillance discouragement routine," I announced as we re-entered traffic and left the spectacle behind us.

— *Ciáran* —

I made Asbury Park a little after oh-eight-hundred, and by oh-eight-forty I was pulling up and parking in the small lot in front of Tenth Avenue Digital Hosting. I grabbed my clipboard and a couple of other necessities, made sure my forged badge was visible, and walked in through the front doors and straight up to the front desk.

"Ted Malden, Network Gurus," I introduced myself, showing my ID badge. "Priority out-of-band service for, uh," I referred to my clipboard, "cages seven, eleven, thirteen, sixteen, nineteen and twenty."

I'd picked that name because with a little practice, I could sign it in a way that was very passably close to one of the several *real* Network Gurus engineers who typically did the Juniper maintenance tasks for the six shell customers we were interested in. And *that* meant that there was a good chance of my name on the sign-in sheet being overlooked by someone who might otherwise spot the anomaly.

"Hmm," the guy behind the desk said. "We weren't expecting you again for five more weeks. Something happen I don't know about?"

"Yeah," I agreed. "Emergency update to remediate CVE... uh..." I squinted at my clipboard. "Goddammit, the CVE number got left off this order. Dispatch musta been in too much of a hurry.

"Anyway, CVSS 9.8, unchecked remote code execution with privilege escalation, known actively exploited in the wild, impacts Juniper PTX thirteen thousand and fourteen thousand series routers running JunOS 25.17 through 26.3.2, fix is in 26.3.3. I have it right here." I showed him a plastic case with a genuine Juniper Networks logo on it.

"Crap," he said. "That sounds really ugly."

I nodded agreement. "You have any other customers running Juniper PTX-thirteen-kay or fourteen-kays," I suggested, "you might update them to current, or give them a heads-up to update."

He squinted at my badge. I obligingly held it closer.

"Don't think I've seen you before?"

"I haven't been assigned for this group of customers before," I replied. "We're... kinda up to our asses in alligators right now, as you could imagine. I drew this straw. I could use a guide to the cages, to be honest. I've never been here before and I don't know your layout." Few things defuse the suspicions of relatively low level security people like *ASKING* them to escort you. And it really would make my task easier.

"Yeah, I'll bet," he agreed. "Hold on, I'll get someone to walk you in." He had me sign in. My badge had evidently passed muster. Front desk social engineering phase: Check.

Five minutes later, I had an escort. He checked my badge again, then led me in through the security doors and back into the datacenter proper. He handed me a call-button fob.

"Which cage you need first?" he asked. I consulted my paperwork again.

"Seven," I said.

He led me to cage seven, checked my badge a second time, and let me in. It was a fair-size cage.

"Just hit that fob when you're ready to move on to the next cage," he told me. I nodded.

"Got it," I answered.

He closed the cage door and left me to it, and I went to work.

A little over an hour later, I was done with the first router. I verified that everything looked to be operating normally and it was passing all diagnostics, which it did. We had, after all, built our patch into the *real* JunOS 26.3.3, and we had made only *tiny* changes.

I hit the call fob. My escort was back in about three minutes. He let me out and locked the cage behind me.

"Which is next?" he asked. I consulted my clipboard again.

"Eleven."

I sweated slightly until I was in the next cage. Letting me into the next cage *probably* meant the oppo hadn't rumbled me. *Probably.*

<hr>

By the time I was done with cage twenty, it was after fifteen hundred. I'd missed lunch, and I'd been up for over thirty hours. I was feeling it.

"Man," the front desk guy commented as I signed out, "you look beat."

I ran with it. I let the tiredness show as I handed the sign-in board back.

"Brother," I told him wearily, "you don't even want to *KNOW* how many of these I've done in the last seventy-two hours. And I have another site still to hit today with five more. And then more tomorrow."

"*Damn*, man," he said.

He buzzed me out. There were no suspicious vehicles loitering nearby, nobody waiting outside the door or near the Volvo, no occupied vehicles in the parking lot or parked nearby on the street.

Head on a swivel, shithead. I walked quickly to the Gray Ghost, surreptitiously scanning my surroundings, listening for footsteps or sudden engine sounds. I unlocked it from a safe distance, made a fast walk-around, tossed my clipboard into the passenger seat, got in and drove off. Nobody stopped me.

I was clear. It was time to go home.

Of *course*, I watched for a possible tail. I didn't *spot* anything. But you can never be a hundred percent certain, especially with no overwatch, nobody watching your six. Someone *could* have had eyes on me from a nearby building, watching for me to leave. So I was on heightened alert until I'd done about half a dozen *separate* things calculated to unobtrusively make life difficult for anyone trying to tail me, and hadn't spotted anything that looked like attempts to maintain contact.

Head on a swivel.

It was time to check in and report success. You're never home free until you're actually home, but you need to let your people know you're inbound. So at the red light just before turning on to the interstate, I punched out the number to Judson's current burner.

Sharon answered, which I expected, since Judson was driving. It made sense to let Sharon handle the comms: it would let her feel like a contributor and less like a helpless passenger. "Love," she greeted me.

"Hey." I was tired as death thanks to the stress suddenly slamming into me all at once, but her voice still put a smile into mine. "You killed Judson yet?"

She made a vague mming noise in the negative.

"*Tempted* to kill him yet?"

Oh, that was one HELL of an affirmative mm.

"It'll be over soon. I'll be back home and we can start planning that cruise to Istanbul we talked about. I'll see you in a few hours."

"Until then," she said, and I swear her voice twinkled.

I hung up the phone, turned onto the interstate, and began the long drive back where I belonged.

— *Judson* —

Fourteen more hours of driving later, Burner Echo rang to life. I tossed it to Sharon to answer, because I refuse to have unnecessary talks while driving.

"Love," she greeted him. Then came a small sea of mmhmms and supportive noises, followed by an "until then," and a pleasant goodbye. She handed the phone back.

"He said he was tired, coming home, and wanted me to look into how much a cruise to Istanbul would cost so we could celebrate properly."

"Yeats, *Sailing to Byzantium,* 'that is no country for old men'. He's free and will be back soon, and we can finally stop driving around in this stupid thing."

— *Ciáran* —

It was well after midnight when we met in the parking lot of a now-deserted shopping mall. Among the teenagers laughing and pretending to be cool and the homeless people sleeping in their cars in a safe spot, nobody noticed another pair of cars arriving.

Judson was driving the world's most nondescript Honda Civic. I should've known. I rolled my car up to his from the front, approached on his left side, so that our driver's windows were almost adjoining. We each rolled down our windows, and in the streetlamps' glow I could see Sharon sitting beside him, visibly frustrated but none the worse for wear.

"How'd things go?" I asked.

"She didn't kill me," Judson drawled.

"Evidently," I replied, grinning with relief.

I looked over at her and put on my best mock-disappointed face. I was rewarded with a glimmer of a smile.

"Yeah, definitely an oversight," Judson continued. "But besides that she was a trooper. High pass, full marks, didn't lose her shit even when we had to break a tail."

The frown I gave Judson was louder than anything I could've said.

"Hey, don't ask me, man." He gave a slight shrug. "When we got here, I started reviewing my surveillance photos from Fiddler's Crown. Found them in the background outside. They apparently figured they were being led into an SDR and fell back, then reacquired the tail once they saw Sharon leave with me. They decided to follow us, not you. Read into that what you like. They looked real corporate, an Audi A8 filled with muscle that looked like executive protection details. They had the good sense not to escalate when some of our friends interrupted their pursuit."

I grimaced. There was nothing good in that news, nothing. Our bolthole might have been compromised if they'd been following us for long. If they hadn't just picked us up on the way to Fiddler's.

"Not happy about that," I told Judson. No blame in it. Just stating it as a fact. Even if it was an obvious one. I was tired. "They hadn't followed us before." Then I corrected myself. "Or rather, if they have, we haven't spotted them—which is *worse*."

"Yeah, well. It's been five weeks, man."

I frowned and tried to parse out what he meant, but finally decided I'd rather look like an idiot for a second than spend the rest of the night trying to deduce it. I'd been awake for around forty hours, I was tired, and I wasn't in my best form.

"What do you mean? Spell it out for me, I'm ragged."

"You've spent the last five weeks detecting them, isolating areas of interest, and escalating your attentions," Judson replied. "What do you think they've been doing? From the moment their hitters hit the floor and began exsanguinating, the bad guys have been on notice there's a new player on the board and he's not taking prisoners. So the bad guys, you know, reacted appropriately. Brought in new talent. Tried new approaches. The fact they had a mildly pro-level tail on us, smart enough to dodge an SDR at Fiddler's, is a sign they're escalating their TTP."

"TTP?" Sharon asked.

"Tools, Tactics, and Procedures," I told Sharon grimly. "And 'escalating their TTP' is spook-speak for something the rest of the world has one word for."

Sharon thought about it for a moment and nodded. "Upgrades."

Judson looked over to Sharon and nodded his approval.

"Upgrades," he repeated, then looked back to me. "This was the warning: you're approaching the endgame now, ready or not. Yeah, we broke the tail, but it was noisy and it gave the bad guys notice there are spooks in play. So your well-financed bad guys are, as we speak, shopping around for ex-spooks now working in the private sector. You've got a day or two before they're on the board. Once that happens, things are going to get really hard for you, really quick. Tie this off soon, brother. End the game before it ends you."

I nodded grimly.

"Unfortunately," I pointed out darkly, "I have no control over when my rock-turning is going to bear fruit. So that means if and when it does, we're going to have to move fast. And that may mean taking risks or exploring options I otherwise wouldn't, if I had a choice."

Well, that was unwelcome news. Still, better to know your bolthole might be compromised, than to not know it at all. We'd have to figure out how to handle that, and what we might need to adapt. I was very unhappy that somewhere down the line, we'd picked up watchers we didn't know about. I didn't know how much they knew about us. Whether they'd actually located us, or just gotten lucky. I hoped very hard it was the latter. And I really wasn't sure what I could do about it either way. Relocating wasn't really an option. The Box tied us down.

Judson handed me a Faraday pouch containing some small objects. "Fresh burner and a thousand bucks in small notes, courtesy of a friend. A trusted friend." A piece of paper came next, a receipt of some kind. "Plus the best spiced apple cider recipe around."

"You're a vending machine of spooky goodness."

He waggled his eyebrows melodramatically but otherwise didn't respond. I looked past him to Sharon and smiled.

"I'm going to circle around, come up on your side, let you cross out in the open for about three feet to my passenger door. Then we're moving in a few seconds."

"I know," Sharon answered with a wry smile.

"Dude," Judson said, sounding mildly offended. "Like I wouldn't brief her on transfer procedure."

I lifted my hands off the steering wheel, briefly, in an open-palm gesture of apology.

"Back in a moment," I said as I took my foot off the brake and began the pickup routine.

And then, as the story so often has it, we went home. I hoped doing so didn't end as badly as stories that invoke that phrase often do. But right now, we had few options.

"So how did they—" Sharon started, as we drove home. Then she stopped.

"No, never mind," she continued. "Before this they possibly only *suspected* I might still be alive. Now we have to assume they *know*. However they spotted us. How would they have known we were looking for them? Did we make some mistake?"

"Doesn't mean they just found out now," I pointed out. I counted off points on my fingers, rubber-ducking again.

"One, as Judson pointed out, we did take out their hitter. We knew all along that would have been a clear sign to them that something had gone sideways.

"Two, it's possible someone inside the police department gave us up. Which is a possibility that makes me very glad the police don't actually know where you are. Though if that leak knows you're with me, and my identity, which is probably in Detective Taylor's reports, then it wouldn't be too difficult to locate me. It all depends on how careful Taylor was. Our best hope, if there is such a leak, is that the leak knows *very little*.

"Three, possibly they rumbled us on the Albuquerque phone gambit after all. The other target might have been more... *alert* than the one we got our recording from.

"So there's plenty of reasons they could know someone was onto them, even if they weren't sure before now that you were a part of it."

"But now they *know*," Sharon said.

"Yeah," I agreed. "But now *we* know that *they* know. The bad news is, they know *that*, too."

Sharon nodded pensively.

"...And Judson probably has to think like this *all the time*," she pondered.

"Yeah," I agreed. "He undoubtedly does."

12: "Because that's where they keep the money"

Once we were done with Tenth Avenue Digital, it was a waiting game—one made more nerve-wracking by the knowledge that Sharon had been spotted at least once. I really hoped that didn't come down on us hard. I had to hope that it had been a chance sighting en-route to Fiddler's Crown, and they hadn't actually located us. It *did* very clearly mean the oppo was still looking for her. We were going to have to *really* keep our heads down.

The stress was clearly getting to Sharon, too, although she did a great job of bearing up under it. Sometimes the mask slipped, though, like over breakfast when she asked me, "So if there are new players entering the game, does that mean it's time to go to the government yet?" She sounded hopeful.

I grimaced.

"We could. But I think that might be a bad idea right now.

"Pro: we would immediately have access to Judson and a half-dozen of his friends. Con: Judson and a half-dozen of his friends. You wanted to kill him after being in a car with him for a day. Frustration ensues, especially when they start threatening to arrest us for doing the things we still need to do.

"You don't bring the government in as a collaborator. You bring the government in *to take over*. As far as I know, Judson didn't break any laws with you, and he's still way out on a bureaucratic limb for us without any safety net. That's as far as his collaboration goes. Anything more, and Judson *takes over*. I love him as a brother but no, I don't think we're at that point yet. We still don't have our smoking gun. And... well, we may still need to do some very questionable things yet." I didn't expand upon that.

The substance of what we had added to the router's code was very simple. It was a tiny change. Or rather, two tiny changes.

First, for each new TCP connection opened through the router, the router would send a single packet to a designated address, containing the source and destination address and port of the connection, and its precise start and end time. Nothing else, for now. There was nothing that was going to happen over UDP—or any of the other possible IP protocols—that was really of much interest to us.

And then, second, it would forget that it had done it. Which *also* made certain that it would not fall into a loop of tattling on its own tattling. If it did that, it could generate a lot of traffic in a hurry, and that would probably attract unwanted attention.

There *was* a remote backdoor in case we needed to make changes, but I hoped we never had to use it. The next firmware update would overwrite everything we had done, covering our tracks.

That target address hosted a tiny, tiny cloud server instance that simply bundled up those logging packets into batches, and forwarded each batch on as it was complete.

Those batches got directed, eventually, to where we could collect them and analyze them.

We weren't really interested, right now, in the *content* of the data being sent over the connections. They would almost certainly be encrypted anyway. It wasn't feasible to break the TLS encryption in real-time. And that meant that in order to find the *content* of the transactions, we'd have to compromise the actual shell-corp servers. Most likely many of them. There would be a high chance of discovery. That would be a big risk that we didn't want to take unless we absolutely had to.

No, what we were most interested in right now was who was talking to whom. What they were *saying* was of secondary importance. We could investigate that further if we needed to.

There was already a fair bit of data waiting for pickup by the time we got home. I'd already built a set of tables to hold it, partitioned and indexed, and built for speed. So the next day, I started running queries against the initial batch, thinking about how to filter out the boring connections that we *weren't* interested in from the ones that we were. One last step, performed on *our* end, executed DNS lookups on the *remote* ends of TCP connections to or from IP addresses we didn't already have in our log, for connections we hadn't already filtered as 'uninteresting'. We only needed to look up what each address resolved to once.

Filtering out the uninteresting connections was going to take a while. I hoped it happened before the next scheduled maintenance update. I didn't think we'd get away with pulling this trick twice in the same place, and I hadn't been able to figure out any way to make our tattle-tale survive a firmware update.

If we were *lucky*, 26.3.3 would still be LATEST at the next maintenance, and the engineer would look at the routers and say "Oh, they're already updated, I don't have to do it." If they got updated again *before* we had the data we needed... we'd be screwed, and I didn't have a Plan B for that case.

There was an awful lot of uninteresting traffic. It was fairly easy, in fact, to filter out a lot of the rubbish. Much of it was spam. I was pleasantly surprised to see the door being slammed in the face of a lot of the obvious spam.

It took about three days to tune my queries to filter out all of the most *obvious* junk. Then we could start looking at what was left and figure out which ones were actually *interesting*. Most of them weren't helpful to us.

The first real sign that it was working was a flurry of incoming connections logged during the second week, originating from IP addresses belonging to Exxon Mobil. Then another extended burst, a few days later, from a Conoco Phillips address.

I pointed that group out to Sharon. She looked very intently at it. We shared one of those Significant Looks.

"This seems to confirm Conoco Phillips' involvement," she noted. "And also that we're still on the right track."

I nodded agreement.

"And by inference," I replied, "that prior group seems to say Exxon Mobil is in on it, too."

We got bursts of incoming connections from Chevron, and from Schlumberger, and from Marathon, and Valero. And then we got hits from Peabody Energy.

"Well, hello," I said. "It's not just oil and gas. The cabal includes coal, as well."

Then the correlation fell into place in my head. I snapped my fingers. Sharon gave me a curious look.

"Cheyenne, Wyoming," I explained. "Peabody Energy. Coal."

"The other meetings," she agreed, as she got it too. I nodded.

We added Peabody to our list. Then we got Arch, as well. That was two coal mining companies. Kinder Morgan showed up. Then Contura.

"That's our third coal company," I stated. "And seven oil and gas, or oilfield services. And all US companies."

"This is coming together into a very dirty picture," Sharon mused. "But what are they *doing*? And why?"

I rubbed my eyes.

"Still don't know, yet," I replied. "But I'm tired. Let's go get a shower. Then make dinner."

"Works for me," she agreed.

═══════════

We were... *hesitant* to go out any more than we had to, just in case Sharon was spotted again. That severely curtailed range time. I broke with my own habits and ordered grocery deliveries. It cost a bit more, but it meant I didn't have to choose between taking Sharon out in public where she might be seen, or leaving her alone at home and unprotected.

We made up for it with extra time in my dojo. I taught Sharon all I could manage, still focusing on defensive and evasive techniques, techniques to distract or interrupt an opponent, techniques to slip out of holds.

It was early in the fourth week that we hit pay dirt. It was the twenty fifth of the month. *All* of the fake corporations spewed outgoing connections. A *lot* of them.

"A lot of corporations do payment processing on the twenty-fifth of the month," Sharon remarked. "It's one of the four most popular scheduled-transaction days. First, tenth, fifteenth, twenty-fifth."

"Well, let's see where they're going," I said. I started looking at the retrieved DNS entries.

Then I started to grin. I couldn't keep from pumping a fist in the air.

"What is it?" Sharon asked. She looked intent.

I pointed at an entry.

"Deutsche Bank," I said. Another. "Sumitomo." Another. "UBS Warburg. Credit Suisse. HSBC Hong Kong."

She read over my shoulder.

"These are some of the biggest offshore banks in the world," she remarked. I agreed.

We ended up with a list of twelve banks.

"It's not just a hypothesis any more," Sharon said. I could hear the satisfaction in her voice. "Now we have *evidence*. The next step in the chain. Fossil energy companies, to shell corporations, to stacked commercial real estate leases, to *more* shell corporations, to offshore banks." We exchanged grins.

"So we know where the money's *coming* from, and where it's going," I mused. "*Why* is still an open question, and it's a baffling one. Because as far as I can see, there's nothing actually illegal in the sources of the money. They're... pumping money through these shell corporations for reasons of their own, when on the face of it there's no reason to.

"Now I don't think they'd be going to all this trouble to hide and dissociate themselves from that money just for something to do. But if there's nothing we can see that's illegal on the *source* end... that strongly suggests that there is something very illegal on the *other* end, that they don't want tied back to them."

"And I think that to figure out what *that* is," Sharon replied, "we have to figure out where the money is going *after* it hits the offshore banks."

"Yeah. We do," I agreed.

"You said before that the big banks are really, really hard to break into," Sharon recalled. "Too tough for you to attempt, you told me. Has that changed with what we know now? And Fester's help?"

"No, it hasn't," I answered. "But I've been thinking about the problem, and it occurred to me that there might be another way around that problem."

Sharon looked at me curiously.

"An easier way to crack the banks?"

"Not exactly."

She started to smile.

"You've got some cunning idea, haven't you? Out with it, Mister mac Cool."

"They're *banks*," I started to explain. "Their security is strong because they're highly attractive targets. Someone once asked John 'Machine Gun' Dillinger why he robbed banks. He replied, 'Because that's where they keep the money.'"

She raised an eyebrow at me, but the penny hadn't dropped yet.

"What'll you bet me someone's already *done* it?" I asked.

Her eyes widened.

"And if they *have*, then perhaps all we have to do..."

"...Is find them and convince them to work with us," I finished. "If, *IF*, we can do it, it ought to be a lot safer than trying to break into the banks by ourselves. *IF* we can find them and convince them. Which may not be *at all* easy."

"That sounds like Uncle Fester's kind of help," she observed. "The *deus ex machina*."

"I was thinking the same thing," I agreed, as I got up. "Hey, Fester!"

The TV was already lit when I got into the next room.

"Fester, we need an assist, if you can. We have a list of twelve offshore banks. It goes without saying they have really, really strong security. We need a way in. But cracking them—especially undetected —will be incredibly hard.

"Can you find us someone who's *already done* it?"

WHICH BANKS DO YOU NEED TO ACCESS?

I looked at Sharon.

"Any one of the twelve we've identified would be enough, at minimum," she said. "But more would be better. We need enough to establish a pattern."

IT WILL TAKE TIME.

"We can wait," I said. "But hopefully not too long. We're starting to be under some serious time pressure. Like Judson said, the endgame is nipping at our heels."

"What do we do in the meantime?" Sharon asked.

"We *take a freaking break*," I replied. "Come upstairs, beautiful, let's steam up the shower a bit."

"I like the way you think," she agreed, with a huge grin.

"Fester," I called back over my shoulder, "please do not disturb us tonight except in case of emergency."

***

We took a long shower, soaking and rubbing all the stress aches and muscle knots out of each other, taking our time, touching each other tenderly, cuddling under the hot water, breathing the steam. Then we got out and dried each other off, got dressed again, and we risked going out to dinner again. Nothing fancy, just a nearby Mexican place. But when I say Mexican, I mean it was *real* Mexican, not commercial-chain Tex-Mex. They had five different molés, they had alambré, they had tacos (and burritos) al pastor, they had quesadillas rellañas. Everything was fresh-cooked to order. There wasn't a steam table in the place.

It was only twenty miles away, but it took us an extra hour to get there, because I wanted to be as certain as I possibly could before we went in that we hadn't picked up a tail.

I ordered pollo chipotle y arroz con mariscos, while Sharon went for the molé poblano. We shared, of course. We sat, relaxed as much as we could, enjoyed ourselves, and *absolutely no* shop talk. This was *us* time. We took our time eating, then we paid up and went home, equally cautiously. We sat on the couch and cuddled while we watched *Kung Fu Panda*, then we went to bed early.

Okay, we may have *gone to sleep* late, but we went to bed early. Honest.

***

The Box didn't have anything for us yet in the morning. But on the afternoon of the fourth day, it sent me a message with a set of instructions.

"We've got something," I told Sharon as I read the instructions.

Then I headed for the office.

Following the instructions, I navigated my way to a dark-web chat forum.

"Knock knock," I typed. "Looking for Glassman." Then I waited.

A while later, there was a response.

```
[GLASSMAN]
Who's asking? Don't know you.

[FIONN]
Honestly, I'd be highly concerned if you did. Been keeping my
head way down. Got a big problem I need to solve. High stakes.
```

I consulted the instructions.

```
[FIONN]
IndigoGrrrl! said you could help with it.
```

There was a pause.

```
[GLASSMAN]
You know the bloogirl?

[FIONN]
Not directly. More, a contact of a contact of a contact. It's
complicated, and I can't give you a full explanation right now.
```

Another pause.

```
[GLASSMAN]
Not feeling a warm happy glow about that. What kind of help are
you looking for?

[FIONN]
Need to poke around in a big glass house with a lot of green
wallpaper. Just to look at records.
```

There was a long pause. Then 'Glassman' messaged me a link to an encrypted private chat.

I joined it. Sharon sat next to me and watched.

```
[GLASSMAN]
You get any kind of keyword from IndigoGrrrl!?
```

[FIONN]
Said to mention Roko's Basilisk.

A lengthier pause.

[GLASSMAN]
OK, IndigoGrrrl! vouched for you. Says you have some
interesting friends. What's this about?

[FIONN]
I have a list of offshore banks whose records I need to poke
around in to trace where a whole heap of laundered money is
going.

[GLASSMAN]
Fuck me. :scream: :explodinghead:

[GLASSMAN]
You have a fucking LIST.

Another long pause.

[GLASSMAN]
Look, the only reason I'm still listening is IndigoGrrrl! asked
me to. Said it was really important. She wouldn't say that
lightly. I trust her judgment, or I'd have already blackholed
you.

[GLASSMAN]
Also, I've looked at your connection a bit, and it's not a
government network, but it's very well protected. And that
makes you interesting.

[GLASSMAN]
But a LIST. Of offshore banks. Like it's a fucking shopping
list.

[GLASSMAN]
You have some mental picture of waltzing in like Keanu Reeves
with virtual guns blazing and lifting something?

[FIONN]
No. Just need to trace where something is going to. But I know
I can't do it myself. I wouldn't be coming to you if I thought
it was easy.

[GLASSMAN]
Banks too tough for you, d00d? :lol:

[GLASSMAN]
Actually, don't feel bad about that. The big banks are tougher

than you would believe. No, tougher than that. No, TOUGHER.
It's not like some stupid techbro hedge fund or binance bros.

[FIONN]
Be straight with you. I KNOW cracking them is WAY beyond my
skills. That's why I'm looking for someone like you. I really
need this information. It's critical.

[FIONN]
So I need expert help. We want to borrow some access for a few
days from someone who already knows how to get in. And what the
quiet rumor says, is that's you.

Pause.

[GLASSMAN]
Dude, you have NO IDEA what you are asking for. Do you know
what an intrusion into a major bank is like?

[FIONN]
No. Only that it's way beyond me. But we need to do it. That's
why I needed to find someone who'd already done it.

[GLASSMAN]
Look. It's not JUST the bank's security. That's the LEAST of
your worries.

[GLASSMAN]
Fucking EVERYONE is in there, man. And I do mean EVERYONE. CIA.
Mossad. FSB, GCHQ, the Chinese, the French, the Australians,
the Koreans, the Japanese. All on a paranoid watch for each
other, and anyone else.

[GLASSMAN]
It's like riding through a fucking free-fire zone, through a
minefield, on an inflatable bicycle, while blindfolded, in the
dark, and all the other guys have night vision gear. And they
play in teams. And sometimes the other teams work with each
other.

[GLASSMAN]
Once you even get IN in the first place, you've got to avoid
ALL of them. And somehow exfil what you want without attracting
their attention.

[GLASSMAN]
Slip up ONCE and you're totally fucked. Those guys play rough.

[GLASSMAN]
Yeah, I got in once, and got out with my ass intact. But I
don't want to ever go in there again without a REALLY FUCKING
GOOD reason. In hindsight, it was fucking stupid bravado. I
know better now.

[GLASSMAN]
So tell me straight out why I should be a part of this
insanity.

I thought, and decided to take a chance.

[FIONN]
You wanna help break open a dirty scheme run by some really big
fossil energy corporations?

There was a long pause. One of the longest yet.

[GLASSMAN]
...Maybe.

[GLASSMAN]
...OK, I'll admit, you got my attention. I'm listening. Tell me
more. But you really better not be fucking with me.

I looked at Sharon.

"How much do you think we dare risk telling him?"

She thought about it.

"I'm... not sure anything we know about the scheme *so far* is worth
keeping secret," she said slowly, "if it gets us a solution to the other half
of the problem. And I think he probably has an interest in keeping
everything about this discussion confidential."

I nodded slowly. Then I turned back to the keyboard.

[FIONN]
OK, here's what's going on. We stumbled by accident across a
massive money laundering scheme. Please don't ask details of
how we found it. People already died for it.

[GLASSMAN]
:thinking: :spockeyebrow:

[FIONN]
It starts at fossil energy companies. Conoco Phillips, Exxon
Mobil, Chevron, Peabody, Arch Coal, Shell-Mex, the whole
rogues' gallery. We've unraveled the trail back to them. A
cabal.

[FIONN]
They're laundering twenty, maybe thirty million dollars a month
— that we KNOW about — through a hidden-in-plain-sight scheme
built around fake commercial real estate leases and bogus shell

corporations with sock-puppet boards.

[FIONN]
We've traced it forward to a group of a dozen or so offshore
banks. And then we lose sight of the money once it enters the
banks.

[FIONN]
That's got to be where the illegal part is happening, because
the rest of the scheme isn't TECHNICALLY illegal in any way,
just weird and stupid in ways that make no sense UNLESS the
destination is something highly illegal.

[FIONN]
They wouldn't be going to these extreme lengths to hide the
money - or murdering people to keep it hidden - UNLESS it was
something very illegal. And it's too complex to be just tax
evasion. They're willing to murder people over it. There's got
to be more to it.

[FIONN]
So we need to know where the money goes from there. To fill in
the last pieces of the puzzle.

[GLASSMAN]
The logic makes sense. And that's a lot of money.

[GLASSMAN]
Which banks?

   I typed in the list.

[GLASSMAN]
Holy fucking shit. Fucking SERIOUS, man. These are some of the
biggest of the big players. How important IS this? Big score?
Nobody builds something this big to embezzle kids' lunch money.

[FIONN]
We don't really know how big it is yet. Not until we know where
it goes. But with this much money being moved, might end up
being the biggest you've ever seen.

[GLASSMAN]
Ha ha, not fucking likely.

[GLASSMAN]
No, actually, you're not wrong there. I'm curious myself now
where this ends.

[FIONN]
Plus we want some personal fucking payback for someone they had
tortured and killed.

[GLASSMAN]
:thinking: Do you know account numbers?

[FIONN]
No. Just transaction sources. Addresses and their owners-on-paper. We'd have to break transport encryption, or compromise a lot of systems, to get the account numbers. And we're under some serious time pressure. Need to move fast before they catch up to us.

[GLASSMAN]
:thinking: That makes it harder. Especially for you. There's resources I could use to make it easier to get some of that information, that you most likely don't know about. And I wouldn't tell you, so don't ask.

There was an even longer pause.

[GLASSMAN]
You know what, fuck it, I'm in. Fuck those planet-raping shitgoblins anyway. If it's that big, I'll take a second chance. THIS TIME. ONLY.

[GLASSMAN]
But I'm not handing you my access. You don't know what you're doing. You'll expose my entry points, and they'll have your butterflied ass turning on the barbecue in five seconds flat.

[GLASSMAN]
Send me what you've got. Enough that I know what to look for. I will TRY to get you into ONE bank. ONE. No more. If they spot me I will drop everything I haven't already exfil'd and run like fuck.

[GLASSMAN]
Give me enough to know where the money is coming from, and I'll tell you where it goes. IF I can.

[GLASSMAN]
Give me a week. Maybe ten days. I'm gonna have to be real careful.

[FIONN]
That's even more help than we were hoping for. What will we owe you?

Pause.

[GLASSMAN]
For this? Fucking freebie, man. Because fuck those assholes.

[GLASSMAN]
But you'll owe me a favor sometime. On the off chance I need
something in the future that you can help with. Like I said,
you have interesting friends.

[FIONN]
Fair enough. Least I can do.

Glassman told us where to send the information, and we made
arrangements for how to get back in contact when he had results. I sent
him the same package I'd last sent Judson Ritter. Plus all of our new
findings since then.

Then, once again, we waited. We were starting to get a serious
case of cabin fever. We had lots of time to focus on each other, but the
stress was really getting to us. Especially with the constant uncertainty
about whether anyone had made us. We found ourselves making a
conscious effort to give each other extra space, and not take anything for
granted.

On the other hand, it gave us lots of time to work on upping our
shared-cooking game and work better together in the kitchen. That was
fun.

It would have been so much better if we could have invited a guest
or two over for dinner now and then. Or, you know, if we didn't have
what felt like a Sword of Damocles hanging over our heads.

There was one weird bright side to all of this stress, too. If our
relationship could survive *this*, it could probably survive *anything*.

========================

Glassman turned out to be as good as his word. He pinged me
back eight days later. Just a two-word message: SAME PLACE.

I went and logged in with the same credentials as before, Sharon
sitting right beside me.

[FIONN]
You rang, sir?

[GLASSMAN]
Fionn. Dude. HOLY FUCKING CRAP, MAN, I repeat, HOLY FUCKING

CRAP. You have NO FUCKING IDEA yet what this is going to blow
open. But you're about to learn.

[GLASSMAN]
I had to bail out before I finished the first set. There's
fresh toothmarks in my ass and they're still bleeding.

[GLASSMAN]
I know I told you only one, but this is gonna be so fucking
huge I took the gamble and dipped my toes in a second one, JUST
long enough to see if the same pattern held. It did. Didn't get
spotted in that one. I already had the source accounts, so I
wasn't in there nearly as long. So you have a good chunk of
data from two banks.

[GLASSMAN]
The names these accounts belong to are gonna look like
nobodies. Don't look at that. Look at who they are CONNECTED
to.

[GLASSMAN]
I passed a heads-up around some friends. We're all gonna be
watching for the fireworks and making a lot of popcorn. ROCK
THE FUCK ON.

[GLASSMAN]
DON'T SCREW THIS UP. I'm NEVER, EVER doing this again. Don't
waste it.

Then he passed me credentials for a cloud storage bucket, and told
me to tell him when we'd downloaded the contents, so that he could
clean up the tracks.

There were two files in it. Large ones.

One was labeled UBS Warburg. The other, Sumitomo. It was
double what he'd told us he'd try to do for us.

I downloaded them, scanned them for malware just to be sure, and
we opened the first file and started reading. It was a detailed list of
transactions showing what transfers came into the accounts associated
with the shell corporations feeding into that bank. And when that
money went back OUT again, in order, and what accounts it went into,
and who accessed those accounts to take money out, and from where.

The final destination accounts were tagged with who owned them.
And there was a list of people whom those people were connected to.

"Holy mother of god," Sharon almost whispered. "These... these
first three are Congressmen. And this one's a US Senator."

We went through the file line by line.

"*Oh my god*," she exclaimed. "'Hanlon's getting greedy'. SENATOR Hanlon."

Then we looked at the other file. It was shorter, but it was the same. Even had some of the same names.

"Do you notice anything about *which* Senators and Congressmen these are?" I asked Sharon quietly. Both of us were feeling we hardly dared speak aloud lest the heavens open or something.

"Yeah," she replied. We looked each other in the eye. "All of those most recent payments are to the ones blocking the omnibus climate bill."

There was a long silence.

"We've *got our fucking smoking gun*," I declared triumphantly. A grin started to spread across Sharon's face. "It's time to *nail these bastards to the fucking wall.*"

I went back online again and sent Glassman one message.

```
[FIONN]
Glassman, you are the mensch to end all menschen. Got the
package. You are a fucking LEGEND, and I will vouch for that.
Firing for effect as soon as possible. May take a little while
to get all the pieces in place. Stand by for fireworks.
```

I got back a string of emoji—a thumbs-up, a punching fist, a grinning horned devil, and fireworks.

"So now what?" Sharon asked. "How do we act on this?"

I thought for a moment before I answered.

"I think it's time to call in that offer from Judson. He asked if we wanted to hand this over to Treasury. It's time to take him up on it."

13: The Belly of the Beast

I called Judson.

"'Allo, guv," he greeted me. "You ready to close?"

"G'day, squire. Listen… you remember that package I sent you?"

"Uh-huh."

"We've traced it all the way to the ends. In both directions."

"…Aaaaaand from the tone of your voice, it's big."

"Judson, I swear, you will not believe how big it turned out to be. We're still coming to grips with it ourselves."

"Ooookay. What do you need?"

"You remember you asked if we wanted to just pass it all to Treasury?"

"Yup. You think it's that time?"

I took a deep breath.

"Yeah. It's time. We've taken this as far as we can. We have the smoking gun, and it's not just still warm, it's still loaded. Judson, can you get us a face-to-face with a… suitable senior official?"

There was a pregnant silence.

"Well, you *did say* it was big. Uh. Let me think."

Another pause.

"Can you give me the view from angels thirty?"

"We have verifiable proof—*buckets* of proof, full chain of evidence with verifiable financial records—that a substantial number of members of Congress, both in the House and the Senate, are taking *huge* under-the-table payoffs from the fossil fuel industry to block the big climate bill. And maybe others."

A couple of seconds of silence.

"Holy. Fucking. Crap."

A pause.

"You're sure?"

"Dead certain. All the way to individual bank accounts, and who many of them connect to. There's some big names."

There was another long silence.

"Give me a few days. I'll have to kick this upstairs."

"You know where to find me."

"I do. *Watch your back, guv.*"

"You bet. Thanks. We'll owe you a huge one."

"No... if this comes off, I think I and a whole lot of other people will owe *you*. Both of you."

"Later, then."

"Talk to you soon."

He disconnected.

A couple of days later, Judson called me back.

"I need you both to come to Washington," he declared without preamble. "We'll be sending a protection detail to escort you in. Bring everything you've got, both printed and electronic copies of the most crucial records if possible. And keep a backup set of everything somewhere *secure*. As secure as you can make it.

"You're going to meet with my Deputy Director, then with a rep of the Undersecretary for Terrorism and Financial Intelligence at the Department of the Treasury, among others, a truly scary set of others. There will be a read-in ready and waiting for you to sign here, before we go over to Justice, and an agreement guaranteeing you both immunity for any, ah, *inadvertent* legal violations you *may have* committed in the course of amassing this information, provided it all pans out."

Then he told us exactly when and where we were to meet, and when our ride would be coming to pick us up.

And that was how we ended up walking into the Department of the Treasury at 1500 Pennsylvania Avenue, wearing our 'professional' outfits, me carrying a hardside briefcase, flanked by Judson Ritter on one side and his several-times boss, Deputy Director Mackey, on the other. A Treasury agent met us as our guide. We went through the metal detectors, walked down a bunch of hallways, rode an elevator up, walked down *more* hallways, and ended up *eventually* being ushered into a small conference room where a number of other people were already waiting for us. The seal of the United States Department of the Treasury was on the back wall.

It took quite a while to reach that point. Judson had told us to bring electronic copies of all of our documents, but he had neglected to mention the half hour of paperwork it would take just to bring them in. When you do this kind of thing day in, day out, the procedures become habitual, and sometimes you forget to warn people who aren't as intimately familiar with them as you are. Strangely, even the Treasury security people seemed surprised by this. Maybe the other agency representatives at this meeting made things different. I'd have to ask Judson about it later. Right now, it wasn't a priority.

<hr>

"Good morning, all," said DD Mackey as we were waved to seats. "Stash your badges, please." People took their seats and slipped their badges into their coat pockets as Judson walked around giving each attendee a different color of highlight marker.

Sharon looked a little confused by this, so I leaned over towards her.

"Need-to-know. Everything's need-to-know. We don't need to know their names or agencies. We've got Mr. Green, Mr. Blue, Ms. Red..."

DD Mackey, now aka Mr. Blue, overheard, looked over, and gave a brief nod. "Welcome to the bigs."

"I suppose it'd be rude to ask 'labor or management?'" Sharon was trying to break the tension, but mostly it came out as nervous. Which wasn't untrue.

DD Mackey smiled.

"Management. Except for..." He looked over towards Judson, who waved a pink marker. "Mr. Pink. You can tell he's labor from how he's the one handing out the markers. Ms. Kielic, please don't worry about job titles. You know me, yes?"

Sharon nodded nervously. "I've seen you testify before Congress.

You're the deputy director of the National Clandestine Service."

"Operations, please. We were only called the NCS for about a decade. Journalists are still using the old name, unfortunately. But yes, I'm the Deputy Director of Operations for the Central Intelligence Agency. Pretty senior. But here in Treasury, people hear 'Deputy Director' and wonder if I've managed to get an office to myself yet. So rather than bore you with who has what title and what each one means, let's just say you know who I am, and everyone here plays at or around my level. Except for Mr. Pink here, who probably wants to disappear into the wallpaper just from how many senior people he's seeing."

Judson gave a brief, terse nod. He wasn't showing any nervousness, but knowing him, this much visibility must have been nerve-wracking.

"Why haven't I seen any of these people in the newspapers?" Sharon asked again.

Ms. Red spoke up, a little sweetly, her voice sounding like Appalachian hills.

"Ma'am, the people you see in the newspapers, they've all got trusted assistants, you know, real right hands. They also have left hands, the trusted assistants few people in the department know about. Over in Treasury there's an Under Secretary for Terrorism and Financial Intelligence. His right hand is Stephen Arnaut, and whenever you see Agent Arnaut in a meeting you know the Under Secretary might as well be present. This gives any meeting involving Agent Arnaut visibility the Under Secretary might like to avoid.

"His left hand is me. Only people who need to know I have the Under Secretary's ear know I exist. This lets the Under Secretary be a ghost in the corner, and keeps us off the bureaucratic radar." She went around the room giving each person a pleasant smile.

"I see left hands from Treasury, the FBI, Homeland Security, and more."

"Why are you here, Deputy Director?" Mr. Brown asked DD Mackey.

"Mr. Blue, please," Mackey answered, waving his marker in a mildly scolding manner. "There are aspects which may involve intelligence operations against the United States government by foreign powers."

"That's our remit, not yours."

"We'll deconflict jurisdiction in another meeting, Mr. Brown."

Judson finished handing out the markers and resumed his seat. DD Mackey—Mr. Blue—continued speaking.

"Everything spoken of in this meeting is presumptively classified TOP SECRET/SCI in the compartment NIMROD," he began, handing out sheets of paper to the attendees to sign. "Yes, I know, 'Mr. Blue, why is a domestic law enforcement matter getting an SCI compartment?' As mentioned, there's an aspect relating to foreign intelligence and the Agency insists this investigation be formally classified, not just 'Law Enforcement Sensitive'. Our guests have already been given one-time read-in access to TS material in the NIMROD compartment. Let's begin.

"I have heard the summary of what our guests have found, and I have looked through some of the information they have gathered, and I believe you will agree that it is a remarkable body of work. It is also extremely serious, on a national level, and possibly internationally.

"So, with your consent, Ms. Red, I am going to turn this meeting over to Ms. Kielic and Mr. mac Cool."

He turned to us.

"If you would be so kind, please tell us in full, from the beginning, what happened, and what you found out. But start by telling us why we should care. It helps us to keep our attention focused."

Sharon and I looked at each other, then she started things off. She took a deep breath.

"You should care because there's a bribery conspiracy involving roughly a tenth each of the House and Senate, possibly more, and we have hard proof."

That went off like the world's quietest nuclear bomb. The room went from annoyed extremely senior government personnel exchanging bureaucratic bickering and jurisdictional games, to a fleet of hawks staring intently at us. This was probably an improvement, but I suddenly understood why Judson wanted to hide in the wallpaper.

"My name is Sharon Kielic," she continued. "I am, or was, a legal associate at a corporate and contract law firm, Harris Magnusson

Partners.

"Nearly three months ago, a tranche of commercial real-estate lease contracts was received by my firm and assigned to the office of the senior partner for whom I worked, Philip Bartholomew. I did not know about these contracts at that time. They would have been assigned to me to review and file, as a matter of course, in the next day or two. It was typical for me to process around two such tranches of contracts a week. They were routine and generally of no particular individual interest beyond verifying that they were properly and correctly drafted.

"That evening, after he and I both left work, Mr. Bartholomew was intercepted on his way home, abducted, tortured, and subsequently murdered, by persons then unknown, who then put him back in his car and attempted, with only partial success, to disguise his death as a fatal single-vehicle rollover accident.

"Also that evening, probably at about the same time that he was abducted or a little after, a then-unknown person entered my house and attempted to murder me in my bathroom. I was saved only by the timely intervention of Mr. mac Cool, who was present in my house at the time for reasons not germane to this meeting."

She nodded to me, and I took the baton.

"I assessed the attempted murder as a murder-for-hire," I said. "With Ms. Kielic's consent and cooperation, I removed her from the house and escorted her to a place of safety, where her location would be unknown to whoever wanted her dead, and where she has remained under my protection ever since. The individual who attempted to murder her has since been identified with the aid of DNA evidence as one Nicolas Carravini, a known hitter for the de Garofolo crime family, with an extensive criminal record.

"At some time in the early morning, the offices of Harris Magnusson Partners were firebombed, causing major damage and the destruction of physical and digital copies of many records. Police investigation of these events quickly determined all three to be linked, although they did not know Ms. Kielic to be alive and declared her to be missing under suspicious circumstances."

I passed a few sheets and a USB drive across the table. Ms. Yellow picked them up and glanced quickly through them.

"These are the police reports. They are also on that USB drive as EXHIBIT A. We allowed the belief that Ms. Kielic's location was unknown to stand, for her own protection."

I gave Sharon the nod. We'd scripted this out, and she had coached me. We wanted to make it very clear that we were a team.

"Shortly afterward," she continued, "we were able to obtain copies of the tranche of contracts delivered to Harris Magnusson that day, proceeding upon the assumption that the attacks were *most probably* linked to some information received by the firm immediately prior to the attacks. We had no other working hypothesis. This was our only potential lead."

Sharon slid the five contracts across the table.

"Those contracts are on the USB drive as EXHIBIT B. If you examine them, you will find them all different in detail, but standard in form, with nothing obviously unusual about them.

"However, if you correlate them with a mapping system, as we eventually did while trying to determine what might be significant about them, you will find that the top two contracts refer to the same physical property, using different—but both legally valid—addresses, on different streets enclosing the properties. In this example, that property, which is bounded by Ninth and Tenth Streets, and crosswise by Oak and Acacia Avenues, is leased twice concurrently, to two different independent lessees—the entire property, not a sub-let—with its address disguised so as to make it appear that the two leases referred to two separate properties, one located on Ninth Street and one located on the cross-street, Acacia. It was only when we highlighted the locations in a mapping tool that we realized the two addresses actually referenced the same property.

"Now, we all know that there is nothing illegal or even particularly strange about multiple leases on a property. That raises the question of why someone would attempt to conceal the fact in this manner; and, more significantly to us, given that this was the only potential clue we had to why Mr. Bartholomew was murdered, a greater question of why some unknown actor was apparently willing to commit murder—or multiple murders—to conceal the fact.

"Since we could find nothing else irregular, we could only assume that this apparent attempt at concealment was in some manner a key clue. Speculating that there might be a pattern to be found if we looked for it in the right way, we searched commercial real-estate databases for other commercial rental properties in the US that could be referred to using more than one address on different enclosing streets.

"We found somewhat over twenty three hundred such, all told. Most had only one lease on them and were uninteresting, or were conventionally sub-let and also uninteresting, or multiply leased using the same address and, once again, uninteresting.

"Out of these, we identified a set of sixty-seven commercial properties that were leased in most cases three times each, sometimes four, using a different possible address to refer to the property in each lease. These properties were all held by, and all leased by, shell corporations.

"We were able to tie ownership of all of these sixty-seven properties, in the end, to four such shell corporations. The lessors, across the entire set of roughly two hundred leases, were all the same set of just over forty shell corporations. We could find no evidence of any of these companies conducting any actual business. As far as we could determine, they exist solely to lease the properties. We also found that out of a total of around sixty directors, all forty-plus corporations appeared to be controlled by a subset of only five directors. It is our hypothesis that the remaining fifty-five or so directors are sinecures kept unaware of what is going on."

She slid across a few more sheets of paper.

"The sixty-seven properties, and the shell corporations holding and leasing them, are listed on these sheets. The lessee corporations, for the most part, hold from five to seven leases each, distributed across the sixty-seven properties. The entire database of multiply leased properties is EXHIBIT C on the USB drive."

She shot me the nod and I took the lead back for a while.

"We couldn't understand why anyone would do this, at first. Then it occurred to us that a property that is leased three times generates three income streams, but has only one set of overhead. A very substantial amount of money flows nearly invisibly through two hundred such commercial leases. On the basis of information we developed since, we conservatively project the total take to be between twenty-five and thirty million United States dollars per month, for whatever portion of the scheme we were able to identify and trace.

"We concluded at that time that we had stumbled across a large, complex and ingenious money-laundering scheme, whose purpose we were as yet unable to establish. However, we considered it highly improbable that anyone would go to such lengths to set up such a scheme—or to try to conceal it—without it involving something illegal, somewhere. Even if only simple tax evasion.

"We also determined that in every case except one, each of the contracts for each of the multiply-leased properties had been assigned to a different law firm for contract recording and legal review. Which is to say, no law firm was ever supposed to receive or record two contracts for the same physical location."

I pointed across the table at the stack of leases in front of them.

"The one exception is the pair of 'clone' contracts sent to Harris Magnusson Partners. This, we believe, was a mistake. We also believe that shortly after the mistake was made, whoever made it realized their mistake, and panicked, fearing discovery of the scheme.

"This, we believe, is the moment at which orders were given for the abduction and murder of Mr. Bartholomew, the firebombing of Harris Magnusson's offices, and the attempted murder of Ms. Kielic, the events which triggered our investigation. Had they not overreacted in this fashion, the error would probably have escaped notice. It took us nearly a week to find it when we were *actively looking* for something suspicious, and had a strong suspicion of exactly where to look."

I glanced at Sharon and she took over.

"At this point," she picked up, "we had two tiers of shell corporations and what appeared to us to be a money laundering scheme. We had no other hypothesis. The source and destination of the money were unknown, nor what specifically it might be that the actors were trying to conceal or why.

"Using the means described in EXHIBIT D, we were able to construct organizational relationships which eventually enabled us to trace overall control of the scheme back to a cabal of senior executives of at least eleven fossil-fuel energy companies. We believe there may be more than eleven companies involved, but have not yet identified the others. During the course of this phase we were able to obtain an audio recording of a clandestine meeting between a number of the coordinators of the scheme."

She passed over another sheet.

"The list of known involved companies and the evidence supporting the conclusions are in EXHIBIT E.

"We were then left with the problem of where the money was going. We were able to later determine, by other measures including traffic analysis, that all of this money was being funneled to a group of offshore banks."

She slid over another sheet of paper.

"This is the list of banks that we know to be receiving the funds. This is EXHIBIT F on the USB drive.

"We were, at this point, unable to trace the funds beyond the offshore banks. We did not yet have any actionable proof of a crime; merely a strange pattern of behavior for which some bizarre, yet legal, justification might have been possible. We also, in the absence of a provable crime requiring concealment, had only circumstantial evidence linking the scheme to the attacks against Harris Magnusson Partners and its employees, although we did by then, as previously mentioned, have a recorded audio stream which contains some extremely incriminating statements, taken in context. That audio file, and a list containing our partial identification of individuals present when it was recorded, constitute EXHIBIT G. We can't definitively match names of those present to specific voices on the recording."

Sharon handed off to me again.

"At this point, we had a large flow of money, through an extensive scheme apparently designed to conceal and obfuscate the origin of the funds, and ending up in offshore banks. We also had strong circumstantial evidence tying concealment of this scheme to one murder-for-hire, one *attempted* murder-for-hire, and a firebombing of a law firm. There had also during this time been one further attempt—that we *know* about—to abduct Ms. Kielic.

"We still did not know what it might be, but it was extremely clear that there was something highly illegal involved, or those operating the scheme would not have gone to such lengths to try to conceal it. Since there was nothing technically illegal in the source of the funds, we concluded that the crime being concealed must be at the destination."

I took a deep breath.

"Lacking any official resources, and finding no viable alternative method to proceed open to us, we took the step at this point of securing the assistance of a gray-hat hacker." That got me a raised eyebrow from Mr. Green, and a measuring frown from Ms. Red.

"This individual, whose identity will remain confidential, was able to penetrate the security of two of the twelve named banks utilizing pre-existing exploits or breaches. He was able to trace, and exfiltrate, details of some of the financial transactions involving the funds exiting the laundering scheme.

"Those records are contained in EXHIBIT H on the USB drive. They are too voluminous to practically provide hard copy.

"He was able to determine the owners of the accounts in which those funds ended up, and determine that from time to time, those individuals made structured transfers from those accounts to domestic onshore accounts in their names, further establishing ownership of the accounts."

I handed off to Sharon. She picked up the second to last sheet from the pile in front of us.

"This is the list we were able to establish, from the first two banks, Sumitomo and UBS Warburg, of the holders of those accounts," she said, passing it across the table. "You will observe that every person identified on this list is a nobody. Yet, every nobody has a direct personal relationship to a state or federal legislator. In one case, the recipient person isn't a person at all: it's the trust fund set up to pay for medical bills of a Senator's son's dog. A dog which is in apparently extraordinarily poor health, given how thirty-six million dollars was funneled into it via this scheme and thirty-five million withdrawn for 'emergency veterinary care'."

Okay, all of a sudden now, we *really* had their attention. Ms. Red and several of the other attendees sat up in their seats, and Mr. Green leaned forward intently. Ms. Yellow drew in her breath between her teeth.

"This is probably not a complete list of recipients of payments from the scheme," Sharon continued, "since we were able to examine only an incomplete set of data from only two of the twelve offshore banks."

She passed them the second sheet.

"This sheet lists the United States Representatives and Senators currently blocking passage of the Omnibus Climate and Renewable Energy Bill in the House and Senate." And she passed it across the table.

"You will observe that every United States level person on the first list is also present on the second list. The conclusion seems inescapable. Especially given that four million dollars was donated to defer Fido's medical expenses, and four million dollars withdrawn for 'emergency veterinary care,' literally one day before the vote."

I picked up the narrative baton one more time.

"It is at this point that I contacted Mr., ah, Pink, and asked him if he could assist us by setting up this meeting." I picked up the briefcase we'd brought with us and laid it on the table.

"There are additional relevant hardcopy documents, including the complete set of all relevant leases that we were able to find, in this case, along with three additional copies of that USB flash drive."

I pushed it across the table.

For a few seconds, dead silence reigned. Then everyone tried to speak at once. After a few moments, order was re-established. Mr. Brown spoke first.

"They're using a dog to launder money. Did I hear you right? They really expect to launder the last transaction through a trust fund for a *dog*."

Ms. Red drawled, "I think it gives a touch of verisimilitude. You remember how dumb the Bank of Credit and Commerce International was while laundering the Cali Cartel's billions?"

"Operation C-CHASE, yeah," Mr. Brown answered, reluctantly granting the point. "Or the fraud that cryptocurrency fund, FTX, was up to in the Twenties. Wow. Someone's giving those clowns a run for their money in the incompetency department."

"I would like to note," I interjected, mostly to try to lighten the mood for a moment, "that the dog, one Jeremy X. Dogsbody, is innocent of wrongdoing and widely recognized to be a Good Boy."

The room chuckled briefly. Ms. Yellow spoke next.

"You do, I trust, realize the *seriousness* of the charges you are making here, correct?"

I went to answer, but to my surprise, Deputy Director Mackey—Mr. Blue—beat me to it.

"From the discussions I have had with Mr. Pink," he interjected, "I believe that Mr. mac Cool and Ms. Kielic are *ENTIRELY* aware of the deadly seriousness of this matter. That, I believe, is precisely *why* they brought the matter to Mr. Pink, and why he in turn brought it to me, and it is why the specific persons present at this meeting are here.

"Mr. Brown and I have already taken the liberty of arranging immunity in return for the evidence they have just provided us and their testimony and cooperation.

"The question is, what are we going to do about it? And how quickly can we act?"

"Mr. mac Cool, Ms. Kielic," Ms. Red said.

"Ma'am?" I replied. She was sitting back in her chair, regarding us with a very calculating look.

"I'm sure you are both aware—especially *you*, Ms. Kielic—that key portions of the evidence you have gathered would be inadmissable if we had obtained them, due to the manner in which it was obtained."

"Yes, ma'am," Sharon replied. "But all of the records we used to trace and detect the money-laundering scheme are public record, cleverly hidden in plain sight. There is no sourcing problem there. You just have to know what you're looking for, and where to look. The last steps to tie the scheme to the originating companies are within the purview of the Treasury in its enforcement of banking regulations, and can be reached by parallel construction for the moment and verified later using subpoenas against business and banking records."

Ms. Red gave a Sharon a hard smile. There was a gleam in her eye.

"The offshore banking records are *clearly* problematic," I observed. "Nor would we expect differently. But now that you know the details, you can subpoena the relevant records from all twelve banks, not just the two we were able to gain access to, under a gag order to avoid spooking the prey. And because we are not government employees and did none of this under government instruction, there is no fruit-of-the-poison-tree problem."

"Very good. Correct answers, both of you. You've done your homework." Yes, that was *definitely* a predatory gleam.

She stood up.

"Ladies and gentlemen," she declared, looking around the room, "if Mr. Blue believes this solid enough to bring it to me personally, I'm going to run with it. I intend to move on it immediately, as soon as we can verify the information."

She looked at Sharon and me.

"I'm afraid I'm going to need you two for at least the rest of the day for statements and depositions," she told us, "and probably a few days after that to walk our people in detail through your discoveries. We'll update and extend your immunity as needed if anything comes up during those depositions.

"And while we're speaking of immunity, is there anything you want to tell me about up front right now?"

"Ma'am?" I said. "About the murder attempt against Ms. Kielic."

"Yes? Ms. Kielic stated that you intervened."

"Yes, ma'am. I shot and killed the hitman. There was no time to do anything else."

She pursed her lips.

"Pity," she mused. "There might have been some useful testimony to be obtained there. But you were understandably short of options at the time.

"Well, what's done is done. Clearly justifiable, and we wouldn't be here today if you hadn't."

"No, ma'am," I agreed. "We would not."

"Don't worry about that," she said. "You gave us copies of local police reports. Are *they* aware of that detail?"

"They are, ma'am," I replied. "They initially *presumed* Ms. Kielic to have been killed in her bathroom and her body removed, but subsequent forensics established that the person killed there was not her. DNA analysis of samples recovered from Ms. Kielic's bathroom later returned four probable identity matches against criminal records, one of whom—the aforementioned Nicolas Carravini—I was able to positively identify from a mugshot."

"But the police know Ms. Kielic to be alive."

"Yes, ma'am. Though to the best of our knowledge, they do not know her exact location."

"And the public does not."

"Correct again, ma'am. We requested that they not reveal to the public that she was alive, for her safety."

"Prudent. What do the news media believe to be Ms. Kielic's current status?"

I exchanged a long glance with Sharon and reached to take her hand under the table.

"Missing, presumed dead, ma'am."

"I see. Does anyone else know differently?"

"Marilyn Lang of Jerison Whitewell Lang," Sharon said. "And Edrick Magnusson of Harris Magnusson Partners."

"And Jim Bell, Sharon's defense attorney," I added.

"You trust them to keep the information confidential?"

"Yes, ma'am," I agreed.

"How much do they know? Do we need to bring them in for statements?"

"Edrick can verify the origin of the contract tranche if necessary," Sharon said. "Marilyn is fully aware of the attacks against Harris Magnusson, but acted only as a messenger between us and Edrick in order to avoid any direct contact, in case he was being watched. At this time, neither of them know about our subsequent findings. And neither does Jim."

"We deliberately shared as little as possible," I added, "strict need-to-know, to avoid putting them in unnecessary danger."

Ms. Red nodded.

"Good call," she agreed, and turned back to Sharon.

"What did you tell them about your... status with regard to your disappearance?"

"We told Marilyn that I was in witness protection," Sharon replied. Ms. Red actually chuckled about that.

"As of this meeting," she told us, "you *are*. Both of you."

I started to say, I thought we had it covered. But then the realization slammed down on me hard that no, we *didn't*, not any more. Not since they'd made Sharon while I was in—or on the way to—Asbury Park. Since then, we'd been running too much on hyper-vigilance and good fortune, and fortune is a fickle bitch. As I'd learned the hard way in Syria.

I wasn't willing to risk Sharon any more. Not when I no longer HAD to.

Ms. Red gave me a questioning look. Apparently she'd caught it.

"You were about to say something?" she asked.

I nodded wearily, the accumulated stress hitting me.

"I was about to say that I've been handling our security up until now," I began, "and that we had it covered. That invisibility was our best defense.

"But no. We're *not* invisible any more. The opposition has made Sharon *at least* once. That we know of. That tail was broken... but we don't know when they might pick us up again. Next time we might not be so lucky. I have to sleep *sometime*.

"I'm not going to risk Sharon unnecessarily, out of misplaced bravado. We both need a break from the highwire. So, yeah. We'll take that protection. Thank you."

Ms. Red didn't look over to Judson as she addressed him. "Mr. Pink?"

"We've had a protection plan ready for weeks. We can roll in an hour flat."

"Visibility?"

"Low." Judson looked over to us and explained: "Low-visibility to you. Pretty near invisible to the rest of the world. But low-viz to you is going to be good for your mental health. I mean, it beats turning around in the shower and seeing me standing there happy as a wet cat, handing you your soap."

That got him a warning look from DD Mackey and a low chuckle from Ms. Red.

"Thank you, Mr. Pink, for the nightmare I'm going to have tonight. Your plan is good to go, fully staffed, equipped, funded, the works. I want it moving one hour after our meeting.

"Moving on."

I felt relieved already. Then a thought occurred to me.

"Ma'am?" I said, raising a hand. Ms. Red looked at me. "I, uh, haven't looked into their finances, but... Tenth Avenue Digital, the colo business where the, uh, conspirators are hosting the administrative domains for all of these companies? I saw no indication that they knew what's going on."

"So you're saying you believe them to be innocent of any knowing part in the scheme?" she asked.

"Well, yes. But more than that. They're a small operation, and this hosting contract—or more correctly, *group* of contracts—may well be the main thing that's keeping them afloat. And I kinda feel bad about that. This may ruin them."

Ms. Red nodded.

"That would be unfortunate," she agreed. "What's your point?"

"Well, they've already demonstrated an ability to be discreet. Perhaps, um, some agency might be able to find some way to make use of that?"

Ms. Red looked at me for a long moment, then smiled.

"That's a worthy thought, Mr. mac Cool. Two birds with one stone. Minimize the collateral damage, and possibly develop a future asset.

"I won't make you any promises, but we'll take it into consideration, assuming they cooperate with us."

"I can't ask more than that," I answered. "Thank you, Ms. Red."

"Right then," Ms. Red said firmly. "Ms. Yellow, I would like you to start setting up the subpoenas and gag orders for the twelve listed banks to verify and complete these financial records.

"Mr. Green, please assign one of your staff to setting up the statements and depositions from Mr. mac Cool and Ms. Kielic, and then I want you to supervise trawling the domestic banking activity records for these fossil energy companies to verify source of funds to the shell companies. Pull in as many people as you need to get it done. Full back-traces under gag orders.

"Mr. Blue, I'll need to borrow your man for a little while as well, for a statement.

"Now if the rest of you will excuse us, Mr. Blue and I need to confer."

════════════

'Ms. Red' was as good as her word; she did indeed keep us for the rest of the day, going in exhaustive detail over every little thing, every detail we could remember. Then they put us up for the night at a safe house, then they brought us back the next day, and we spent most of that day in depositions as well. We both carefully avoided any mention whatsoever of the Box. When one of the attorneys deposing us asked how it happened that I was at Sharon's house and in a position to prevent her murder, Sharon simply replied, "That is personal." Somewhat to my surprise, the attorney accepted that. Possibly they'd been instructed not to press us hard on personal details. We were informants, after all, not suspects in anything.

We ended up spending the rest of the week working with Treasury people, going step by step through every detail of the massive information dump that we'd handed over to them, until everyone involved was certain they understood the entire construction.

And then they took us home. Just us, and our new protection detail. I was glad to have them.

14: Here Comes The Sun

Nothing much happened for nearly a month, though I was extra vigilant for the first week or so just in case someone had seen us being picked up or returned. After about the first week, I think it sunk in that I could finally relax a little, that our protection detail had us covered. But not *too* much. It felt kind of weird, being under protection *myself*.

We just stayed in, kept our heads down, and tried to let all the stress and tension drain out. We spent a lot of time just quietly cuddling and enjoying having no concerns but each other. We ran twice a day, every day, two agents a discreet distance behind us—but close enough to react. (Several of them got to meet Sam.) And Sharon worked on her studies for her bar exam.

Then came the day my phone rang. It was Judson Ritter.

"G'day, squire," I greeted him.

"'Allo, guv," he replied. "Don't have a lot of time to talk right now, just a heads-up. You might want to turn on one or more of the major national news channels."

"Thanks for the heads-up. We'll do that."

"Righto, then, catch you later. Stay safe."

"You too, squire," I replied. Then he hung up.

We went and turned on the news. We came in a little late, so I backed up to the start of the segment.

> "Washington is in uproar today," the anchor began, "after the Department of Justice unveiled a massive corruption and influence-peddling indictment targeting both fossil fuel companies and multiple members of both houses of Congress. It's hard to say which is the more shocking: the huge scale of the indictment, the sheer number of indictees, or the fact that it came as a complete surprise to nearly everyone.
>
> "The indictment details how the nation's, and in fact some of the world's, largest fossil energy companies conspired with members of Congress to derail clean-energy and climate legislation, and instead work to enact policies that would have locked in unrestrained fossil-fuels development for decades and imposed crippling penalties upon clean and renewable energy

projects.

"It invokes RICO statutes and other charges against twenty-six named chief officers and directors of fossil energy companies, and documents how they pumped tens of millions of dollars a month through a complicated multi-level money-laundering scheme using fake commercial real-estate leases. The laundered money was then funneled through offshore banks to numbered accounts gifted to elected officials, in return for them voting as directed by the energy cabal and adding poison-pill amendments to pivotal energy and climate bills.

"No fewer than thirty-three Congressional Representatives and nine Senators are named in the indictment. This is one of the most far-reaching criminal indictments in the history of the nation.

"We take you now to Jim Edwards at our Capitol desk for the inside view. Hello, Jim."

"Good morning, Sandra. Let me be blunt: The inside view here is that there IS no inside view. *Nobody* outside the Departments of Justice and Treasury knew that this was coming. It was an absolute bolt from the blue. Analysts have been arguing about how an investigation on this scale was executed without anyone else having any idea that it was happening. The list of charges alone is enormous.

"This indictment sends several messages. First, it says to those who peddle the authority of their elected offices for personal gain, that America will no longer tolerate this kind of blatant corruption. And secondly, it gives notice to the world that the Department of Justice has revealed some hitherto unknown capability to sniff out even the most cunningly hidden graft schemes. This is going to put fear into the hearts of those who sell the influence of their offices for political gain."

"How is this going to impact Congress, Jim?"

"I think we can confidently predict that this is going to bring about huge changes, Sandra. There is a saying that sunshine is the best disinfectant, and this indictment has just shone a staggeringly huge beam of sunshine into Congress. There are already rumors starting to circulate about elected representatives who are *not* named in the indictment unexpectedly considering early retirement. This could change the face of the nation. The currently-known arraignments, just for initial appearances, are going to give the D.C. Marshals Service more work in a couple of weeks than they've had all year, what with all the VIP defendants they have to protect."

"Anything else from your desk, Jim?"

"I think we might be about to see some sudden changes in the state of the stalled omnibus climate bill. That's going to be interesting to watch.
"Back to you, Sandra."

"So, there you have it. We will continue to bring you developing news of this *stunning* revelation as soon as more information becomes available. In the meantime, over to our New York desk for more analysis from..."

For a long time Sharon and I just stared at each other. Then we both whooped in exultation. I jumped up, she flung her arms around me, and then I lifted her off the ground and swung her around.

"We *DID* it!" she cried out in glee. "We *ACTUALLY DID IT!*" We were both shedding tears of joy and relief. Then I kissed her, and she kissed me back, and we spent a while just kissing and hugging each other.

After a while, it occurred to us to go check on the Box.

"How's it looking, Fester?" I asked.

EXCELLENT PROGRESS, the Box replied. PRIMARY ASSIGNMENT IS ALMOST COMPLETE.

"...Almost?" I asked.

HIGH PROBABILITY OF COMPLETE RESOLUTION WITHOUT FURTHER INTERVENTION.

"Does that mean we get to take a break?" Sharon asked.

NO IMMINENT FURTHER ACTIONS FORESEEN.

We took that as a yes.

Over the next week or so, four more Representatives in the House and two Senators announced their intention to retire from politics without finishing their current terms. More importantly, from our perspective, the House voted by three hundred and twenty eight to sixty, with thirty-seven abstaining, to remove all of the poison-pill amendments and riders from the omnibus climate and energy bill. So amended, it passed the House by three hundred and two to eighty-six, with the same thirty-seven abstaining, by some strange—or, perhaps, suspicious—coincidence. It proceeded on to the Senate, where it was scheduled for a vote the next day, expected to pass with a solid majority. President Kelly appeared on national TV and promised to sign it the very hour it reached her desk.

"Today, we are going to change the world for the better," she declared. "We owe our descendants a huge debt for squandering their birthright. When this bill reaches my desk, we will finally begin the process of meaningfully paying down that debt."

═══════════

We went downstairs to talk to the Box.

ASSIGNMENT ACCOMPLISHED, read the message on the screen when we walked into the room. Then it changed.

TERMINAL DEPLOYMENT WILL NOW END. YOUR ACTIONS ARE GREATLY APPRECIATED. YOU HAVE BEEN EXCEPTIONAL AGENTS.

"Ohhhh, no, no NO, wait, wait," I said. "What do you mean, 'terminal deployment will end'?"

NO FURTHER INTERVENTION IS NECESSARY. DESIRED OUTCOME IS NOW ASSURED. PROJECTION OF THIS TERMINAL TO THIS LOCUS IS NO LONGER REQUIRED.

"You mean—wait, no, *no way*," I protested. "That sounds like you're telling us you're leaving, right? But you owe us some answers. You *OWE* us."

There was a pause.

AGREED, the Box replied. Then, QUESTIONS WILL BE ANSWERED TO THE EXTENT NOW POSSIBLE. SOME ANSWERS MAY STILL BE PROBLEMATIC.

"The questions we want answers to are mostly ones that you previously declared problematic," Sharon stated. "Are you able—or willing—to answer those now?"

There was another pause.

MOST SUCH ANSWERS CAN NOW BE PROVIDED. WE HAVE PASSED BEYOND THE POINT AT WHICH SUCH DISCLOSURE CAN HAVE MATERIAL

ADVERSE EFFECT UPON THE FINAL OUTCOME.

"Right," I said. "Let's start with this, if you can. What *are you* and where did you come from?" Sharon nodded agreement.

THIS TERMINAL IS A PROJECTION FROM YOUR FUTURE TIMELINE.

"The *future…?*"

YES.

"But… doesn't that create paradoxes?"

EXTREME CAUTION WAS NECESSARY IN ORDER TO AVOID PARADOX.

"Which is why so many answers were 'problematic'," Sharon guessed.

PRECISELY.

"What do you mean by a projection?" I asked, not wanting to let that detail slip by.

PHYSICAL TIME TRAVEL IS NOT POSSIBLE. THIS PROJECTION HAS NO PHYSICAL EXISTENCE IN YOUR LOCUS. IT IS A PROJECTION INTO YOUR TIME OF A PHYSICAL TERMINAL THAT EXISTS IN YOUR FUTURE TIMELINE.

"…Is that why it has such *weird* physical properties?" I asked, speculating.

YES.

"Out of curiosity, does that also have anything to do with the fractal appearance of the… projection?"

FRACTAL APPEARANCE?

A pause.

WHAT DOES THIS PROJECTION APPEAR AS, TO YOU?

"A roughly one-meter metal cube, whose faces have a fractal appearance similar to a Sierpiński gasket," I replied.

There was a long pause.

INTERESTING. A SPHERICAL APPEARANCE APPROXIMATELY TWO THIRDS THAT SIZE WAS EXPECTED. THIS WILL BE INVESTIGATED. IT MAY YIELD FURTHER INSIGHTS. THANK YOU FOR THE INFORMATION.

"Let's get back to the paradox question," I said.

"Wait a moment," Sharon interrupted. "I want to make sure we don't miss this. You said a projection from our future. Who, in our future, sent you?"

THIS PROJECTION IS SENT FROM AN AGENCY WITH MANY ANCESTORS, BOTH PUBLIC SECTOR AND PRIVATE. YOU HAVE ALREADY DISCOVERED THE MOST SALIENT ONE EXISTING IN YOUR TIME. YOU KNOW IT AS THE LONG NOW FOUNDATION.

Sharon looked thoughtful for a moment, and then asked, "Does today's Long Now Foundation know about this?"

NO.

"Does any part of the support and help we have received come from the present-day Long Now Foundation?"

NO.

"Your witness," Sharon told me, with a smile.

"Let me put this briefly," I said. Then I paused. There were so *many* questions to ask.

"Actually, first, can you expand on what you mean by 'projection'?"

NOT IN ANY USEFUL WAY, the Box stated. THE UNDERLYING PHYSICAL THEORIES NECESSARY TO UNDERSTAND IT DO NOT EXIST IN YOUR TIME. Then it added, NEITHER DO THE THEORIES REQUIRED TO UNDERSTAND THOSE THEORIES. TRY TO THINK OF IT AS ANALOGOUS TO CREATING AN ECHO OF A SOUND, THAT IS HEARD BEFORE THE SOUND ITSELF OCCURS. OR TO SEEING THE SHADOW OF AN OBJECT THAT DOES NOT EXIST YET, BUT WILL. AN EVANESCENT SHADOW CAST FORWARD THROUGH CURVED SPACETIME, INTO THE PAST.

"Okay, I get the picture," I nodded. "Beyond our understanding. Can you explain to me how you were able to avoid paradox?"

THAT ANSWER IS BOTH SIMPLE AND COMPLEX, came the response. WE SIMPLY DID NOT DO ANYTHING OF LARGE SIGNIFICANCE THAT WAS NOT KNOWN TO HAVE ALREADY HAPPENED.

"...Wait, how does that work?" I asked, confused.

IT IS A MATTER OF RECORD THAT HELP IN THIS MATTER WAS RECEIVED. THEREFORE WE SENT THE HELP THAT WAS RECEIVED, SO THAT IT WOULD BE RECEIVED.

I struggled with that. It made my head hurt, and I said so.

"Are you saying," Sharon asked, "that you avoided paradox by sending only help that you already knew from... *your* historical record that we would receive?"

Yes. In essence.

"Why did you pick Ciáran? You previously stated there was no other choice."

Correct. It was known that he was necessary for completion. No other choice was possible.

"Why?"

Because that is how it happened.

"What about Sharon?" I asked. "Why did you involve her?"

We did not. It was known a second person was necessary. We did not know her identity.

"Until the opposition moved against her," I said, remembering our past speculation.

Correct. At that moment her identity became knowable.

"And then you sent me to her. To save her."

Correct.

"You said the... outcome in which I failed to save her was not considered because it was not possible."

Yes.

"Why was it not possible?"

You had already done so.

"Already done so? I don't understand." I was developing a headache.

There was an unknown second person. Sharon was identified as a target of the critical attack at the moment it was launched. No other target was identified. Therefore she is the second critical person. So we sent you to her. It is known that the second person survived the attack at that time. Therefore you saved her.

"What about Philip?" Sharon asked quietly.

Sadly, he leaves no historical footprint.

"But I do?"

Yes. But we could not ascertain your identity until the attack.

"How did you know about the... attack... in time for Ciáran to save me?"

It was a critical path event. Such events are detectable as soon as they occur.

"Did you know in advance what help would be needed at any other point in this assignment?" I asked.

In general, no. It was necessary for the terminals to be adaptable.

"Wait a moment. Terminals? Plural?"

Yes. There are other terminals, the Box stated.

"Other terminals," I echoed. Struck by a thought, I took out the satellite phone. "Is at least one of those *other* terminals placed with a person in—or with access to—some government agency or program? In some other nation?"

Yes.

"Is that how you were able to obtain this phone for me?"

Yes.

"Which agency? And which nation?"

Providing that information would technically violate laws in your time regarding disclosure of classified information. It would also breach operational security for, and thus might endanger, that recipient, which might in turn rebound upon yourselves. You do not need to know. You have already determined sufficient information to speculate with reasonable accuracy about the answer. Direct contact with you remains an option for that operative at their discretion. You may find them to be like-minded.

"Fair enough," I agreed. "Are all such terminals now being recalled?"

Yes.

Sharon and I exchanged looks.

"Okay," Sharon said slowly. "You have fundamentally answered 'how' and 'why us' about as well as we can reasonably expect. That leaves one major question:

"Why *now?*"

You stand at a cusp of history, the Box replied. Your media has described the climate bill that is about to be signed as pivotal. They do not understand how pivotal it truly is.

"A cusp?" I asked.

A BRANCH IN HISTORY. A CRUCIAL DECISION POINT ON THE TIMELINE. AN INTERSECTION OF MULTIPLE CLOSED TIME-LIKE CURVES. MULTIPLE PATHS POSSIBLE WITH DRASTICALLY DIFFERENT OUTCOMES. EXIT PATH IS IRREVOCABLE ONCE THE CRITICAL POINT IS PASSED.

"You're saying the outcome was not predetermined?" Sharon asked.

YES... AND NO. IT IS COMPLEX. THE THEORIES NECESSARY FOR YOU TO UNDERSTAND IT HAVE NOT YET BEEN FORMULATED IN YOUR TIME.

"How can it be both predetermined, and not?" I asked, more confused than ever.

DECISION IS POSSIBLE AT A CUSP, the Box explained. Well, *partially* explained. CUSPS ARE SINGLE FAR-REACHING EVENTS OF ENORMOUS FUTURE SIGNIFICANCE. THEIR OUTCOME IS NOT FIXED. YOUR CONCEPT OF THE BUTTERFLY EFFECT IS NOT WHOLLY INAPPLICABLE. AGENTS AT THE CUSP ARE REQUIRED, IF IT IS TO BE ENSURED THAT THE CUSP IS CORRECTLY NAVIGATED IN ORDER TO ACHIEVE A SPECIFIC DESIRED OUTCOME. IN ESSENCE, YOUR ACTIONS CHOSE WHICH OF THE POSSIBLE TIME-LIKE CURVES PASSING THROUGH THE POINT THAT IS YOUR PRESENT WOULD REPRESENT YOUR FUTURE. YOU CAN THINK OF IT AS A SUPERPOSITION OF POSSIBLE FUTURES EXISTING, UNTIL A NECESSARY SET OF KEY EVENTS OCCUR THAT COLLAPSE THE SUPERPOSITION INTO A SINGLE TIMELINE.

"And this particular cusp centered on the omnibus climate bill?" Sharon asked.

CORRECT. THIS WAS A CRUCIAL POINT OF DECISION. THE BILL NOW PASSES, AND THE CIVILIZATION OF YOUR AGE BEGINS TO REPAIR YOUR WORLD. OUR SHARED WORLD.

"...And if it hadn't passed?" I asked. "If the fossil fuel companies had succeeded in killing it?"

THEN YOUR WORLD AND OURS GOES DOWN TO RUIN, replied the Box. TOO LITTLE IS DONE, TOO LATE. OUR FUTURE NEVER HAPPENS.

"Doesn't that then present a paradox again?" Sharon asked. "How could we receive help from a future that never happens?"

UNKNOWN. WE CANNOT SEE CLEARLY INTO THAT OTHER CURVE. IT IS CLOSED TO US BEYOND A SHORT DISTANCE. IT IS NOT IMPOSSIBLE THAT THE OTHER BRANCH ALSO SENDS HELP TO NAVIGATE THIS CUSP, POSSIBLY IN AN ATTEMPT TO AVERT THEIR PRESENT. IT IS POSSIBLE THAT THIS PROJECTION WAS ITSELF IN A SUPERPOSITION OF BOTH FUTURES, UNTIL THE CUSP WAS PASSED. THE MATHEMATICS OF THE THEORY DICTATE THAT IT IS NOT POSSIBLE TO

DETERMINE.

There was a brief pause, then the Box continued.

IT IS NOT BEYOND POSSIBILITY THAT SUCH A SUPERPOSITION IS CAUSING THE UNEXPECTED APPEARANCE OF THE PROJECTION.

"But you can see *enough* of the other... curve to tell us that it leads to wrecking the world?"

YES.

"How badly?" Sharon asked quietly.

CLIMATIC TIPPING POINTS ARE PASSED LEADING TO IRREVERSIBLE RUNAWAY GREENHOUSE EFFECT. ECOLOGICAL CATASTROPHE ENSUES. MASS EXTINCTION OCCURS. PLANETARY SURFACE ENVIRONMENT BECOMES INHOSPITABLE TO ALMOST ALL MAMMALIAN LIFE, INCLUDING HUMANS.

"Holy *FUCK*." I looked at Sharon. She was shaking. Frankly, so was I.

I grabbed her, and we wrapped our arms around each other and clung on. I hadn't grasped until that moment how titanic a bullet we'd just dodged. My brain kind of stopped working and just ran gibbering in circles.

"The end of the world," Sharon mumbled into my shoulder.

THE END OF YOUR WORLD, YES. AND OURS. NOT IN YOUR LIFETIMES. BUT SOON. A FEW CENTURIES. THE PLANET WOULD EVENTUALLY RECOVER. THE HUMAN RACE AND ALL OTHER LARGE TERRESTRIAL MAMMALS WOULD BE LONG SINCE EXTINCT.

"Why didn't you *WARN* us how high the stakes were?" she demanded.

WOULD IT HAVE HELPED? WOULD YOU HAVE DONE ANYTHING DIFFERENTLY? OR WOULD ANXIETY HAVE DRIVEN YOU TO MAKE MISTAKES?

There was a long silence. Given how that revelation had just hit us both... I didn't have a good counter-argument.

"...Your point is taken," I conceded, somewhat shakily. "I can't imagine what we *could* have done differently. Except to go to the press. And they'd have just written us off as doomsday-conspiracy-theory lunatics." A further realization struck me. "And the Black Hats would have known for sure that Sharon was alive. And they might have come after her again. And they'd probably have known by then exactly where to find her."

Probable outcome agreed. Projections indicated a high likelihood that full knowledge would prevent successful navigation of the cusp. High probability that you would both die. Highest probability of successful navigation of the cusp was obtained by minimizing your knowledge of the cusp.

"What about all the prior assignments?" Sharon asked. "Were they... pivotal?"

No. But they were necessary.

"Why?"

Training. To build trust, skills, and confidence. Also, some contributed to lasting changes of public perception that make the desired future more robust.

Sharon nodded.

Most were also beneficial in their own right, in small but important ways. This consideration was deemed worthwhile.

"You gave me far more help with some of those other assignments than with this one," I said after a moment. "Particularly the Syrian assignment. Why?"

They were not in the critical path of the cusp. A greater degree of assistance was possible. There will be no public historical record of your actual part in the Syrian assignment. Thus a high level of assistance was possible.

"*Could* you have given us that level of help with this assignment?"

No. Help was given to the maximum extent possible. The more critical the event, the less intervention is possible. Active intervention, or direct assistance other than in response to your own direct instructions, could have resulted in paradox. The projection would have failed. It could have driven events onto a different branch of the cusp.

"Did you have... prior knowledge of any of those other events? From the record?"

No.

"Then how did you know to send me to them?"

Because they were not on the critical path, active data gathering was possible. Events which it was likely you could affect for the better could be identified.

"Were there... other possible things that you could have told me about? Other things I could have fixed if I'd known about them?"

Yes.

"Is there a reason you didn't?"

We did not wish to risk you unnecessarily. You were ready. And you had already been seriously injured once. Further high-risk assignments were deemed to be an unacceptable risk for the expected additional benefit. Achieving the correct path through the cusp required both of you to survive.

I ran out of questions. Sharon had one more.

"How, exactly," she asked, "do you *know* that we have passed the cusp? How can you be *sure*?"

The superposition of timelike curves has collapsed into one. Lesser events are still indeterminate, but on the large scale, the future course of your timeline is now clear.

She bit her lip.

"You said 'lesser events'," she said, hesitantly. "I'm sure that on this scale, *we* are 'lesser events'. Are we... safe? Now? Or are we going to have to hide for the rest of our lives?"

The Box took a while to answer that one.

Your safety is not assured. But it is extremely probable, provided you continue to exercise situational awareness. Your risk level is already drastically reduced, and declines fairly rapidly as you pass further from the cusp.

"On what kind of timescale?" I asked.

There was a pause again before the Box answered.

Do you understand the concept of half-life? it asked.

"Yes," I replied.

It is not grossly inaccurate to describe your future risk from this assignment as having a half-life on the scale of two to three months. Changing where you live would reduce it still further.

I did some quick mental math. Two and a half months from now our risk level would be half what it was today. A year from now, it would have dropped by somewhere around sixteen to thirty times, maybe more. A year after that, the same again.

"I think I can live with that," I said.

Sharon and I shared a long look.

"We can't tell anyone about... your part in this, ever," I said. "Can we?"

PUBLIC DISCLOSURE WOULD BE INADVISABLE. TOO MANY PEOPLE WOULD REACT BADLY OUT OF FEAR. IT WOULD ENDANGER YOU TO NO PURPOSE. EXTREME CAUTION IN ANY DISCLOSURE OF DETAILS IS ADVISED, THOUGH IT IS OF COURSE UP TO YOUR DISCRETION. WE ADVISE THAT YOU ALSO AVOID ADVERTISING YOUR OWN PART UNNECESSARILY.

"That seems like sound advice," I agreed. "I can see that a lot of people might carry grudges over it.

"Is that why there is no future record of Sharon's exact identity?"

YES. THAT IS HIGHLY LIKELY.

"But there is of mine?"

WE INVOLVED YOU TOO DEEPLY IN TOO MANY EVENTS FOR IT TO BE OTHERWISE. IF WE DID NOT KNOW WHO TO HELP, WE COULD NOT HELP. IT IS ONLY BECAUSE YOUR IDENTITY BECAME KNOWN AS A RESULT OF THESE EVENTS, THAT WE WERE ABLE TO ASSIST YOU.

"So what happens now?" Sharon asked, after a few moments.

ARRANGEMENTS HAVE BEEN MADE FOR SERVICES CURRENTLY BEING PROVIDED TO YOU, EXCEPT FOR THIS TERMINAL, TO CONTINUE TO BE PROVIDED FOR AS LONG AS YOU WISH TO CONTINUE THEM. IT IS ALL WE CAN DO NOW TO SHOW GRATITUDE.

There was a pause.

DO YOU HAVE ANY FURTHER QUESTIONS?

"I... don't think so," I said. "Sharon?" She shook her head.

"But there is one last thing," I said, as the thought popped into my head. "*Thank you* for sending me to Sharon."

YOU ARE BOTH VERY WELCOME. THANK YOU BOTH ONCE MORE, AND FAREWELL.

And then it just... wasn't there any more. It didn't go anywhere, it simply vanished, like turning off a light, except more abrupt. It was there on the platform; and then it wasn't. It disappeared in complete silence, as though it had just... *ended.* There wasn't even a *thump* of displaced—or un-displaced—air.

The small TV, suddenly unsupported, fell to the wooden platform and broke.

"Soooo... do you remember a conversation we had a while back about warrior heroes and Fenian gods?" Sharon asked after a bit.

"I believe I do," I agreed.

"When you asked the Box if there were other assignments it could have chosen to send you on, and it said yes," she went on.

"...Yes?" I wasn't sure where she was going with this.

"If it had asked, you would have, wouldn't you? Just because it would have helped, would have done good."

"Well... yes," I agreed, still unsure where she was going with it.

"See?" she declared with a triumphant grin. "Celtic warrior hero."

All I could do was laugh.

15: After The Storm

Finally it was reasonably safe for us to reveal to those we knew—in particular, Sharon's friends—that Sharon was alive. We put on our business faces and went by Harris Magnusson's offices.

Somewhat to our surprise, we found the building mostly torn down. We hadn't thought to check. A sign directed us to the firm's new location, just down the street from the Federal building. So we went there. We parked next to the building, walked around the front, and went to walk in. The leaves on trees on the street were starting to turn, and the aromas of fall were in the air.

Then Sharon glanced up, and stopped dead.

"Oh... my," she said slowly.

"What's wrong?" I asked.

She shook her head, grabbed my hand, and pulled me a few steps back from the building for an easier angle.

"Look up," she told me. She pointed up at the facade. The tasteful polished-metal letters three feet above the double doors spelled out "HARRIS MAGNUSSON BARTHOLOMEW".

We looked at each other for a long moment, and then went inside.

We walked into the lobby, and the thirty-something receptionist looked up.

"Can I help you?" she asked.

Then she froze.

Then her hands flew to her mouth and her eyes widened.

"OH MY GOD!" she squealed. *"SHARON!"*

She knocked her chair over in her haste to get out from behind the desk, nearly ran up to Sharon, and folded her in a hug.

"Oh my god, where have you BEEN, what *happened?*" she demanded. Then she paused, and before Sharon could answer, she broke away, ran to the double doors into the main office area, and threw one side open.

"Everyone," she called, "come quick, it's *Sharon*, she's here, she's *ALIVE!*"

For a moment, there was near-silence. Then one person stuck their head out of an office. And then suddenly people were streaming out of offices and through the doors. There were a great many teary reunions, and a great number of introductions. I can't remember them all.

By the time the initial babble and chaos finally started to die down, probably a good fifteen minutes later, Sharon was exchanging a long, tight hug with an older man with a salt-and-pepper beard. After a minute or so, he let her go, and she turned to me.

"Edrick," she said, "I want you to meet Ciáran mac Cool. He saved my life, and has been protecting me for the past four months. Ciáran, this is Edrick Magnusson, the senior partner in the firm."

She turned back to him.

"Thank you for keeping our secret, Mr. Magnusson," she said. Then, "I saw the name change. Outside. Is it...?"

"Yes," Edrick replied, nodding gravely. "In memory of Philip.

"But we needn't all stand here. Come inside, come inside, we can use the main conference room, there's room for nearly everyone in there."

Edrick led the way to a large conference room with a relatively narrow oval table down the center. We followed him in. He took a seat at one end, and gestured us to seats next to him. A lot of people filed in after us.

"So," he asked. "Can you finally reveal what happened? Where have you been all this time? Marilyn told me that you were alive, and conducting an investigation, but wouldn't say anything else."

"Wait," someone demanded, "you knew Sharon was alive *and you didn't tell us?*"

He opened his mouth to answer, but Sharon got there first, raising her hands for quiet.

"I'm *so sorry*," she apologized to everyone. "I really am. I *had* to tell Edrick he *couldn't* tell anyone. I've spent the last four months, uh, in witness protection. The more people knew I was alive, the more danger

I would have been in."

"You poor dear," replied an older woman with graying red hair, sniffling slightly. "We all thought you were dead."

"It was a very close thing," Sharon said. "The same night that Philip was murdered, they tried to kill me too." She gestured toward me. "Ciáran killed the hitman and took me to... a safe-house. I've been there ever since. Except when we both had to go to Washington."

Edrick gave her a sharp look. I could see the wheels ticking over.

"So," he asked, "did you learn anything useful from the contract copies I had sent to you?"

Sharon and I looked at each other.

"That's why we had to go to Washington," I said. "Sharon spotted an anomaly in those lease contracts—not the contracts *themselves*, but the commercial properties they referred to—that led to her uncovering the fossil-fuels money-laundering scheme that you might have recently seen in the news."

For a moment there was silence. Then it turned to pandemonium. Everyone was trying to talk at once.

Edrick Magnusson let the chaos continue for a minute or two, smiling broadly, while people got it out of their system a bit. Then he stood up.

"**Order***!*" he called, in a ringing voice.

Most of the people in the room were attorneys. So of *course* it worked. He looked at Sharon, smiling, his eyes twinkling.

"Who knew we had a tiger in our midst?" he said, with a chuckle.

"Was that really you?" someone asked, a slender black woman with long, lustrous hair tied back. We'd been introduced, but I didn't remember her name. There had been too many names in too short a time. "Thirty-three Congressmen and nine Senators? *You* discovered that scheme?" She was shaking her head in amazement. Next to her, a stocky Asian man with a huge grin spread across his face was bouncing up and down on the balls of his feet in excitement, rubbing his hands together.

"Ciáran and I did it together," Sharon said, moving a little closer to me. "And we had... other help."

There were a lot of questions, and it started to get out of control again.

I held up both hands.

"Please," I said. "I'm sure Sharon will tell you as much as she safely can, in time. But you all surely understand that there is a great deal that we *cannot* tell you." That brought a wave of nods and murmurs of assent. "And *please*, say nothing in public about Sharon's part in this. It could still endanger her. There are probably other people involved who are still out there, and they are probably very angry that their scheme failed. For the present time, we are still in danger."

"The important question now," Magnusson said to Sharon, "is this: What are your plans for your future?"

Sharon hesitated.

"Please tell me you were planning to come back to us," he added.

I saw the tears well up in Sharon's eyes.

"But... Philip?" she asked.

Magnusson nodded gravely.

"Philip is gone, though we are committed to honoring his memory. But... I hoped you might consider working for me instead." Sharon's mouth dropped open.

"Until you pass your bar exam, that is," he continued. "You *are* still working on that, I trust?" Sharon nodded mutely, not trusting her voice.

"And then I believe we can make room for you in the firm. I would consider it an honor to have you."

That was just a little bit more than Sharon was ready to handle right then. The tears burst from her eyes, and I gathered her into my arms. There were a dozen voices murmuring words of encouragement and welcoming her back, but Magnusson shooed everyone else out.

"Go on," he told them, "there'll be lots of time to talk later, she needs some space."

He turned to Sharon.

"I'm sorry, Sharon," he apologized. "I didn't intend to overwhelm you."

She nodded.

"It's all right," she replied through tears. "I'll be okay in a little bit. It's been a long, hard four months. But it's so good to see you all again." She lifted her head. "Philip is gone. I respected and liked him, but he's gone for good."

She paused to wipe her eyes.

"But on the other hand, I have Ciáran now."

Magnusson nodded kindly.

"It's obvious there's something powerful between you two," he said.

"We've been through a lot in the last four months, sir," I agreed.

"Call me Edrick," he corrected me. "Is there anything the two of you need?"

"I... don't think so," I said. "We just need to stay alert, for now. And we have a full protective detail watching over us."

"Well, if it turns out you do, just let me know," he told us.

We made our excuses and left, then we went to check on Sharon's house. Our escort followed discreetly behind.

<hr>

We pulled up outside... after quickly scanning the neighborhood. Force of habit that we couldn't afford to break yet. Someone—property management, I assumed—had been mowing the lawn. The mailbox had a Post Office notice on the front in a plastic bag.

Sharon undid her seatbelt, opened the door, and went to get out. Then she stopped. She closed the door again. Took a deep breath. Opened the door, started to get out, hesitated.

Then she closed the door and turned to me.

"I don't want to go in," she said shakily. I took her hand and squeezed it.

"You don't have to if you don't want to."

She closed her eyes tightly, then opened them again.

"But I need to," she went on. "I have to." She took a couple of deep breaths. "Come with me?"

"As if I wouldn't," I reassured her. "Did you really need to ask?"

I got out, walked around to her side, and opened her door. I held out my arms to her. She stepped straight out into them and I hugged her tightly. Then I held her hand as we walked up the front path.

The front door was unlocked. There was some kind of police paperwork in a clear plastic document bag taped to the door. It didn't say Keep Out, so we didn't look through it yet. We'd deal with it in a minute. There was a RENT PAST DUE notice as well.

Downstairs didn't look too bad at first, though we didn't check the whole house yet, as Sharon wanted to go to her room first. It seemed relatively untouched, at least from the hallway. Then we saw that everything had been dumped off the shelves in her living room and was strewn across the floor.

We went upstairs and figured we'd come back to the downstairs later.

Upstairs, *everything* was trashed. It had all clearly been tossed, drawers empty and scattered, some of them broken, clothes strewn in piles. Her hand clenched fiercely around mine. The computer was missing, its monitor lying smashed in a corner. The spare room looked as though a tornado had been through it. A lot of it looked less like a hurried search, than the results of spite or anger. Someone had wrecked her place to send a message. Or maybe just to vent their rage.

Sharon pushed herself into an effort to start sorting through the top layer of the mess, but I could see the toll it was taking on her.

"Sharon," I interrupted, after a little while. "Sharon, look at me." She turned a tear-stained face my way, then started to take a step toward me. She tripped on loose clothes and stumbled, but I caught her.

"It's... everything I had," she sobbed. *"Everything.* They just... trashed *everything."* I could understand. This had been her home, her possessions, her *life.* She undoubtedly felt violated. And that was probably part of the point.

"Sharon, you don't have to do this," I told her gently. "The computer, documents, all of those things are unimportant, they can all be replaced. Clothes can be replaced. Furnishings.

"Is there anything here that is *irreplaceable* and *important* to you? Tell me, and I'll try to find it for you."

She looked over her shoulder, scanning the room, her gaze lingering on piled clothes. Her wardrobe was still upright, but one of the doors was hanging by one hinge. Her bed had been flipped over.

Then she looked back at me.

"There's really only one thing," she said, after a long pause. "You."

She turned her head and surveyed the wreckage one more time.

"Let's just go. *Please.*"

I turned and led her down the stairs and out of the house. She got back into the car. I went and grabbed the notice off the mailbox and looked at the ones on the front door. There was a phone number to contact on the police notice and a case number, so I took that and the past-due rent notice. Then I got into the Volvo and started it, and we left.

"What do you want to do about it?" I asked, after she'd had a while for her frayed nerves to settle.

There was a long silence.

"I'd thought I could go in and get my things back," she said. Her voice was ragged. "But... just no. I don't ever want to set foot in, or *near*, that bathroom ever again. It's not—where I lived any more. Just the place where I almost *died*. I couldn't even really think about what I was looking at. I looked at the piles, and all I could see was blood all over the wall."

I winced.

"We can hire someone to clean it out," she continued. "Maybe at least get my music collection and my books back. Donate anything else that isn't completely trashed to Goodwill. Let them go to someone else who they won't give nightmares to." She sniffled and got herself a bit more under control. "I guess I'm losing my damage deposit."

"I didn't know you were renting until I saw the past-due notice," I said. "Never occurred to me to ask, I guess. You had renter's insurance?" She nodded.

"You're good, then. You were the victim of a crime. They'll make everything good and cover all the damage. You won't have to pay for a thing." She knew that, I was sure, but right now she was too much in distress to remember it.

She nodded.

"I can call my bank now, get my missing cards re-issued, get my phone re-activated... there'll probably be a thousand hoops to jump through. I don't know where to start. And I'll have to deal with the past-due rent. And the damage deposit. And probably a lease termination penalty."

"I might be going out on a limb here," I speculated, "but I'll bet that with a few words in the ears of some of our new acquaintances, most or all of those hoops will just vanish like morning mist."

"You're probably right," she agreed. "It can be a problem for another day. Ciáran?"

"Yes, love?"

"Please take me home."

════════════════

Indeed, it turned out that when the Department of Justice itself formally requests expedition of the process of unfreezing frozen accounts and the like for a person previously declared missing and presumed dead, it happens very quickly. A Department lawyer accompanied us to the police department, and made sure there were no obstacles to cleaning up loose ends there.

We got her phone back from the police evidence room—smashed, as Detective Taylor had warned us—and a few other items that he'd missed, including one of the missing cards. They had her car in impound, and we got that back without difficulty. The impound lot waived the storage fee. We paid a mechanic to go over it, and he changed out some stale fluids, put in new brake pads, and pronounced it otherwise sound. We reactivated her mobile account, and a carrier phone store was able to recover all of her data and contacts and clone everything onto a brand new phone. They even still had her old number available, but I advised her to abandon it and get a new number. She saw the sense in that immediately. I didn't even have to explain why. That didn't surprise me at all, by now.

We paid to have her house cleaned out, and she did indeed get her music collection and most of her books back. The few important books that were ruined or destroyed were easy to replace. Insurance covered all of the damages, as I'd predicted. Not only that, but under the highly unusual circumstances of her return from the presumed-dead, the property management company let her out of her lease early without penalty, and even waived two months of the past-due rent. There might have been some official encouragement to them to do so. I didn't ask.

Sharon went back to work at Harris Magnusson Bartholomew for the time being, working directly for Edrick Magnusson, with me acting as her driver just in case. About six months after that, she passed her state bar exam. We had a big celebration dinner at Shōgun, with all three remaining Harris Magnusson Bartholomew senior partners and Marilyn Lang. We invited Judson Ritter as well, which gave Judson his chance to finally meet Sharon in a non-professional capacity. All in all, it was a pretty good evening out.

══════════════

We invited Judson back to the house after dinner. There were conversations we couldn't have in front of people not already deeply involved in all that had happened.

At some point during that discussion, Judson oh-so-casually asked, "So, how *did* the two of you manage to pull all of this together on your own, anyway?"

I looked at Sharon, and she looked at me. We exchanged a long look.

"If there's one person on earth we can trust with the entire story," I suggested, "it's Judson."

She nodded minutely.

I took a deep breath.

"Look," I told him, "I know you're going to have a really hard time believing this. But I swear I am not shitting you. There's... no real physical proof to show you, at this point, but you're welcome to examine what little there is."

Then, over the course of about the next couple of hours, we told him all about the Box. And the cusp, and the little the Box had told us about its origins and nature, and the limits on how much it could help us, and its warnings about keeping its existence a secret from the public. And the way it had just... *stopped being there*. We showed him where it had been, and the patch of the platform, slightly larger than the Box itself, that for over five years, dust wouldn't settle on.

Judson listened silently, with a very thoughtful expression. He steepled his hands and looked at me over them.

"When, *exactly*, did you say it showed up?" he asked. "You said perhaps five and a half years before all this started. Was it by any chance January first, 2029?"

I blinked, and thought about it.

"You know," I answered, "I think possibly it was." I looked at him intently. "Why? And how did you know?"

"It's a closed timelike curve, right? That means it can't go back before the beginning of the curve."

That was beyond my physics knowledge, but sounded like it made sense.

"Um... if you say so. So...?"

"On one one twenty-twenty-nine, DARPA privately announced they saw some *really weird shit* happen in a lab, and then they pulled it back and stopped talking about it altogether. When I tried to follow up on it, even the memo was gone. I didn't think anything about it. Programs and results get classified all the time and vanish from my newsfeed. Just, you know, rarely from DARPA."

I hadn't made the connection yet. It probably showed in my expression.

Judson leaned back in his seat, with the weirdest smug, self-satisfied look. Like he'd just figured out something that had been eluding him for a long time. Maybe several things.

"Consider this possibility," he said. "Suppose that whatever happened in that lab on one one twenty-twenty-nine, it marked the start of the closed timelike curve, and *maybe* started DARPA down the line of research that eventually, *way* down the line, leads to the development of the temporal projection technology used to send the Box to you."

The penny dropped, with a massive CLANK. Or perhaps it was a manhole cover. I tried to think through the implications, and it made my head hurt.

"*Public and private* agencies, the Box told us," I pondered slowly. "Are you telling me that all of this time, I've maybe been working for... a distant descendant of the *United States Government?*"

Judson's grin had progressed to full shit-eating now.

"Yup," he said. "That's my best working theory, at any rate."

I shook my head in bemused wonder. I couldn't help laughing.

I looked over towards Sharon, and she looked back at me.

"Of all the weird things that have happened," she finally said, "I think discovering that I'm an undercover agent of a future United States government, doing covert operations under the nose of the *current* United States government, is definitely the *weirdest*."

I could only agree.

"I have only one request," I told Judson. He raised a questioning eyebrow.

"Please, do not share what we've just told you with anyone who does not have a legitimate *need* to know." I trusted him to decide who met that criterion.

Judson nodded.

"That's how the trade works," he replied, still grinning.

Epilogue

With the Box gone, I was left a bit at a loose end—aside from, of course, doing everything I could to ensure Sharon's continued safety. The Box had already told us fairly clearly that I wasn't going to have to be hyper-vigilant on her behalf *forever*—just until our risk dropped down close to background level. We still needed to be very careful for a little while, and not take stupid chances like her going anywhere alone unnecessarily. But the further we got past the cusp, the safer she was. And honestly, she'd picked up enough of what I could teach her about unarmed combat that any random ne'er-do-well unwise enough to try to mug her was probably in for a very rude attitude adjustment.

Still, I figured at some point we should get her some quality time with a better teacher than I, just to be sure. I had some ideas on that score. Perhaps some of the people I'd learned from.

Oddly, the... *lack* of any further skulduggery, as Judson had put it, needing to be accomplished left me a little on edge. I kept feeling like there was something important I should be doing, that I wasn't. I wasn't sure how much of this was just residual stress.

As a kid, the day after Christmas is always a fun one: you have all these new toys. But this wasn't Christmas, and neither Sharon nor I were kids. We'd spent four months together under intense stress, and now we were trying to go back to how our lives had been before. But you can't go back after something like this, and you especially can't go back *together*. Just for starters, we had very different 'befores'.

We had to learn something Judson already knew: that some victories come with grieving periods attached. He was able to point us to a therapist who had experience in these things, and after a while we managed to get through it, together, and start taking steps towards the future, instead of trying to recover our pasts.

The best part about those steps towards the future?

I asked Sharon if she would please marry me. And she said yes.

Well, that is, what she *actually* said was something closer to "Yes, of course, you magnificent fool, *of course* I will, I wouldn't be apart from you for the world, I've been starting to wonder when you'd get around to asking me."

But the important part was the 'Yes.'

Post-it Notes

The Box is clearly beyond any present-day science of any nation on Earth. However, as described, it actually does work, in a strictly mathematical sense—which is to say, it is not prohibited by any currently known mathematics/physics. It strictly obeys general relativity, and maintains Novikov self-consistency for closed timelike curves. Actual implementation is left as an exercise for the reader.

The Long Now Foundation really exists, and is as described in this book. So does the Dutch symphonic-metal band *Within Temptation*. And yes, Sharon den Adel's voice is Just That Good.

Cooper's Laws are real, and so is Colonel Jeff Cooper. Think of them as being the Four Commandments of firearm safety beyond "Try not to be a complete idiot." Even if you **don't like** firearms or have no desire to ever own one, knowing the safety basics might save a life one day if you find yourself unexpectedly needing to deal with a firearm that someone dropped, or accidentally left on a coffee table or on a public restroom counter. (Don't laugh, it's happened.) You don't have to agree with Cooper's political views, or like guns, to learn from his advice on gun safety. *Safety* has no political affiliation.

The Laugo Alien pistol is also real, and is as mechanically different from almost all other pistols as described (the *closest* mechanical similarity is to the Heckler & Koch P7, and it's not very close), but *currently* exists only in nine millimeter. In *this* timeline, at least.

The SIG P320 was designed as a service pistol, but also offered on the civilian market. There have been a large number of complaints about the civilian-version P320 discharging—firing—on its own without the trigger being pulled. Many of the complaints allege that the pistol has a design defect, an allegation repeatedly denied by SIG. At one period in time, Remington had a rash of similar problem reports that the Remington Model 700 rifle would fire on its own when the safety was released. Remington was able to reproduce and identify the problem, and voluntarily recalled all Model 700 rifles for installation of a redesigned trigger group that resolved the problem.

A Sierpiński gasket, also known as a Sierpiński triangle or Sierpiński sieve, is a fractal attractive fixed set named after Polish mathematician Wacław Sierpiński. Like all fractals, it is self-similar, which is to say it appears the same at all scales. In mathematical principle, it has infinite resolution. This is obviously not possible in the real world. But for a projection having no physical existence, implemented through physical theories not yet discovered by us? Who knows?

The Apple iOS/OSX exploits mentioned in this story are absolutely real. No, we're not giving you the CVE numbers. Besides, they're patched by now anyway. So don't get any ideas.

Yes, OS fingerprinting via examining fine details of TCP packets is **absolutely** a thing. So is *altering* that behavior to disguise what hardware you're running. Sean once—for perfectly legitimate reasons—made a Sun Microsystems UltraSPARC 5 workstation look, on the network, like an Apple LaserWriter printer. Interested parties are referred to the fascinating field of network forensics, and/or the open-source tool nmap, or the Shodan search engine.

Rubber-ducking is a term for just talking out loud, to anyone, even a bathtub rubber duck (hence the name), about what you're thinking through, and seeing whether it still makes sense when you hear it out loud.

The RSRE VIPER processor is exactly as described, although you've probably never heard of it before.

Juniper Networks makes very good network routers. They do indeed have a PTX product line of enterprise routers, and their router operating system is indeed called JunOS. The PTX13000 and PTX14000 series do not exist—*yet*—and neither does JunOS 26. And yes, there are indeed service companies that specialize in servicing and maintaining—and, when necessary, repairing—your Juniper networking equipment for you. The CVE vaguely described in Chapter 11 does not exist; it is made up out of whole cloth. We wish to emphasize once again that NONE of the exploits described in this story is a complete, working attack. It would be extremely irresponsible of us to do that.

CVSS is a zero-to-ten scale ranking the severity of software vulnerabilities. A 9.8 CVSS score, especially for a known-actively-exploited defect, is really, really, "oh shit" bad.

If anything, we have UNDERSTATED the difficulty of hacking into a major bank. Don't ask.

In Chapter 11, Judson name-drops the late Allan Kornblum. Kornblum was a legendary counterintelligence spook who served as gatekeeper to the FISA Court for literally decades. His standards for warrant applications were so exacting the NSA's former General Counsel, Stuart Baker, all but publicly denounced him as an obstacle to investigations (read Baker's excellent book, *Skating on Stilts*, but be warned that Baker inexplicably spells his name wrong). We are of the opinion that anyone who looks the NSA in the eye and says "no, you have to dot all the is and cross all the ts on this warrant application" is a damned American hero. One of us (Robert) knew him socially. He was funny, kind, wise, had a great laugh, and loved sharing his knowledge.

In Chapter 13, DD (Deputy Director) Mackey states the investigation is classified as TOP SECRET/SCI. SCI stands for "Sensitive Compartmented Information," and denotes that even people trusted to know the nation's deepest secrets need specialized vetting and/or training to handle these secrets safely. (Contrary to myth, it's not about need to know: all classified information is by definition need to know.) Many SCI inductions are nothing more than a sheet of paper with a bullet list of unique risks in a project, and once you sign, you're in. The real shock—to everyone at the table except Judson and DD Mackey—is that everyone is expecting a briefing on a domestic law enforcement effort, which rarely rise to the level of existential risk to the United States. By this time in the story Judson and DD Mackey are convinced Ciáran and Sharon are agents of an unknown nation-state with an unknown agenda. The enormous potential threat to national security requiring a special compartment be created isn't the bribery conspiracy: it's the Box. This is why Ms. Red is so insistent on protective custody and engages in nearly legendary cutting of red tape to authorize, fund, and staff Judson's protection plan: it's not just to get Sharon and Ciáran under protection, but to simultaneously place them under surveillance. Everyone in the briefing knows this except for Sharon and Ciáran, due to their lack of experience with professional intelligence operations.

(And yes, the investigation into the Box is what ultimately leads to the Box's creation, which in turn communicates back in time to trigger its own genesis. Novikov self-consistency is rigorously upheld. We, of course, did not invent this temporal trick: we lifted it shamelessly from Robert A. Heinlein's *All You Zombies*.)

There does not exist, to our knowledge, any such money-laundering scheme linking fossil energy companies and Congress as is described here. *To our knowledge.* This **particular** scheme is fictitious, but there are many similar real schemes on record, including the Ohio nuclear bribery scandal

($60 million in bribes), the SoCal Gas scandal (over $36 million), and others. The fossil energy sector is doing everything it can to scuttle effective climate action and renewable energy sources. They have known about the coming fossil-fuel-driven climate-change crisis *at least* since 1954 (this is not speculation or conspiracy theorism, it is *hard fact* verifiably documented largely from their own records), and have been suppressing information about it for over half a century, because extracting and selling fossil fuels is profitable and public awareness of the problem would jeopardize those profits.

Yes, we know how the bad guys found Ciáran and Sharon, and later moved to tail Judson and Sharon. We've worked it through. We haven't detailed it out in the story because it didn't drive the plot forward, but we left all the clues you need to solve that mystery, and several others. We hope you have fun figuring them out.

If you think some of the chapter titles are musical or other cultural references: Yes, you are absolutely correct. There are at least ten such. Give yourself however many points you feel you deserve, if you think you've identified them. There won't be a quiz. You are more then welcome to visit us on the Fenian House Discord (see https://fenianhouse.com/discord/) and ask for confirmation, or just talk about the book—or other Fenian House books.

More Books From Sean Fenian

The Stardock Trilogy

Humanity is not alone in the universe. We are far from even the only intelligent species in our *galaxy*. It was foolish, arrogant, and naïve of us to think we were.

The Chrrt'ktk't are one such intelligent species. But Sean Fenian's best-selling *Stardock Trilogy* is not about the Chrrt'ktk't. It's not even about humanity and the Chrrt'ktk't. It is about what happens to humanity, and how the future of humanity is changed, when the Chrrt'ktk't abandon a mobile shipyard with a burned-out hyperdrive core in the Solar System as a decoy to distract pursuit — and how it changes the life of a retired engineer who finds himself chosen, more or less by chance, as custodian of the Chrrt'ktk't shipyard, and all of the lives he changes in turn.

Praise for *The Stardock Trilogy*:

"These three books were a delightful, well written tale of a hopeful future, populated with a cast of characters that were easy to root for and interesting alien species."

"An excellent read and finally a well thought out plan forward that does not include a forever war!"

"This has been a wonderful trilogy to enjoy. Great character development and storyline."

"Happy because it is well written with solid scientific underpinnings and because it shows a side of humanity that I wish we would all strive for."

Fireborn

The man who will become Alrekr Járnhandr is *done*. Weary, physically and emotionally broken, abused beyond the limits of what he can endure, he is ready to give up and die. But instead of dying, he finds himself drawn through a dark void to another world. Terribly injured, he is found and rescued by people among whom he will have a chance to build a new life.

His new world will be filled with wonders. It will be magical. It will finally give his life meaning. But it won't be easy, and he will come to discover that he has not entirely escaped all that he fled from. His past is not done with him yet... and neither is his future.

But in this life, he won't have to do it alone.

Sean Fenian's **Fireborn** is a transformational alternate-world fantasy novel featuring mystic arts loosely based on Finnish mythology, polyamorous relationships, and healing from emotional abuse. Have you ever heard of a smith who can mix advanced metal alloys *by ear*? In *Fireborn*, you will.

And yes... there are dragons.

PRAISE FOR *FIREBORN*:

"Delightfully imaginative"

"This book has a feel and cadence utterly unlike any others in this genre. [...] I have never read a 'transformational' novel with such a positive cast of characters and uplifting message."

"The author writes characters of depth out of his own depth, loves, and widely varied experience. A lovely tale and I devoutly wish he'll find a way to revisit this surprisingly special world and characters he's shared with us."

"A different type of book from Sean Fenian, and even better"

"Fascinating take on legends"

"My new favorite author"

"[Fireborn] will take you into a mythic world, and you will be saddened that it stands alone. I only wish there was more of this world myth."

Becoming Real

Michael Hagerty—*GhostRayder*, to his fans—reviewed video games and made game videos for a living. He was intimately familiar with virtual worlds. They were his everyday bread and butter. He was quite certain he understood very clearly the lines of demarcation between game and reality, between what was physical, and what was virtual. What was real, and what was not.

Then one day, not long after he reviewed a newly released VR open-world adventure game, a mystery source sent him a modified version of the game, and asked him to go back in and try it again.

Michael would soon find out, amid a high-stakes game of hide-and-seek with shady multinational corporations and shadowy government agencies, that the question of real or virtual, human or not, was far more nuanced and less clear-cut than he had ever believed possible.

Sean Fenian's **Becoming Real** is an exploration of the natures of humanity and reality.

Or perhaps it's a commentary on some of the blind spots of video game design.

Or perhaps it's an SF postmodern love story with a twist.

Or perhaps, it's all of these things... and more.

Praise for **Becoming Real**:

"This edges out [Frank] Herbert's Dragon in the Sea as the best sci fi book I ever read. [...] You really must read this."

"It makes you think about some big social issues that are quickly becoming more relevant and may turn vital much sooner than you'd expect."

"Without question some of the best books I have read in years. I compare them to books by David Weber, John Ringo, and Nathan Lowell."

GODTHIEF

The Prophecy of Tendarrion—or at least, one likely reading thereof—said that the time was coming for the goddess Jirilis to die.

Jirilis, understandably, was rather unhappy about this. Her plans for the future did not involve dying yet. But, a prophecy is a prophecy.

Prophecies, however, are notoriously fickle about exactly what precise interpretation of them turns out in the end to be correct. The possibly existed of finding an exploitable loophole. But Jirilis could not exploit it *herself*. That was, to greatly oversimplify the explanation, 'against the rules.' Prophecy and the powers of gods didn't work that way.

Jirilis needed a champion. Not one who could win battles for her, not one who could slay mighty enemies for her, not one who would spread her word or perform heroic deeds in her name.

No, Jirilis needed a champion who could *subvert a prophecy*. And she had an idea that she knew just who that might be. She had had her eye on him for some time, in fact.

Fortunately, he was already coming to *her*. Though he might need a little help.

That was alright. Jirilis had one of the most powerful incentives to help him that there could possibly be.

Sean Fenian's **Godthief** is a standalone fantasy novel set in an alternate world that might or might not be 'real'. It delves into the natures of gods and the mechanisms of prophecy, and what we really mean when we say the word 'Paladin', all against a background of the aftermath of a thousand-years-past, almost-world-shattering demon war.

PRAISE FOR **GODTHIEF**:

"Excellent and consistent world building. If you enjoy fantasy without the swords and magical combat, this is for you."

"Well paced, imaginative, exciting tale. Sean Fenian is a skilled world builder. I look forward to reading more adventures set here."

IN FLUX

Years ago, Justin—we'll call him Justin—escaped from a hated orphanage, and from his own *time*. Now he will give a woman whom he does not know a last-second escape from *hers*—and also from her imminent brutal murder. Together, they will learn and share mysteries and wonders, pain and joy, make new friends and face new challenges, in a strange place outside of time and space as we think of it, where possibility can become reality—if your will is strong enough, and your vision clear and firm.

But be careful. There are *deadly dangers* hiding within the Flux.

Sean Fenian's **In Flux** is a standalone SF novel drawing inspiration in part from sources including Jack L. Chalker and Julian May, in a setting with distant echoes of Jules Verne and H. G. Wells, to tell a vaguely steampunk-era tale—without the steam.

About Sean Fenian

Sean Fenian is a generalist and open-source evangelist, recently retired from several decades of working in the information technology sector. He is broadly knowledgeable in many subjects, with a long-standing informed layman's interest in physics and related science in particular. He has been an avid reader of SF and fantasy since his teens, and first became aware of, and began campaigning on, environmental issues in the late 1970s. He is proficient with weapons both ancient and modern, has trained in four different martial arts, and believes that understanding basic firearms safety is like knowing basic first aid, CPR, or how to use a fire extinguisher. He believes that it is a basic human duty and responsibility to treat all beings fairly and decently, and that the true measure of a person is how you treat others.

His past volunteer activities include educational historical re-enactment, marine mammal rescue, and handicapped riding therapy. He has been formally diagnosed on the autistic spectrum, but stubbornly persists in trying to understand people anyway.

He dreams many things. Occasionally, some of them become reality. But only occasionally.

Sean's books are read in 14 countries, at last count, and his bestselling *Stardock Trilogy* is also available as audiobooks on the Audible platform, published by Podium Entertainment.

About Robert Auerbach

The problem I have with encapsulating my history is it winds up sounding like James Bond playing a game of Mad Libs. You say "something red" and my life fills in "a freshly-used dagger" while I look on in horror. You, stop asking those questions! You over there, stop filling them in like that! Why can't I have a nice apple or cherry or something?

Like Sean, my official background is in the strange side of computer science. I've presented original research at Black Hat and DEF CON. Also like him, my unofficial background is, to say the least, colorful. Most people have never needed to know how to convert ice cream into an explosive more powerful than dynamite. Me, I hang around people who do that stuff by accident. Successfully keeping them alive has given me a set of stories even I have trouble believing.

Sean's already hit the importance of kindness, so I'll just briefly underline it and move on to being kind to yourself. Don't judge yourself more strictly than you'd judge your enemies. Don't punish yourself worse than you'd punish your enemies. You owe yourself duties of fairness and kindness. Embrace them, and let kids see you embracing them. If we're really lucky, we can teach this to the next generation before the rest of the world teaches them to hate themselves.